AMERICANUS REX

For Dorinda.
Hope You Enjoy it.

10/16/09

300 Book Sold

Published by Workplay Publishing
Bluffton, Ohio 45817
workplaypublishing.com

ISBN 0-9842122-0-5

Cover design and layout by Alison L. King
Illustrations by André Swartley

PRINTED IN THE UNITED STATES OF AMERICA

Americanus Rex

BY

ANDRÉ SWARTLEY

WORKPLAY PUBLISHING

For Kurt Vonnegut, author of the bravest book I've ever read

PROLOGUE: A BEACON OF PEACE

.

1

Sunday, November 10, 1968

Stage lights hung like a row of tiny suns from the ceiling of the Seattle Center Opera House, raining white heat down onto the 1968 Miss Washington contestants. A trickle of sweat rolled down the side of Liza's nose to the corner of her mouth. She flicked her tongue at it, tasting sweat, and hoped the cameras were aimed at someone else.

"Now comes the part where we get to hear these lovely ladies' voices," the host announced, flashing his straight teeth in a smile that undoubtedly dazzled the audience members close enough to see it. On stage with him, Liza could smell the Brylcreem in his hair. "It's my favorite part of the pageant, the personal interview. We'll begin at the top of the alphabet with Miss Dorothy Anstett, who I believe grew up just north of us in Kirkland, isn't that right?"

Liza scanned the second row of the audience for her father and once more found him directly behind the judges, watching her with equal parts hope and encouragement.

"With the last name Bennett," her father had calculated during one of their many rehearsals at home, "I'm guessing you'll be one of the first interviews. That's not great because judges have short memories. But you'll also have the highest IQ of anyone up there by fifty points. Just say something that makes it impossible for them to forget you. You'll blow them out of the water as long as you keep you head."

"You mean as long as I don't think about how I'm conducting a supposedly hard hitting interview while parading around in front of half the state of Washington in a bathing suit?" she'd said irritably. "And besides that, I doubt you'd like to hear another contestant's father imply that I must be stupid just because I'm pretty enough to stand on that stage."

"Of course not, I didn't mean that." His brow had furrowed. "Sweetheart, I know the pageant isn't your first choice for a way to pay for college, but wasn't the effort to become Miss Seattle worth this year's scholarship? To have the next three years paid off as well...maybe if your mother or I were still working full time, we could—"

"It's okay, Dad. She needs you at home."

Liza's eyes wandered now to her mother, who sat in the audience beside Liza's father, wearing large Jackie Kennedy sunglasses. Her hand rested lightly on his forearm the way it nearly always did these days, as if she were afraid she might need to be guided somewhere even while sitting down.

The audience was applauding.

"Next we'll speak to our very own Miss Seattle, Elizabeth Bennett."

Suddenly Liza's hair itched furiously. Another bead of sweat ran down the inside of her left thigh. Still, she knew her smile betrayed neither of these feelings, nor the plethora of other discomforts that came with standing on a hot stage in a sky blue bathing suit before hundreds of people.

"Thank you, Bert. It's wonderful to be here."

Say something that makes it impossible for them to forget me, she reminded herself.

"Elizabeth, I don't want to pry but we've learned that a rare disease recently blinded your mother."

She swallowed to cover her surprise at such a personal statement. One of the judges, a small, goateed Oriental man, watched her intently, his long and delicate fingers folded across a yellow legal pad resting on the long judges' table in front of him.

"That's correct, Bert," she said. "Although shingles isn't all that rare of a disease. It's caused by the same virus as chicken pox. It was only the severity of my mother's case, the way the virus attacked her face and eyes, that was so unusual."

"Well, you and your family have our condolences. I'm sure this has been a difficult time for you."

"My parents are strong people. I'm very proud to have them here tonight."

The audience applauded again. Liza's parents nodded encouragingly in the second row.

"Elizabeth, I know that you are partway through your first semester of a Mathematics major at the University of Washington."

"With a focus in Geometry, that's correct."

"But your application to this pageant also states that you have a love for poetry. You write poems in your spare time?"

She nodded, her tight red curls bouncing in her peripheral vision. "Good poetry offers the same beautiful and timeless precision as Geometry. Why else would we still study *The Iliad* and the Pythagorean Theorem unless they worked as well as anything we've come up with in the centuries since they were created?"

The Oriental judge and one of his colleagues, a stern looking woman with graying hair tied back in a tight bun, dipped their heads and scribbled on their legal pads. Liza tried not to let her smile widen too much. No pageant judge ever born would forget a contestant who equated Homer and Pythagoras.

Three more years of full scholarships, please God.

"Do you participate in any extra curricular activities on campus, or do math and poetry take all of your time?"

"Yes, actually. A classmate of mine named Hollace Cornell and I just recently started a campus peace club with a mission statement borrowed from the late Dr. Martin Luther King: 'We still have a choice today: nonviolent coexistence or violent co-annihilation.'

"The peace club has written letters encouraging President Johnson to seek peaceful, creative resolutions to the Vietnam Conflict rather than destructive ones; we educate other students about war propaganda and the psychological dangers of dehumanizing other cultures; and every night we meet in the student union to watch the new CBS news program with Walter Cronkite."

"You sure sound like a busy young lady," the host said. He might have spoken the same way to a kindergartener who had just told him she used her spare time to organize tricycle races. "Last question, then. Since you are obviously interested in the cause of peace, if you become Miss Washington, how will you use your visibility and influence to advance world peace?"

Liza wasn't sure that even Miss America would have the visibility or influence to do much about the Vietnam Conflict, at least not by virtue of winning a beauty pageant, but of course she couldn't say so here.

However, before she could formulate a more acceptable answer, her mind conjured an image of such ferocity that she forgot all about Bert, the judges, and the cameras recording her every curve.

She saw herself, still in a blue bathing suit but no longer on a stage. She stood at the jagged, snowy summit of Mount Rainier, the highest peak in Washington and the whole continental United States. Raised in her hand like a torch was the Space Needle, the six hundred foot marvel of architecture that had dominated the eastern bank of Elliot Bay since Seattle had hosted the 1962 World's Fair. A ball of furious, torrential light blazed from the top spire of the Space Needle as if Liza had reached up and pierced the heart of the brightest star in the universe as easily as a chef preparing shish kebabs.

Yet that was not the most incredible part of the vision. Below Liza, boiling around the foot of the mountain, were millions upon millions of men locked in combat. Some thrust spears at one another, teeth bared in animal ferocity; some swung wicked curved blades in deadly arcs; still others fired pistols, cannons, and machine guns—earth's long history of war playing out all at once.

Even as Liza watched, the light from her captured star began to pour over the battlefield. Where the light touched, swords hung still at the fighters' sides and the cannons ceased their deep thunder. The throng faced upward as one toward Liza and her beckoning torch, as if the light she shone down on them were too mesmerizing for them to tolerate their own violence.

"Elizabeth?"

She blinked rapidly. Bert inched the microphone's round head closer yet to her mouth and cranked the wattage of his grin to Lunatic.

She felt breathless and a little unreal—Saint John's dreams recorded in the book of Revelation could have been no clearer or more intense than what she had just seen—but she felt her own grin widen just the same.

Bert wanted to know what she would do to advance world peace? Never before had she so completely or confidently known the answer to a question.

"I will light a beacon of peace from the top of the world," she told Bert and the hundreds of pageant spectators laid out before her.

She turned gracefully on her heel and took her place in the line of contestants once more, the afterimage of the star atop the space needle still burned into her imagination.

It was only when she heard quiet, uneasy laughter ripple through the audience that she realized what she had said. How very *little* she had said. Her father's face, a pale oval among hundreds in the darkened Opera House, wore an expression halfway between exasperation and dismay.

For one wild moment she considered bolting to center stage and wrenching the microphone from Bert's hand to explain what she had meant, but he had already called the next contestant, Caroline Buss of Fircrest, Washington.

Forty minutes later Miss Dorothy Anstett wore the diamond tiara and Liza filed offstage with a knot of other contestants who had been cut from the roster of finalists. She assumed she had been unanimously disregarded by all of the judges after her interview, but the Oriental judge tracked her down outside the dressing room after the show.

"Miss Bennett, I want to commend you on your bravery tonight."

"Excuse me?"

Between his ratchety, muddled speaking voice and a spiraling black cord that ran from a node in his ear to a bulge under his jacket lapel, she wondered if he might be partially deaf.

"Very few people could make so profound a promise in a place like this." He made a simple gesture that seemed to encompass the entire Seattle Center Opera House with his slender hands.

"I'm sorry, what promise?"

"To light a beacon of peace from the top of the world," he said as if it should have been obvious. "A grand and terrifying endeavor, but only as grand as the determination behind it." His black eyes sparkled fiercely as he looked up at her. "When you spoke onstage, the force of your will rebounded through the cosmos. Truly inspirational."

He bowed slightly, standing very still until she thanked him, at which time he stepped out the door and vanished down the hallway.

"At least *one* of them had an imagination," Hollace Cornell groused when Liza told him about it later.

In the days following the pageant, Liza couldn't decide whether her father or her boyfriend had taken her defeat harder. But aside from the utter strangeness of her episode with the Oriental judge, the surprising truth was that losing the pageant didn't bother her much. The problem of lost scholarship money became almost nonexistent when she took on part time jobs pouring coffee at a little upscale café in the Pike Place Market and running the Math Tutoring Lab on campus every weeknight.

Liza also quickly discovered she had indeed said something that had made it impossible for people to forget her, although it'd had nothing to do with Pythagoras or Homer. An editorialist for the *Seattle Times* had described her beacon of peace comment as "a perfect symbol of the pageant contestants' staggering beauty and simplicity of mind."

The *Seattle Post-Intelligencer* had been kinder in tone, but far more patronizing: "Miss Seattle, Elizabeth Bennett, stole hearts in the audience with her achingly sincere, if naïve, promise to "light a beacon of peace from the top of the world" during her onstage interview."

She didn't mind being attacked personally—she knew she wasn't vapid or simpleminded, and so did the people whose opinions mattered to her—but she was still troubled that her one comment had been used to classify all of the other pageant contestants as bimbos as well.

Liza put the pageant behind her and spent the next three years focused on her studies, her jobs, the Peace Club, and, when she had time, her relationship with Hollace Cornell. Mercifully, the newspapers lost interest in her quickly, and by the end of her senior year she believed the world had at last forgotten about her gaffe in the pageant.

She found out otherwise after the University of Washington announced that she would graduate *Summa Cum Laude* and as valedictorian of her class. While her speech at the UW graduation ceremony was mentioned favorably in most printed accounts, the *Post-Intelligencer* connected her graduation address to her performance in the Miss Washington pageant, once again with rather patronizing results.

"'We admire Liza Bennett's drive to forget past embarrassments and use her time at the university to improve herself,'" she quoted sourly to Hollace over dinner the night after the graduation ceremony. "I haven't forgotten anything."

"I know that," Hollace said nervously.

They were sitting at a small round table in the Space Needle Restaurant, high above downtown Seattle. A curved bank of windows circled the entire restaurant, slowly revolving to offer dizzying views of Queen Anne, Mercer Island, the Business District, and Bainbridge Island across the bay. Buildings, cars, and boats twinkled against the black backdrop of night.

"I *can't* forget," Liza went on, turning away from the windows. "Salvador Dalí was full of crap. The persistence of memory doesn't look like a bunch of melting clocks, it looks like a woman standing on a mountain in a swimsuit and shooting starlight at a bunch of men so they'll stop killing each other. What good is a persistent memory or a perfect idea when you have no hope of realizing it in life?"

"There's always hope," Hollace said. He glanced through the windows too, but immediately turned back to her, looking slightly green.

"What am I supposed to do?" she demanded. "Strap on my old blue bathing suit, stride up to the foot of the Space Needle, and heave it into the air like an Olympic weightlifter?"

"No, you accept the beacon of peace as a part of yourself," Hollace said. "I know you hate it when I play psychologist with you, but something spoke up—or woke up—inside of you that night. I'm sure it will make sense eventually. You'll just have to keep your eyes open."

"It doesn't matter if I keep my eyes open or closed," she said softly. "I see it all the time."

"I *know*," Hollace repeated. "Why else do you think I brought you to the top of the Space Needle to propose?"

"What?" she asked, her eyes widening.

But something in her mind had just clicked into place, making her quite forget about the article in the *Post-Intelligencer*. Last September she and Hollace had entered a wager that whichever of them graduated in second place would be obliged to propose marriage to the other. In the flurry of activities and responsibilities surrounding graduation, she'd completely forgotten.

"I brought you up here to propose," Hollace said, now smiling cautiously. "Lord knows there's no other reason I would voluntarily eat a meal six hundred feet above the ground."

She reached across the table and pulled his face toward her with both hands and kissed him over and over. Their plates clinked against the stems of their wine glasses with the sudden movement. Two nearby couples were staring when they parted, but Liza didn't care.

"Yes, of course I'll marry you, yes," she babbled as Hollace clumsily slid a modest—though still wonderfully sparkly in the restaurant's low lighting—diamond ring onto her finger.

They married before Christmas. Another two years found both of them with a post-grad degree apiece and faculty positions at the University of Washington. Liza felt like she'd barely adapted to the teaching side of the educational desk when her four-year review came around and she was awarded a full professorship and an appointment as the first faculty sponsor of the Campus Peace Club.

Despite the rush of time that whipped past her like wind, Liza managed to do what Hollace had suggested the night he'd proposed: keep her eyes open. And she discovered that keeping her eyes open and waiting, much like losing the Miss Washington crown, weren't so bad after all.

When she became pregnant, part of her wondered if her unborn child would play some role in bringing about her beacon of peace. The thought flared doubly through her labor pains when her bewildered obstetrician passed her brand new son to the OB nurse and declared that Liza's baby hadn't been alone in there—that the tests during pregnancy had somehow missed the presence of a twin brother or sister.

"Twins?" Hollace barked, squeezing Liza's hand.

Fifteen minutes after Hollace Benjamin Cornell, Jr. declared his entrance into the world with a squall, Imogene Elizabeth joined the party, adding an outraged bellow of her own.

The ten years following Ben's and Imogene's spectacular births, while wonderful beyond Liza's wildest imaginings, brought her no closer to her beacon.

2

Wednesday, June 19, 1991

Ben watched his mother close the book she'd just finished reading to him. One curl of dark red hair tumbled over her eye and she brushed it away. "*The King's Stilts,*" she read from the cover. "Dr. Seuss sure wrote some strange ones, didn't he, babe?"

Ben nodded, but he didn't smile. He'd smiled once already tonight at a funny voice his mother had done while she was reading and one of the sores by his mouth had broken open again.

The bedroom door swung open with a creak. "Sorry I'm late, Liza," Ben's father said, shrugging out of his tweed coat and leaning down to kiss her. "How you doing, kiddo?" he asked Ben. "Did you see Dr. Logan today?"

Ben nodded again. He yawned, attempting to keep his mouth immobile, and his teeth chattered with a fit of shivering.

Hollace's mouth turned down. "Still running a fever, is he? What did Logan say?"

Liza shrugged, but Ben thought his mother looked as nervous as she had at Dr. Logan's office today. "He checked Ben and Imogene both, head to toe. He didn't find any further sign of chickenpox on Imogene besides that one sore above her eyebrow, and even that one is fading now, but…"

She gestured at Ben as if to say, *See for yourself.*

Ben looked solemnly up at his father. "I'm sick enough for both of us."

His father laughed in surprise, and his mother smiled. Ben didn't know what was funny, but he was glad he'd made his mother smile for real for the first time all day.

"That's a direct quote from Dr. Logan," she agreed. "Imogene took off running like she thought she might get in trouble when Logan asked me if I was sure she had brought home the infection. For being a pediatrician, sometimes he doesn't have the best grasp on how to deal with ten-year-olds. I considered explaining that it wasn't her fault that her grandmother went blind and nearly died from the chickenpox virus, but a packed waiting room didn't seem like the best place to lecture a screaming child about hereditary vulnerability to disease."

Hollace reached down and rubbed her neck absently. "I just saw Imogene out on the couch reading. I didn't know a ten year old could look so despondent. Did Logan give Ben a prescription?"

"Chicken soup and a lot of sleep," Liza said, standing from the little desk chair she'd sat in while she read. Ben thought she looked pale. "Speaking of sleep, little man," she said to him. "I'm sending your sister in and then you guys need to go to hit the hay, all right?"

Both of his parents acted ready for him to protest and seemed almost disappointed when he didn't. Sleep sounded very good right now. The only time his body hadn't itched or shivered or just outright hurt in the last week had been while he slept.

They left his room, swinging the door almost shut. But they didn't go far. He heard them speaking softly in the hall.

"You look tired," Hollace said. "I'm sorry I couldn't go with you today."

"I know. Why were you so late?" Liza asked, her voice slightly muffled. Ben could picture her leaning her head on his father's shoulder.

"Myra Johns wanted to talk to me."

"Name sounds familiar."

"Franklin's daughter. I had her in Psych 101 as a freshman."

"What'd she want?"

"To talk to you, actually. She's enrolled herself in the Miss Seattle pageant. Hoping to make some scholarship money like you did."

Liza grunted. "And she wanted some tips about what not to say in your onstage interview?"

"Quite the contrary. Apparently she found a film of you in the archives at the university library while she was researching former winners of pageants in the state."

"Good girl. Sounds smart."

"She said she'd heard the things the newspapers said about you after the pageant, but she wondered why she hadn't heard about everything else you said. Your allusions to math and literature."

Ben heard his mother take a deep breath and release it like she did when he and Imogene were tormenting each other, but when she spoke again she didn't sound angry. Just very tired.

"As long as she's aware of the stereotype they'll try to squeeze her into, and that some people can hold onto stereotypes for, what, twenty-three years now?"

"Oh, she's aware of the stereotype. Doing her best to smash it to pieces with a four-oh GPA in all of her pre-med classes. I did mention to her that not all of the judges thought you were a dimwit. She loved what the Asian judge said after the show about the force of your will rebounding through the cosmos."

"If the force of my will rebounded through the cosmos, my babies wouldn't be sick," she sighed.

Ben listened to her slow footfalls travel down the hallway, heard her tell Imogene it was time to brush her teeth. Five minutes later Imogene shuffled into the bedroom, head turned downward. Tangles of red curly hair, so much like their mother's, hung over her eyes. When she sat down on her bed she finally looked at him.

"I didn't mean to bring home the infection, Benny."

He didn't say anything. He'd never seen his sister so serious before.

"Mom says you need sleep, so I'm going watch you all night and make sure you're okay."

She seemed almost ready for him to argue, just as his parents had been ready for him to argue about going to sleep, but he only nodded. Apparently satisfied, she turned and leaned against her bed's headboard, knees pulled up to her stomach to support the book she had brought in from the living room.

"You should read the one Mom read to me tonight," he told her, lifting it off the bedspread and setting it on the stand between their beds. "It's about a kingdom covered in water where the king walks on stilts everywhere."

"Go to bed, Benny."

"And there's a bad man named Lord Droon who thinks the king is silly and tries to hide the king's stilts. And he says a little boy who works for the king has measles and locks him away. Measles are like chicken pox," he clarified wisely.

"Don't scratch," Imogene said. "Doctor says you'll get Frankenstein scars."

He'd been raking away at the little orange scabs on the side of his neck without even realizing it. He dropped his hand, trying not to sulk.

"I just thought you might like the book."

"I'll read it if you go to sleep," she sighed. "We can talk about it in the morning, okay?"

"If you want," he said lightly, trying to mask his relief.

He knew Dr. Seuss was for littler kids than he was, but *The King's Stilts* had scared him. One picture in particular, of Lord Droon in his black robe and black hat with the little wire sticking out of it, refused to leave his mind. Ben had asked his mother if she thought Droon had a radio hidden under his hat. She had laughed and said there weren't radios back when kings had lived in big castles, and even if there had been, a radio under your hat would be pretty uncomfortable. Ben had pretended to laugh too, moving his lips as little as possible, but it hadn't changed the simple fact that he didn't like Lord Droon. He didn't like the mysterious wire in his hat or the black goatee that jutted from his chin like the point of a knife.

Ben vaguely heard Imogene trade the book in her hand for the one on her desk and slide back onto the bed. That was good. He didn't know if she would be afraid of Droon also, but even if she was, being afraid together was better than being afraid alone. Maybe she would even have an explanation for that creepy wire…

His eyes flew open. He had no idea if he'd been asleep for five minutes or five hours. The little lamp on the nightstand between his bed and Imogene's was still on, and he rolled his head to the left to see if she was still awake.

Despite her promise to watch him all night, she had fallen asleep. She was still sitting up, head resting heavily against the tops of her knees. But Ben registered these details distantly. A third person in their room was taking up all of his attention.

I'm still asleep, he thought wildly, his eyes darting from the little man's carefully trimmed goatee to the gleaming, needle-thin silver wire sticking up from the band of his hat. *Of course I am. I don't even itch.*

And he didn't. Not his arms or his neck or the wide patch of skin above of his butt that had itched relentlessly for the last two days. But this realization gave him little comfort. All of the other too-real details in his room—the wadded Kleenexes on Imogene's bedspread (she must have started crying again after he fell asleep), the box of Transformers in the corner beside the wooden writing desk he shared with his sister—told him he was wide awake. This was nothing like his typical good dreams of marrying Theodora Lilly at school or even the bad ones where he ran panicked through a darkened house, flipping light switches that never turned on.

The small man in the chair, grinning widely, shook his head as if to concur that Ben certainly was not dreaming. The grin made Ben feel more scared because the Lord Droon in the Dr. Seuss book had never grinned at all. Of course, the Droon in the book also hadn't looked Chinese like this one did.

"Your mother and your sister are very upset," Lord Droon said. His voice sounded like it was coming from a TV in another room: tinny and a little fuzzy.

"I'm sick enough for us both," Ben told him in a shaking whisper he hardly recognized as his own.

Droon nodded enthusiastically. "You would like to get better? For your mother and your sister as well as for yourself?"

The man coughed suddenly and the bedroom filled with a smell like burned matches.

"I don't itch right now," Ben whispered.

"Indeed not," Droon said. "Even so, you are still very sick. You may die from your illness."

His long fingered hands gently lifted Imogene's pink diary from the writing desk. The diary had originally been very thin, but Imogene had stuffed it with folded school notes, movie tickets, stickers, and ribbons from school contests. The whole mess was held together by a simple plastic lock Ben had opened countless times with a paperclip.

"There is a piece of paper in this diary that can make you better. Don't you think your sister would trade that one small thing if it could make you healthy again?"

Ben was starting to think he might be dreaming after all. He remembered his father saying that people usually dreamed about whatever had been in their minds when they fell asleep. Well, Lord Droon had been foremost in Ben's mind, and here he was, asking for a page out of Imogene's diary. In fact, Imogene would probably enjoy hearing about this dream in the morning, as long as Ben remembered to leave out that he'd opened her diary all those times.

Droon grasped the square corner of a piece of pink notebook paper and slid it upward, out of the diary's closed pages.

"Hey, my sister didn't write that one," Ben protested as Droon unfolded the page. "It's a letter from her penpal in Phoenix."

"Dulcinea Montero de Frutas," Droon read from the bottom of the letter. "Your sister's penpal has a lovely name."

"Sure that's the one you want? There's better stuff in there."

Droon nodded slowly, his eyes darting over the words written on the pink page.

"Well, just don't tell Gene I said you could have it," Ben said, figuring he might as well cover his tracks, dream or not.

Droon's grin widened. "Agreed." He delicately refolded the pink notebook paper and slipped it into the inner breast pocket of his black jacket. "Sleep now. We wish you a speedy recovery."

Ben's eyelids suddenly drooped. Could you fall asleep in a dream? "Thanks," he yawned. "See you later."

Droon coughed again, but this time Ben was too close to sleep to care much about the smell.

"Yes," he rasped at the edge of Ben's consciousness. "You will."

Strangers in Accord, Part 1

1

Wednesday, August 24, 2011

Low green hills and irregular patches of farmland rolled to a hazy horizon outside Imogene's window, partially blocked from her view by the short silver slant of the regional jet's wing. The Ohio River wound lazily along the border between Ohio and Kentucky like a fat brown snake. This was her second flight of the day and she was growing restless. At least this leg, from Cincinnati to Charleston, was only supposed to be about a third as long as the first one from Los Angeles to Cincinnati had been.

The pilot came on the speaker and confirmed a flight time of just under an hour. "And it looks like we'll have a nice, smooth ride, folks," he finished.

Imogene took a deep breath and willed herself to calm down. She could still barely wrap her mind around the idea that she was at last flying to West Virginia to visit her brother. It had been a year since she and Ben and their father had spent a sizzling August day in the back of a Budget moving van, stacking Ben's few belongings along the metal walls of the van.

She leaned forward and rifled through the seat pocket in front of her, found a discarded copy of *USA Today*, and skimmed the front page. Her father had always disdained this particular newspaper as "a mental laxative for a mentally diarrhetic society," and a story at the bottom of the page—"Pilots Report Second Wave of UFOs Over Gulf of Mexico"—probably wouldn't change his mind. But Imogene suspected Ben might be interested in this article as a possible source for the book he was writing on UFOs and bigfoots and who knew what else. She tried to read the article, but after restarting it a third time and still comprehending little of it, she decided she was too antsy to read.

She glanced at the man in the seat next to her and saw that he was still asleep. He hadn't so much as cracked an eyelid since the pilot had powered up the jet's engines back on the tarmac in Cincinatti. The man was so small that if not for his meticulous black suit and tidy goatee, Imogene would have guessed him to be a child traveling alone. The toes of his shoes dangled off the floor despite their enormously thick soles.

Short-man complex, anyone? her brother's dry voice intoned in her head.

The shoes themselves were as black as the man's suit and shone like mirrors. His whole wardrobe, especially the black fedora currently tilted over his eyes, made him look like he had just stepped off the set of *Guys and Dolls*. The only part of his get-up that wouldn't have jived with Nathan Detroit & Co. was a long, straight silver wire, the top three inches of which gleamed above where he had tucked it into his hat band. Only his mouth and chin were visible under the brim of the fedora, his angular Asian features softened by sleep.

The man had also been on her first flight from LAX, though he'd sat across the aisle from her on that one. As far as she'd been able to tell, he'd slept through that entire flight as well. When he'd sat down directly beside her on this flight she had joked, "We must have bought our tickets from the same agent. You stopping in West Virginia too or going farther on?" He had appeared not to hear and made no reply.

Imogene found herself unabashedly studying him—that wire in his hat reminded her forcefully of...*someone*. It evoked an old memory, almost certainly from childhood. Had one of her dad's colleagues at the University of Washington worn a hat like that, or had she actually met this man before? She decided she would ask him when he woke up.

As if responding to this thought, his hand rose, thumb upraised, and pushed the brim of his hat upward to reveal dark, almond shaped eyes. They crinkled at the corners with a smile, sharpening the already sharp lines of his face. He rummaged in his black bag, pulled out a liter bottle of Evian water, and took a long drink.

She returned the smile, cheeks burning. There was no point in trying to pretend she hadn't been staring at him while he slept. "So what's bringing you all the way across the country? Do you have family in West Virginia too?"

For a long moment Imogene thought he was just going to ignore her again, but he finally said, "I will be traveling farther on to attend a reunion."

His voice surprised her. It was raspy and flat, though somehow not unpleasant, and carried no accent. Like his clothes, his voice reminded her of the 1940s, specifically of her father's nostalgic collection of radio dramas in which urgent narrators spoke of Elliot Ness speeding toward Capone's hideout, or the Shadow knowing what evil lurks in the hearts of men.

He looked down at the *USA Today*, now closed and folded in half on Imogene's lap. "You have read this?"

Her cheeks reddened further. "My brother has a thing for UFO's. I was just going to show—"

"No," he interrupted, flipping the newspaper with long, slender fingers so that the top half of the page showed. "Here."

"'President to Discuss Fallout from "Red October Sky" with European Leaders,'" she read the headline aloud. "Is this about that plane that went down in Alaska the other day?"

"Much has happened since then. Read," the man invited.

Imogene shrugged. What else did she have to do?

ALASKA—An aircraft piloted by ranking officers of the Russian and Chinese Air Forces crashed into the Pacific Ocean early Monday morning. The pilots' bodies were recovered by the Coast Guard, along with several large pieces of the craft identified as being similar in composition and size to components of the space shuttle and other supraorbital vehicles. However, further salvage was halted when unsafe levels of radiation were detected from the underwater wreckage.

The Russian and Chinese governments have declined to answer questions from the President and other NATO leaders about the craft, its mission, or the unprecedented military cooperation between two of the world's largest nuclear superpowers. Top analysts in the military have suggested that the downed aircraft would be the perfect first-strike weapon.

A member of the National Security Administration, speaking on the condition of anonymity, shared that the intelligence community had already dubbed the craft the "Red October Sky," in apparent reference to Tom Clancy's novel, The Hunt for Red October *and Homer Hickam's* October Sky. *Despite its clever nickname, the craft is no joke, as the NSA member stressed. "A squadron of such aircraft attacking from a low orbit could deploy enough firepower to vaporize all of America's largest cities in a single strike."*

Underlining the seriousness of the situation, the President met this morning with Secretary of Defense and the Joint Chiefs of Staff. In a press conference afterward, he encouraged journalists to "keep a level head" in their coverage of this story. "I've already heard too much speculation about the so-called Red October Sky carrying nuclear weapons, for which there simply is no evidence. Panicking at this point could turn a troubling situation into an apocalyptically dangerous one."

Imogene quickly flipped to the page that contained the rest of the article.

The President believes there is also no compelling evidence that either Russia or China plans to launch a nuclear attack on the United States or anyone else. However, he also stated, "anything is possible." If it were discovered that the Red October Sky is actually a deployment vehicle for nuclear weapons, the President said, "I won't hesitate to take whatever action I must to keep America safe."

The President cited the apparent military cooperation of Russia and China as "further evidence of the truly staggering depths of globalization," of which, he said, we saw only the barest hint during the worldwide economic crisis in 2008 and 2009.

The theme of globalization was even more present in the President's plan to deal with the current situation. "The unilateralist foreign policy of my predecessor fits our current world about as well as an outhouse fits on a commercial jet. For good or for ill, globalization has become the truth of our world, whether in business, ecology, scientific discovery, and yes, even war. So it is with the safety of the full global community firmly in mind that I will travel to Paris tomorrow for a week-long summit with my European counterparts. Their concern is as great as our own."

The Council of Paris, as the summit is being called, will give the Russian and Chinese governments a week to volunteer the answers they owe to the rest of the world, said the President, adding, "The Council will also give us a chance to come up with an appropriate plan to protect ourselves if we must."

Imogene looked up. "Have you read this?"

"Oh yes," the man said gravely.

"The President isn't taking his own advice very well, is he?" she said. "'Apocalyptically dangerous'? And what kind of editor would allow the term 'fallout' to be in the title of an article about nuclear weapons?

It's just going to scare a lot of people."

"Then you understand the situation," the man said, sounding relieved. "You must also understand that it has always been people like you, not governments, who instigate meaningful changes in history."

"I don't know about that," Imogene said, caught off guard. "I just grew up talking politics around the dinner table with my dad and brother, so I keep up with the news as well as I can. What's your interest in the Council of Paris?"

Before the man could answer, his small body contorted with a wild, deep-throated hacking and Imogene caught a whiff of something like the hot sulfur smell of a match being swiped across emery.

"Are you okay?" she asked. "Do you need me to call the flight attendant or something?"

The man shook his head. He took another long pull on his water bottle and slumped against the back of his seat, the bristles in his goatee glistening. "All nations will eventually be dragged into this war if we do not intervene. It is a proven cycle of humanity."

"So…" Imogene floundered. Whatever this guy's health problems might be—asthma, emphysema, and clinical paranoia came to mind— Imogene decided that the topic of conversation was making him feel worse. "What do you do?" she finally asked.

"I am something of a diplomat," he wheezed.

"You know, I thought you looked familiar. Is it possible that I've seen you on television before?"

He shook his head again and smiled widely for the first time. His teeth were square and very white. "I am told there are many people in the world who look like me."

He upended the Evian bottle and drank until it was empty, then slid it back into his bag and pulled out a fresh one. He twirled a long, tapered index finger in the air. "Recycled air."

The two of them sat in companionable silence for a few moments. The new bottle of Evian crinkled in the man's grip as he twisted off the lid.

Imogene suddenly remembered a line her brother repeated at every opportunity. "Hey, did you know that Evian is naïve spelled backwards?"

The man momentarily looked alarmed, then broke into wheezing, shaking laughter, and drained half of his new bottle of water before he calmed. He tipped his fedora over his eyes and appeared to go to sleep once more, the water bottle still clutched tightly in his long fingers.

2

Ben was waiting for Imogene behind the security cordon at the end of the terminal. His dark hair, which had never carried a trace of the deep red in her own, was cut shorter than she'd ever seen it. He wore khaki slacks, which by some miracle seemed to have been ironed, and a black button down shirt that was far more formal than the occasion demanded. But the lopsided smile that spread across his face when he saw her was a hundred percent Ben.

"Queen Gene!" He pinned her arms to her sides in a spine cracking bear hug.

"Hi, Benny," she gasped. The sterile walls of Charleston's Yeager Airport ("West Virginia's Gateway" boasted a framed poster on the brick wall) blurred through tears that had nothing to do with her brother's painful hug.

Last year when she had interviewed to be Teddy Roth's assistant at the Roth Art Gallery in Los Angeles, Teddy had noticed in her personal information that she had a twin brother.

"Can you and your brother communicate telepathically?" he'd asked with the brusque humor that Imogene had quickly learned was his idea of charm. "Or kill people with your brains like those kids in *Village of the Damned?*"

"No, nothing like that," she had answered, laughing because Teddy had wanted her to laugh and because she had wanted the job.

She'd told Teddy she and Ben were as normal as any brother and sister: they had grown up picking fights, cheating each other in Monopoly, and sitting in their respective chairs at the dinner table. They weren't B-movie monsters. But since their mother had died they had shared a sort of electric completeness, like touching wires to the two posts on a battery to power a light bulb, whenever they were together. Watching his moving van pull out of the driveway last summer had been the worst moment of her life since her mother's funeral.

She blinked hard. "It's really good to see you."

"Yeah, you too," Ben said easily. He released her and reached down to grab her carryall. "This all you brought?"

"I'm only here a few days. Oh, before I forget," she added, "I saved you an article about pilots in Mexico reporting UFOs. It's there in my bag. I didn't know if you needed anymore sources for your book."

He nodded as if he'd heard this news already. "Second wave of sightings there in the last ten years. But the Gulf UFOs are pretty small potatoes right now. The conspiracy nuts on the internet are burning holes in their keyboards typing blogs about how the Red October Sky—that nuclear jet that crashed in Alaska—was actually a UFO that our military shot down. Complete garbage, of course. Have you heard about that?"

"Yes!" Imogene said, smacking his arm lightly for emphasis. "The guy next to me on the plane showed me an article all about it in the paper. He seemed really nervous about the whole thing."

Ben grimaced. "Well, the President has already been called the return of JFK, so why not give him his own missile crisis?"

"To me, the scariest part was how the anonymous source in the article was talking about vaporizing American cities, and the President talking about the apocalypse."

Ben shrugged. "No government on the planet is dumb enough to start a nuclear war. No matter where you're from, getting your electorate blown up isn't the greatest bullet to have on your record when campaign season comes back around."

"When did you become a cynic?" she asked, only half-joking.

"When my alternative was to live in complete terror," Ben said. "Look, I've spent my summer doing research in chat rooms with guys who proudly wear aluminum foil hats and pull out their dental fillings with needle-nose pliers. Even with a mysterious nuclear jet boiling in the ocean off the coast of Alaska, I have to trust that the leaders of the world have more sense than that."

He opened the door leading to the parking lot and held it for her. "Thanks for saving the article, by the way. I'll definitely give it a read when we get back to Accord."

"How far is away that?"

"An hour, but most of the drive might as well be on a treadmill. Trees and hills, hills and trees. Anything else happen on your trip?"

"Not really. Just that weird guy in the seat beside me. He looked exactly like somebody I know. I never did figure out who. He wore this black Indiana Jones hat with a wire sticking straight up out of the band."

Ben seemed to miss a step, but when Imogene glanced over at him, he had caught up with her again. He clicked a keychain fob to unlock his Prius, his skin unusually pale in the early evening light. "Sounds like Lord Droon from that old Dr. Seuss book Mom read us. Did he have a goatee too?"

Imogene's mouth fell open. "Lord Droon? That's perfect," she laughed, sliding into the passenger seat of Ben's car.

He stood outside for another moment.

"Hey, you all right?"

He climbed into the driver's seat and tossed Imogene's carryall into the back before reaching over the center armrest to clap her on the thigh. "You're in West Virginia now." He still looked pale, but he spoke with his usual humor and waved his arm expansively at the gray sea of parking spaces and airline hangers visible through the windshield. "Home to the Appalachian Celts, the Mothman, and of course the main reason I came out here: the Men in Black."

"Men in Black? You mean like the movies with Will Smith and Tommy Lee Jones?"

"Hardly," Ben grimaced. "In those movies the Men in Black were government agents that policed 'illegal aliens' living in the US. Cute, but pretty far off the mark. The real Men in Black come to your house and threaten you to keep quiet about a UFO you saw, or ask ridiculous questions about how your toaster works. Honestly, if the strangest thing you see in West Virginia is some guy dressed up like a Dr. Seuss character, you should ask for your money back."

"The Droon guy on the plane wore all black," she mused. "He didn't say anything about toasters, but he was a pretty odd duck. Did I just have my first Men in Black sighting?"

"No," Ben said shortly. "They're not known for riding airplanes. Like I said, they usually come to your house."

Ben had been correct about the heavily forested geography around Charleston. Fifteen minutes beyond the parking lot toll booth, the already sparse commercial and residential buildings gave way to spruce trees that cast long crisscrossing shadows on the low hills surrounding Highway 35. Even with the early evening sun still visible over the horizon, Imogene had little trouble imagining a humming silver saucer rising from behind the hill to their left, or a hairy man-shaped monster—perhaps a cousin to the famed Bigfoot sighted frequently in forests not too far from their home in Seattle—roaming through the trees.

"Have you seen any of those things you mentioned?" she asked. "The Mothman or whatever?"

Ben favored her with a horrified glance. "Of course not."

He pointed through the windshield. "See that big rocky hill way up ahead? That's General's Peak. Third highest point in West Virginia. My apartment in Accord is about a mile from the trailhead."

She stretched her arms as best she could in the confines of the car. "Pretty," she yawned.

"You want to call Dad and let him know you got here alright? Maybe you should do that now since we still have most of the ride ahead of us."

"I can't, remember? He's kayaking in the Boundary Waters with his Psych department cronies for their yearly civilization purge. No TV, no cell phones, no e-mail. He's probably soaked to the bone and having the time of his life at this very moment."

"Right, right," Ben nodded. "Who *wouldn't* be thrilled to get hypothermia in August?"

He hummed a few bars of some tuneless song, obviously stalling at something. "You aren't hungry, are you? I've got some granola bars in the glove box, and supper might be a little late."

"They fed us on the plane," she said suspiciously. "Why?"

Ben's fingers drummed the steering wheel. "No reason."

"Why, Benny?" She heard their mother's voice in her own.

Ben heard it too. "Well, *Mom*," he said, "Wednesday Church starts at eight and I wondered if you needed to eat beforehand."

She gaped at her brother. "*That's* why you're so dressed up. And when I moved you were so afraid Los Angeles would change *me?*"

He attempted to appear indignant. "Excuse me for wanting spiritual nourishment."

"Ben Cornell communing with religious conservatives," she marveled. "Dad would choke on his organic hummus."

"First Pentecostal does go a little heavy on the God-and-Country idea," he admitted. "But do you think these people would let me teach in their school—science, no less—if I didn't go to church with them?"

Imogene pondered this. Her brother attending a church, even a church that likely did not share the ideologies on which she and Ben had been raised, was not terribly shocking in itself. And she would happily join him if he wanted to go tonight. But he was hiding something.

He tried a different approach. "I can research my book in church too, you know. Religion is a major source of UFO lore. Remember that old spiritual?" He took a deep breath and sang, *"Ezekiel saw the wheel, way up in the middle of the air."*

"You've been practicing," Imogene noted.

He raised his eyebrows. "A wheel of fire in the sky. Flying saucer, anyone?"

"No need to get defensive," she said mildly. "I was just having trouble picturing you in a small town church pew. There's nothing wrong with it."

He gripped the wheel in both hands and grumped, as if to himself, "Just because Los Angeles is full of godless heathens, I guess nobody can go to church anymore."

3

They stopped at Ben's apartment in downtown Accord, but did not go inside. Ben parked the car in the alley below the apartment and ran Imogene's carryall up the wooden staircase that led to his door and chucked it inside. He suggested they walk to the church, and Imogene agreed readily after her full day of sitting.

"Is it far?" she asked.

"Five minutes, and that's if we take our time," Ben said, setting off briskly across Main Street.

Three minutes later Imogene saw the First Pentecostal Church of Accord for the first time.

"Kind of takes your breath away, doesn't it?" Ben said thoughtfully.

The church's narrow square steeple rose perhaps thirty-five feet into the air—higher than any other building Imogene had seen on the walk from Ben's apartment. The church gleamed white in the evening's dying light, its heavy wooden siding clean and almost supernaturally straight. Warm, golden light shone through a row of simple stained glass windows that peaked in gothic arches. Less inviting was a high brick wall with wrought iron gates surrounding a small cemetery.

At the main entrance of the church, a middle aged man and woman greeted Ben and Imogene with warm handshakes.

"This is my sister, Imogene," Ben introduced her.

The couple offered Imogene a "Welcome, sister," and a folded program of the evening's service. The inside of the sanctuary, like the outside, fit Imogene's expectations of a small town church. Antique light fixtures depended from ceiling fans hanging over the entire length of the center aisle, but most of the light they created was immediately sucked up by the heavily varnished ceiling and walls. The stained glass windows lining the western wall of the sanctuary glowed faintly with the evening's remaining light. The strongest two lights in the church illuminated the American and West Virginian flags that hung on sturdy wooden poles behind the pulpit, both frocked in faded gold fringe. Ben stopped at a pew four rows from the front end of the sanctuary's long center aisle and motioned for Imogene to sit.

Every pair of eyes in the room seemed to watch her sit down. She opened the program, cheeks burning, and read that the service would begin with a hymn led by someone named Priscilla Hemphill. Imogene imagined a barrel torsoed woman with wide hands and a wider vibrato. However, five minutes later, a radiant, trim twenty-something in a white cotton dress stood from the front pew and invited the congregation to sing "A Mighty Fortress is Our God."

Imogene heard snatches of harmony even though the hymnal contained only the melody. Although the lyrics were stirring, the music felt flat and rather drab inside the dim church. Mostly the people seemed content to let Priscilla Hemphill's soprano voice drift prettily above their own.

Imogene sang along, but let her eyes wander over the first three rows of the congregation. All of the women wore dresses, and although the temperature was at least in the mid-eighties, Ben was the only grown man in short sleeves. Most men wore slacks or jeans with cotton or chambray shirts open at the collar. Imogene noticed two boys of about twelve staring at her and Ben from a couple pews up. The dark haired one threw a quick wave to Ben. An elderly man in blue denim overalls that seemed to have been starched and pressed for the occasion hushed the boy at once before glaring sternly over his shoulder at Ben.

But Mr. Overalls didn't waste much time in returning his attention to the young woman leading music. He, like the rest of the congregation, seemed to have trouble looking anywhere else. Between Priscilla Hemphill's sparkling gray eyes and precise, lyrical voice, Imogene thought she might know why Ben was so interested in church all of a sudden.

The congregation sang "Amen" and Priscilla seated them with a gesture. Imogene immediately pulled Ben's pen out of his pants pocket and scribbled a note on the back of her program: *Have you asked her out?*

Ben's mouth turned down in a grimace. He took the pen back and glanced around discreetly before writing, *Engaged.* He seemed ready to write something else, but simply capped the pen and looked forward again.

The two boys Imogene had seen earlier read the evening's scripture, after which a man with a sleek helmet of black hair—listed in the program as Pastor Ephraim Wallop—delivered a sermon on the sin of complacency.

In the front pew, Priscilla Hemphill listened raptly beside a broad-shouldered, handsome young man. He listened to Pastor Wallop as well, but glanced down at Priscilla every few seconds, apparently to make sure she was still there. When she took the pulpit after the sermon to lead another hymn, Imogene noticed that the young man did not sing with the rest of the congregation. He stood silently, watching Priscilla with pride that seemed almost dangerously fierce.

Imogene tilted her head at the man and wrote to her brother, *Fiancé?*

Ben smiled uneasily. *Brother,* he wrote in tiny script. He scratched out both her question and his answer and stuffed the paper and pen into his pocket.

Before the song ended, the wooden double doors at the back of the sanctuary clunked quietly. Priscilla Hemphill's eyes rose over the congregation and her face broke into a smile of such surprise and elation that Imogene guessed it would melt the heart and knees of any man toward whom it was aimed.

She craned her neck backward and saw an odd little man—today was her day for odd little men, it seemed—in a plaid flannel shirt tucked into work weary jeans. He wore thick, purple-tinted glasses under a thick straw-colored bale of hair. She estimated him to be about her and Ben's age, probably close to thirty anyway.

The congregation stopped singing. There was no Amen this time. The voices, including Priscilla Hemphill's, simply died out halfway through the stanza. The only noise in the sanctuary was a horsefly buzzing against one of the stained glass windows.

As Priscilla watched the flannel man, her smile faded. Her perfect brow creased with worry. The congregation looked at her, then at the flannel man, then back. Had their movements been more coordinated they would have looked like fans at a tennis match. Except for Priscilla's brother. He focused only on the flannel man, his eyes smoldering with such untethered hatred that Imogene wanted to duck behind the pew.

Finally Priscilla spoke. "Gary, thank God you've come back. We were all so worried, weren't we?" If anyone in the sanctuary had been sharing her worry, they kept it to themselves. When the man didn't answer, Priscilla pressed on, "What happened? Where have you been?"

"I have to leave," the flannel man, Gary, said. His voice was flat and matter-of-fact, the auditory antithesis of Priscilla's.

Priscilla stepped cautiously from the pulpit to the center aisle, her eyes never leaving Gary. "You've already been gone for a week, baby."

Gary tilted his head upward, as if listening for something. "I can't marry you," he said. He sounded confused. "I have to leave."

Priscilla continued her slow migration up the aisle, gray eyes wide.

"Gary, you're scaring me, and you're scaring our friends. If you need help, anyone here will be glad to give it to you."

Gary cocked his head again—Imogene could have sworn his eyes flicked to hers for an instant, but it happened too quickly to be sure—and said more loudly, as if speaking to the entire congregation, "I will light a beacon of peace from the top of the world."

Ben stiffened. The wind rushed out of Imogene's lungs with only a soft whisper from her lips. She felt like she had been kicked in the gut.

Gary's head straightened on his shoulders and he smiled for the first time, apparently pleased with himself. He turned on his heel and left the sanctuary.

Priscilla Hemphill stood in the center aisle with one hand clutching the back of a pew and the other her throat. When the big wooden double doors thumped shut she winced, then heaved herself into motion and ran out after her fiancé.

4

Imogene expected the church to erupt into the hushed, excited whispers one might hear in a movie courtroom after a surprise confession. However, without any spoken directions, the congregants shuffled quietly from the sanctuary, one wary gaze occasionally meeting another before returning to the floor. Pastor Wallop had taken the pulpit again, perhaps to deliver the evening's benediction, but now he simply watched his flock corral themselves through the double doors.

Ben laid his hand on Imogene's shoulder and steered her into the exit line. She twisted around to see how Priscilla's handsome-scary brother was faring. He sat again on the front pew, his head now bowed. Imogene saw the broad, tense line of his shoulders and the back of his sandy hair. He might have been praying, except that his shoulders and upper back were vibrating under his shirt as if he were clenching his fists so tightly that his whole body shook with the effort.

The dark haired boy who had read the evening scripture with his friend waved again to Ben on his way out of the church but Mr. Overalls shooed him along. Ben and Imogene were among the last outside. The sky had gone to full dark and the waning thumbnail of the moon cast almost no light. Eerily bright starlight illuminated the mostly empty sidewalks.

"Where did everybody go?" Imogene asked. "Did they all start running once they got outside?"

Ben didn't answer. His hand stayed on her shoulder and steered her left when the sidewalk branched. Once they were completely alone, he finally let out a heavy breath. "Holy crapfish. Did you hear what Gary said?"

"Of course I heard it," Imogene hissed. "Do you tell Mom's beacon of peace story to everyone you meet? I hope you also tell them how brilliant she was."

He looked as flabbergasted as she felt. "I haven't told anyone about—"

He suddenly cocked his head like Gary had done in the church.

"Okay, Benny, you're freaking me out."

"Hush a second!" he whispered sharply, head still cocked.

All visible sidewalks and roads were still deserted. A silence more complete than Imogene had ever heard in either Seattle or Los Angeles had settled over the town.

Wait…she *did* hear something. On the other side of the long brick cemetery wall to their left. A woman's voice.

Ben grabbed her hand and pulled her over to the wall. He flattened himself against the bricks and inched toward the cemetery's arched entrance gate.

The utter strangeness of the situation finally struck her. She had always been used to her brother indulging his imagination, but sneaking along a wall like a secret agent in some gritty crime show? What next? Would Ben briskly draw a service pistol from his belt, spin through the cemetery entrance, and demand the owner of that voice put her hands in the air?

Ben didn't draw any firearms from his belt, but he did tilt his head into the entrance for an instant before pulling it back. *Priscilla and Gary,* he mouthed to Imogene before leaning in again.

Imogene yanked him back toward her and whispered, "Those people have every right to solve their problems privately. Let's just go home."

His head drooped, but not in defeat. "I know you're tired, and it must seem like your alien chasing brother has finally waved bye-bye to real life, but that guy back there was nothing like the Gary Pritchard I know. There's something really wrong with him. What if he hurts Priscilla?"

She had no answer to that. She had little practice acting against her brother's wishes. Plus she had to admit the mysteries of what Gary had meant by lighting a beacon of peace from the top of the world and where he had heard that phrase were too great to ignore.

Ben was peering into the cemetery again. Imogene stepped carefully around him to see for herself.

Gary sat on a tombstone. Priscilla knelt in the grass in front of him, clutching his hands.

"It's okay if you don't want to tell me where you've been for the last week," Priscilla was saying. "And if you're not ready to get married, I can give you all the time you need."

Gary stared over her head toward the craggy mountain Ben had called General's Peak. Starlight reflected in the thick lenses of his glasses.

Priscilla wrung his hands more tightly in hers. "We can find a counselor in Point Pleasant, or even Charleston if you don't want people to know about it. But I need you to tell me what's wrong. *Please.*"

Gary finally seemed to notice her. He turned his face down from the mountain in the distance and met her eyes.

"Yes," Priscilla said encouragingly. "Just tell me what's wrong, baby."

Gary shook free of her grip like a horse swishing its tail to drive away a pesky fly. He may as well have punched her in the face. She fell back so hard that Imogene heard her teeth click together.

Gary slid off the tombstone and ambled toward the iron gate at the opposite end of the cemetery. He swung it open and stepped through, his eyes never leaving General's Peak. The gate's rusty cry seemed too loud and close to Imogene's ears.

Priscilla stood slowly, looking after him. When it was obvious he wasn't coming back, she turned and walked dazedly toward the arched entrance where Ben and Imogene hid.

Imogene jumped backward out of Priscilla's line of sight. She and Ben padded swiftly to a dark recess between the church and cemetery wall.

They needn't have moved. Priscilla stared straight ahead as she glided past. Her footsteps made no sound on the sidewalk.

Imogene could now admit that Ben had probably been right about staying behind. Gary had treated Priscilla so coldly that he might have hurt her if she had pressed him. Imogene doubted she would ever be able to forget the image of Gary shaking Priscilla loose.

"Can we please go home?" Imogene whispered.

"I want to make sure she gets home okay," Ben said, maneuvering himself from the recess.

Priscilla had advanced about a block northward, a pale shade floating above the sidewalk. The night still seemed too dark, too quiet.

"I hope you put all the people from that church in your book," Imogene said softly. "Aliens, every one of them. The way they just lowered their heads and left the sanctuary without saying a word…"

"They were embarrassed," Ben said, still watching Priscilla. "Pride is a big deal here. People know each other's business inside and out, but not because they broadcast it in public like Gary did." He sighed in sudden frustration. "You know, Gary's dad runs the general store in town. I doubt anyone will shop there for a week. In the morning we ought to pay him a visit at the store, just for support. He serves a pretty mean breakfast. You still eat like a horse, right?"

"Wait," Imogene interrupted, "are you saying Gary's dad made him break up with Priscilla?"

"No, but people won't know what to say to him now. I don't know, maybe everyone will just pretend like it never happened."

"They did a fine job of it in church," Imogene agreed.

She wondered how many of the houses they walked past contained people who had attended tonight's service. No porch light challenged the darkness on either side of the street as far as she could see. Maybe they were at their windows, hiding behind drawn blinds as she and Ben secretly pursued Priscilla across town.

Imogene shivered.

Up ahead, Priscilla had apparently reached her home. She ascended the concrete steps to her front door and opened it without using a key. She tripped over the aluminum jamb and went to her knees. For the first time since leaving the cemetery she uttered a loud sob.

Ben ran a hand over his face.

To Imogene's surprise, Priscilla took hold of herself and stood before walking the rest of the way inside her house.

Ben sighed again. "Alright, come on," he said, laying a hand across Imogene's shoulders. "I've got a bottle of wine back at home and I think we both…"

But his voice died. Across the street, plainly visible in the yellow glow of her kitchen's overhead light, Priscilla had turned around as if to close her door, but hadn't yet moved out of her doorway. Her face pointed downward, and she seemed to be staring at dark grass and dirt stains knee-high above the hem of her dress where she had kneeled in the cemetery. An almost frightening look of determination had come over her face.

She took three firm steps from her kitchen back onto the concrete stoop outside her door. In one swift motion she reached down to the hem of her dress and yanked it off over her head. Underneath she wore a conservative white cotton brassiere and underpants to match.

Imogene gasped as loudly as her brother. She was forcefully reminded of the photographs she had seen of the healthy, curvy contestants in the 1968 Miss Washington pageant, her mother included. Priscilla had the body of a woman who had spent her life working hard and eating well. Nothing like the coked-out skeletons that Teddy brought to his exhibit openings at the gallery in Los Angeles.

"I don't belong to you anymore, do you hear me?" Priscilla thundered at the star filled sky. She crumpled the dress and flung it on top of a metal trash can standing beside the stoop. Her hands strayed to the bra straps running over her shoulders, but fell away. "No part of me," she finished.

This last might have come across as petulant or sullen—the cry of a child saying she didn't *want* to be Gary's dumb old wife *anyway*—but did not. For the second time that evening Imogene was reminded of her mother's declaration in 1968 that she would light a beacon of peace from the top of the world. Imogene had seen a recording of the televised pageant many times in her life, and each time she had literally trembled at her mother's words, the same way she now trembled at Priscilla's.

Having apparently spoken her peace, Priscilla stood a moment longer on the stoop, motionless, proud, and strong, lit from behind by the single fixture in her kitchen. Time itself seemed to have stopped…

…Until the neighborhood lit up in a white-purple flash.

Imogene suddenly found herself on the ground behind a low, scraggly juniper bush, Ben's arm pressed across her back. An unnaturally loud whirring came from somewhere to their right and Imogene knew with bizarre certainty that the sound was a Polaroid camera discharging a photograph. Someone had just taken Priscilla's picture.

Or theirs.

She listened for rustling grass or speedy footfalls on concrete but heard neither. Through the loose thatch of juniper, she saw Priscilla's head cast about, but she didn't throw her arms across her chest or show any other sign of modesty. The woman acted more like she was waking from a dream than searching for a peeping tom with a camera. Slowly, purposefully, Priscilla stepped back inside her house and closed her front door on the night.

Imogene looked over into Ben's wide eyes. "Can we *please* go home now?" she whispered.

5

Ben's step lightened once Priscilla's house and the memory of that single white-purple flash of light were behind them. Rather than walk past the church again, Ben suggested they cut over to Main Street so Imogene could see downtown Accord "in all its glory."

"You know, even if someone did take a picture of Priscilla in her underpants," he said, "that picture will never see the light of day. This town handles the Hemphills with kid gloves for a lot of reasons, not the least of which is Cody's temper. He's the brother you saw at church."

Imogene recalled too clearly the hate Priscilla's brother had shown for Gary in his facial expression alone. Combine that hate with the muscle quivering under his shirt and she could see why people here were not eager to get on his bad side.

"Plus their dad Earl died last April," Ben continued. "They raise horses on their ranch and he was rolled under an unbroken stallion. Freak accident."

They covered the last few steps to the corner of Main Street in silence. The neighborhoods through which she and Ben had walked had continued to look, to Imogene, unnaturally dark. Main Street was not exactly Times Square but it did at least sport arc sodium street lamps on the corners of every block. A four way traffic signal hung on crisscrossing wires over an intersection two blocks to the south, flashing yellow for north/south traffic and red for east/west.

"Like something out of a movie, isn't it?" Ben said proudly.

"A western, maybe," Imogene said.

The business district on Main Street consisted of two- and three-storey brick buildings, some with flat, painted façades. Large, occasionally elaborate Closed signs were posted in every window. A lighted second floor window down by the traffic signal seemed to be the only inhabited space in the whole row of buildings. A canvas awning below the window read *Pritchard's Corner, Gen. Mdse.* Hadn't Ben said Gary Pritchard's father ran a general store downtown?

Ben pointed at a faded blue and white corrugated tin shed across the street from where they were standing. "That's Cody Hemphill's garage. He's the town mechanic. He's honest and competent enough, but I wouldn't trust a squeaky tricycle to the two guys who work for him."

Now it was Imogene's turn to point. "Who's that?"

A hunched figure shuffled into the orange disc of a streetlamp down by Pritchard's Corner.

"Yeah, who in the world *is* that?" Ben echoed. He sounded amazed that there could be a person in town he didn't recognize.

If not for the dress and pink afghan around the person's shoulders Imogene would have been hard pressed to identify her as a woman. She was uniformly round and walked with a thick wooden cane.

"Do you think she's the one who took the picture at Priscilla's house?" Imogene asked doubtfully.

But Ben was already trotting out from the shadows on an intercept course with the woman. "Excuse me!" he called loudly.

The woman kept walking. Imogene adjusted her opinion of the

woman's mobility. She was quite fast, even with the cane.

Ben stepped in front of the woman, blocking her progress up the sidewalk. "Excuse me," he said again, this time in the polite, no-nonsense tone Imogene supposed he used with misbehaving students in his classroom.

The woman stuck out her cane and braked hard. "The quickest way to get excused, young man, is to stay out of my way. This train doesn't exactly stop on a dime."

"I'm sorry, miss," Ben said. "I just wanted to ask if—"

"Miss!" the woman snorted, pushing large, owlish bifocals up the bridge of her nose with a gnarled finger. "The accent gave you away quick enough, but now I *know* you don't belong here." She braced her palms on the head of her cane and leaned upward until her nose nearly touched Ben's. "If you're the one who took Curtis you can be sure I'll see you again. And this cane ain't just for walking."

She flexed her hands on it and eyed Ben and Imogene in turn, obviously ready to make good on her threat.

"Curtis?" Ben said. "Curtis Garfield? Has something happened to him?"

The woman squinted with new distrust.

"I'm his science teacher. Ben Cornell. This is my sister Imogene."

"Hello, dear," the woman said shortly, not offering her own name.

Imogene smiled nervously. She would not have chosen this setting for her first personal introduction to a resident of her brother's hometown.

"Look, if something has happened to Curtis I want to help," Ben insisted.

The woman's grip relaxed on her cane, though she still looked ready to spring forward at a moment's notice. Imogene had no doubt she could knock either one of them into the gutter if she wanted to.

"I've heard your name, of course, even if we haven't properly met. I'm Agnes." The woman did not hold out her hand. "Do you know Curtis's grandfather Calliope?"

"Sure, the big guy in the overalls sitting beside the two boys at the service," Ben said.

"I wasn't at the service, but that would almost certainly be him," Agnes said. "He called me tonight for the first time in over ten years, saying Curtis disappeared sometime during what Calliope called the 'exodus' from Wednesday Service." She spat the last phrase as if the words tasted of wormwood. "Curtis apparently wasn't at home when his parents got there either."

"We were at the church," Ben said. "Curtis read scripture with Jamie Hemphill. The service definitely ended…abruptly," he decided. "But that was probably only thirty minutes ago. Maybe Curtis went home with Jamie and lost track of t—"

"It doesn't take thirty minutes to run through the town's phone tree, Mr. Cornell," Agnes interrupted. "And I wouldn't have believed that Calliope Garfield would call me to say the Rapture was happening outside my kitchen window. A thread of panic has been running through town since Gary Pritchard disappeared last week, and even thirty minutes is too long for a boy to be missing these days."

"Somehow I doubt that Gary's return tonight would do anything to soothe that panic," Ben said darkly. "What can we do to help you find Curtis?"

Agnes hesitated. "Calliope asked me to check General's Peak. I know it better than anyone in town."

At the mention of the mountain she looked ready to spring off north again, but she simply resettled her afghan. "Tell you how you can help. If you all have keys to the elementary school, take a swing through on your way home. Children do sneak in there on occasion."

The woman resumed her rapid pace up Main Street but stopped again and turned back after only a few steps. "Imogene, was it? Well, I doubt if anyone else has said it yet, so I'll speak for the town: welcome to Accord."

Accord Elementary was a squat, unimpressive rectangle of yellow brick and narrow windows at the western edge of town, five minutes' walk from Main Street. Imogene caught a glimpse of swing sets and a small jungle gym behind the school building. Beyond this meager playground was a jagged black screen of spruce trees that extended as far as Imogene could see in either direction. The road she and Ben had followed from the center of town terminated in the parking lot.

She'd heard that living in a small town felt like living in a bubble at times, but Accord seemed to fit that description literally. A bubble of humanity surrounded by wilderness.

Ben unlocked the front door. "The school should be locked all day but now that it's almost September teachers have started coming in and getting their rooms ready for the first day of school."

"When do you start?"

"First day of class is two weeks from tomorrow." He ushered her through the door and locked it again.

Nothing about Accord had felt familiar or safe to Imogene so far, but Accord Elementary finally broke the trend. Like all schools she had attended or visited, the building smelled of equal parts industrial cleaner, cafeteria food, and the somehow hectic odor of small children. Single bars of fluorescent lights gleamed dully along the hallway ceiling.

"My room's third on the left," Ben said. "But we'll check the others first."

The first room they checked was empty save a few rows of student desks, a wooden teacher's desk and a single tall cupboard, the latter being the only place a child could easily hide. Ben dipped his head under the teacher's desk and swung open the cupboard doors before switching the room's lights back off and locking the door. Besides the layout of the student desks and a few posters on the walls, all of the classrooms they examined were identical. There were maybe twenty rooms in the whole school.

"Wait," Imogene said as she noticed placard outside one door that read *Miss Hemphill.* "Is this Priscilla Hemphill, the song leader?"

"Yup," Ben said, unlocking the door. "Priscilla teaches first grade."

Unlike the other rooms, there were no posters on the wall and all of the desks were scooted to one side of the room. Only a single row of hanging files on the teacher's desk showed that Priscilla had any intention of returning to the classroom someday.

"Last year she was the first to get her room ready for the students, but her wedding is in a week or so," Ben explained. "*Was* in a week, I guess."

After they had checked every other room, they returned to the one Ben had claimed was his own. "I'm almost ready for the kids," he said proudly, flipping on the lights.

Stuffed three ring binders and manila folders littered the teacher desk and floor. He scooted these out of the way with his foot so he could open the room's only cupboard, which was equally crammed with school materials and a seemingly random assortment of textbooks and novels. Imogene noticed fondly that Ben had a poster behind his desk with a silver flying saucer hovering over a grove of pine trees. The poster's caption read *I WANT TO BELIEVE* in large white letters.

"Have you told your students that you're writing a book?"

Ben shrugged. "Not yet."

"Your colleagues?" she asked as nonchalantly as she could manage. Back at church she had imagined Ben mostly admiring Priscilla Hemphill safely from a church pew. She had trouble imagining his relationship with her as a coworker.

Ben glanced at her reproachfully.

"Am I that transparent?" she laughed.

"More," he said. "I did mention my book to one of the other teachers, Abe Penrod. He also wrote a book, a two-volume sleeping pill called *The Rich History of Accord*. It's in the public library if you're interested." He flipped off the lights. "Which I guarantee you're not."

"What about Priscilla?" Imogene pressed.

Ben shooed her out the door and locked it. "What do you think? She's engaged to a good ol' boy, and her brother is a Neanderthal with anger management problems." He sighed. "The first time I sat next to her in the faculty lounge, my hands were shaking so badly I dumped coffee in her lap. Thank God it had cooled."

On their way out of the building he stopped at the main office.

"Hang on. I want to call Curtis's parents and see if he's home."

He leafed through a thin, stapled packet that Imogene realized must be the Accord telephone book, and dialed. "Emma Louise? This is Ben Cornell calling from the school. I heard Curtis was MIA tonight and I wanted to make sure—" He brightened. "Hey, that's great. Where was—? Oh. Well, you have a good night too."

He squeezed the phone tightly and hung up. "She said Curtis turned up at home a few minutes ago, but wouldn't say another word. I had that kid in my class everyday for a year and his mother still acts like I might sell him crystal meth or feed him to a pack of wild pitbulls or something."

He grunted tiredly. "See why I'm having trouble researching my book?"

6

The next morning Ben burst into his bedroom—he'd given Imogene his bed and slept on the couch in the living room—at 8:00. Imogene's body clock insisted that it was only 5:00, but Ben harassed her until she pulled on some clothes, tied her hair back, and dragged herself down to Pritchard's Corner with him for breakfast. A single whiff of the mingled scents of coffee and frying potatoes drifting through the front door of Pritchard's Corner woke her more fully. Her stomach growled loudly.

"That a girl," Ben said, smiling. He entered the store behind her and latched the door. A leather strap covered in gold sleigh bells jingled merrily on the knob.

They walked down an aisle lined with shelves stacked ten feet high on either side with…stuff. Imogene had never seen anything like it. To her left were shallow boxes of sledgehammer and axe heads with various sizes of wooden handles on pegs above them. To her right were racks of t-shirts, socks, and baseball caps. The aisle itself was a tidy jumble of bins, crates, and shelves, all crammed with items for sale. Nails and screws, footballs and basketballs and Frisbees, work gloves and steel toed boots, garden hoses and sprinkler heads...

"I thought you said this was a hardware store," she murmured to Ben.

"*General* store," he corrected. "A real one. Businesses like this don't exist in Seattle anymore, if they ever did. It's the only place I've ever been where you can buy a lawnmower and a rhubarb pie at the same cash register."

Indeed, she saw the front end of a green John Deere riding lawnmower poking from a distant corner of the store and a line of beautiful golden pies under the counter covered in cellophane. A hand lettered sign in the pastry display case read:

Ma's Homade Pies
Slice...$1.50
Whole............$8.00 ($10 for requested filling)
Baked daily by Meredith "Ma" Hemphill

Priscilla's mother? Imogene wondered. Or maybe grandmother?

Before she could ask, a stocky man in an apron pushed through swinging saloon doors at the back of the store. In one hand he carried a plastic bag that appeared to be wrapped around some type of long, thin tool. When he saw them he stuffed the bag quickly under the counter.

"Gary's dad," Ben muttered, quite unnecessarily. Aside from the deep crow's feet around the man's eyes and a retreating hairline, he could have been Gary Pritchard's brother. Even the frames of his square tinted bifocals matched his son's.

"Ben," Gary's father said kindly. His shoulders made a broad, straight line under his buttoned work shirt, and his back showed only the first hint of a stoop although Imogene guessed he must be nearly old enough to retire. "Welcome. How did that screwdriver you bought work out for you?"

"It was a delight," Ben assured him. They shook hands. "Glenn, this is my sister Imogene. She's visiting from out west."

Glenn released Ben's hand, then grasped Imogene's in a firm shake. "Your sister." He sounded relieved.

"I wanted to give her a taste of real Appalachian cooking, but without the squirrel meat. You making Lee's Specials this morning?"

Glenn smiled tightly. "Griddle's been running for an hour. Two Specials coming up." He produced two coffee mugs from under the register and invited them to fill up while they waited for their food.

"I don't think he liked your joke," Imogene said when Glenn had turned his attention to the spitting griddle behind the counter.

Ben filled his coffee mug from the urn and ushered Imogene to a small booth with an orange Formica tabletop and benches. "Something's got him distracted this morning. After last night's little production at church he probably thinks the whole town is whispering about him and his son this morning. Like we're doing," he added.

Imogene did not hear anything past *this morning*. As soon as she'd sat down, her attention had locked onto the person walking past the store's front windows.

"What in the world's wrong with you?" Ben asked, turning in his seat to follow her gaze.

The sleigh bells on the front door jingled again. Imogene heard the soft thump of rubber soles on hard wood before the new customer stepped into full view. The man was dressed in a black two-piece suit with a starched white shirt and black tie. Imogene did not need to see his black fedora with the silver wire sticking up from the band, nor his tidy goatee, to know he was the same man who had sat beside her on yesterday's flight.

"That's the guy," she hissed. "Lord Droon."

Ben's throat seemed to have locked. His Adam's apple worked soundlessly.

Droon—until Imogene learned his real name, this ridiculous moniker from Dr. Seuss would have to suffice—padded to the counter on his thick-soled shoes.

"Water?" Droon said politely. His voice had the same raspy, radio-drama quality Imogene remembered from the airplane.

"You," Glenn breathed in obvious recognition. He reached under the counter.

He's going to kill him, Imogene thought suddenly. *He's going to pull an antique shotgun from under the cash register and blow him away.*

But Glenn did not draw a shotgun, antique or otherwise. Instead he held up the plastic bag he had carried through the swinging saloon doors and shook it in Droon's face.

"Are you the one who gave these to my son?" he demanded. The plastic bag shook quietly in his fist. "Are you responsible for making him do...what he did?"

Lord Droon blinked rapidly. "Bottled water?" he wheezed in that same polite tone. "Naïve?"

Glenn's fist and the bag in it slowly lowered. "Please. Gary's all I have left," he said huskily.

Droon's whole body shuddered. "I mean Evian. How silly of me?" The words made sense but his tone seemed almost a plea.

When Imogene had met Droon on the airplane he'd seemed odd but at least he'd been personable. Now he acted as if he might be mentally handicapped.

Glenn glanced over at Ben and Imogene before stuffing the bag back under the counter. He collected himself enough to retrieve a liter of Evian from an upright cooler and handed it to Lord Droon. "That's a dollar-twenty."

Droon smiled at last and placed a large wad of what appeared to be fifties from his jacket pocket on the counter. He tipped the water bottle upside down over his open mouth.

"You, uh..." Glenn pulled one crumpled bill from the pile and rang up the water. "You have to take off the lid." He reached for the bottle and unscrewed the cap.

Droon smiled gratefully. This time the water flowed in loud *glup-glup* sounds into Droon's open mouth. He did not appear to be swallowing, but not a drop fell onto the floor.

When the bottle was empty he said, "More please. To go."

"I can see why a case doesn't last you long," Glenn said. He seemed to have calmed slightly since the plastic bag had disappeared under the counter again. He retreated back through the saloon doors.

Imogene turned to her brother. His face was still quite pale but he no longer appeared to be choking. He had produced a small reporter's notepad and was scribbling furiously.

"Is that for your book? The guy's a weird cookie, but you said yesterday you didn't think he was a Man in Black. And I seriously doubt he's an alien either. Why would someone with his own spaceship fly coach?"

Ben ignored her.

Glenn reemerged through the doors with a case of twenty-four Evian bottles wrapped in plastic. Droon's slender fingers curled eagerly around the bottom of the cardboard case while Glenn made correct change for the fifty he had taken off the counter. Droon accepted the money and stuffed it back into his pocket with one hand. Imogene thought he must be awfully strong to hold twenty-four bottles of water so easily with one arm.

"I gave nothing to your son," Droon said, suddenly more eloquent. "You shouldn't worry about him."

Glenn's eyes hardened. "That's my last case of water. You'll need to shop elsewhere from now on." He turned back to the griddle, where Ben's and Imogene's breakfasts now showed appetizing browned edges.

Droon left the store as quietly as he had entered, having no trouble operating the doorknob in spite of his burden.

Ben finished scribbling and stowed his notepad just as Glenn Pritchard delivered their breakfasts. Imogene's stomach rumbled again at the mountain of eggs, potatoes, and sausage swimming in thick gravy on her plate, but she didn't pick up her fork.

"Are you okay, Mr. Pritchard?" she asked. The man's cheeks were ashy below wet, pink eyes.

"I'm sorry you folks had to see that," Glenn said heavily. "I can usually keep myself together better than that. Just having Gary go missing on the anniversary of the day my wife Esther and I learned about what happened to Annette all those years ago…"

"Annette?" Imogene asked.

"Our daughter," Glenn said heavily. He shifted his weight suddenly, as if his body were trying to walk him away from their table, but his mouth needed to talk to someone. His mouth won the battle. "She died in Iraq in 1993. One of the first female casualties in the war. Gary was only twelve at the time. Esther took it so hard she moved north on her own. It's been just Gary and me since then." He absently removed his glasses and scrubbed them on his apron.

"I'm so sorry," Imogene said.

"Well. The day Gary took his temporary leave last week, that Chinese fellow showed up in my shop asking for water." Glenn glanced toward the door as if to make sure Droon had gone. "Been here everyday since."

"So he and Gary aren't friends?" Ben prompted.

"Not that I know of," Glenn said. He seemed pleased to be moving away from the subject of his deceased daughter and absent wife. "That first day I asked him what thirsty work brought him to Accord, and he said he was a reporter covering the collapse of the Silver Bridge up in Point Pleasant." He blew briskly on his bifocals and slid them back into place against the bridge of his nose. "Problem is, that was over forty years ago."

"Christmas of sixty-seven," Ben agreed.

Glenn nodded. "There were loads of his type around here back then. I had just opened the store and more visitors passed through here in a day than we see in a year these days. A lot of nosy college kids, but plenty of his sort too, driving black Cadillacs and asking strange questions."

Imogene hoped Ben would also ask about the plastic bag Glenn had shaken in Lord Droon's face, but he only thanked him for the food.

"You're welcome," Glenn said, managing a smile. "I hope you enjoy your breakfast. One hundred percent squirrel free. Dig in," he invited, then retreated behind the store's front counter once more.

7

Imogene dug in. Shiny pools of hot grease swam into the empty spots on her plate. "This is terrific," she said, shoveling more onto a wedge of toast with her fork. She glanced over at Glenn Pritchard, who appeared to be taking inventory of a series of crude paintings hanging on the wall behind the counter.

"No wonder he seemed so upset this morning when Droon came into the store," she said. "So Glenn met Lord Droon here in his store, I met him on the airplane yesterday, and, if your expression when Droon walked in here was anything to go by, you've seen him before too. Don't deny it, Benny."

"I deny nothing." Ben leaned back and sipped his coffee. "Look, I came out here to write a book about UFOs, aliens, unexplained phenomena, right?"

She nodded. None of this was news to her.

"Except those things are just side notes. The Men in Black are the real stars of the story I want to write, not flying saucers or Bigfoot. And statistics show that if you see unexplained phenomena once, you're much more likely to see them again."

"So you're saying that Lord Droon was the unexplained phenomenon you saw...once." Her brother nodded. "I don't know if I'd classify him as an unexplained phenomenon. The guy's weird, I'll give you that, but you and I saw weirder at the Pike Place Market back home when we were growing up. Remember that blind guy with the ferret named Jesus?"

"I saw Droon when we were ten," Ben said. When Imogene didn't respond, he went on. "Remember those last couple days when I had the chickenpox?"

"Of course I remember."

She set down her fork. A familiar distant ache settled hard in the pit of her stomach. Her memory of those few hellish days seemed as eager as ever to come rushing back after two decades. She and her mother sitting in an examination room on identical chairs with brown *faux* leather cushions while Dr. Logan's fingers gently probed the red sores on Ben's body. The paper covering the examination table had crinkled dryly with Ben's fever shakes.

Dr. Logan had turned to look at Imogene, at the fading red mark above her left eyebrow. "You say Imogene brought home the infection?" he had asked her mother.

"She came home scratching a red bump on her forehead, and Ben got it soon after that. It just never took over her like it did Ben."

The doctor had leaned over to press his fingers once more against the skin above her eyebrow. Imogene remembered steel-gray bristles of hair growing out of the top of his nose. She remembered smelling cinnamon and a sour, yellow odor she always associated with the doctor's office.

"Well, we can be grateful the chickenpox never got hold of her," Dr. Logan had said, "but Benjamin is sick enough for both of them."

I brought home the infection, she remembered thinking. She hadn't known the word "infection," but she'd suspected it had to do with the welts covering every part of Ben's body, some of them red, some purple, some with hard orange scabs like crystals.

She had run out of the examination room, down a long white hallway, and all the way to the waiting room before her mother had caught up to her and pulled her close.

"I didn't mean to do it!" she had wailed into the front of her mother's shirt. "Is Benny going to die?"

"Shh," her mother had said, rocking her. "Of course not. He's going to get better very soon. You don't have to be sorry about anything."

And Ben *had* gotten better very soon. His fever had cooled the next morning and the welts had begun to fade a few days later.

But the chickenpox had not finished with the Cornells. Before the single red mark on Imogene's forehead had disappeared entirely, similar red marks had appeared on her mother's arms. Then on the sides of her neck. Then on her eyelids. If Ben had been sick enough for two people, their mother must have been sick enough for the whole world. Her skin had eventually become so clogged with chickenpox that they'd had nowhere else to go except inside her body. They had marched down her throat and strangled her as surely as if a pair of meaty hands had slowly squeezed her windpipe closed. No steroid or anti-inflammatory medication had been able to touch them. She'd died one week after the visit to Dr. Logan's office.

"I saw Droon in our bedroom the night before my fever broke for good," Ben said, interrupting Imogene's grim memories. "He was reading your diary."

"*What?*" Goosebumps flared on her forearms. Somehow the thought of Lord Droon breaking into their childhood home—into their *room*—was still less disturbing than the image of him sitting in the dark, reading her diary.

"He told me he could save me if I gave him something out of your diary. I think it was a letter from your penpal in Phoenix. The little girl Mom found for you when you wanted to learn Spanish. What was her name?"

"Dulci," Imogene said, her insides turning colder yet. The last letter she'd received from her friend had been about Dulci's brother Ramón and a bully at school, but Imogene had only read it once because she'd lost it around the time Ben had recovered and their mother had died.

Ben smiled without any real amusement. "In the morning, the idea of trading my life for a piece of paper was too ridiculous to say out loud, so I never told you about it."

"Benny, it *is* ridiculous. You had a dream."

"I got better," he said stubbornly.

She had no answer to that. When Benny had gone to sleep that night twenty years ago she had been convinced he would not wake up again. Yet here he was, drinking coffee across from her, a healthy thirty year old man.

"In high school I read an article in one of Dad's psychology journals about the Smiling Man," Ben went on. "That's what head doctors call him. Usually he wears a plaid shirt and just sits or stands near your bed, grinning like an idiot. People wake up in the middle of the night, see him, and get so scared they usually cover their faces or roll over and squeeze their eyes shut. Dad's journal tried to pass it off as some Freudian subconscious waking dream, even though in every case people claim they are not just awake, but lucid, when they see him.

"Anyway, the jump between the Smiling Man and Men in Black isn't terribly wide. A lot of Men in Black lore involves ominous smiling men. Which is why," he finished expansively, "I thought I'd come to West Virginia, where unexplained phenomena are a part of everyday life. I didn't consider that no one here would *want* to talk to me about it. The hubris of having a psychology professor for a father, no doubt."

The sleigh bells on the front door tinkled again. Ben's head whipped around. "Is he back?"

But the new customer was Cody Hemphill. He was tall enough that Imogene could see his head moving above the various shelves and display bins in the store. She heard the clump of his work boots on the wood floor with steps as heavy as Droon's had been light.

The air around him seemed crisp, charged with an invisible electric current. Two other young men—one taller that Cody, but scrawny, with a hooked nose like a witch; the other only a few inches taller than Droon, with a thick body like a blacksmith's—stayed in formation a few feet behind him as if to avoid getting shocked. Imogene imagined that if Cody's fingertips brushed one of the shovels or axe heads on the shelf next to him the static discharge would blow him and his buddies backward through the front windows.

He spared the Cornells a single disinterested glance on his march to the counter. "Mornin, Glenn."

"Cody." Glenn's hands were clasped tightly on the sides of the cash register.

"I closed the garage for today. Me and Wash and JT went up the Peak to see if we could figure out who made that picture of my sister." His fists worked at his sides.

"Picture?" Glenn managed, trying and failing to sound surprised.

"You ain't heard?" Cody's tall friend said eagerly, but quieted under Cody's sudden glare.

"Last night," Cody said, obviously straining to keep his voice calm, "on the face of a flat white rock on General's Peak, someone made a picture of Priscilla in her underclothes."

"We don't know the pecker's real name," the shorter friend said helpfully. "Signed it 'Americanus Rex' instead of a real name, like he's some kind of fucked up dinosaur. Course I wouldn't put my name to anything so trashy either."

"Yeah," the tall one said, once more excited. "You can see the bumps on Priscilla's nipples." His voice cracked on the first syllable of *nipples*. "Right through her titty purse."

Cody rounded on them. His sand-colored bangs swept prettily across his forehead. "If you two don't show more respect for my sister and for Glenn's place of business I'll take a shiny new pair of pliers off that shelf and rip out your tongues." He turned back to Glenn. "I apologize."

Glenn spread out his arms and pursed his lips as if to say *Hey, we're all friends here.* His hands returned quickly to the sides of the register.

"I heard there was some little gook in town acting funny and asking questions. We're going to find him and ask some questions of our own. Thought I'd see if Gary wanted to join us. Show him there's no hard feelings for what he done last night."

Sure, Cody, Imogene thought. *And your two friends are the town doctor and chess champion.*

The hate he had shown for Gary Pritchard in church was not the sort either to develop or dissipate in a single night. Imogene wasn't sure who would receive worse treatment at the hands of Cody and his goons: Gary Pritchard or Lord Droon.

"I haven't seen Gary since, ah," Glenn fumbled, "earlier this morning. He's still upstairs in bed, matter of fact. Bad fever." He hesitated. "Gary feels terrible about what he said in front of everyone last night. He hasn't been right since he came back. Can't even seem to tell me where he's been, if you want the truth. Doc Jacques has seen him twice already for brain tests."

Cody nodded as if Glenn's words sounded utterly sensible but his hands remained in tight fists. "Well, it would have to be something serious to make Gary do what he done in church last night, wouldn't it? Wish him well for me when he wakes up. We'll be around town all day if he gets to feeling better."

Glenn smiled. "I'll be sure to tell him."

Cody turned and brushed past his goons, who once again allowed him a few feet of space before following. Once the sleigh bells on the front door clanged with their exit, Glenn released the breath he had been holding and let go of the cash register. He snatched the plastic bag out from under the counter one more time and bustled to the front door. After a quick check through the windows to make sure Cody had departed for good, he stepped outside.

Imogene and Ben silently watched him disappear into the alley around the corner of the store and reappear moments later, empty handed. Ben stretched, rubbing his stomach theatrically as he called across the store to the counter, "Terrific as always, Glenn. What do I owe you?"

Glenn rang them up robotically, pounding the keys on his antique cash register. When he delivered their check and made change at their table, Imogene thanked him as warmly as she could manage. Glenn shuffled away wordlessly and disappeared through the batwing doors behind the counter.

Outside, Ben stretched again, turning his face up to the sun. "Dumpster," he muttered as soon as the door jangled shut behind them. "You stand guard."

The dumpster in question was on the way back to Ben's apartment. Imogene leaned over to adjust the straps on her sandals while Ben ducked into the alley to retrieve the plastic bag. Heat was already baking off the sidewalk, coaxing tiny beads of sweat from her toes.

She heard the rustle of plastic as Ben tucked the mysterious bag Glenn had thrown away into the rear waistband of his shorts. He joined her on the sidewalk and they strolled back to his apartment.

"Last night you said a photo of Priscilla Hemphill in her underclothes wouldn't ever leave the photographer's closet," Imogene said once they had turned into the alley that led to his apartment.

"You saw Cody Hemphill in there," Ben retorted. "Would you do anything to piss that guy off? Except I'm not sure Cody was talking about a photograph. He said somebody *made* a picture of his sister and it was on General's Peak. And his friend Wash said somebody signed the picture. Neither one of those guys speaks the King's English by any means, but something about what they said doesn't jive with a Polaroid."

"So what were they talking about?"

Ben glanced behind him. "If Glenn's response to whatever is in this plastic bag is anything to go by, we'll know as soon as we look inside."

8

Imogene kicked her sandals off inside the apartment door and dropped onto the puffy red couch, where Ben had volunteered to sleep last night. She was once again surprised at how clean Ben kept his place. Although, she reasoned, she had been here for less than twenty-four hours. The truth might come out soon enough. But for now the wooden floor of his living room—which melted into a small kitchen and dining room—was free of dust bunnies and shoe scuffs. The only messy part of the apartment was a wooden writing desk across from the couch, wedged between the two bookshelves bursting with sci-fi and fantasy novels. Ben's laptop sat on the desk, nearly invisible among black cables, loose papers, science textbooks, and three stained coffee mugs. A well worn rolling desk chair only confirmed the sense that this was where he spent most of his time when he was at home.

Ben dumped the contents of the plastic bag on the coffee table in the middle of the living room and plopped down on the couch beside her. He stared at what had fallen from the bag, then looked inside the bag as if to make sure he hadn't missed something.

A metal tube of paint, creased and rolled like a used tube of tooth-paste, sat on the table. Beside it was a long calligrapher's paintbrush with a fat wooden handle and sparkling globs of silver paint like beads of mercury stuck in the bristles.

"So Gary painted a picture of Priscilla?" Imogene ventured. "Is he an artist?"

Ben considered this. "You're really asking several questions there. I'm not sure if you noticed, but Glenn had a few of Gary's paintings for sale in his store. A series of landscapes hanging behind the counter?"

Imogene nodded. "It looked like Glenn was inventorying them this morning. Those were landscapes? They weren't very good."

Ben gingerly lifted up the brush. "I *think* they're landscapes. There's some green in them that could be trees. Or possibly a mallard duck."

"I get it," she said. "Gary wants to be a painter, but he stinks out loud. Then who made this picture Cody was talking about? Who around here could be good enough to paint a recognizable portrait of Priscilla Hemphill?"

Ben set the brush down again and sat back, rubbing an index finger across his upper lip as he always did when thinking hard. "You know, I remember that after Gary and Priscilla got engaged last year, the talk in the teacher's lounge turned toward the Pritchard family, specifically Annette—Gary's sister who was killed in Iraq."

Imogene nodded.

"Apparently her death sparked Gary's interest in painting. But he only wanted to paint pictures of his sister. I guess his mother got freaked out about all the barely recognizable paintings of her daughter strewn around her son's room, so she burned them all and forbade Gary from ever painting Annette again."

"Oh my word. And that's when she left Accord?"

"Or shortly thereafter. Gary quit painting altogether until he and Priscilla got engaged, which is when he started doing those landscapes down in the store."

"So maybe Gary wasn't satisfied with landscapes," Imogene suggested. "And he switched his earlier portrait obsession from his sister to his fiancé."

"Makes sense to me," Ben said easily.

Imogene frowned. "*Except,* Cody and his buddies were positive that the picture up on the mountain was of Priscilla. If Gary is such a lousy painter, how could he have made a recognizable portrait, even with a photograph to help him along?"

Ben took a deep breath. "That might be where our friend Droon comes in. Gary's disappearance, his behavior since he got back—all of it is classic contactee behavior. And after what Glenn said about Droon being around since Gary first disappeared—"

"Hang on," Imogene interrupted. "Contactee behavior?"

"You can ask anyone in West Viriginia," Ben said quickly. "Or Dad, for that matter. There have always been people in the world who claim to have been contacted by beings from other worlds or dimensions, and afterward those people have the tendency suddenly to leave their families, change jobs, or demonstrate new abilities in art, music, or language."

Imogene felt her left eyebrow rise. "Give me an example."

"Moses is probably the most famous case. God spoke to him from a burning bush and suddenly he was able to single handedly rob the Pharaoh of his entire workforce and drown the Egyptian army when they tried to stop him."

"Benny, the Bible is not a history book. The story of Moses alone is so full of allegory, metaphor, and specific references to several different cultures that—"

"If you want a modern example," he persisted, "how about a guy named George Adamski? He claimed he was contacted by Venusians in 1950."

"Venusians."

Ben grinned. "When an interviewer asked him what the alien looked like, Adamski said, 'his trousers were not like mine.' Possibly one of the greatest quotations in human history."

She clapped politely. "Good stories, Benny. I'm totally convinced."

But he wouldn't be put off. "Think about your first impression of our buddy Lord Droon. The first thing you mentioned to me at the airport was his clothes. Like the little details of his appearance encapsulated his overall strangeness for you. Is it so ridiculous to think that Adamski met someone like that and was struck by an odd pair of pants?"

She held up her hands in acquiescence. "Fair enough. Theories aside, what about the actual picture of Priscilla? What's Gary trying to do? Why paint a portrait on a rock on top of a mountain? In silver?" she added, frowning at the tube of paint on the table.

Ben sat forward on the couch suddenly, obviously excited. "I don't think it's a coincidence that he mentioned a beacon of peace in church before painting Priscilla. The message of peace also fits the contactee profile. The 'aliens,'" Ben wagged his fingers in the air to make quotation marks, "or whoever contact people like Gary, frequently prophesy the end of the world. At the height of the Cold War in the 1960's there were loads of contactees who said aliens had warned them of a nuclear holocaust that would destroy all humanity. You'd be surprised at how seriously the US government took those warnings."

That gave Imogene a nasty jolt. On the airplane Droon had claimed the upcoming Council of Paris would almost certainly be a preamble to war. *All nations will eventually be dragged in,* he had promised.

She cleared her head with a little shake. "Are you sure you never told anyone here Mom's story?"

"Positive. People here hardly know me, and the story's only good if you know how unlike Mom it was."

"So that takes us back to Gary Pritchard. Supposedly untalented as a painter, but one hell of a mind reader." She picked up the soiled calligraphy brush and spun it around absently in her fingers. "I've never seen paint like this. It looks like liquid metal."

Ben reached for the tube of paint and began unrolling it. "Gary probably took it off a shelf in his dad's...oh, you're not going to *believe* this."

She looked up from the brush. Ben was staring at the unrolled tube, the smile on his face part satisfaction and part…terror?

"What?" she demanded.

He held the tube up to her face so she could read the label.

DroonCorp
Fine Nonremoveable Paints Since 2011

The words "Silver Lumine" were printed near the bottom of the tube in the same unremarkable black font.

"What is this?" she asked, unconsciously leaning away from the tube as if it might strike like an angry cobra. "Benny, tell me the truth. Did you know about the Droon guy before I got here? If this is some practical joke that you and your West Virginia buddies are playing on your sister, it's not funny at all."

"Calm down," he soothed, though he did not appear to be particularly calm. "Stuff like this always happens to contactees."

"I thought Gary Pritchard was the contactee, not us."

She realized she was still holding the paintbrush and threw it onto the coffee table. A bright bead of silver paint—or Silver *Lumine* paint, according to the impossible label—dripped onto the wood. They sat quietly for a moment, tube and brush lying discarded on the table in front of them.

"What eventually happens to all the contactees in your stories?" she asked.

"They're shunned by society. Most eventually disappear. Or commit suicide." He glanced up at her, eyes twinkling. "But their lives are never boring."

Rapid pounding on Ben's apartment door made them both jump. Ben swept the paint and brush back into the plastic bag and shoved it under the couch.

"Who is it?"

"Misser Cornell?" a high, breathless voice called from the other side of the door.

Ben went through an immediate and surprising transformation: his posture straightened and he affected a scholarly frown. "Curtis?" he said, opening the door.

Two boys of about twelve stood on the top step outside Ben's second-floor apartment. The one in front had dark hair, slicked with sweat at his temples. The other had similarly sweaty blonde hair that fell across his forehead, almost covering his large gray eyes. Imogene recognized them as the two boys who had read scripture during the church service last night.

"I know you probably don't want students to visit you at home…" the dark-haired boy began before he noticed Imogene. "I'm sorry, sir. I didn't know your ladyfriend was callin."

Ben's teacher persona cracked and he fought back a wide grin. Imogene struggled as well. She doubted so formal a child existed anywhere on the West Coast.

"Boys, this is my sister, Imogene."

"Curtis," the dark haired boy introduced himself. "Pleased to meet you." He stepped over the threshold in the apartment.

"Jamie," the blonde boy said in a much softer voice.

Imogene immediately understood that Curtis was the boy she and Ben had searched for in Accord Elementary last night. And she didn't need anyone to tell her the blonde boy's last name must be Hemphill.

Ben motioned for the boys to sit on the couch with Imogene. He rolled his desk chair over to the coffee table and sat down. "Now, how may I help you? Does this have something to do with where you got off to last night, Curtis?"

Curtis nodded slowly and swallowed. "I hung around the cemetery after Wednesday Night Church because I wanted to hear what Mr. Pritchard and Miss Hemphill were talking about. That's one reason I wanted to talk to you." He cocked an eyebrow in mild reproach. "If I can give you some advice, you ought to hide yourself better the next time you eavesdrop, sir."

"So noted, Mr. Garfield," Ben said formally. "Although none of us should have been listening to Gary and Priscilla's private matters."

Curtis nodded impatiently. "Anyway, I thought about following Miss Hemphill back home—Jamie would want me to look after his sister."

"I had to go home with my brother," the blonde boy said in that same soft voice.

"Of course," Ben said.

"But I seen you all head after Priscilla," Curtis continued, "so I followed Mr. Pritchard up General's Peak."

"At night?" Ben demanded. "Curtis, listening to a private conversation is impolite, but hiking that mountain in the dark is just plain dangerous. The first time I heard about Aggie Mills breaking her leg in half up there I had nightmares for a week."

Again the impatient nod.

"Curtis, does your mother know you're here?" Imogene asked gently.

"No, ma'am. Jamie's neither. We're s'posed to be buying milk and hot dogs at the general store."

"Then we won't interrupt you anymore." She glanced meaningfully at her brother.

"Yes, ma'am. And Mr. Cornell, no disrespect to Aggie Mills, but a retarded baby could crawl up the Peak at night if it kept to the trail. Plus me and Jamie hike up there everyday in the summertime."

Both boys straightened up with obvious pride. "We know the trails better than Aggie Mills ever did," Jamie said, more confidently now.

Curtis went on, "I followed Mr. Pritchard all the way to the top. There was another man waitin for him."

"Did you know him?" Ben asked.

"No, sir. Was a short fella had on a black preacher suit."

Did he wear a hat with a silver wire sticking out of the band? Imogene almost asked. *Was there a letter in his pocket written by a little Spanish girl?*

"He wasn't one of Cody's friends, Wash or JT?"

Curtis shook his head.

"And you had never seen him before?"

"I never seen anyone from China before, except on TV."

Imogene and Ben exchanged glances. Ben leaned forward, elbows on his knees. "You're not telling me a story?"

Jamie gave his friend a clear I-told-you-so glare—obviously he had expected no one to believe Curtis's testimony—but Curtis seemed not to notice.

"Of course not, sir," the boy said, sounding truly horrified. "Leastways I think he was from China. He had them eyes." He pulled at the edges of his own eyes with his index fingers.

"Okay, I understand," Ben said quickly. "Please don't do that again, though."

Curtis dropped his hands. "The Chinese, um, the preacher man handed Mr. Pritchard a photo and asked if Mr. Pritchard could paint the lady in it. He coughed a lot but I could understand him okay."

"Are you sure the man was talking to Gary Pritchard?"

"Yes, sir. Mr. Pritchard signed a funny name instead of his own when he was done painting. American something. But it was definitely Mr. Pritchard. He painted the lady on this smooth white rock. I don't know if they dug that rock up or what, cause it was never there before."

"Was the picture of someone you know?" Ben said.

Imogene almost reprimanded him for asking questions to which he obviously knew the answer—whatever Curtis had seen was certainly the picture of Priscilla Hemphill that had Cody and his friends so riled this morning—but then she realized her brother was only playing the responsible journalist.

Curtis nodded rather miserably. "I thought I'd have to come back in the morning to see the picture but Mr. Pritchard was done in like a minute. He moved real funny. Back and forth."

He held one arm out in front of his body and swung it smoothly to the left, then zipped back to the right and started moving left again, unexpectedly reminding Imogene of the budget inkjet printer she had used to print her papers in college. She knew that the photo-realistic artist Chuck Close achieved amazing likenesses of his subjects by dividing photographs into careful grids, which he then transferred to the canvas and filled with colorful spirals. But she had never seen anyone paint in horizontal slashes like Curtis was describing. Besides that, she'd read that Chuck Close spent days or *weeks* on a single portrait, not one minute.

The boy's arm fell to his side. "I went and looked at it after they all left. At first I just…" His feet suddenly seemed to interest him a great deal.

"You won't get in trouble for being honest," Ben said.

Curtis shot a pained glance at Jamie, who shrugged uncomfortably in return. "At first I just looked at her body. She was only wearin underpants and a brassiere. I thought she was pretty. I swear I didn't know it was Jamie's sister until I saw her face."

"It's okay." Ben frowned. "Have you boys told anyone else about this?"

They shook their heads.

"Why are you telling me?"

"You ain't from here," Curtis said, as if Ben should have known this already. "Do you think we ought to tell our moms?"

Ben rubbed his upper lip and exhaled softly through his teeth. "I won't tell either of you what to do. Part of growing up is making those decisions by yourself."

The boys' shoulders slumped in unison.

"But I will say that you have to tell your parents if you think the painting or the man you saw wearing the preacher suit are dangerous in some way. Do you think that?"

Curtis rubbed his own upper lip, copying Ben's gesture perfectly. "No," he decided. "But I think it might be bad for Priscilla if the whole town knew there was a picture of her in her lace things."

Jamie nodded rather gratefully.

Ben stood. "That's very mature of you. Both of you."

The boys followed him to the door, beaming at each other. "Bye, Mister Cornell. Thanks." Curtis turned around. "Ma'am," he said to Imogene, reminding her so strongly of an old John Wayne exit line that she had to cough to cover a sudden spate of giggles.

With Curtis and Jamie safely gone, Ben reached under the couch and brought out the plastic bag. "*Los niños y los locos dicen las verdades,*" he said. "The eighth grade Spanish teacher has it on her wall. Means, 'children and fools speak the truth.'"

He lifted the paintbrush out of the bag and studied it again. "I wonder why Droon wanted Gary to paint Priscilla. We ought to hike up General's Peak and have a look at this picture. Maybe Droon himself will be up there. We can also ask him what he wanted with Dulci's letter twenty years ago. We'll have to wait until dark, of course. I can't even imagine how Cody and his lapdogs might respond if they found us snooping around Priscilla's portrait today."

"Let's think this out," Imogene cautioned. "Art is my job. The scene that kid described is impossible. No one paints a recognizable portrait in one minute. Not even a caricature."

"A trifle," Ben said dismissively.

"Second," she pressed on, "how can you be so positive that the Lord Droon we saw this morning has anything to do with the man you saw—and might have hallucinated—when we were ten years old?"

"Gene, you seem to be forgetting that last night Gary Pritchard, a person I have met a handful of times and never really talked to, quoted the finale of our family's favorite story, then painted his fiancé on a rock because a Chinese man in a black suit told him to. *And,*" he pointed the handle of the brush at her, "this happened the very same day you arrived in town. I'm just saying maybe we should go up there and have a look."

10

The afternoon passed without anymore surprises, for which Imogene was grateful. Ben transferred his written notes from Pritchard's Corner to his laptop and then leafed through a few of the books on his shelf, occasionally jotting something down.   By the time they finished washing the dishes from supper—Ben cooked a lovely mushroom and sausage spaghetti—the sky outside the kitchen window had made the shift from blue to red to deep purple.

Ben hung his dish towel on the refrigerator handle. "You ready for a hike?"

"To the top of the world," Imogene agreed.

"Hardly. General's Peak is still at a lower elevation than Denver, Colorado. But I guess for a guy like Gary Pritchard, who's never been more than a hundred miles from home, it might as well be Mount Everest."

He retrieved the plastic bag with Gary's paint and brush from the coffee table and tucked it into the left cargo pocket of his shorts.

"What are you going to do with those?" Imogene asked.

"Compare," he said simply.

She understood his caution; there must be a thousand hoaxes out there for every genuine contactee story. She had failed in the last few hours to come up with a rational explanation for the DroonCorp label on the tube of paint, but as for the matter of Gary painting a portrait in less than a minute, she would cry hoax about that "trifle," as Ben had called it, until she lost her voice. Or until she saw some proof of it for herself.

She tightened the Velcro straps of her sandals while Ben rummaged through his kitchen drawers for a flashlight. He found a Mag-lite small enough to fit in a car's glove compartment and clicked the rubber button. A feeble orange beam played across the kitchen.

"I guess if the batteries die we can always follow the retarded baby up the trail," he chuckled, stuffing the flashlight into his other cargo pocket. "Can you believe those kids?"

The air outside was still warm, but carried a distant touch of the coming autumn. Imogene was glad she had elected to wear a long-sleeved pullover instead of a t-shirt like her brother.

"Even if Curtis keeps quiet about what he saw, I can't imagine Cody will do the same thing," she told Ben as they reached the bottom of the staircase. "You think other people in the town have the same idea we do once they hear? To go up the mountain and see for themselves?"

Ben unlocked the car and shrugged. "They may have the same idea, but the *cojones*? Pretty sure we'll be alone up there tonight."

Main Street, with its corner streetlamps and lone traffic signal flashing through the car's windshield while Ben drove, still reminded Imogene a movie, except now instead of a western, she imagined the setting of every horror movie she had ever seen. Small town at night, dark windows, light breeze. Even the creaking of the traffic signal on its wires sounded ominous.

Ben sighed blissfully. "The quiet took me awhile to get used to. There's something peaceful about an empty street at night."

"Hmm," she said.

But in the half mile between the last building on Main Street and the foot of General's Peak, Imogene purposefully abandoned her negativity and luxuriated in the wind blowing through their open windows and the sharp, somehow clean scent of spruce trees lining the road.

Ben veered right into a circular gravel turnout, the tires coaxing fine white dust into the air. The clearing turned a hazy, shadow-filled red in the glow of the brake lights, then went completely dark as Ben shut off the car.

Before they had even stepped out of the car an angry voice crowed from the trees just ahead of them: "What do you think you're doing?"

Ben whipped the tiny Mag-lite from his pocket and spun to face the source of the voice.

Imogene's eyes still had not adjusted to the new darkness but her ears worked just fine. She heard a rapid scuffling sound moving toward them across the gravel. "Instead of driving that fancy car of yours, you could have just sent fliers to the whole town to let them know you were coming here," the harsh voice continued. "Or better yet, you could've sent them right to Cody Hemphill and his drones."

The scuffling shape resolved into a round, vaguely human shape in the darkness. The fringes of knitted afghan flapped against the figure's shoulders.

Imogene blinked gravel dust from her eyes. "Agnes?"

"Hello, dear."

Ben's flashlight finally centered on the approaching woman. The strange scraping Imogene had heard was of course the sturdy wooden cane in the woman's hand.

Agnes squinted at Ben. "Kindly get that thing out of my face before I lose my night eyes and ruin my good leg."

The flashlight quickly disappeared into his pocket again.

"That's better," Agnes said. "Now Mr. Cornell, if you and your sister are planning a nature hike I suggest you come back in daylight. And if you all are hoping to gawk at Priscilla Hemphill I suggest you get back in that auto of yours and go back home."

Imogene remembered this same woman informing them last night that her cane "ain't just for walking," and inched back toward the car.

"Agnes…" Ben repeated, sounding awed. "Wait, you're Aggie Mills, aren't you? I can't *believe* I missed the connection last night. I even talked to Curtis Garfield today about how you broke your leg climbing General's Peak when you were a little girl. I thought you were dead."

She shifted her weight, no more than a dark silhouette against the darker background of trees. "One of the pitfalls of being a ghost," she said dryly.

"Is Priscilla Hemphill actually up there?" Imogene asked.

The cane creaked as Agnes regarded her. "Might as well be," she said finally. "But if you're looking for a burlesque show, you can turn right back around and go home. Gary Pritchard didn't paint any dime store pinup."

"So Gary really did paint her. Did he use these?" Ben asked. Imogene heard a whisper of Velcro as he reached into the pocket containing the plastic bag. He pulled out the paint tube and brush, the bristles of the latter glowing strangely in the moonlight.

Agnes breathed in sharply. "Who gave you those?"

"Glenn Pritchard tossed them into the dumpster by his store this morning."

The older woman's sour silence expressed quite plainly that the idea of them dumpster diving behind Pritchard's Corner did nothing to improve her opinion of their motives.

"Listen," Imogene said, suddenly very tired of all of the cloak-and-dagger suspicion. "We're here because last night in church Gary Pritchard repeated something our mother said a long time ago, before she died. We have to see what he meant by it and the answer might be at the top of this mountain. If you're worried about what we'll do when we get there, how about you take us there yourself? You said you know the trail better than anyone, and our flashlight is almost dead. Please."

Agnes studied her at length and must have found what she saw acceptable. She rotated her sturdy bulk toward the trailhead and said, "You all just try and keep up."

11

Thirty minutes later, sweat pouring dark rings under her armpits and around her collar, Imogene regretted wearing long sleeves. *Maybe if Droon is up there he'll share some of his Evian,* she thought with macabre amusement.

"Almost there," Agnes called over her shoulder. She wasn't even breathing hard.

"You're kidding," Ben wheezed from the back of the group. The wet circles under his arms were inches away from meeting in the middle. "I just found my rhythm."

Ahead and to Imogene's right, the curved tip of a tall, pale boulder peeked over what appeared to be the mountain's final ridge, glinting oddly in the starlight. Directly ahead, Imogene saw a deep shadow yawning through the middle of the path. Agnes braced her free hand on top of her cane and pushed down like a pole-vaulter, leaping the gap and landing spryly on her right leg without slowing.

"My favorite part of the hike," she cackled.

"To the right, Gene," Ben instructed.

A clear path wound through a stand of scraggly trees, circumventing the gap. Imogene had to dodge several poking branches but she considered the dodging preferable to missing a step and plummeting into that stony gap.

Agnes had added another five yards to her lead in the meantime. Shortly, though, the trail flattened out. A screen of spruce trees fenced the right side of the path from the summit, and to the left was empty space over a dark patch of landscape. Imogene could barely make out the flashing traffic signal in downtown Accord. A dim clamshell of red-purple light remained in the west and the sliver of the moon sliced a white grin in the sky, but the rest of the world had surrendered to the clear blackness of night.

"Never saw this many stars in Seattle, huh?" Ben said, rolling his head on his shoulders.

"I didn't know there were such things as stars until I read about them in school."

"Get a move on!" Agnes hollered. "You're fifty paces from seeing something a lot more interesting than the stars."

It was more like twenty paces, actually. As soon as Imogene stepped around the screen of spruce trees, the terrain opened wide to reveal a broad skid of red sandstone with a tall white boulder standing starkly at its center. Over six feet high and roughly rectangular, most of the boulder's surface was as roughly textured as the ubiquitous chunks of sandstone littering the mountaintop, but the side of the rock facing Imogene and the others looked like it had been chiseled and sanded to make it as flat and smooth as possible. On that flat surface, glittering as brightly as the stars overhead, was an unmistakable silver image of Priscilla Hemphill rendered in bold light and shadow.

As remarkable as the stone and portrait were, Imogene immediately noticed that there was already another person on the summit. Wearing blue jeans and standing before the boulder as one might stand in front of a mirror was the real Priscilla. Her painted self seemed to be studying her in return, framed in the smooth, flat face of the boulder as Priscilla had been framed in her own kitchen door last night after church. At the portrait's left ankle was the inexplicable looping signature that Curtis Garfield and Cody's friend Wash had mentioned. Even at this distance Imogene could plainly read the words *Americanus Rex,* though she still had no idea what name might mean. Nor could she explain the enormous, cartoonish breasts woven into the capital *R* of *Rex.*

The boulder on which Priscilla had been painted wasn't limestone or any other regular type of light-colored rock, as Imogene had initially believed. She now guessed it might be a massive hunk of milky quartz, though at over six feet high, two feet wide, and another two feet deep, it was easily the largest such stone Imogene had ever heard of. Furthermore, it had no place on a sandstone mountain like General's Peak. The translucent rock captured enough light from the moon and stars that it seemed to glow from the inside.

But even more arresting than the unusual stone was the portrait itself. Imogene certainly understood why Curtis had spent so much time looking at Priscilla's painted body before moving on to the face, although the portrait lacked the cheap sexuality Cody's friends had hinted at. The painted woman on the boulder was simply *alive.* She had weight and depth and incredible power in her stance. The soft curve of muscle in her thighs seemed to flex under her weight.

"Oh my sweet God," Ben said huskily beside her.

Curtis had told them that Gary painted for less than a minute. Despite herself, Imogene determined that such a feat would at least be humanly possible, if absurdly unlikely. She had no ready genre for Gary's style, but she decided "high contrast photo realism" might come close. All of the depth and detail in Priscilla's portrait came from the contrast between light and shadow. Gary had only painted shadows, leaving the eyes of his viewers to create Priscilla's remaining features in the blank areas of stone. The overall effect was that of a person caught forever in the instant of a bright flash photograph.

Which was, of course, exactly what had happened to Priscilla last night.

"Is this what Gary meant the other night in church?" she asked Ben through numb lips. "Is this what a beacon of peace looks like?"

"Are we on top of the world?" he responded nonsensically, the white stone reflecting deliriously in his eyes.

It's just the way Mom looked onstage in her bathing suit at the Miss Washington pageant, Imogene thought, and after the last twenty-four hours, the similarity surprised her not one bit.

Agnes was shuffling forward. "Priscilla, dear. I didn't expect you up here so soon," she said warmly. "Looking at your portrait is like seeing an angel through the doorway of heaven itself, isn't it?"

Priscilla didn't answer, and Agnes didn't press her. They and the Cornells might have spent the entire night rooted before the stone, studying every curve and shadow of Priscilla's portrait, but something heavy crashed through the bushes to their right. Before any of them could do more than turn toward the sound, Cody Hemphill burst onto the summit of General's Peak.

"Prissy!" he screamed. "Don't look at it! Oh, Prissy, please don't look!" He did not spare Agnes, Ben, or Imogene a glance even though they must have been in his line of sight.

Priscilla still seemed not to notice that she had company until her brother reached her side.

"I'm sorry I couldn't protect you from seeing this…" Cody trailed off, momentarily losing his train of thought in the glowing swim of lines on the boulder. He tore his eyes away. "This *sick bullshit!*" he screamed.

He grabbed his sister's arm presumably to pull her back down the mountain. "Pritchard will pay for this. Wash and JT and me'll find him, I swear to G—"

Priscilla tore herself from his grasp with such sudden ferocity that Cody nearly lost his balance.

"Take your hands off me," she commanded breathlessly. "The only sickness here is coming out of your mouth."

Cody must have had fifty pounds on her, but his knees visibly trembled under her terrible gaze.

"What would you protect me from, huh? A strength—" She floundered for words, hands clenched at her sides. "A *peace* with who I am that I've never shown anyone, including myself? Is *that* what you're afraid I'll see?"

He took an uncertain step backward, his empty hand still raised as if to bear her away down the mountain.

"I don't need you to protect me from myself, Cody. If that's the only way you know how to be my brother, you can just leave me alone."

She turned her back on her brother and marched past Agnes, Ben, and Imogene without another word.

Cody watched her go, slumped against the boulder's flat, polished face. When she disappeared around the row of spruce trees he made no move to follow. Imogene's heart ached for him despite her fear. Over a space of perhaps three seconds she doubted she had ever seen so deeply or clearly into another person's emotions as now she saw into Cody Hemphill's.

But the moment passed. In one second he was a confused, pitiable child, and in the next a raging weapon. A deep, rough growl began low in his throat and crawled out his mouth like an alligator emerging from a sewer pipe.

He spun toward the portrait with astonishing, liquid speed. His fist lashed out and connected against the smooth face of the boulder with a horrid crunch of bone. The growl turned into a scream of pain and he bent in half, clutching his knuckles.

Imogene and Agnes gasped in unison. Cody's eyes rose to study them. Hollow fear splashed into Imogene's stomach, nearly doubling her over as well. But Cody seemed to have little interest in them. He leapt into motion after his sister, flattening the same bushes through which he had entered earlier.

Agnes recovered first. "Come, children," she said briskly, moving back toward the path down the mountain.

Imogene nearly argued. She wasn't even close to finished with her study of the portrait. The glittering curves and blobs of silver paint that formed Priscilla's painted body, the huge milky stone that was most definitely glowing in the starlight…

But Agnes was right. The real Priscilla was more of a priority right now. They found her collapsed halfway down the trail. Imogene neither saw nor heard Cody nearby. Agnes crouched beside Priscilla with only the most perfunctory use of her cane and wrapped her in a motherly embrace.

The younger woman let her cheek rest on the soft pink afghan covering Agnes's shoulder. "I knew something had come between Gary and me in the last couple weeks, I just couldn't admit it to myself. Not until last night when I saw the grass stains on my dress where I'd…*knelt* in front of him. I got rid of that dress. I'd never felt so clean in my life. So free."

Abruptly, she looked up at Agnes and started. "But what are you doing up here?" Then she peered past Agnes, first at Imogene and then her brother. "Ben?"

"Evening," he said awkwardly, and introduced Imogene once more.

Priscilla finally disengaged herself from Agnes and stood. "Pleased to meet you."

"You too," Imogene answered. This night was getting more surreal by the minute.

"May I walk you home, dear?" Agnes asked Priscilla.

Priscilla nodded. In the moonlight filtering through the trees, her gray eyes and blonde hair seemed to send out the same silver shimmer as her portrait.

Imogene wanted to ask a hundred questions—about Gary, about Droon, about the Beacon of Peace—but she held her tongue, as did her brother and Agnes. All three of them walked behind Priscilla, watching the glow radiate from her as if it could light their path.

12

A heavy white dust cloud filled the gravel turnout at the foot of the Peak as if a car had recently passed through, spinning its tires wildly. Other than that they saw no sign of Cody or anyone else.

Although Agnes had offered to walk Priscilla home, she now seemed heavy on her feet for the first time all night. Both women accepted Ben's offer to drive them home. Imogene sat in the rear passenger seat beside Priscilla and stared out the window. She still believed that following Priscilla had been a better choice than staying to study the portrait, but she could not get the glowing image out of her head. Maybe after they dropped off Priscilla and Agnes she would ask Ben if he wanted to hike back up the mountain. Curtis's assessment of the trail had been accurate, if politically incorrect; after completing the hike once, Imogene knew she would have no trouble finding her way a second time. Without Agnes's daredevil antics, of course. No wonder the poor woman had busted her leg when she was a kid.

"Everyone strapped in?" Ben asked.

All the way into town, the only sound in the car was the quiet rising and falling whine of the engine.

"Turn left here," Agnes commanded at one of the first intersections they came to, just before the road straightened out and became Main Street proper. "Unless you want to read about yourself in the newspaper, complete with speculation as to why you were in a car with old Aggie Mills and the newly single Priscilla Hemphill."

Aside from a few more words of direction from Agnes, silence reigned in the car until Ben pulled up to the curb in front of Agnes's little house. As she heaved herself from the bucket seat, Priscilla spoke for the first time since they had gotten into the car.

"I'm sorry for what the church did to you, Aggie. You certainly are not a she-demon from hell."

Agnes, now fully outside the car, crowed with laughter. The sound was rough and unexpected and wonderful. "I'll stitch that onto a wall hanging if you don't mind." She sobered. "I'm not the only person this town has underestimated. Or taken for granted."

She held Priscilla's gaze a moment longer, then put a hand to the small of her back and stretched up, her face disappearing from Imogene's view. "Goodnight, loves," she said loudly and slammed the door.

Ben pulled away from the curb. "I can't believe I'd never met her before," he said to no one in particular. "Neat lady."

Imogene wanted to ask Priscilla what the church had done to Agnes, but she supposed too many cans of worms had already been opened tonight.

Ben was driving toward Main Street and the town's single traffic signal, but slowed down suddenly. "What in the world's all this?" he muttered.

Imogene leaned forward and looked out the windshield. Rows of people blocked the road like spectators for a late-night parade.

"I guess I'll go around," Ben said.

"No," Priscilla said. "Something's happening. Can you let me out, please?"

When Ben had pulled to the curb, all three of them exited. They walked to the edge of the crowd in a triangle with Priscilla at the leading point.

Since arriving in Accord, a sense of unreality had settled so deeply over Imogene that reality seemed like some other place, as far away from her now as West Virginia was from Los Angeles. But even the strangest events she had witnessed—Lord Droon turning up in Accord after sitting next to her on the airplane, the ethereal glowing portrait of Priscilla Hemphill painted on a smooth-faced rock—could still have rational explanations.

That all changed when she looked over and between the heads of the townspeople lining Main Street. The elusive Gary Pritchard stood in the middle of the street with a Polaroid camera hanging on a thin plastic strap around his neck. A rolled green sleeping bag rested by his right boot. Ten feet away and a full head taller stood Cody Hemphill. An old brown pickup was parked diagonally in the middle of the street behind Cody, the driver's side door hanging open.

Imogene shuffled to her right to get a better view, which she found just in time to see Cody raise a pump-action shotgun and aim it at Gary's head.

"Cody, no!" Priscilla yelled.

Cody did not acknowledge her. Nor did any of the silent townspeople. Her head swung side to side in search of a break in the crowd.

"We been through a lot this year," Cody announced loudly. He spoke with a politician's calm, reasonable tone. "It wouldn't be honest to my family or my town if I didn't stand up to this little pervert for how he embarrassed my sister. Putting her on display like a cheap whore. You all seen her at church, heard her angel voice. She don't deserve what he done to her. And less'n half a year after buryin our daddy."

"Cody, no," Priscilla moaned.

"Cody!" Ben shouted.

He plunged into the crowd and yanked the calligrapher's paintbrush and paint from his pocket. Imogene grabbed his arm, but he pulled out of her grip.

"Gene, Cody will kill Gary if we don't do something," he said quickly. "I'll be okay. You take care of Priscilla."

She nodded numbly. She knew about Cody being capable of killing Gary. She'd seen the murder in his eyes after he'd smashed his knuckles against Priscilla's portrait.

"Can't you talk to your brother?" she demanded of Priscilla.

"I've never seen him like this," Priscilla said shakily.

"Come on, think! There's got to be something we can do," Imogene said, glancing around desperately. Weren't there any police in Accord?

But it was too late. Ben had already breached the inner edge of the crowd, the paint and brush held high in a single fist.

"I'm the one who painted your sister," he said, strolling into the street to plant himself in the no-man's-land between the barrel of Cody's gun and Gary Pritchard's head. "Hey, you dumb hillbilly ass-hole, you've got the wrong guy."

Cody's eyes—and his aim—stayed on Gary. "My beef ain't with you, Cornell. You ain't the one who disgraced my sister."

"Oh Benny, please be careful," Imogene whispered. She felt Priscilla's small, sweaty hand grasp hers. She squeezed back.

Sweat now hung in beads on Ben's forehead. "Wrong again. I've always had the hots for Priscilla and I figured painting her naked was about as close to scoring with her as I would ever come. If a couple other guys in town get off on it too, so much the better."

At last Cody focused on him.

"That's right," Ben said.

He edged away from Gary toward the side of the street, the gun barrel tracking his every step. The paint and brush fell from his hand and clattered in the street.

"The thing is, I've realized I'll never get your sister. So I'm going to leave town forever. I won't even pack up my stuff. I'll just get in my car and go. Nobody has to get hurt and you'll never have to worry about this again."

All throughout this speech he kept backing slowly toward the crowd. He glanced behind him, probably to see how easily he could melt into the line of people on the curb, but he saw something that stopped him in his tracks. Incredibly, he seemed to forget all about Cody Hemphill and the shotgun aimed at his head. His cheeks flush with anger, turning a ruddy purple in the orange light from the arc sodium lamp on the street corner.

Imogene craned her neck and saw Curtis Garfield's face, long and pale with fear, hovering chest-high among the townspeople gathered on the opposite side of the street.

"You people brought your *children* to see this?" Ben said, his voice dangerously quiet.

To Imogene's astonishment, the gathered people of Accord heard him. *Listened* to him. A hundred sets of eyes blinked as if waking from a dream. A hundred abashed faces turned from her brother's wrathful gaze.

Then several things happened very quickly. First, Gary Pritchard finally seemed to realize what had fallen from Ben's hand. He said, "Hey, my paint!" with the same childish glee someone might express at finding fifty cents in a pay telephone.

Cody's eyes widened until Imogene could see the orange-red light of the streetlamps reflected in them. His knuckles, already swelling from their furious encounter with Priscilla's stone portrait, whitened around the wooden stock of his shotgun.

"Benny, look out!" Imogene yelled. "Everybody get down!"

The only person who moved was Curtis Garfield, who crouched into a ball amid the forest of legs around him.

A determined look came across Gary's face. He lifted the paintbrush from where it had fallen in the street and stuffed it into the barrel of Cody's gun with prissiness befitting a flower shop owner filling a vase until the brush's fat handle would slide no further into the barrel.

"This is the kind of moment you'll want to forget later, but you shouldn't," Gary told Cody bossily, and raised the Polaroid to his eye.

Hard ropes of muscle in Cody's forearm tightened as he squeezed the trigger.

Imogene had watched enough cartoons as a kid to know what happens when someone stuffs a cork into the barrel of a gun. She clapped her hands to the sides of Priscilla's head and pulled her to the ground.

13

The combined flashes from the camera and the gun burned orange-green blobs in the center of Imogene's vision. Cody Hemphill's body flew backward, trailing smoke like a GI-Joe figurine strapped to a bottle rocket. Imogene heard a complicated crunch as he struck the pavement.

Gary seemed not to notice how close he had come to a messy death. The photograph *whirred* out the front of his camera and he waved it back and forth absently while he waited for it to develop.

Priscilla broke free of Imogene and crashed through the crowd like a running back. Imogene saw a mess of flailing arms as several people were knocked flat in her wake, many taking others down with them. Finally in the open, Priscilla ran toward her brother's inert form.

Gary simply continued waving the photo back and forth. The only other movement came from behind the crowd on the other side of the street: a short, dark figure moving north up the sidewalk. Imogene only saw it for an instant before it disappeared around the corner of the post office.

She stepped gingerly toward her own brother through the gap Priscilla had created moments ago. Ben's eyes looked glassy and his mouth hung slightly open, but he appeared unhurt. Unsure of what to do, she simply grabbed his hand.

"I have to go to the airport now," Gary declared in a golly-ain't-this-a-fine-evenin-for-a-stroll voice.

He pocketed the photograph, hefted the green sleeping bag, and started up the street. Faces on both sides of the street followed him in unison. He passed within five feet of the two Hemphills without a glance.

"Gary! Please don't leave!" Priscilla cried, fear and despair giving her lyrical voice a raw edge. But she remained beside her injured brother, who had begun to stir feebly.

When Cody whimpered, Priscilla shouted for an ambulance. The townspeople only watched Gary silently until he vanished around the gentle curve of road leading to the base of General's Peak.

Even then, whatever spell had been cast over the town did not break. The people began shuffling slowly toward their homes. The ones Priscilla had knocked over regained their feet and their positions in the herd.

Priscilla cried out again for an ambulance and was again ignored. She launched into a litany of names as faces she knew passed by: Cal, Gordon, Rosie, Verna, Jack, Emma Louise, Andy.

And so on. She might as well have been shouting random words or numbers for all the response she got.

"*What is wrong with you people?*" Imogene yelled, suddenly furious. First what had happened in the church, and now this? "Don't you care about anyone but yourselves? Don't you—"

Ben squeezed her hand. "Do you have your cell phone?"

She patted her pockets and shook her head. "I didn't want to take it up the mountain in case I tripped or something and broke it."

"Never mind. Can you run to my apartment and call the paramedics? I'm going to stay with Priscilla."

* * *

Imogene dialed 911 on Ben's telephone and told the operator in Point Pleasant that a man was badly injured and they could find him on Main Street in Accord. The operator seemed satisfied with those directions and told her an ambulance would arrive as soon as possible.

She hung up and tried not to shiver. If she allowed herself even one little twitch, she had a feeling she wouldn't be able to stop. She splashed water on her face, dabbed away the moisture with Ben's hand towel. The urge to bury her face in the towel and either cry or scream nearly overpowered her, but she simply hung the towel back on its ring above the light switch and left the apartment.

The ambulance had arrived by the time she returned to Main Street, though she was sure she'd called fewer than ten minutes ago. She saw two large blond male paramedics strapping Cody Hemphill to a wooden board, which they lifted easily onto collapsible gurney. The ambulance driver performed a three point turn as the paramedics worked so that it would be facing south again for the drive back to Point Pleasant.

Priscilla stood off to the side, clutching her elbows, Ben's arm wrapped protectively around her waist. When the paramedics had loaded Cody into the ambulance, Priscilla climbed inside with them.

"Call if you need anything," Ben told her. "Even if it's in the middle of the night."

She nodded distractedly as the rear doors slammed and the ambulance roared into motion. The driver did not turn on the emergency lights or the siren. Imogene guessed he would not meet much traffic between here and Point Pleasant, especially considering how quickly he had arrived here. She waved to him, hoping the gesture conveyed some of her relief and gratitude for the competence he and his colleagues had shown tonight.

As the ambulance rolled past her, one of Accord's lonely streetlamps shone into the cab and Imogene saw the driver for the first time. He smiled brightly at her and tipped his black fedora.

A strangled squawk erupted from her mouth. She broke into a run behind the ambulance.

"Gene!" her brother yelled.

But the ambulance had gathered speed quickly and was already nothing more than red tail lights against the black landscape. Even those disappeared shortly.

Ben caught up to her. "What was that about?" he breathed.

"Did you see who was in the cab?"

"Those big Swedish looking guys?"

"The one up front. It was Droon."

He studied her. "Gene, I think we both need some sl—"

She exploded. "*Is that any weirder than anything else we've seen tonight?*" She tried to relax. None of this was Ben's fault. "I got a clear look at him for a second or two. It was him, I know it was."

The full weight of all she had seen tonight suddenly crashed on her. "Benny, I don't think I can stay here anymore. I know all this is why you moved here—to find the Men in Black and write your book—but I can't handle it. I thought you were going to die tonight."

A vision of Cody with a shotgun to Ben's head passed through her mind and she loosed a single loud sob. Ben helped her back to his apartment with a firm hold on her shoulders.

Once they were back in his apartment she regained enough control over herself to clutch a mug of chamomile tea in both hands. She blew little gusts across the steaming liquid, elbows propped on the kitchen table.

"How can you live like this? A mysterious man in a black suit screwing with people's lives, a town bully threatening to blow away his sister's fiancé..." She trailed off.

Ben poured a mug of his own from the stainless steel teapot on the stove, unperturbed as ever despite her hysteria. "Actually I'd almost given up on the book. I told you the truth when I picked you up at the airport. I didn't see any of that stuff until you showed up."

And there it was, plainly, almost nonchalantly stated. *I brought home the infection,* she thought suddenly, her cheeks and scalp tingling madly.

Ben sipped his tea. "Wow that's hot."

The same despair that had come over her when Ben had waded out to face Cody Hemphill returned now. She was poisoning her brother again, not with chickenpox this time, but with her simple presence. At least this time she could think of a remedy. She set her mug on the table and walked into Ben's bedroom, where her carryall still lay on the floor where she had set it last night before going to sleep.

Ben followed her, frowning. "What're you doing?"

Her clothes were still in the neat piles she had made last night on Ben's dresser. The shirts went first into her carryall.

Ben was beside her in a flash. "Hey, I *chose* to put myself between Gary and Cody tonight. You didn't put me in danger any more than you put that gun in Cody's hand."

The pile of shorts and capris went on top of the shirts.

"Sleep on it," he insisted. "One night. If you still want to leave in the morning I'll take you to the airport, no questions asked."

She reached for the pile of bras and underpants, her shining red curls—those constant reminders of her mother—hanging in front of her eyes. "What if Droon comes back tonight for us? Don't you dare laugh, Benny. If he could intercept my phone call and get himself an ambulance, I doubt he'd have much trouble figuring out where you live."

"No one's laughing," he said mildly. He walked briskly to a small closet beside the bedroom door and withdrew a tightly rolled sleeping bag. "Think you could stand sharing a room with your brother again? You still take the bed, of course. If that weirdo tries to pull something dodgy on us, at least we can deal with him together, right? Go team."

"Go team," she agreed, and even managed a weak smile.

A few minutes later he tossed one of the couch cushions onto the sleeping bag for a pillow. He latched the bedroom door, stripped to his boxer shorts, and crawled into the sleeping bag. Imogene sank her head gratefully onto her own pillow, falling asleep even as Ben reached up to switch off the lamp beside his bed.

She slept deeply, which was a welcome surprise.

14

The world outside Ben's windows was still dark when Imogene's cell phone jangled a loud electronic rendition of the song "It's Raining Men." She rolled onto her stomach, clawed through her bag, and flipped open the phone. The digital readout said 5:52. "Teddy?"

"Genie!" her boss's voice barked in her ear. "Get your ass on the next plane to London."

"What?" She cleared her throat.

"Wow, you sound terrible. Go buy a large coffee and the first available ticket to Heathrow. I don't care what it costs, but save your receipts. Oliver and I will pick you up at the airport if we can."

She pulled a notepad—not unlike her brother's—from her carry-all and scribbled. Saving receipts meant this would be a business trip, which made sense to her rapidly clearing mind. London had always been Teddy's favorite vacation destination and therefore his playtime. She had never been invited to join him there, and she would not have believed that anything short of the resurrection of Picasso would interrupt Teddy's playtime.

"Wuzgoinon?" Ben mumbled from the mouth of the sleeping bag.

"What's going on?" Imogene asked Teddy in a more coherent echo of her brother.

"You'll think I've gone completely bonkers."

She bit her lip to keep from laughing. If Teddy wanted to have a gone-bonkers contest, she had no doubt she could lay him flat in round one.

"This new artist just came on the scene in Germany," he explained. "And I mean *just* came on the scene. They found his first piece a couple hours ago. I wouldn't even know about it except Oliver's got such great connections."

An understatement if Imogene had ever heard one. Oliver Hume, Teddy's best and perhaps only real friend, was the curator of the Tate Modern Museum in London. Aside from the people who held curator positions at the Louvre and Manhattan Guggenheim, Oliver probably had the best connections in the art world of anyone on the planet.

"I want you over here to do some very important research," Teddy went on. "Oliver's bringing the piece to the Tate as we speak and I'm acting pretty much as his gofer right now. Hell, I'd hand-feed him grapes if it scored me a piece of this Americanus Rex thing."

All remaining traces of sleep vanished. She felt her knuckles go white around the cell phone. "What did you say?"

"I knew you'd think I was crazy," Teddy said giddily. "An artist calling himself Americanus Rex just painted the most incredible portrait inside a cathedral in Dresden, Germany. From the footage I saw, some giant naked Amazon babe seems to be the centerpiece. It should arrive at the Tate sometime tonight."

Imogene struggled to work out a timeline in her head. When exactly had Gary walked up Main Street last night? Could he possibly have made it to Germany in time to—

Teddy laughed, interrupting her thoughts. "Supposedly the artist drew a huge pair of tits into his last name. I think I would call bullshit if I hadn't already seen the painting on the BBC."

Any question whether Teddy's Americanus Rex might not be connected to Gary Pritchard died immediately. Maybe Curtis Garfield's insistence that Gary had painted Priscilla's unearthly portrait in under a minute had not been so far off after all. Although even Gary's talent as an inhumanly quick painter did not explain how he had gotten from West Virginia to Germany in the last ten hours.

Once again she heard Gary's voice ringing through the First Pentecostal Church of Accord: *I will light a beacon of peace from the top of the world.* Priscilla's portrait was a good start, but Imogene had failed to see its connection to world peace. Maybe painting his fiancé had been a warm-up for the real thing.

Which brought up the question of what she should tell Teddy about the painted rock still up on General's Peak. Whether Gary had intended Priscilla's portrait to be his beacon of peace or not, Imogene had never seen a more beautiful or emotional piece of art in her life. The thought of it sitting unseen on top of that mountain made her sick to her stomach. However, she had no more claim to the rock than Teddy did. Maybe she would still be able to track Priscilla down and talk to her about it yet this morning.

"I'll be in London as soon as I can," she told Teddy.

"Call me when you get to Heathrow."

The line clicked. The words *Call ended* flashed on the screen of her phone.

"London?" Ben asked. He also sounded wide awake now. "Let me guess. Master Teddy wants you to drop everything and fly across the ocean for him *right now.* What, does he need a pair of pants ironed? Don't let him do this, Gene. He okayed your trip out here three months ago."

"He needs me to do some research, but I think—"

"Why can't you stand up for yourself? This is the only vacation you've had in the last year."

"I think Gary Pritchard painted in Germany last night," she said.

Ben had pulled on a pair of jeans while she was on the phone. Now he paused halfway inside an old t-shirt, arms up in the air, dark hair visible through the neck hole. After a moment he pulled the shirt the rest of the way down.

"That's impossible."

"You're the one with the lowdown on UFOs," she countered. "Maybe Droon picked Gary up on General's Peak and dropped him off in Germany. Some kind of celestial taxi service."

Ben rubbed his palm across his stubbly cheek.

Inspiration struck Imogene. "You could come with me. You said you don't have to be at school for another two weeks and you've always wanted to see London. I could tell Teddy I need you to help me research. He might even pay for your ticket."

Before he could answer, the knob on the bedroom door twisted with a creak of old springs and Priscilla Hemphill stepped into the bedroom, startling them both badly. Imogene's cell phone slipped from her grip and clattered on the hardwood floor.

"I let myself in last night," Priscilla told them softly. "Your door was unlocked and I was scared to go home. My brother..." she broke off.

Imogene shot Ben an incredulous glance. After everything that happened last night, he still had not locked his front door? And besides that, how had Priscilla known where he lived? But she answered the second question for herself after a moment's consideration: everybody in a town like this must know where everybody else lives. In the case of her brother, an outsider who worked with children, the town newspaper had probably published his address the day he arrived.

"Is Cody alright?" Ben asked Priscilla.

Imogene thought his ability to ask that question so gently, especially when Cody had been ready to kill him only hours before, was a testament to his feelings for Priscilla.

The woman's face was inscrutable. "He's gone."

Ben stepped closer but still did not make physical contact. "Oh, man. I'm sor—"

"I'm not saying he's dead," she interrupted firmly. "He's just not in the hospital anymore. I went to the bathroom in the middle of the night, and when I came back he was gone. No one at the hospital could find him. I caused a scene and an orderly brought me back to town. I couldn't bear the idea of spending the night alone in my house, and you two were the only ones who helped me last night when Cody got hurt. I slept on the couch," she finished, rubbing her neck and looking terribly young.

Ben seemed paralyzed, five feet still separating him and Priscilla. "Do your mother and Jamie know?" he finally asked.

Priscilla shook her head and inhaled deeply, as if steeling herself against imminent unpleasantness. "May I use your telephone?"

"Of course. It's out on the desk by my computer."

While Priscilla called her mother, Ben strapped on his cooking apron and pulled some eggs, fresh vegetables, and ham out of the refrigerator. Imogene wanted to pack the last few items she'd left beside the couch last night, but hung back in the kitchen and chopped up the vegetables to give Priscilla some privacy.

"How long will it take you to pack a bag?" she asked Ben, scraping a pile of onions and garlic from the cutting board into a frying pan.

He shrugged, tossing the sizzling contents of the pan with practiced flicks of his wrist. "Half-hour. While I do that, you can call the—"

He looked past her out into the living room. "What's the matter?"

Imogene turned to see Priscilla looking pale and distraught.

"I heard you say earlier you're going to London," she said, "and that Gary painted again. You're going to find him, aren't you? I'd like to come with you. I'll just need to pack some things and tell my little brother goodbye. He should be at his chores in the stables soon."

The Cornells met this declaration with a thick, baffled silence. "How did your mother handle the news that Cody is gone from the hospital?" Imogene attempted.

"I was right about Cody being alive. He's at home now. Sleeping, but Mama says he'll be alright." Priscilla lowered herself gracefully into a chair at the kitchen table, her back ramrod straight.

"Are you sure you don't want to be at home with your family right now?"

"Mama says I'm not welcome anymore." If possible, her back straightened even more. "She said that if I hadn't let Gary paint me Cody wouldn't have gotten hurt."

Ben pivoted slowly away from the stove, the frying pan still in his hand. His eyes were wide and his mouth worked in soundless rage. "Priscilla, this is not your fault."

"Gary's picture captured me in a moment I never believed would come in my life," Priscilla said, more loudly. "It wasn't Gary's moment to share, but now that he has, I'm not going to bury my head in the sand for shame, no matter what Mama says. I would like to come to London with you, if I may."

"Okay," Imogene said slowly. "Then it's only fair you know what you're getting into. Do you remember what Gary said Wednesday night in church?"

Priscilla spoke without hesitation. "'I will light a beacon of peace from the top of the world.'"

Imogene tried not to shiver. "Our mother said those exact words in a beauty pageant over forty years ago."

"It's been sort of our family's catchphrase since she died," Ben said. "The story's pretty long, but…"

He seemed to realize he was still holding the frying pan and set it back on the stove. "Tell you what," he told Priscilla. "Go home and do whatever you need to do before we leave. The flight to London will take around ten hours—more if we have a long layover in New York or DC or wherever—and that should be plenty of time to fill you in about our mother and the UFOs that we think took Gary to Germany."

Imogene supposed Ben could have been more delicate in his delivery, but at this point there was little to be gained from beating around the bush. She retrieved a pen and paper from a drawer in the kitchen island and sat back down next to Priscilla.

"I'll make you a list of everything I'm packing for the trip, if you're still interested."

Priscilla glanced over at Ben, who had returned his attention to the omelets, then back to Imogene, her gray eyes clear. "I'm still interested."

Interlude: The Historian

1

Friday, August 26, 2011

A matter of hours before Imogene woke up to the jangle of her cell phone, the sun had already risen on Dresden, Germany and sat high over the Elbe River, winking on the crests of gentle waves. Tankers and tour boats drifted lazily under the stone Augustus Bridge, greeting one another with blasts from their foghorns.

Ellen Ramsey, walking across the bridge above the boats, dug her thumbs miserably under the padded straps cutting into her shoulders. It seemed like she'd had to resettle her backpack every few seconds on the long walk north from Dresden's bustling Hauptbahnhof to the cathedral laden Altstadt. A short night in a youth hostel's bunk—clearly not designed for people over six feet tall—had neither alleviated her jetlag nor soothed her aching muscles from sitting on an airplane for eleven hours yesterday. But, she supposed, if dorm life at the University of Washington over the last four years had taught her nothing else, it had at least given her the ability to function on little sleep.

Ellen's mother had begged her to plan her post graduation capstone history tour in the United States instead of Europe. "Colonial Williamsburg isn't too far from the Hamptons," she had pointed out. "You could take Eugene's key to the condo, spend a couple days watching people ride horses or make those triangle hats and buckle shoes, and then head up to the condo to relax."

"Or, isn't Williamsburg near Busch Gardens?" her father had coaxed.

"Busch Gardens," Ellen muttered now. At least her parents had still paid for the trip like they'd promised.

She blinked hard against the sun and pulled out her *Rick Steves' 2011 Germany* guidebook. A photograph of Rick Steves assured her with an enthusiastic thumbs-up that before World War II Dresden had been in the company of Budapest and Florence as one of the most beautiful cities in Europe.

Directly ahead, at the end of the Augustus Bridge, rose the single spire of the Katholischen Hofkirche, whose name Ellen translated as the Catholic Church of Hope. It was one of the few buildings that had not been totally destroyed when the Royal Air Force firebombed the city in 1945. She had learned this fact and others about the end of World War II as a history major at UW. She hadn't found much real emotion in the firebombing of Dresden until a few weeks ago, during a 400 level summer elective—Ellen had already graduated, but the summer course was a brand new joint offering from the History and Psychology departments, and was recommended for any students thinking about graduate school in the future—called Psychology of Warfare.

The instructor, Professor Hollace Cornell, had spoken of the Dresden bombing with righteous disgust: "Early in the war, in a show of arrogance and superiority, the German *Luftwaffe* had bombed London for fifty-seven nights in a row, killing over twenty thousand civilians. The Germans called this tactic *Blitzkrieg,* or Lightning War, and they conducted costly daylight bombing raids throughout Great Britain, focusing on cities and civilians rather than military targets. It was Hitler's idea that British morale would be a far greater loss than a few military factories.

"Four years later, the English Parliament had learned that lesson well, and decided to apply it for themselves. The city of Dresden was a perversely logical choice for their revenge, with its renown throughout Europe as the Jewel on the Elbe."

Here Cornell had pulled off his wire-frame glasses and fixed the class with his hazel eyes. "The allies had actually bombed Dresden twice before, each time striking only railroad supply lines that ran through the city. But on February 13, 1945, only three months before Germany's unconditional surrender, their government and military were already in shambles. What better way to show a broken Germany that it had no power, and its enemies no mercy, than literally to melt a center for art and religion?"

One rule of air raids that went largely unbroken throughout the war, according to Professor Cornell, was that churches and public places like parks were spared from destruction. However, the Royal Air Force had known where the citizens of Dresden would seek refuge—"Many of whom were American and British prisoners of war," Professor Cornell pointed out, again removing his glasses—and ordered a second wing of bombers to focus their fire on those same parks and churches. Stained glass windows in churches all over the city had exploded inward, showering the people inside with hot glass.

The most obvious symbol of the Allied attack on morale had been the Frauenkirche, Dresden's startling and unique Church of our Lady. Ellen could now see its enormous central white dome peeking above the nameless rectangular building to her left. This morning she had already encountered hundreds of postcards showing the Frauenkirche in various states of ruin since the war, the earliest showing only three skeletal fingers, nothing more than a few bricks unconquered by fire and gravity, poking up out of extensive rubble. Professor Cornell's excitement about what the Germans called the *Wiederaufbau*—or "Rebuilding" as Rick Steves translated it—of this famous church had been the main reason Ellen had included Dresden on her itinerary.

"Estimates of civilian casualties in Dresden range from 35,000 to 160,000. Many of the records were destroyed either in the bombing or after the war by the allies," Cornell had said. "Yet even at the lowest end, it represents the largest number of civilian dead in a bombing on the European continent. How many of you heard a word about Dresden in school?"

A fourth of the class had raised their hands.

Ellen settled her pack on her shoulders yet again and leaned on the western railing of the Augustus Bridge. Professor Cornell had mentioned several times the psychological impact of standing in the presence of history, especially because events deemed historically significant frequently involved mass death. She had visited Ground Zero of both the Oklahoma City bombing and the World Trade Center in New York, and on both occasions had experienced the same hollow quickness of breath she felt now, as if the ghosts of the people who had died here were doing somersaults through her guts.

Ellen forced the image from her mind. She had not come to Dresden to wallow in the sadism and hate of the war. Even Professor Cornell, a self proclaimed bleeding heart liberal with a vocal disgust for all forms of violence, had suggested that she'd wallowed plenty already in her Senior Thesis, "Might Makes Right: The Vanishing Illusion of 'Just War.'" No, she had come to Dresden to study and celebrate what Cornell had called Germany's profound power of recovery.

She began walking again. Mounted on tall poles on the far bank of the Elbe, toward which the Augustus Bridge now aimed her, a giant banner read, *Friede auf Erde: Musik von U2 und anderen Gruppen. 20 August.*

Peace on Earth, she translated. Courtesy of the Irish rock band U2 and "other groups," whoever they might be. And that felt perfect after the German editorial she'd read on the train this morning, in which the writer had speculated wildly about the possible implications of the Russian and Chinese militaries apparently joining forces to build what the American media were calling the Red October Sky. The German editorial had gone as far as recommending western Europeans to start building fallout shelters for a possible nuclear apocalypse.

When Ellen had initially heard about the Council of Paris a few days ago, she had hoped it would take some of the piss out of the media's obvious fear mongering. But in the days since the Council had been announced, the American media in particular had begun to spout vague, official sounding concerns about Russia's and China's massive nuclear stockpiles, and how easily those stockpiles might be aimed at New York and Washington, DC from fancy supraorbital jets. Not exactly the sort of language to curb panic. Hell, three days ago, most Americans hadn't even known the term "supraorbital," and now it seemed like the national media's catchphrase.

Ellen forced herself once again to shake off her dark thoughts. "I'm on vacation," she reminded herself.

Anyway, it wasn't like she could personally do much to convince heads of state that another Cold War—or a hot one, for that matter—was an unspeakably lousy option for a world moving ever onward toward what the President himself had described as a centralized global economy and culture.

She took a deep breath and cinched the thick waist strap of her backpack to ease the weight from her shoulders (maybe she would leave a few items behind at the next youth hostel) and set off for the gap between the wide stone steps of the Katholischen Hofkirche and the rectangular building hiding the Frauenkirche.

She estimated the Frauenkirche to be only a block or two away, but the narrow, meandering streets surprised her. The central dome of the cathedral disappeared and reappeared continuously behind the high storefronts of countless small pubs, bakeries, butcher shops, and shoe stores, filling more of the sky each time it did.

"At least I'm going the right direction," she muttered to herself, squeezing between a sausage vendor's cart and a high rack of postcards, taking care not to topple the latter with her swollen backpack.

The streets were half as wide as those in any city in the States but somehow the Germans found room to park cars on either side and still pass two abreast driving. Tourists and native Dresdeners drank coffee and smoked thin cigarettes at heavy iron tables on the sidewalk. Ellen lost herself in the symphony of many mixing languages, bicycle bells, and car horns as she walked.

At last, a half hour after she had stood on the Augustus Bridge, Ellen stepped into an open square dominated by the bone white dome of the Frauenkirche. Across the square to her right, the glass façade of an upscale hotel reared upward almost as high as the Frauenkirche itself. Colorful flags representing ten different countries hung limply over the revolving front doors. To Ellen's left was another long row of shops. A few of the proprietors were still setting up outdoor stands with the usual fare of postcards, shot glasses, and collectible spoons.

The square could have been in any city in western Europe, in other words. Except for the Frauenkirche itself, which stood at the square's center, still hemmed in at a couple spots by bright orange construction fencing. Professor Cornell had shown the class digital photographs of the church as it had looked when he last visited a decade ago: high scaffolding had covered the top half of the building. Now the entire church stood naked in the sunlight. To Ellen it looked like a mix between a gothic cathedral and a mosque. Instead of the typical cruciform layout of European churches, the foundation of the Frauenkirche looked almost circular from Ground level. Four thin towers rose to form the points of an equal armed cross surrounding the massive central dome.

With the fame of the *Wiederaufbau* project and its hugely publicized completion in 2006, Ellen had expected the church's wide front staircase to be swarming with tourists, but she only saw two. One wore a jet black suit and 1940's-style felt hat as if he were an FBI agent instead of a tourist. The other wore jeans and a flannel work shirt. They stood on the top step in front of the church's tall main door, looking into the crowded square. Upon closer inspection, Ellen noticed with some discomfort, they actually seemed to be looking at *her*. They were still too far away to tell for sure, but…

She casually studied her immediate vicinity for any point of interest besides herself. An American couple to her right argued loudly in

English, jabbing fingers at a city map so large that each of them held up one side of it; a Dresdener on a gas powered scooter droned past her into the maze that led back to the Augustus Bridge.

Suddenly she laughed and rubbed both hands over her face. "What are you doing?" she mumbled into her palms. She was getting to be as paranoid as her mother, assuming she was important enough to be watched by strangers.

She decided that tonight she would pay extra for a hotel room with a king size bed. Perhaps even one in yonder five star palace with all the flags above the front doors. Her parents certainly wouldn't begrudge her the extra money, if they even noticed. She could lay diagonally and her feet wouldn't even hang over the edge. And she could take a long, hot shower before bed. Oh yes. She closed her eyes and willed the imaginary water to relax her aching shoulders.

But she *couldn't* relax, and it had nothing to do with the weight of her backpack.

She opened her eyes again, the feeling of being watched stronger than ever. She looked back at the front staircase of the Frauenkirche, simultaneously hoping the men were gone and knowing they weren't. The shorter man—the one in the G-man costume—was now pointing in her direction. Paranoid or not, it was time to get out of here.

Her head swung from side to side again, ignoring the arguing couple and the flow of tiny cars and bicycles on the narrow streets, searching from some avenue of escape. A large sign to her left read *Frauenkirche historic tours every quarter hour.* A large red arrow pointed off toward a distant side entrance of the church. She probably knew as much of this church's history as any local guide, but a tour meant other people, and other people meant safety.

She risked a glance back at the G-man and his flannel-wearing sidekick. There was still a chance, after all, that she *was* overly paranoid and working on too little sleep.

The men were gone.

Ellen followed the arrow pointing to historic tours, her heart pounding in her throat. Two more red arrows directed her to the mouth of a low, dusty door in the white rock of the Frauenkirche marked *Eingang/ Tour Entrance.* She did not know when the next tour started, but there should be other people waiting inside.

She pounded through the door, the straps of her backpack cutting red hot ruts into her shoulders every time her feet hit the pavement. Her breath came in great hitches. Sweat poured down her chest and back, soaking her halter-top. Her well worn volleyball shoes danced down the shallow stone steps leading to the starting point of the tour— at least she hoped that's where they led.

The red arrows finally directed her into a dark, cool room with stone walls, floor, and a low ceiling. About fifty black molded plastic chairs, not unlike those in which Ellen had spent the last four years listening to countless lectures, but without the attached desks, were set up in front of a platform with a podium on it. A collapsible projection screen on a thin metal tripod stood behind the platform. The walls to Ellen's left and right contained three square recesses each, seven feet wide by seven feet high, showcasing religious art and artifacts behind glass. Only the closest recess on her right was unprotected, though Ellen saw a tall, thick pane of glass propped beside the recess, as if waiting to be installed.

Aside from these items, the room was deserted. No stragglers from a previous tour, no visitors waiting for the next one.

Panic nearly took her then. Pins and needles of approaching numbness tickled the balls of her feet, her fingertips, her cheeks, even her teeth. Only once in her life had she been so afraid.

"You are twenty-two years old," she said suddenly. Her voice rebounded loudly off the stone walls. "Not fourteen. This is childish and stupid. *Scheissdumm,*" she added, enjoying the harsh sound of the German curse in the small room.

After a few moments of determined stillness, she managed to slow her breathing. Her trembling muscles quieted. She jostled her pack into its appropriate position on her shoulders and felt cold sweat spreading across her back and under her arms. She had run close to a block under the burden of a 43-pound backpack, after all.

Although a block seemed a paltry distance compared to how far she'd run when she *had* been fourteen years old.

A groan rose in her throat but she clenched her teeth and focused the sound into a fierce growl. "No," she vowed to the empty, echoing room. "I will *not* think about that right now."

She shed her pack onto the basement floor and dabbed at the sweat stains on her shirt where the shoulder straps had lain. The cool, damp basement air played across her wet shirt and set her shivering. She unzipped the top pouch of her pack and drew out another top. She looked around the room again; her halter had a built-in bra, so in the few seconds it took her to remove it and put on the dry one, she would literally be topless. But she saw no cameras hanging from the ceiling or walls, and the only entrance or exit was the staircase she had come down, on which she would easily hear anyone before they could see her.

She grabbed the hem of her halter-top in both hands, meaning to pull it off over her head, but a painting in the open recess caught her eye. She drifted across the room, wet shirt momentarily forgotten.

A beige placard printed in German, English, and French titled the painting as "Pleiades and Azazel." Ellen read the English notes:

> This is one of many works of art that was stored in the underground catacombs of the Frauenkirche at the beginning of World War II in order to preserve Germany's rich history of art. Unfortunately the artist of this piece chose not to sign his name, perhaps due to the fact that the painting's subject matter would have been highly controversial. It is one of the only paintings in the world inspired by the Biblical verse Genesis 6:1, in which "the sons of God went into the daughters of man." One clever girl named Pleiades climbed Mount Herman and promised to marry the slyest of the angels if he revealed the true name of God. However when he did so, she spoke God's name and escaped to Heaven.

In the painting, Pleiades had apparently already tricked her angelic suitor. She floated above the sharp peak of a mountain, radiating a terrible and beautiful silvery light. The angel Azazel looked nothing like angels Ellen had seen in other Renaissance paintings and Hallmark cards—the ones with white robes, harps, and luxuriant dove wings. Azazel was an unnaturally tall, dusty gray shape vaguely resembling a human with huge, horribly intelligent glowing red eyes and bat-like wings folded in leathery peaks behind his back.

Ellen tore her eyes away from the painting to read the rest of the placard:

> *This painting dates back to the early Fourteenth Century, which is especially noteworthy considering the artist's attention to three-dimensional depth. The earliest successful use of the artistic vanishing point is typically considered to have been invented by Italian artist and engineer Filippo Brunelleschi, approximately 100 years after the estimated creation date of "Pleides and Azazel."*

Yes, she thought. This was why she had come here: a seven hundred year old painting, peerless in both content and style. And yet this church alone abounded in history and art to a degree that such a painting—which had probably outlived the oldest artifact in Colonial Williamsburg by four centuries—had been relegated to the basement.

And the subject matter didn't hurt either. A woman who escaped sly monsters by outthinking them? When Ellen got home she might have to find a poster of this painting and hang it over her bed.

She looked left and found her reflection in the thick glass partition that was currently propped against the wall, but would eventually separate visitors from "Pleiades and Azazel." Aside from looking like an entrant in a wet t-shirt contest, Ellen approved of what she saw. Her body still carried most of the muscle she'd built during volleyball season, but that was mere periphery. Much more important were her eyes, which stared back at her, clear and determined.

A loud, rapid clacking suddenly echoed through the basement. Although Ellen would never have expected to hear that sound in the context of a cathedral basement, she recognized it easily: someone behind her was shaking a can of spray paint.

She spun around guiltily, positive she would see a uniformed Frauen-kirche staff worker. The basement room she'd stumbled into was obviously being prepared for some type of presentation. She opened her mouth to apologize—her brain was already forming the German sentences—but closed it again without saying a word. The man before her was no Frauenkirche worker, but he did indeed hold a white aerosol can in one upraised hand, his index finger resting lightly on the spraying mechanism. Ellen recognized him as the man in flannel who had pointed at her from the steps of the Frauenkirche earlier. Adding to the surreal tinge of seeing a real life flannel wearing American farmer in Germany was the old fashioned Polaroid camera hanging around his neck on a thin plastic strap.

"What are you doing with that?" Ellen asked him, gesturing at the spray can.

In answer, the man's eyes flicked past her into the recess containing "Pleiades and Azazel," then returned to her face.

"What—" she began again, but it was only reflex. She suddenly knew he meant to deface the painting behind her, as completely and surely as she'd known he and his friend were pointing at her in the city square.

Her first instinct was to tackle him. Or maybe send a well aimed Tae Bo kick at the bridge of those ridiculous purple tinted glasses. She knew she had the strength and physical advantage to do either one and end the guy's plans for good.

But hadn't she written her own Senior Thesis to dispute the fallacy of might-makes-right?

She didn't tackle or kick. Instead she threw out her arms to protect the painting. Her fingertips didn't quite meet the sharp stone corners where the room's main wall dipped into the painting's recess. She had a moment to wonder why the museum staff hadn't just hung the final glass partition over this recess whenever they'd done the others.

"You're not touching this painting," she told the man, bending her knees and positioning her feet so that her body shielded as much of the recess as possible.

He shook the can again, the little metal bearing inside it clacking madly. His eyes remained on her face.

"That's fine," she told him, nodding. "Spray paint me if that'll get your rocks off. I won't fight you. But I also won't move."

The man looked delighted. However, rather than spraying her face or any other part of her body, he set down the can of paint and raised the Polaroid to his eye.

"Wait," Ellen said.

A purple-white flash exploded in the dim basement, leaving green and blue spots dancing in her vision. A loud mechanical whirr echoed through the stone room as the camera disgorged the photograph.

Ellen blinked rapidly, trying to gain her sight back. She was forcefully reminded of an old movie that had ended in a ridiculous scene with Jimmy Stewart in a wheelchair, using a flash bulb to blind an advancing murderer. That scene didn't seem quite as ridiculous now as it had before.

She heard a heavy scraping sound on the floor just a few feet ahead of her. The man was dragging her backpack away.

Stealing my stuff? she thought frantically. Her passport and all of her money were in there.

She finally took an uncertain step away from the recess, but she didn't lift her foot high enough. The front edge of her shoe clipped an uneven stone in the floor and she overbalanced. She thought she was falling forward, but her sight hadn't even cleared enough to watch the stone floor rush up and slam her in the face. There was one final supernova of bright spots as her head collided with the floor, and then the world went completely dark.

2

The one time Ellen had gotten sloppy drunk had not been at her twenty-first birthday party, as had been the case with several of her friends in college, but seven years earlier, after she had returned home from that miserable trip to Colorado Springs with Coach Zell. When Ellen had described the trip to Corinne, her best friend since fifth grade, Corinne had broken into her father's liquor cabinet and busied herself with progressively more ridiculous concoctions. Ellen's last clear memory of the night was Corinne pouring vodka and cranberry juice over a jiggling pile of Jello shots from the miniature refrigerator inside the liquor cabinet.

Now, trying to keep her entire face squeezed shut against all light and sound, Ellen realized she must have gone on another incredible and totally unmemorable bender last night. She remembered some movie or other describing dying of thirst as a hangover that finally kills you. Ellen didn't know if she was dying of thirst, but this hangover might just kill her anyway. Her tongue felt heavy and fibrous as if a sheep had crawled into her mouth and died.

She smiled at the image, the slight movement making her head pound harder if that was possible. An involuntary groan caused the bones around her nose and eyes to rattle alarmingly. A sharp, singular pain jabbed between her eyes as if she had snorted a bumblebee into her sinuses and it was stinging her head from the inside.

"*Guten Abend,*" said a voice made of lightning and thumbtacks. "Good evening, yes?"

Ellen raised her hands to cover her ears and felt an uncomfortable tugging in the top of her right hand.

"Quiet," she whispered, feeling the bumblebee buzz again.

Bits of memory from this morning were coming back to her. There had been no bar. No alcoholic bender. Just the G-man and flannel farmer on the front steps of the Frauenkirche. The flash and belabored whirr of a Polaroid camera in a dim stone basement.

"Good evening," a second voice said, deeper and less accented than the first but still female. "I am Doctor Müller. Do you remember what happened? The paramedics told us you tripped on a stone in the floor of the *Frauenkirche.* The bones in your nose shifted upward, but broke before they could puncture your brain."

Now that Ellen was more awake, the skin on her face felt tight and swollen like a water balloon about to pop. Her hands instinctively came up to her face but they met thick gauze and cold, plastic lumps that would have been familiar to anyone who had played as many organized sports as she had: ice packs. Only her mouth, chin, and the underside of her nose seemed to be uncovered.

Holy shit, I'm really hurt, she thought.

"I was able to reset the bones in your nose without surgery, though your eyes have swollen shut and you will have bruises for many weeks. I think you have broken your nose before?"

"Did he rape me?" Ellen whispered.

There was a heavy silence.

Holy shit holy shit holy shit. Please not again.

"We found no evidence to suggest sexual assault of any kind."

A single sob of relief burst from her mouth. Cold laces of spit landed on her chin. "Are you sure?"

"I am positive," the doctor said. "You have an IV in your hand and you can press the button for more drugs if the pain becomes too great. We have tried to contact your parents with the telephone number and e-mail address on your tourist information card, but they have not responded."

They're at the condo in East Hampton, Ellen tried to say. Only a hiss of air came out.

"Is there someone else we can contact?"

Rick Steves, she thought deliriously.

After a moment the doctor said, "I will come back. Nurse Hofer can bring you food when you are ready to eat."

Ellen's mother called her cell phone in the middle of that first night. Ellen was awake; she had little use for day and night since her world was constant blackness. Nurse Hofer pulled the telephone from her backpack and handed it to her.

"Thank God!" her mother shrieked. "We were on the beach all day and I just got the message from that awful German hospital. What a cruel-sounding doctor. And a woman no less! I told you Europe was dangerous. I told you not to go."

"I'm fine, Mother," she said weakly.

"Are you crying?" her mother demanded. "What has that woman done to you? Oh, my poor baby."

"The hospital is very nice and—"

She grabbed a Kleenex from the ever-present box by her left leg and honked carefully into it; the pain was better now, probably due to the constant ice packs and medication, but the pressure of blowing her nose still didn't feel too stellar. A large wet gob thudded into the Kleenex. She balled it up and tossed it to her right, where she supposed there must be a mountain of slimy red tissues. Dr. Müller had said her sinuses would drain blood and mucus for another day or so.

"It's very nice and clean," Ellen finished.

The "clean" part would hopefully calm her mother, who knew nothing of Germany except what she had seen in grainy black-and-white footage on the History Channel.

"Eugene and I will be on the next flight to Germany to bring you home," her mother said, either not hearing or not trusting Ellen's promise of cleanliness. "Your father thinks we can get there and come back inside of 36 hours and then you can receive proper treatment over here."

Ellen guessed her sinuses would literally explode if she spent even an instant in a pressurized airplane cabin but did not say so. "I have to stay here at least until the swelling goes down. The doctor is very nice and…" What would soothe her mother? "…clean?"

"And I simply can't believe they're calling it *art*," her mother went on. "I suppose it's incredibly lifelike, but that just makes it worse. The hospital e-mailed us the article from some newspaper or other but it's all in German. I know fashion is different in Europe but you don't have to display your body like some common prostitute. Your father had to take *two* pills when we got home."

"Mom, what—"

Another gooey mess rocketed through her sinuses and she held the phone away from her mouth while she coughed and snorted into a new tissue.

She brought the phone back to her ear in time to hear her mother say, "…call again after we buy your tickets home…*Yes,* Eugene, I'll tell her. Your father is relieved you're not dead. We love you and we'll see you very soon."

Nurse Hofer, whom Ellen still had not seen, was kind enough to check in with her regularly for the rest of the night. Ellen asked each time if the nurse knew what her mother had been talking about on the phone. *What* was very lifelike? But Nurse Hofer always gave the same enigmatic answer: "You must see for yourself, yes?" Ellen quit asking.

The next morning, after a breakfast of a gritty strawberry-flavored nutrient shake, Nurse Hofer and Dr. Müller turned on the lights, so to speak. It took the nurse about a minute to remove all of the gauze and ice packs. Ellen felt her head being tugged in concentric circles, reminding her of trashy junior high horror movies that always ended with the Mummy coming unwound to reveal nothing but dust and a jawbone.

"Keep your eyes closed for a moment, yes?" Nurse Hofer said softly. "The lights will be very bright."

As the last bandage over Ellen's eyes came off, the room's fluorescent lights pounded fiercely through her closed eyes as though her eyelids had grown transparent overnight. This new light made the Polaroid's flash seem like the feeble spark of a firefly at dusk. Both of Ellen's arms, including the one with the IV needle, flew up instinctively to protect her eyes. Nurse Hofer caught them.

"Ah ah. *Vorsicht.* Careful," Dr. Müller warned. The word came out *Kyar-fool.* It was the first time the doctor had spoken with a noticeable accent. "You must not put too much pressure on your nasal bones. Your eyes will adjust rapidly."

It was true. Ellen's pupils must have grown to the size of dimes under those bandages, but they were shrinking again to let in a more tolerable amount of light. She fluttered her eyelids and found they didn't open very far. A purple and yellow mountain rose in the center of Ellen's vision and disappeared somewhere between her eyes. Her *nose?* She closed her eyes immediately and breathed deeply against a wave of nausea.

Gentle fingers probed the bruised mound between her eyes. "You are healing quickly," said Dr. Müller approvingly. "I asked if you broke your nose before because we found a hard facial mask in your ruck-sack—I hope you do not mind that we searched your belongings, but we had to call your family. The mask we found should adequately protect the bones as they heal. You will need to wear it for as long as the bruises remain, although I think that is better than stitches and scars?"

The mask wasn't such a big deal. Ellen had had to wear it for most of the volleyball season after taking a spike in the face from a Penn State hitter, and she'd only brought it to Europe because her mother had pestered her until she agreed to do so. Far more traumatic was the unspoken question of how soon they would force her to go home.

"And today you can see what Nurse Hofer has been saving for you," Dr. Müller continued.

A brief internal battle followed this statement. In the end curiosity overcame self pity. Ellen opened her eyes to their maximum squint and saw her first glimpse of Dr. Müller. She was a small woman with short blonde hair, the very picture of what Ellen had expected Nurse Hofer to look like. Despite Ellen's first impression of lightning and thumbtacks, Nurse Hofer's voice had turned out to be high and bright and soft, Tinkerbell's voice. However, the woman standing beside Dr. Müller was no Tinkerbell. She was probably close to Ellen's height— over six feet for sure—and angular. Ellen wondered if Nurse Hofer had heaved her from the paramedics' gurney onto this bed all by herself. Small blue eyes peered brightly at Ellen over a slightly upturned nose. Pale skin and hair, large teeth. A very Nordic package.

And in those heavy Nordic hands was a newspaper, which Nurse Hofer passed wordlessly to Ellen. Block letters at the top of the paper read *Sächsiche Zeitung*. Ellen thought it meant *Saxony Times*, but that title didn't explain why she was on the cover. At least, her *image* was on the cover. There was no mistaking it despite the shimmering silver in which she was painted. She had been painted on the seven-by-seven pane of glass that had been propped against the wall in the basement of the Frauenkirche. Someone had now propped it in front of the collapsible projection screen on the black platform that Ellen also recognized from the Frauenkirche. There were more silver marks on the projection screen in the background of the shot, but they were out of focus.

There was a long article below the photo as well, but for now Ellen couldn't take her eyes from the picture. She remembered well enough how she had been dressed—almost not at all, as her mother had so tactlessly mentioned—when she had found the painting of Pleiades and the angel, and her portrait reflected her memory perfectly. The silver portrait of Ellen wore a thin halter top soaked to the point of transparency, shoulders and extended arms shining with sweat, fingertips floating inches from either edge of the glass pane. Her face showed no trace of panic from her dash into the basement, but radiated the simple, immovable resolve she had felt to protect the seven-hundred-year-old painting "Pleiades and Azazel" from defacement.

All of these details in Ellen's painted face and body rose from the simple contrast between painted light and shadow, with the blank spaces in the glass representing the parts of her skin and clothing that had been illuminated in the Polaroid's flash, and the areas of silver paint representing the parts of her that had been hidden in shadow.

He did all this with a can of spray paint?

The newspaper's headline read, *Americanus Rex: Das neue Gesicht der Kunst.*

The new face of art, she translated.

She skimmed the article. Her German skills were not quite up to a direct translation, but she caught the most important details. The painting had been discovered in the basement room by the Frauenkirche's tourism director, Hermann Klein, and a German television news crew that was filming a feature for the anniversary of the Frauenkirche's reopening. Klein insisted that he had finished setting up the room only fifteen minutes before bringing the news crew inside.

Ellen saw no mention of herself or the paramedics who Dr. Müller had said brought her to the hospital. Had she already been in the ambulance by the time the news crew reached the basement? Almost certainly. No news team she had ever heard of would ignore an injured woman in favor of a new painting. That meant the man who'd painted her had also called the ambulance.

All in fifteen minutes?

In the article, Hermann Klein theorized that Americanus Rex had painted the pane of glass ahead of time and waited until just before the news crew was scheduled to enter the room to set up his little exhibit. Ellen knew better. However the flannel farmer had done it, he must have painted her in under fifteen minutes and then carried her—possibly with the help of his friend in the black suit—up to street level to await the ambulance.

She believed Klein's statement that he was just as surprised as his companions to discover the new portrait on the pane of glass. But surprised or not, he was skilled enough as a publicist to turn the situation to his advantage. "*Ich bin immer der Meinung gewesen*," he was quoted as saying, "*daß die Frauenkirche ein starkes Symbol des Friedes ist. Der Krieg nur zerstört, aber Friede baut irgendetwas wieder auf. Hoffentlich kann die Kanzlerin an der gleichen Meinung von Americanus Rex und mir kommen, während den Council of Paris.*"

Ellen looked up at Dr. Müller. "Okay, I understand why this Klein guy says the Frauenkirche is a symbol of peace. When he says war can only destroy, but peace can build anything, he's talking about how the Frauenkirche was rebuilt after World War Two, right?"

Dr. Müller nodded. Nurse Hofer beamed proudly at Ellen.

"But why does he think Americanus Rex is painting for peace? And what's he saying about the German Chancellor?"

Nurse Hofer took the paper from Ellen's hands and began flipping through it.

Dr. Müller frowned apologetically. "It is very complicated, yes? The Chancellor is attending the Council of Paris with your President and other world leaders at the moment. Many Germans, like Herr Klein, believe your President hopes to convince us to commit our militaries against Russia, similar to the way George W. Bush convinced some of the European nations, including our own, to support the war in Iraq in 2003. I think Herr Klein is using your painting and the public's strong curiosity about Americanus Rex to gain national momentum for a peaceful solution to the Council of Paris. I believe you would call it a 'grass roots' movement?"

"Yeah, that's the right word," Ellen agreed, "but that still doesn't explain why Herr Klein thinks my portrait has a message of peace."

"Since the Council of Paris began, your President's position seems to be that the best protection against a mighty military is an even mightier military. Herr Klein asserts that your portrait embodies a stronger sort of protection without the threat of violence."

Ellen nodded slowly, trying to take it all in.

Dr. Müller made a frustrated noise in the back of her throat. "I think I am not explaining correctly. My English…"

"Is excellent," Ellen assured her. "I understand, but it just seems like a real jump from motherly protection to a call for world peace."

Dr. Müller smiled as if she had expected this response.

"What?" Ellen asked.

"Americanus Rex also wrote a message to go with your portrait."

Nurse Hofer returned the newspaper to Ellen, now open to a new page containing four more photographs: a close-up of Ellen's painted face; a wide shot of the stage where the portrait had been found; Americanus Rex's bizarre signature, which appeared to contain absurdly large cartoon breasts in the *R* of *Rex;* and a photograph of the projection screen Ellen had seen on the little stage when she had first entered the basement. The man who painted her had sprayed a sort of poem on the screen, at which Nurse Hofer was pointing.

The Tower of Babel has betrayed us. Rather than making us into gods, the Tower has driven wedges between all people in the universe to form the spokes of the Wheel of War. We must uproot the failed Babel and carry it to the top of Mount Olympus. Only there can we pierce the heart of the brightest star in the universe to make a torch, the light of which will cause all life to weep with joy until the wheel of war shudders to a stop.

Ellen read through the poem twice without stopping. The part about making a torch out of a star tickled some distant memory, possibly from her time at the university, but she couldn't put her finger on the memory itself.

She turned to Dr. Müller again. "Can I visit my portrait? Go see it in person?"

Dr. Müller made another one of those apologetic expressions. "The answer to that question is certainly too complicated for my English."

Ellen doubted this, and opened her mouth to say so, but Dr. Müller went on.

"I can tell you that the painting will probably come back to Germany in the future, but I do not know if it will return to Dresden at that time or go to another city."

"Where is it?"

"*Großbritannien,*" Nurse Hofer answered.

Ellen made the translation. "England?"

"London," Dr. Müller clarified. "It has been moved temporarily to the Tate Modern Museum in London."

Ellen laid the newspaper on the white sheet covering her legs. "How soon can I leave?"

Exhibition in London

1

Saturday, August 27, 2011

The customs line at Heathrow Terminal 4 swarmed with the usual fare of travelers. At least Imogene supposed they were usual. She was much too tired to pay attention to anyone besides herself and her traveling companions at the moment. Priscilla had never flown on an airplane before, but she had not seemed to suffer motion sickness during the flight, possibly because all three of them had been far too caught up in the stories of the Miss Washington pageant, chickenpox, and Lord Droon's antics to notice any turbulence. Now, however, after nearly eight hours on the airplane, Priscilla looked more than a little worse for wear.

"Feels pretty good to stand up and stretch, huh?" asked Imogene.

Priscilla's back abruptly straightened into her normal flawless posture. "I keep thinking the next place we get to will have fewer people than the last." She offered them a waxy, if good humored, smile. "I thought the Charleston airport was crowded."

"You'll get used to it real fast," Ben assured her. He squeezed her hand, but let go quickly.

"I'll be fine. Do you need to call your boss, Imogene?"

"Good thinking," Imogene said. "Maybe Teddy can get a car here for us by the time we get through customs."

But when she thumbed the power button on her cell phone, a message popped onto the screen: *1 New Voicemail.* It was from Teddy. "Genie," his recorded voice barked into her ear. "Sorry, babe, I'd hoped to have some transportation lined up for you, but you'll have to get to the Tate Modern on your own. Once you get to the museum, find someone with a walkie-talkie and ask them to page Dr. Hume."

"Perfect," Imogene said, snapping her cell phone closed irritably. Well, Teddy paid her to be a problem solver.

They cleared customs thirty minutes later.

"What's the plan?" Ben asked.

"We're meeting Teddy at the Tate Modern Museum."

"How do we get there?"

"I'll let you know when I figure that out." She made her way to a tall desk under yellow sign with a black lowercase **i** inside a black circle. "Hello," she said. "I need to get to the Tate Modern as quickly as possible. What would be the best way?"

A thin blonde man with wireframe glasses glanced up from his computer screen. "Normally it would be a cab, but you'll never find one this time of day." He pulled out a tiny map of the London Underground and launched into a series of names. "Go down the escalator behind you. An airport shuttle will take you to the Heathrow Tube Stop. From there, take Picadilly Line in the direction of Cockfosters and ride until you reach South Ealing. Switch to District Line and get off at Blackfriars. From there just follow the street signs to the museum."

Imogene scribbled furiously before accepting the map. "Thank you very much."

She found Ben and Priscilla in front of a news kiosk, both of them staring in open wonder at the front page of a copy of *The Times* in Ben's hands.

"What's going on?" she asked.

Ben handed her the paper, pointing at an article halfway down the front page. "Didn't you say we're going to the Tate Modern Museum?"

The article's title read, "Tate Modern Offers £10000 Reward." She glanced up at her brother, then quickly read on.

London: Tate Modern Museum curator, Dr. Oliver Hume, is offering £5000 to anyone who can provide the museum with certifiable information on new artist, Americanus Rex, whose first controversial portrait was discovered in the Frauenkirche (Church of Our Lady) in Dresden, Germany yesterday. According to Dr. Hume, the reward will double if the information leads to the discovery of a new painting.

Dr. Hume's interest likely stems from the surprising fact that the original portrait did not remain in Dresden. Frauenkirche Tourism Director Hermann Klein contacted Hume shortly after discovering the portrait and offered temporary ownership to the Tate Modern Museum. Said Klein, 'The German public already knows how the Council of Paris must end. We can delay our possession of the portrait if it helps Great Britain realize the same thing.'

When the Times *asked Dr. Hume if he was afraid Americanus Rex might bring bad publicity to the Tate Modern, he responded, 'The best art stirs controversy. And that's doubly true when art speaks out against the mistakes of established governments or institutions.' Adding his own bit of trademark cheek, Hume said, 'Personally, I think Americanus Rex will cause more trouble for the Prime Minister than for me.'*

The trouble to which Hume referred comes not from the painting itself, but the printed message found with the portrait. In it, Americanus Rex refers to the Tower of Babel and the Wheel of War, both of which are thought to be condemning references to the U.S. organised Council of Paris, which the Prime Minister has been attending since Thursday. Despite widespread concern from British citizenry about the summit, the politically beleaguered Prime Minister has hinted that he plans to throw in his lot with the Americans.

No matter the outcome of the Council of Paris, Americanus Rex's first portrait will be accessible to visitors of the Tate Modern Museum for one month, beginning 29 August.

Imogene whistled through her teeth. "The Tate's setting up a new exhibit in two *days?* Teddy sometimes takes a couple weeks."

Ben accepted the paper back from her. "All this effort for one painting," he mused. "Just imagine what they'd do if they knew about—"

He broke off and glanced at Priscilla. She was still staring fixedly at the article.

"They would want to put my painting into a museum too, wouldn't they?"

"That's certainly a possibility," Imogene said slowly. "Priscilla, I'm sorry about the way your friends and family reacted to your portrait. And no one would blame you if you wanted it to stay on General's Peak for the next fifty years, but I hope—"

"I could never be ashamed of the way Gary painted me," Priscilla interrupted.

"I don't think you should be," Imogene assured her. "I just want you to know that many people probably won't see your portrait the same way you do. To some people, my boss included, your portrait will probably look like a pile of money. Especially if that newspaper article is any indication."

Priscilla only nodded. She leaned over and replaced the newspaper on its shelf.

Imogene watched her in quiet wonder. She had spent the last year of her life surrounded by art, yet she doubted that she would be able to keep as cool as Priscilla was now if someone had painted such a deeply personal portrait of her.

"So how do we get to your museum?" Ben asked.

Imogene held up the miniature map of the London Underground. "We're taking the subway."

2

Twenty minutes and one shuttle ride later, the three of them stepped off their second long escalator of the day. A prim male voice echoed through the station, "Now arriving, Picadilly Line to Cockfosters Station. Mind the gap."

Imogene felt a gust of warm, oily wind ruffle her hair. A moment later a boxy silver train clacked noisily into view and stopped with a high whine. The train's doors slid open, loosing a colorful cocktail of humanity: families draped in luggage, sleek business men with well-worn carryall bags, uniformed airport and Tube employees.

"This is us," Imogene announced.

She snaked through onto the train through the right half of the train's portal while the last of the previous passengers disembarked through the left. Ben and Priscilla bunched at her heels as if afraid the train's door might slide closed on them.

The trip to South Ealing took another twenty minutes. Once in the station proper, the three of them followed a series of arrows and signs until Imogene found an electronic billboard showing arrivals and departures.

"Where are we going?" Ben asked. "Maybe we should ask someone again."

Imogene found what she had been looking for, and pointed at a tunnel about fifty feet ahead of them. "District Line toward Upminster," she said, unable to keep the satisfaction from her voice.

As if to punctuate her victory, somewhere in the crush of travelers ahead, a tourist snapped photograph, the flash rebounding through the dim tunnel like white-purple lighting. Priscilla blinked confusedly, apparently failing to grasp why anyone might want a picture of a dingy subway tunnel.

Ben's eyes followed the path of Imogene's pointing finger, equally annoyed and impressed. "Good grief, how can you understand where these signs are telling us to go? I'd get lost and die of starvation down here."

"I drive in Los Angeles," she said simply. "Now, our next train doesn't get here for eight minutes. You guys need a bathroom?" Ben and Priscilla shook their heads. She unshouldered her carryall and handed it to Ben. "I'll be right back."

Despite these words, wading through the commuters took her over a minute, due in part to a women's field hockey team that filed through the station behind their coach like a row of colossal ducklings. Eventually Imogene reached a door next to an oblong white placard on the wall that read *toilet* in bold lowercase letters. She recalled Teddy's numerous complaints that you had to pay "50p to pee" in London, but inside Imogene found no "toilet guard," as Teddy called the restroom attendants, nor any coin-operated locks on the doors.

She also noticed that, unlike American restrooms, the stalls were equipped with sturdy doors that reached all the way from the floor to the ceiling. She swung open the nearest of these and let out a startled cry. Directly at eye level, her own face peered back out at her from the stall's navy blue back wall in glittering silver.

Imogene understood immediately that the camera flash out in the tunnel had not come from a regular tourist, but from Gary Pritchard's Polaroid. The similarities between Priscilla's portrait and this new one on the restroom wall were too numerous to deny. As in Priscilla's portrait, Gary had created tremendous detail and depth simply by the use of light and shadow. Except where the silver paint in Priscilla's portrait had represented shadow, in Imogene's portrait, the unpainted patches of dark blue tile served as shadow, and the silver paint defined the lighted portions of Imogene's skin and clothing.

Her painted body was turned slightly to the side, left arm upraised in precisely the same pose Imogene had struck only minutes ago when she had located the tunnel leading toward their final train ride. Her painted eyes were clear and calm, the mouth set in a satisfied line. Even her beloved carryall had made it into the portrait, slung between her breasts and riding her hip like an adventurer's satchel.

Imogene remembered being pleased with herself when she had located the sign for Upminster, but the painted version of her looked positively exalted, as if pointing toward some glorious horizon only she could see.

But if Gary had painted her as she looked only a couple minutes ago…

"He's still in here," she whispered to herself.

She stepped left and wrenched open the door to the only other stall, but the second stall was empty. There was no other place in the little restroom where a person could hide. Somehow Gary had escaped.

Behind her, the door to the station cracked open and Imogene leapt back into the first stall, nearly ripping the door off its hinges as she yanked it shut and turned the lock.

"Are you *quite* alright, Miss?" came the muffled voice of a properly horrified English woman.

"Fine, thanks!" Imogene bellowed with as much sincerity as she could muster.

This either satisfied or frightened the woman into silence. Imogene heard the other stall door click shut, but the other woman was already the furthest thing from her mind. She had realized that her portrait was not pointing to an invisible horizon as she had originally thought, but to another of the stall's navy blue walls, on which Gary had painted words in his gleaming liquid mercury paint.

Silver Lumine, her shocked brain reminded her.

She recognized the childish scrawl as easily as she had recognized her own face, although she had not seen it in a very long time.

Estimada amiga (dear friend),
   Yesterday my brother Ramón beat up a bully at school for kicking a smaller boy. Ramón said he just wanted to help the small boy but Mama said 4th grade is to old to hit people. Tonight she invited the bully and the smaller boy and their parents to super at our house. Ramón and the other two boys are playing Transformers in his room right now and are very loud. Boys are so weird. I helped make torrjas for dessert. I will ask Mama if I can send you one.
Besos y abrazos! (kisses and hugs)
Dulcinea Montero de Frutas

Gary had recreated, misspellings and all, the last letter Imogene had received from her Spanish penpal, Dulci. The same letter Ben claimed he had traded to Lord Droon in exchange for his own life twenty years ago.

Is this a beacon of peace? Imogene wondered, just as she had done in the presence of Priscilla's portrait on General's Peak.

"Of course it is," she said aloud, her voice calm and firm.

Imogene's eyes trailed down her portrait's curvy torso, cast in silver highlights against the blue restroom wall, and followed the long, sturdy legs as they straddled the pipe leading from the back of the toilet into the wall. She was not at all surprised to see, beside her portrait's left ankle, a hastily scrawled signature reading *Americanus Rex* with the top half of the *R* in *Rex* transformed into two pendulous breasts. Finally she returned her study to her own face, bright and terribly alive. The portrait's expression said she knew the world would follow where she pointed.

Imogene jumped as the English woman exited the other stall. How long had Imogene been in here? Long enough for Ben and Priscilla to worry that they would miss their train?

Well, Imogene had lost interest in the train, and she guessed her brother and Priscilla would too once they saw this.

She cracked open the stall door until she was sure she was alone, then slid through the outer door into the station. Her eyes raked the crowd but neither Ben nor Priscilla was tall enough to stand over the sea of humanity in the station.

One familiar face did pop out of the crowd ten yards to her left, but seeing it gave her no comfort.

At five feet tall, Lord Droon certainly have been hidden by passing commuters, but everyone in the station gave him a wide berth. He was rubbing what looked like a long paint roller against a poster on a wall between two storefronts, smoothing the air bubbles out of the glue holding it to the wall. The poster said:

Americanus Rex's Dresden Portrait
A New Exhibit at the Tate Modern
Opening Monday 29 August

Apparently satisfied that the poster would stay where it was, Droon turned toward Imogene and showed his square white teeth in his unmistakable grin. On the two occasions Imogene had crossed Droon's path before, he had been practically unable to talk except with the aid of large amounts of water. He suffered no such handicap today.

He opened his mouth wide and bellowed, his voice rebounding through the Underground station like that of a circus ringmaster with a bullhorn, "*Americanus Rex has painted in the women's lav! The artist bloke from today's* Times!"

In the few seconds of muted chatter following Droon's proclamation, Imogene saw several people glance down at copies of today's *Lon-*

don Times tucked under their arms or in purses or briefcases, before facing up toward the bathroom she had just exited.

Droon's voice came again, this time from deep within the crowd to her right. He was a quick little guy. *"Isn't there a ten thousand pound reward on offer from the Tate Modern?"* he shouted jubilantly.

The commuters responded to his voice in an eerily concerted movement, like a flock of pigeons wheeling toward a dumpster of donuts. Imogene backpedaled until her shoulders slammed against the wall beside the bathroom door. The pigeons continued to flock.

Near panic, Imogene yanked open the bathroom door and locked herself in the stall again, throwing her back against the inside of the door to barricade it. Fists began hammering on the door. From the sounds, more and more people were shoving their way into the restroom. The door bucked against her back as someone outside gave it a hard kick, but it held in its sturdy frame.

"Benny!" she screamed, but heard no reply from her brother.

And even if he had answered, she could never have opened the door to let him inside with her. The surging crowd in the bathroom could crush them both as easily as the ocean tide could dash a canoe against a coastal cliff.

Another kick rattled the stall door on its hinges, this one hard enough to pitch her body momentarily forward. She immediately threw herself backward again, bracing her body against the door with her legs. Yet even as she strained, her eyes returned to her portrait, tracing the smooth lines of her composed expression and pointing hand.

Imogene felt her panic and desperation begin to ebb away. Without breaking bodily contact with the door, she slipped her hand into the pocket of her capris and dialed Teddy's cell phone number.

3

The door held until the police arrived. Imogene had no idea how long she had been sitting on the tile floor in the stall, but her legs were shaking from the constant strain of pressing backward against he door. She heard the sound of the crowd being pushed backward until it was reduced to a dull roar out in the station. A male officer rapped on the door with his nightstick and asked her to come out of the stall.

When she didn't answer at once, Teddy's sharp voice echoed through the small room. "Genie?"

She scrambled to her feet, unconsciously brushing floor grit from the seat of her pants, and opened the door.

"Thank God," Teddy breathed, peering over her shoulder.

Aside from his clothes being unironed—Teddy kept an automatic steam iron in his bedroom in Los Angeles so that he could wake every morning to freshly pressed clothes—he looked as controlled as ever.

"Bravo, Genie. It's Americanus Rex, all right. How in the hell can he get so much depth from dichromatic contrast? The guy is like Ansel Adams with a paintbrush. Far freaking *out*."

He finally looked back at Imogene, tilting his head to study her over the tops of his tiny square Armani glasses. His widow's peak, sculpted dirty blonde without a thread of gray at forty-three, shone with hair gel in the bathroom's fluorescent lights. "So what the hell happened? Are you okay?"

She nodded, pressing her palms against her eyelids. "Where are Ben and Priscilla?"

"Who?" he asked without much interest, eyes locked once again on her portrait. "Oliver, you gotta see this."

"Well bloody move," a brisk tenor voice suggested from somewhere behind Teddy. Imogene hadn't even realized anyone else was in the room with them.

Teddy rarely talked about Oliver except to condemn the cost and breadth of the man's shoe collection. "His closet is like a gay Valhalla," Teddy had remarked with his usual tact after his last London trip.

Ever her father's daughter, Imogene had bristled. "There's nothing wrong with being gay."

"Of course there's not," Teddy had said shortly. "And if Oliver *were* gay, I'm sure he'd value your approval. All I meant was that gay guys typically like footwear, and Oliver has more shoes than Imelda Marcos and God put together. Lighten up."

Teddy now obeyed Oliver's command and backed himself awkwardly out of the stall, allowing Imogene her first glimpse of Dr. Oliver Hume. He strode into the stall and greeted her with a formal tilt of his meticulously shaved head.

"Miss Cornell," he said, taking her hand.

He was younger than she had imagined, with skin the color of dark chocolate. His grip, while pleasantly firm, felt like velvet under her fingers. She suppressed a ridiculous urge to ask him what type of moisturizer he used.

"It's nice to meet you finally," she said.

"Likewise," he said with another tilt of his head. Unlike Teddy, he had not yet even glanced at the painting.

"Dr. Hume, my brother and his friend are still out in the station."

"Go find them, by all means," he said, gesturing to the London bobby just inside the door. "But come back here quickly, please. I would like to ask you about all this."

He turned around and faced the painted toilet at last. Without her even realizing it, he had traded positions in the stall with her while holding her hand, as if they had just completed some type of ballroom dance maneuver.

"Astounding," he said, drinking in the portrait's silver face.

Even more astounding to Imogene, he dropped to his hands and knees on the stall floor and peered at the underside of the toilet, the wooden soles of his shoes sticking up in the air. His outfit had probably cost more than Imogene's plane ticket—his *shoes* had probably cost more than her plane ticket—and here he was, practically mopping the restroom floor with it. Several unpleasant hairs and dust bunnies stuck to his tailored black trousers and the sleeves of his sport jacket.

Imogene left him to his study and slipped past Teddy out into the station. The police had set up a blockade of waist high yellow caution tape in a fifteen foot radius around the bathroom door. Ten bobbies in black peaked hats stood calmly in front of the fences.

"Which is your brother?" asked the one who had followed her out of the bathroom.

Several cameras flashed as she stepped out the door, her heart jumping with each one. In addition to the regular cameras, she saw several arms holding cell phone cameras over other people's heads. Her eyes flicked across the crowd, sure that she would see Gary Pritchard and his bulky Polaroid, but the photographers only seemed to be curious tourists. Some of them undoubtedly hoped to send their pictures to the Tate Modern for a chance at the reward money.

Ben and Priscilla stood near the front of the crowd, looking tired and worried. Ben's shoulders sagged in obvious relief when he saw Imogene emerge from the restroom.

"That's my brother," Imogene told the bobby, pointing. "The tall one with the green backpack. The blonde woman beside him is with us too."

The bobby nodded and, after a quick comment to a colleague guarding the makeshift fence, escorted Ben and Priscilla back to the bathroom. More cameras flashed as Imogene hugged her brother.

"What happened in there?" he asked, releasing her.

"Did either of you see Gary Pritchard leave this bathroom?" she asked.

"Gary was here?" Priscilla asked.

"I wasn't looking," Ben said. "I heard someone shouting about Americanus Rex and then the people stampeded. There must have been some police officers just above the station on street level because they got here almost right away. When you didn't come out…" His face had gone quite pale.

Priscilla put a calming hand on his back. "You're okay," she said to Imogene. "That's what's important."

"I *am* okay," Imogene agreed, mostly for her brother's benefit. "But there's something else that's pretty important too."

"Did Gary really paint again?" Priscilla said. "Like Ben said, we heard the shouting."

"He did, didn't he?" Ben said, beginning to smile. "And you were the first one to find the painting. Remind me never to use the word 'coincidence' again."

"He painted *me*," Imogene said. "Before I went into the bathroom." She pulled them inside before either one could say anything else.

"—should have no trouble removing the toilet itself, though the tile may present a trick," Oliver was saying.

"Yeah, but who owns it *right now?*" Teddy demanded. "In the States, any type of art on public property belongs to the local municipality."

"Which in this case is the London Assembly," Oliver agreed. "After negotiating with the German Chancellor for the Dresden piece, this one will be no trouble at all. I know a bloke in the Assembly who would tear up Trafalgar Square for the right price."

"I'll pay it," Teddy said immediately. Oliver raised an eyebrow. "I know, I know, the Tate can display it for the first month. But Genie's my employee. No one else is getting her portrait."

Imogene considered asking if "no one" included her, even though she was the one who had been painted in the first place. But now was not the time for such quibbles.

She cleared her throat. "Dr. Hume, Teddy, this is my brother Ben and our friend Priscilla."

Ben shook Teddy's hand politely enough—Imogene had an idea he still had not quite forgiven her boss for cutting off her vacation in Accord—but when he saw Imogene's portrait for the first time all the tension seemed to flow out of his body.

"Holy crap," he breathed, shaking hands vacantly with Oliver.

Oliver smiled broadly. "It's a joy to meet you as well, Ben. And Priscilla," he added, maneuvering himself past Ben to peck Priscilla on both cheeks. She blushed furiously. "Please," he said, gesturing toward the stall.

"Dr. Hume?" said the bobby, who had once again taken up his post at the door.

"Of course." Oliver took Imogene's arm and led her over to the bobby, explaining quickly, "The London police usually do not respond to graffiti in a public toilet, but they received an emergency call about a riot in this station."

The bobby pulled a small pad of paper and a pen from his shirt pocket. "Since you seem to be the person portrayed in the artwork that started the riot, could you please explain how it started?"

Imogene quickly described her arrival at the station, how a man in the station had taken her photograph—she did not reveal Gary Pritchard's name; she could not stand the idea of him being arrested before she could ask her growing pile of questions in person—and how another man putting up a poster in the station had shouted something about Americanus Rex and the reward from the Tate Modern.

The bobby's eyes flicked to Oliver with poorly veiled disapproval.

"I ran back inside the bathroom just to avoid being trampled," she finished. "That's when I called my employer, Teddy Roth, who informed Dr. Hume."

The bobby scribbled on his pad. "Why didn't you unlock the door when I knocked?"

Imogene opened her mouth, then closed it again. How could she begin to describe her mental state during the delirious minutes she'd spent barricading the door and staring up at her portrait?

"I guess I was in shock," she said lamely. "I'm sorry."

The bobby seemed unimpressed, but he wrote down her answer.

"You don't need to apologize for anything," Oliver assured her. He turned to the bobby. "Thank you for your rapid and professional response here. Your supervisor will hear my thanks as well."

"Just doing my job, Dr. Hume," the bobby said, but his back straightened as he slid the pad and pen into his pocket again.

"I'll phone the London Assembly to come remove this graffiti straight away," Oliver said. "Get you lot back to your regular work."

"Remove the graffiti?" Imogene repeated as Oliver steered her back toward the restroom.

"To preserve it, believe me," Oliver said softly. He held the door for her and followed her inside. "Teddy?"

Teddy, like Ben and Priscilla, still appeared lost in the portrait. *More victims of Americanus Rex,* Imogene thought, remembering how everyone up on General's Peak, herself included, had been unable to look away from Priscilla's portrait for very long.

"Oi! Chuck!" Oliver barked.

Teddy blinked a few times. "What?" he said petulantly. Imogene fought back a bubble of laughter.

"I want you back at the Tate immediately. Tell the lads working on the Dresden Exhibit that they'll have a new piece to install alongside it. More pressing than that, however, the Cornells and Miss Hemphill look exhausted. I'm sure Imogene in particular would like to be gone before the press discover it is her likeness on this wall. There will be time for such revelations soon enough," he added with a meaningful look in her direction. He handed Teddy a key. "Take them all to my flat on your way to the museum. I'll pay the fare, naturally."

"Aw, man," Teddy complained. "What if you need me to do something here?"

Oliver raised an eyebrow.

"Fine. Forget it. Come on, Genie."

4

The interior of the Black Cab reminded Imogene of the limousines Teddy typically rented for the guest artists he featured in his gallery. Two beige upholstered bench seats faced each other, separated from the driver by a clear partition. Imogene and Teddy sat on one seat, with Ben and Priscilla across from them. Imogene gave her account of being painted while the other three listened in solemn, wide-eyed silence. At least until she got to the end.

"Wait wait wait," said Teddy. "*How* long between when you think he took your picture and when you found the portrait?"

"A minute and a half, maybe two."

"Bullshit," Teddy said simply.

Ben blinked. "Excuse me?"

"There's no way," Teddy said. "That would leave him less than a minute to work. Plus he apparently had time to make himself scarce without you seeing him? Gimme a break."

"I'm sorry, I didn't realize you were there," Ben said.

Imogene aimed a warning glance at her brother. The last thing she needed right now was to waste her energy putting out territory fires between Ben and Teddy. Ben leaned back and crossed his arms, scowling.

Teddy seemed not to notice. "Let's build the scene here," he said. "Let's say the guy had this painting planned for a couple days. Or even just for the morning. He could have painted the words in the stall before you got there."

Imogene believed this was just what had happened. The presence of written words in a bathroom stall wasn't much to get worked up about, no matter how many women visited the stall before Gary could paint Imogene herself. It was the portrait that gave the words context and meaning. Further evidence of premeditation, if she needed it, was the fact that Droon had apparently kept the letter he'd pilfered from her diary for twenty years and passed it on to Gary Pritchard.

"But that was *you* in there, Genie," Teddy raved. "And not just your face. Your clothes—hell, those *sandals* you're wearing were painted right there. Nobody on the planet is that good, that fast."

Ben spoke up again. "I don't suppose it occurred to you that you don't know as much about this as Imogene does."

Teddy faced him calmly. "I'm having a business discussion with my assistant. And excuse me for saying it, but you know less about the situation than either of us."

Ben glared at him but, blessedly, kept his mouth shut. Imogene had an idea that Priscilla's hand covering his on the seat might have something to do with his restraint.

"You asked me what happened," she told Teddy quietly.

He snorted and turned to stare out the window, tapping rhythmlessly on his thigh.

"How are *you* doing, Imogene?" Priscilla asked into the thick silence. All three of them turned to stare at her.

"I'm okay."

Teddy frowned. "Why wouldn't you be?"

Priscilla's gray eyes flicked to Teddy. "Has anyone ever painted your portrait, Mister…"

"Just Teddy. And no, actually."

Unless Imogene was asleep and dreaming—which was a distinct possibility, considering her day so far—her boss was actually fidgeting under Priscilla's gaze.

"Allowing someone to create an image of you makes you vulnerable and takes trust. You can imagine that would be doubly true with an image as surprising and public as Imogene's has already been," Priscilla said.

Teddy cleared his throat. "Quite right. Genie's a real trouper. Well done," he said, clapping Imogene on the thigh. He pulled out his cell phone, clicked a few buttons, and held it to his ear.

The cab slowed at an intersection. Visible outside the driver's side windows was a low, wide bridge clogged with pedestrians, cars, and city busses over a stretch of gray water.

"Is that the Thames?" Ben asked.

Teddy nodded, phone still pressed to his ear. "Battersea Bridge. This is where the river turns south. You can't see it from here, but the Tate Modern is directly east of us, and the London Eye—the big ferris wheel—is right where the river bends south…son of a bitch," he finished in a mutter, jabbing the End Call button with his thumb. "The fifteen minutes we were in that bathroom today is the longest Oliver has been off his phone in the last twenty-four hours."

Imogene abruptly remembered why Teddy had called her to London in the first place. "You said Oliver would have a new Americanus Rex piece from Germany in his museum before we got here?"

Teddy nodded enthusiastically. "Arrived around four this morning, and Oliver already has a press conference scheduled for tomorrow night. The exhibit opens to the public on Monday."

"Yeah, I saw the poster," Imogene said dryly.

"It's definitely by the same artist who painted you in the subway," Teddy said. "The guy must have heard that the Dresden portrait was coming here and hopped the first train to London." He laughed suddenly. "Two portraits in two days. This Americanus Rex guy works so fast that I almost believe he painted you in thirty seconds."

Imogene had no trouble catching the disapproval in his final comment. "I don't know how he did it, but he's done it before."

Teddy shrugged. "I'll give you that. The timeline of the Dresden portrait feels pretty wonky to me too. Somehow this Rex guy moved the portrait into the room where it was discovered in a fifteen minute window. But he could have..." he broke off, frowning again. "Wait, how did you hear about that already?"

She took a deep breath. "I'm not talking about the Dresden portrait. Mine today in the subway is actually his third one. We think," she added.

Teddy's frown deepened to the point that he was glaring at her over the tops of his tiny square glasses. "From the beginning," he commanded, resting his palms on his knees and leaning back into the plush bench seat.

She struggled to decide where the beginning actually was. Telling Priscilla their story on the airplane had been easy, relaxed, and intuitive. Teddy, she knew, would want the same story in the length of a memo.

"His real name is Gary Pritchard," Priscilla interjected. "He was my fiancé. But he called off our wedding the same night he painted me on a tall white stone. It glows like silver fire and is the most beautiful thing I have ever seen."

She paused, looking at Teddy the way she might look at a first grader who had just thrown a paper airplane in her classroom. "You might also find it interesting that the only person who saw Gary make my portrait claimed he did it in under one minute, precisely as Imogene has said about her own. Furthermore, we were with her in the subway, and I saw a camera flash just before she left us."

Teddy's mouth hung slightly open. He was most certainly fidgeting now, but he was not the type of man who could be caught flat-footed for very long.

"Well," he finally said, "the only part of that story I can put on a museum placard is the guy's real name, which I'm sure Oliver will be grateful to have. Is there any more impossible nonsense I should pass on?"

"Actually," Imogene said. "There is one more thing."

Teddy threw his arms wide. "Bring it on!" he said, his expression equal parts amusement and exasperation.

"All three of us saw Gary in West Virginia about ten hours before you called me."

Teddy calculated. "That's not impossible," he decided. "Just ridiculous. I'm relieved, actually."

Five minutes later the Black Cab eased to a stop on a street called Earls Terrace in a part of London that Teddy told them was the Royal Borough of Kensington and Chelsea. He pointed to a handsome six-storey building covered in tall windows and balconies. "Ride the elevator to the top floor and turn left. Oliver's place is at the end of the hall. You can't miss it."

He held up the apartment key, hesitating. "Are you sure you don't want to go to the museum right now? I know Oliver said you should take a nap, but the Dresden Exhibit is pretty spectacular, unfinished or not."

Imogene accepted the key, but handed it, along with her carryall, to her brother. "Why don't you guys go ahead? I'll be back tonight."

"You sure?" Ben asked, sliding across the bench seat and stepping out into the sunny afternoon. "The exhibit will still be there tomorrow, and we didn't get much sleep the last couple nights."

"I couldn't sleep now anyway," she said truthfully.

He shrugged, taking Priscilla's hand to help her out of the cab. He didn't let go—and neither did she—as they walked slowly up the sidewalk toward the glass front doors of Oliver's building.

5

Teddy had barely swung the cab door shut before he leaned through the partition and barked, "The Tate Modern."

He faced Imogene as the cab pulled away from the curb. "Why didn't you tell me about that Priscilla chick's portrait when I called? Hell, if I'd known it was there I would've given you an extra day to package the thing up and ship it to LA."

Maybe I should have stayed at Oliver's flat after all, she thought wearily. At the notion of answering Teddy's question, the previous two mostly sleepless nights seemed to crash over her head like dark ocean surf.

"First," she said resolutely, "I wasn't positive it was even the same guy until what happened today. Like I said, we had just seen Gary in Accord a few hours before you called. The idea that he had already made it as far as Germany seemed too crazy to believe."

"As crazy as a photo-realistic portrait in thirty seconds?" Teddy asked mildly.

"Second," she pressed on, "he painted Priscilla's portrait on a six foot high boulder on top of a mountain. The thing must weigh a thousand pounds. I don't know how I could have shipped it to Los Angeles with an extra week to work with, let alone a single day."

Teddy considered this, then gave a curt nod. It was, Imogene knew, as close as he would come to admitting that she was right.

"So what's this Gary like? Why have I never heard of him?"

She bit her lip. So far she had accepted her brother's rationales—taken almost exclusively from his volumes of Men in Black lore and the testimony of people who believed they had been contacted by aliens—for Gary Pritchard's bizarre behavior and skills. But such tales of the occult would cut no mustard with Teddy.

"He's about my age," she said. "Close to thirty, anyway. I know that Priscilla's portrait was the first one to be seen by the public."

"When was that exactly?"

Imogene tried to calculate. "My body clock is so screwed up. I think three days ago."

"Three days," he mused. "Three portraits. Three countries. And enough political influence to start arguments between heads of state."

"What do you mean?"

Teddy shrugged. "I don't know all the nuances. A couple hours after Oliver learned about the Dresden portrait, he had already negotiated some kind of deal with the German Chancellor to bring the portrait to England for a month. Said he convinced her that having such a timely and stirring piece of art in London might swing British support away from a likely war agenda at the Council of Paris."

"The Council of Paris again," Imogene said.

"There wasn't much about it on TV when I left home, of course," Teddy said. "But the Red October Sky and the Council are big news over here. On mainland Europe too. The German Chancellor apparently agreed right away to attend, but Oliver says that's just because she wants to make sure she keeps the German military out of what she calls the prelude to World War Three."

Droon's grave voice rasped through her mind once again, telling her, *all nations will eventually be dragged into war.*

"I heard a similar idea recently," she said. "West versus east all over again, but this time with nuclear space jets and the largest armies in history killing each other with other twenty-first century weapons technology."

Teddy shrugged again. "Like I said, I don't know much about it. World politics are Oliver's bag, not mine. All I know is that about an hour after he hung up with the Chancellor, he got a royally pissed off call from the Prime Minister."

"The Prime Minister of Great Britain?" Imogene said incredulously.

"Scout's honor," Teddy said. "Oliver runs in slightly different circles than we do."

"But I still don't get why the German Chancellor let Oliver have the painting at all?" Imogene asked. "If it was discovered in a church in Dresden, wouldn't that make it property of the state, like you and Oliver were saying about my portrait belonging to the London Assembly?"

"Right, but from what Oliver told me, the tourism director at the Frauenkirche is a real peacenik. Probably because his church got blown up in World War Two. And like I said, most Germans are already pretty vocal against the Council of Paris. So the Frauenkirche guy decides a highly public antiwar portrait could make a bigger difference in England, which apparently supports the more aggressive American position on Russia and China. Add to that the Frauenkirche guy's relationship with Oliver from when the Tate helped restore a few pieces for him a few years ago, and," he clapped his hands in a *Ta-daa!* gesture, "there you have it."

"Antiwar portrait," Imogene murmured. "The *Times* mentioned that the Dresden portrait makes references to the Tower of Babel and…"

"The Wheel of War," Teddy supplied. "Rex wrote this strange little poem. You'll see for yourself in a few minutes."

The cab buzzed past the Battersea Bridge again without stopping.

A few blocks later it turned right and thumped over the threshold of a far plainer bridge. Simple concrete pylons rose from the concrete legs supporting the bridge and flashed past the cab's window, stuttering Imogene's view of the Thames River.

Teddy sighed happily. "Can you imagine seeing the Globe Theater—that's the little white building over there on the left—on your way to work in the morning instead of endless concrete barriers and cars farting smog on the 405?" He leaned back and sighed again. "Ah well. Enjoy London while you can. We'll be sitting in LA traffic again before you know it."

They rode the rest of the way to the museum in silence. The cab dumped them onto a huge concrete pavilion surrounding an equally huge rectangular black building. A brick chimney rose a few hundred feet from the center of the building. Imogene easily recognized the Tate Modern Museum from photographs Teddy had shown her of his earlier trips.

At the museum's front doors, Teddy strode past long lines of visitors, suffering their curious looks and occasional glares with his usual smugness. "I keep telling Oliver he needs to charge admission to get into this place," he said loudly. "There's hardly room to breathe in here on the weekends."

"Excuse us," Imogene said to a young couple in the doorway as Teddy brushed past.

Inside, Teddy made a sweeping grand gesture with his arm. "The Tate Modern Museum." His chest puffed up. "Oliver gave me keys to his storeroom and prep area."

Imogene stared up into the museum's main hall, an immense rectangular room long and high enough to make her head swim with vertigo. The hall was open all the way up to the seventh and highest floor. The north side consisted of two tall banks of windows overlooking the Thames. The south side comprised seven levels of balconies on which visitors milled about like ants on a layer cake. Imogene nearly cried out when she saw a teenage boy on the fourth balcony leaning over the railing to snap a picture of three enormous metal towers at the far end of the hall, but she immediately realized that at least five other tourists were doing the same thing from different balconies.

"Oliver set up the Dresden Exhibit on the walkway right above us," Teddy was explaining. He pointed up to a twenty foot wide platform spanning the gap between the first balcony and the bank of windows. "I told him he was nuts when he said he would open the exhibit to the public on Monday, but I think he's actually going to pull it off."

He forged through the line of visitors and swiped a keycard through an electronic lock on a door marked *Museum Personnel Only.* "We'll take the stairs."

A wide, poorly lit concrete staircase led them up to the first level of the museum. "The exhibit is mostly set up already, but the landing here is roped off from visitors until Monday. Which is good, since now Oliver also wants to set up your portrait before then, complete with display cases and information placards for both pieces."

She followed him through the door onto the long, bridge-like platform she'd seen from below. Tall canvas curtains shrouded the entire platform like a beige fumigation tent. A museum guard in a gray plastic chair near the door waved Teddy past without a word. Visitors on their way up to the third level openly studied the two of them as Teddy lifted the curtain flap and ducked inside. The platform was set up like a small auditorium. A center aisle ran between five rows of black molded-plastic chairs that had been bolted onto raised floor partitions. Subtle seams showed where the new partitions had been pushed together.

"What are the chairs for?"

"They serve two purposes. Most importantly, there were similar chairs in the room where the painting was originally discovered. Oliver guessed that since the painted glass was moved in front of them, Americanus Rex must have meant them to be an extension of the portrait. Second, Oliver always hosts a handpicked group of journalists before opening a big exhibit, and they'll need a place to sit. His carpenters built a new floor for this whole platform in a couple of hours," Teddy marveled. "Feels just as solid as the original."

"Huh," Imogene grunted.

Her real attention was on the figure painted on an inch-thick square pane of glass in front the chairs. She estimated the pane to be six or seven feet square. The painted woman covered much of the pane's height, despite her knees being slightly bent in a protective crouch. Imogene sensed no fear in the woman's posture, though neither did her features convey any threat.

Like Priscilla's portrait, the painting should have dripped with sexuality but did not. Imogene sensed great physical power in the woman's shoulders, which showed sleek striations of muscle under taut skin as she raised her arms. A kind of persuasive power lay too in the dignified, determined cast of her eyebrows and firm line of her mouth.

Blasting away any further doubt that Gary Pritchard had painted this portrait was the same vibrant silver hue he'd used in Imogene's portrait and Priscilla's. Oliver's people had erected a black velvet curtain behind the stage, making the portrait's metallic brilliance all the more startling.

Imogene looked away with difficulty. Bolted to the floor beside the painted woman was a vinyl projection screen on a rickety metal tripod, contained within a heavy cask of museum plexiglass. Like the stall walls in Imogene's portrait, the screen contained a message that Gary had painted in careful silver lettering.

"'The Tower of Babel has betrayed us,'" Imogene read softly. "'Rather than making us into gods, the Tower has driven wedges between all people in the universe to form the spokes of the Wheel of War. We must uproot the failed Babel and carry it to the top of Mount Olympus. Only there can we pierce the heart of the brightest star in the universe to make a torch, the light of which will cause all life to weep with joy until the wheel of war shudders to a stop.'"

Not an exact match to what her nineteen year old mother had said about carrying the Space Needle up Mount Ranier, but identical in both tone and purpose.

"Far out, huh?" Teddy asked almost reverently. "See what I meant by the words perfectly fitting the portrait?"

Imogene did. With the incredible poise, strength, and height of the painted woman, the abstract ideas of uprooting the Tower of Babel and piercing a star did not seem abstract at all. Imogene could easily envision this woman toiling up the snowy cliffs of Mount Olympus with the mighty Babel cradled in one straining bicep.

"Protecting us from ourselves," Imogene whispered.

"What'd you say?"

"Who is she?" Imogene asked more loudly.

"No idea," Teddy said. There was no mistaking the disappointment in his voice. "I mean, she's got to be German, look at the size of her. But she didn't have the presence of mind to stick around and claim her portrait the way you did."

Presence of mind had had nothing to do with discovering her portrait in the station, but Imogene didn't say so. She and Teddy stood in silence before the towering woman on her pane of glass for a very long time.

6

After a small and unsatisfying supper in the Tate café, Teddy finally agreed to head back to Oliver's flat. Oliver still had not returned either to the museum or his home. Imogene found Priscilla sleeping deeply in the empty bedroom (Teddy's belongings were strewn throughout the other extra room in heaps to which Imogene would have attended if she'd had the energy). Ben had fallen asleep in a chair next to Priscilla's bed. Imogene sat down on the unclaimed half of the bed and removed her shoes…

…Then sunlight. And the smell of frying pork wafting under the bedroom door. At some point in the night Ben had given up his chair and created a makeshift pillow on the floor from the folded undershirts in his duffel bag. Priscilla had not moved at all. She lay on her back, snoring lightly.

Imogene blinked hard and rubbed the sleep from her eyes. She lifted her carryall, tiptoed over Ben, and latched the door softly behind her.

At the stove, wearing a white apron over a salmon colored dress shirt and a brightly striped tie, Oliver supervised several sizzling pans with a spatula.

He beamed at her. "Don't you look dishy in the morning."

She was unsure of what "dishy" meant but she felt like she had just crawled out of a sewer. Oliver, in contrast, looked ready to stroll down the nearest fashion runway, spotless apron and all.

"Good morning, Dr. Hume."

"Oliver," he corrected, expertly flipping sausage links in a frying pan.

"Oliver, then. I need to take a shower. Is Teddy in the bathroom?"

He rolled his eyes. "He was up and pestering me before six. I finally gave him my personal museum key and told him to sod off. Towels are in the closet behind you." His eyes twinkled. "Teddy told me you are even more adventurous than he when it comes to food, so I've made a traditional English breakfast to celebrate the new exhibit."

"It smells wonderful."

Oliver nodded, grinning like an oyster shell, as her father might say. "After your shower we'll eat. And we'll talk," he added meaningfully.

He was humming to himself when she emerged from the bathroom twenty minutes later with fresh clothes and a much improved spirit.

"Sit," he invited. "Right. I've got fried eggs, bangers and mash, black pudding, beans on toast, and tea, naturally."

She sat on one of the stools at the raised counter by Oliver's stove. "What are you going to eat?"

His dark eyes widened and he let loose a startled laugh. He piled a generous helping of each food he had mentioned onto a plate for her, then repeated the exercise for himself. Imogene speared a wedge of toast covered in baked beans with her fork and took a bite.

"Oh yeah that's good," she mumbled.

Oliver bowed his head slightly in thanks. Between the excellent food and his easy personality, Imogene felt herself relaxing. Oliver tucked into his food with the same swift, elegant movements Imogene remembered from yesterday.

"Teddy tells me there is a third portrait of your friend Priscilla in the States. Painted on stone, this one. Our Americanus Rex doesn't seem to like canvas, does he?"

Imogene nodded, swallowing. "He and Priscilla were engaged. His name is Gary. I don't know if Teddy told you."

"Yes. Gary," Oliver repeated, drawling the *r* in exaggerated mimicry of an American accent. "I suppose not every great artist can be called Michelangelo. So is her portrait as revolutionary as the two I have seen?"

"At least."

She quickly explained that she thought the painted boulder was made of quartz or a similar type of stone that reacted to light, as did the paint that came out of the tube her brother had lifted from Glenn Pritchard's dumpster.

"Brilliant luck," Oliver hissed. "My lads at the museum haven't been able to classify the type of paint used in the Dresden portrait. Not even if it is oil or water based. In fact, they haven't even been able to scratch a sample from the pane of glass or the nylon screen."

Imogene wrinkled her eyebrows apologetically. "The label on the tube of paint did say it was nonremovable. Aside from that, I can only tell you the color was called Silver Lumine, made by a company called DroonCorp."

Oliver sighed. "That's a start. I must tell you, I've had my post at the Tate Modern for ten years and I have never planned a stranger exhibit. Acquiring the piece, which is usually difficult and fraught with paperwork, was simple and absurdly quick. Yet nailing down the type of paint used in the portrait was impossible until you mentioned it. And I have to deal with the political complaints that always accompany a piece like this, obviously."

"Because it has an antiwar message?"

"That's part of it," Oliver agreed. "Certainly no one has missed the fact that two of the five countries involved in the Council of Paris have now been visited by Americanus Rex. Three, including your friend's portrait in the States. But more troubling are the intellectual pugilists in the British media condemning the Dresden portrait as misogynistic. They say the combination of revealing clothing and her stance of protection is a disturbing window into a rapist's mind. Rubbish, if you ask me."

Imogene rubbed her forehead, as if to massage all of this new information directly into her brain. "If everyone has already seen the Dresden portrait on TV, don't they know it's actually a statement *against* the hatred of women? I don't think I've seen any piece of visual art that portrays women more positively or powerfully than Gary's portraits."

Oliver stood suddenly and retrieved a newspaper off the kitchen counter. "I almost forgot to show you today's *Guardian*."

She accepted the newspaper and felt her jaw drop. The day's top headline read, *Americanus Rex in London*. Below this were two color photographs in which Imogene prominently featured. The larger picture was of the painted bathroom stall, and the other showed her and Ben in a relieved embrace outside the bathroom stall with a uniformed bobby to their left and Priscilla to their right. The caption read, *American tourist Imogene Cornell, Americanus Rex's second public subject (middle left), remains unhurt while Rex's first subject is still missing.*

Imogene felt her temper flare. "Why would they try to make Gary seem dangerous?"

Oliver looked troubled. "Normally I would say it's because danger keeps people buying newspapers, as I'm sure you well know. This time, though, I'm afraid it's a cultural issue."

"You mean British culture?"

"As far as newspaper sales go, yes. But the stories in our media are only a symptom a greater problem in world culture. Ten years ago, when the airplanes struck New York, the Pentagon, and the empty field in Pennsylvania, hundreds of millions of people all over the world cried out in support for the United States and against terrorism. That support turned to concern, then outright horror at how the American government and culture galvanized people's fear into unthinking patriotism and aggression.

"Four years later, when a terrorist organization set off bombs in

London's subway system, the government and people stood together for the opposite reason: to show that we would not let fear rule us or dictate our actions. There were blokes in the Tube stations selling T-shirts with the Underground logo and the words *Not Afraid.*

"Then came Christmas of 2007, when a bomb exploded at Barajas airport in Madrid. The Spanish government had flights running again within a matter of hours, and Spaniards marched through the streets in support of their government and denial of terrorism. Once again the message was obvious: acts of violence and murder can hold no power over the behavior of a thinking society.

"Each instance seemed a step in the right direction. The attacks were sobering reminders of the hatred and desperation in the world, but we still believed the seductive culture of fear hadn't spread to Europe. Yet now an artist calling for a peaceful solution to the admittedly troubling situation of the Red October Sky is being portrayed as a madman because his practices are unusual."

Imogene sat quietly for a moment, digesting all of this.

Oliver's teeth flashed suddenly. "Sorry, love. I hadn't meant to deliver a speech."

"No, it's okay," she said quickly, smiling herself. "In fact, I wish my father had heard you just now. He'd make you his best friend."

"Sounds like a wise man," Oliver said gravely, pouring fresh boiling water over the small canister of dried tea leaves in his mug. "So in any case, we've got the politicians and the press involved. Now all we need is the unnatural speed of Rex's painting to reach the public so that political conservatives can tie him and J.K. Rowling together in some kind of conspiracy to encourage the practice of witchcraft."

He noticed her surprise. "Oh yes, Teddy relayed your insistence that Rex had a maximum window of two minutes."

"And you don't have a problem with that?" Imogene said cautiously.

"I'm absolutely gob-smacked, naturally," Oliver said. "But I won't deny a new type of genius simply because I haven't seen it in action. Besides that, Rex would not be the first artist with peculiar habits. Er-nest Hemingway, for example, supposedly composed his stories while standing nude at a typewriter."

He seemed to debate something as he poured more hot water into her mug as well. "Would it surprise you to learn," he finally said, "that the subject of the Dresden portrait shared with me a certainty similar to yours about Rex's inherent goodness? Not to mention the impossibly short time in which he must have painted. In fact, she and I also enjoyed a high minded political conversation. Your father would adore her, I have no doubt."

Imogene's eyes widened. "Teddy said you never found out who the woman in Dresden was."

He nodded. "That's because Teddy doesn't know yet. She is a young American woman called Ellen. She's here in London already, but has asked me not to reveal that fact or her name to the press."

"How did she know to contact you?"

"The whole of the European Union knows her portrait is at the Tate Modern. That story has likely been printed in twenty languages in the last two days. Ellen located the Tate quite easily on her own, so when she introduced herself to me yesterday evening, I invited her to a pub for fish and chips. For someone so large, she handles her alcohol poorly," he added with professional disdain. "She's probably six-foot-seven."

"Didn't anyone else recognize her? The *Guardian* obviously connected me to my portrait easily enough."

"You were right outside the door of the room where your portrait was found," he reminded her. "Besides that, Ellen's nose is broken and she is wearing a sort of medical mask until it heals. I would've had trouble recognizing her myself if I she weren't so bleeding tall and I had not spent so much time studying her portrait."

"You don't think someone attacked her, do you? I mean, if people are saying her portrait anti-feminist propaganda or something…"

It was a short jump in logic between Cody Hemphill trying to kill Gary for painting his sister and some zealot beating up a woman who appeared in artwork supposedly demeaning her own sex.

"Definitely not," Oliver said at once. "In her words, she 'tripped over her own feet' after Americanus Rex took her picture in the Frauenkirche's basement. But it would be much easier for the media to claim Americanus Rex is dangerous if Ellen, looking the way she does at the moment, accidentally found herself on the front page of a newspaper the way you have done."

"So how do we keep the media from finding out about her?"

"That's…not the only option," Oliver said slowly. "We could try to keep her identity under wraps, which shouldn't be all that difficult as you and I are the only two people besides the woman herself who know that she is in London. Or, I could try to convince Ellen to reveal her identity tonight when I unveil the Rex Exhibit, now featuring your own portrait as well as hers, to the press. She could assure them in her own words that Americanus Rex is not dangerous except to war hungry politicians. I prefer this latter option, naturally."

Without waiting for her to respond, he swabbed the remaining baked beans on his plate with a triangle of toast and popped it into his mouth.

"Heavenly," he said, standing. "Well. I've got an exhibit opening tomorrow, haven't I? Please invite your brother and Priscilla to the Tate when they wake." He pulled a plastic Museum Staff pass card from a kitchen drawer. "This will get you past the guard by the exhibit. You can find me there when you make your own decision."

She had lifted her mug of tea to take a drink, but she paused with the mug an inch from her lips. "What decision is that again?"

"Do all Americans have such short memories?" he asked in mock exasperation. "The Rex Exhibit now has two stars instead of one, as I've just said. I would love Ellen to speak her mind about her portrait tonight at the press event, and it follows that I was also rather hoping to see you entertain questions about yours."

Her mug clinked on the saucer as she set it back down.

"The decision is yours," Oliver said, shrugging into a black sport jacket of exquisitely thin silk as he opened the front door. "I won't lie and tell you it will be easy."

She didn't even have to think about it. "I'll be there."

Already out in the hallway, Oliver stuck one of his gleaming shoes in the doorway to keep it from closing. His head popped back through the opening. "Teddy has no concept of how absurdly fortunate he was the day you walked through his door, does he?"

The question disarmed her so thoroughly that she had no idea how to respond. However, Oliver nodded curtly as if she had answered aloud. "I thought not. Until this evening, then."

His head disappeared through the doorway once more and he was gone.

7

The Tate Modern's Sunday visitors seemed even more curious about the curtains surrounding the Dresden Exhibit than the Saturday visitors had been. Two women close to the cordon stopped their steady shuffle up the ramp between levels and studied Imogene as she led her brother and Priscilla from the *Museum Staff Only* door toward the exhibit. The first young woman pointed and spoke excitedly to her friend, who, Imogene saw with flabbergasted amusement, quickly raised her cell phone to snap a photograph.

Ben glanced reproachfully at Imogene. "Who are you, Miley Cyrus? That's the third time since we got here."

Imogene flashed the pass Oliver had given her to a thick torsoed woman in a museum uniform. The guard squinted at the card and waved them toward the tent with the robotic movements of a police officer directing traffic. Ben ducked inside the canvas flap currently serving as the Dresden Exhibit's front door. Tomorrow, Imogene knew, the canvas tent would be gone entirely and the platform would support an extra fifteen tons of eager foot traffic from the moment the Tate Modern opened until it closed.

Before she could follow her brother inside, though, Priscilla's hand closed around her upper arm.

"Look."

Priscilla did not point at whatever Imogene was supposed to look at, nor did she need to. At the other end of the hall, where the ramp that led past the Dresden Exhibit dumped museum visitors on the Tate's third level, was an extremely tall woman with short blonde hair sticking out from under a white baseball cap. Light from the museum's bank of windows reflected off a slick transparent mask covering the upper half of the woman's face.

Imogene had told Priscilla and Ben what she knew of Gary's third subject over breakfast in Oliver's apartment, along with a description of the Dresden portrait and the Tower of Babel speech. Ben had been shocked into atypical silence by the speech's similarity to their mother's beacon of peace vision, but Priscilla had seemed more interested in Ellen herself.

"Does she have anyone with her?" she had wanted to know.

The idea that Ellen was in London alone, especially after being painted by Gary, had seemed to worry Priscilla a great deal. Perhaps because London seemed so huge and alien to her despite the friends she had close by.

Imogene considered offering to pursue Ellen alone while Priscilla got her first look at the Dresden Exhibit, but she knew Priscilla would refuse. Although Priscilla had clearly been moved by Gary's portrait of her, the artistic aspects of this trip were Imogene's specialty, not hers. The way Priscilla had upbraided Teddy for ignoring Imogene's emotional state yesterday in the cab had proved that much.

Imogene handed over the pass card and gestured to the *Museum Staff Only* door. "Lead the way."

They caught up with Ellen ten minutes later, in front of a freestanding sculpture of a gasoline pump. The artist had removed the pump's nozzle and replaced it with a nasty looking black machine gun with a brown wooden stock. And where a normal pump would have read *Unleaded Gasoline,* this one had the words *Unnecessary Deaths.* Red numbers clicked steadily higher in the pump's digital face. The sculpture certainly lacked the subtlety of Gary's portraits, but Imogene found it effectively disquieting nonetheless.

Priscilla showed no interest in the sculpture. She walked directly to the tall woman, stopping within a foot or so of her back. "Ellen?"

The woman spun around, her eyes as wide as they could get within the swollen mound of bruises. Her clear plastic mask sparkled almost wetly in the museum's powerful lights. She wore a white sleeveless vest of some slick, elastic material and a small backpack on a wide black strap running diagonally across her chest. The center of her baseball cap was embroidered with a very familiar purple and gold *W* (Imogene fought a ridiculous impulse to pump her arm and shout, as she had done so many times during her four years at the University of Washington, "Go Huskies!"). Below the cap, Ellen's straight blonde hair hung down to her chin in a simple, elegant sheet that reminded Imogene of shampoo commercials.

Ellen tensed as if to bound away like a gazelle. One look at those long, muscular legs convinced Imogene that she and Priscilla would never catch her if she did. She seemed even taller in person than on the pane of glass where Gary had painted her, and a lot younger.

She can't be much more than twenty, Imogene thought, holding out her hand gingerly as if to allow a strange dog to smell it. "We're friends of Oliver Hume. My name is Imogene and this is Priscilla. We—"

She glanced around, not eager to invoke another tidal wave of cell phone photography. "We have something in common," she said at last.

Recognition flashed in Ellen's eyes. "He painted you in the subway station." None of them needed her to clarify who *he* was. "I saw you in a newspaper this morning," she said, accepting Imogene's hand in a firm grip rough with calluses.

Before Imogene had a chance to confirm this fact, Ellen, still grasping her hand, yanked her forward into a crushing hug. Imogene laughed in breathless surprise, helpless to pull away or even move, her right cheek mashed against the taller woman's collar bone.

"I can't tell you how relieved I am to meet you," Ellen's voice came from somewhere above Imogene's head. After a brief squeeze that evacuated the rest of the air from Imogene's lungs, she let go.

"The feeling is mutual," Imogene assured her, smiling and rubbing her breastbone.

Priscilla took over. "We figured, since you already got in touch with Dr. Hume, you needed to talk out your experience. I know I do."

Ellen's chin nearly came to rest against her sternum as her gaze shifted downward from Imogene to Priscilla. "You too?"

Priscilla nodded.

"She was actually the first one," Imogene put in. She tried not to wince as another camera flashed behind her.

"Well, I'd hug you too, but the yokels are starting to rubberneck," Ellen told Priscilla briskly, settling the strap of her backpack over one of the powerful shoulders Gary had captured so perfectly with his mysterious paint. "So where do you guys want to go?"

Imogene led them up a series of ramps and escalators until they reached the café on the seventh level. They passed hundreds of museum visitors and earned hundreds of stares—most of them aimed at Ellen, who would undoubtedly have drawn stares even without the unusual plastic mask and bruises on the upper half of her face—but no one seemed interested in photographing the three of them, a fact that relieved Imogene mightily.

The line in the museum's café reached all the way out the door. Imogene invited Priscilla and Ellen to sit at one of the two open tables while she bought three coffees. Priscilla said she would fill Ellen in on Imogene's story and her own so that Ellen would only have to tell hers once when Imogene got back. However, the line was so long that by the time she'd weaved through the last few circular tables and sat down, Priscilla was already listening raptly to Ellen. Ellen spoke with such easy familiarity and confidence that Imogene wished Priscilla had taken longer in telling their stories so she could have heard Ellen's from the beginning.

"I'm sure my parents are freaking out but—oh thanks," Ellen said, taking a slurp of coffee.

"What's the matter with your parents?" Imogene asked.

Ellen grinned sheepishly. "That's why I reacted the way I did when you guys came up behind me. I sort of discharged myself from the hospital in Germany without telling them, and I've been worried that they might have Interpol track me down or something."

Priscilla distrustfully eyed the froth on her latte before looking up at Ellen. "Are you sure you don't need to go to a hospital here? Doesn't it hurt?"

"A little. I broke my nose before playing volleyball. That time hurt worse. The girl was huge."

Imogene believed her. Anyone Ellen would describe as huge must have been positively monolithic.

"And this new accident happened in Dresden, right?"

Ellen nodded. "That's what I was just telling Priscilla. My parents bought me a trip to Germany as a graduation present. I majored in history," she explained. "And over the summer I took a course about the psychology of warfare, and…what?"

Imogene was shaking her head, but she couldn't quite bring herself to be surprised. "My dad was very excited when the university let him teach a war psych class. So what did you think of Professor Cornell?"

Ellen's eyes tried to widen again among the bruises. "Your dad? You mean…" Her gape slowly melted into an astonished smile. "So your last name's Cornell, then? Or are you married?"

"Nope."

"That's just so weird," Ellen went on. "I mean, what a coincidence."

Get used to it, sister, Imogene thought.

"Your mom!" Ellen shouted suddenly.

At first Imogene thought Ellen was making one of the tragically unfunny "your mom" jokes with which Ben had been so enamored in his early high school years, but the timing made no sense, and Ellen wasn't laughing.

"I *knew* the poem with my portrait seemed familiar," Ellen said. "It fits almost exactly with what your Mom said about lighting a beacon of peace at the Miss Washington Pageant, isn't it?"

That finally surprised Imogene. "Has Dad started telling his classes about that?"

"No, not at all," Ellen assured her. "The only time he mentioned her in class was when he talked about founding the campus peace club with her in the late Sixties. The peace club got so big during the Bush years that a friend of mine started another peace organization just for women on campus. One of the first things we did was research past female students and professors at UW who took stands for peace. My friend found that old recording of your mom in the archives and asked your dad to come tell us the story behind the beacon of peace."

"I bet that would have meant a lot to your mother," Priscilla said to Imogene.

Deep, startling fondness welled up inside Imogene for these two women she hardly knew. "I'm sure it would have too. Ellen, why don't you finish telling us about Dresden. We won't interrupt again."

"That's fine."

Ellen gave her head a little shake before resuming her narrative. She took only a sentence or two to find her groove again. Imogene thought it was no small wonder that Priscilla found Ellen engaging. She spoke with great animation and enthusiasm. In fact, Imogene had an idea she would speak animatedly and enthusiastically for as long as a person would let her. For someone as reserved as Priscilla, Ellen must seem as exotic and noisy as a parrot from the African Congo.

Imogene and Priscilla listened to the increasingly familiar tale of Droon's and Gary's hijinx, this time in Germany but otherwise not so different from Imogene's experience, at least until Ellen's dash into the Frauenkirche's basement.

"I found a painting down there," she said. "It was of a girl who tricked the angels into telling her God's name so she could get to heaven."

Ellen looked down at her hands, which were now curled tensely around her paper coffee cup. "When I was a freshman in high school my volleyball coach promised me what I thought was a slice of heaven: a chance to play for the US Olympic Team. Can you imagine?"

The pain of this memory was obvious even through the bruises, but Ellen's eyes were dry and hard behind her mask.

"I went to high school in Florida, but the Olympic Training Center is in Colorado Springs, so Coach Zell and I flew there together."

Uh-oh, Imogene thought.

"My parents were going to come along, but someone t-boned my dad's BMW the day before we were supposed to leave and both of them went to the hospital instead. They signed the consent papers for Coach and me to go to Colorado alone. I mean, we still had different rooms reserved at the hotel," she added, her voice oddly insistent.

Priscilla nodded sympathetically, but her expression broadcast the same growing horror that was currently souring the latte in Imogene's stomach.

"Well, there was a mistake," Ellen said bitterly. "I still don't know if it was real or planned. We got to the hotel late after the first string of tryouts at the Olympic Training Center, and instead of the two rooms we were supposed to have, there was only one. The tryouts had filled most of the local hotels, so there was pretty much no way to get two rooms in the same hotel."

A muscle in Priscilla's jaw twitched.

"In the middle of the night he came into my bed. Afterward, as soon as I could tell he'd fallen asleep, I got dressed and I ran. First downstairs and outside to a taxi, then to the airport. I've carried my parents' credit card since I was twelve, so I used it to buy a ticket on the next flight back to Miami and got another taxi home from the airport early the next morning. My parents were back from the hospital by then. They knew something had happened, but I couldn't tell them exactly what. I was just so embarrassed. I told them I had been cut from the team after the first set of tryouts, which wasn't true, but I knew they'd believe that's what had upset me. I'd never been cut from any sports team."

She snatched a napkin off the table and absently wiped a sheen of sweat from her palms. "I'm sorry. You guys didn't ask for that. But I guess you can see why the Pleiades painting spoke to me."

"Is that why you came here?" Priscilla asked after a moment.

Ellen shrugged, already looking less tense. Whether she knew why she had told her story or not, the act of telling seemed to have calmed her. "Partly. My nurse in the German hospital brought me a newspaper two days ago that had pictures of what Americanus Rex had painted in the church. Right away I knew that it was good. That it was right."

Imogene and Priscilla nodded together.

"I've learned to watch men very closely since I was fourteen, and I've seen the way they look at me." She rolled her eyes. "Even with a broken nose and two black eyes. That painting wasn't just about my body, although I'm not naïve enough to believe my body and my size have no part in it. Of course, my clothes were the first thing my mother noticed about the portrait. On the phone she basically asked me what I was thinking dressing like a hooker in a foreign country."

"Nice," Imogene growled before she could stifle it.

"That's not your fault," Priscilla said softly.

Ellen seemed not to hear either of them. "There was something else too. This, like, relationship between the Pleiades painting in the church and the one of me. Just seeing a photograph of my portrait in the newspaper made me feel like somehow I could also rise up and...I don't know."

Imogene smiled a little self-consciously. "Change the world?"

Ellen seemed to wince, but transformed the gesture into a slow nod. "Out loud, that sounds worse than melodramatic, but, yeah. I felt like I could change the world."

8

Imogene invited Ellen to come see the unfinished Dresden Exhibit—
she still had never seen her portrait in person—but Ellen declined.

"Dr. Hume already said I could come tonight after the museum
closes. And anyway," she added apologetically, "I'm not quite ready to
see it with other people around. No offense."

Imogene understood, and she guessed she wasn't the only one. Priscilla had responded poorly indeed when Cody had interrupted her first
viewing of her portrait. Imogene wondered how she might have responded to her own portrait if Teddy, or even Ben, had been with her
at the moment she'd stepped into the painted bathroom stall for the
first time.

"Can we meet you later tonight or tomorrow?" Priscilla asked. "Get
to know each other for real?"

"Tonight I have to call my parents. Try to explain why I ran away
from the hospital and came to London instead of going home." The

corners of her mouth curled downward as if she did not look forward to such a call.

"Tomorrow lunch, then," Priscilla persisted.

Ellen smiled. "That'd be nice. Until fish and chips with Oliver last night, I'd eaten every meal alone on this trip. Except when Nurse Hofer fed me through a straw."

She began gathering up her paper and napkins. Imogene stayed her hands with her own.

"I need to ask you something."

Ellen watched her expectantly, but that one sentence was as far as Imogene got. How could she ask Ellen to appear for the press event tonight? She could point out that she had already promised Oliver she would be there herself—and she had only been painted yesterday—but guilting Ellen into a media appearance seemed far worse than letting her hide from the public if she wanted to.

Even as Imogene thought these things, Ellen's smile suddenly became more knowing. "You want me to talk to the press tonight, right? Publicly declare my support for Americanus Rex and world peace?" She laughed. "Don't look so surprised. Remember, your Dad himself told me the beacon of peace story, and Priscilla told me about it again while you were in line for coffee. Plus, you've already said you're friends with Dr. Hume, and he brought up the newspapers every five minutes during our supper together."

Imogene felt her cheeks redden. How many times had she underestimated or misjudged strangers in the past couple days?

"Hey, I didn't mean to embarrass you," Ellen said, touching Imogene's forearm. "I've never had to publicly stick up for something I believe in, and I respect people who do." Her smile faded. "I realized I had to speak at Dr. Hume's press conference when I saw that today's newspaper said I was 'missing,' like I'd been kidnapped or something."

"Yeah, Oliver showed me that," Imogene said sourly.

Ellen went on, "In class, your dad called that sort of mass manipulation the Culture of Fear. He said it's one way governments keep their people hating an enemy's culture in times of war, the same way the American military has taken to calling their enemies 'bad guys' like they're acting out some old GI-Joe cartoon."

Ellen's green eyes, bright and sharp in their bed of purple bruises, locked on Imogene's. "I'll be standing by my portrait when the press arrives at the museum tonight. The newspapers will hear right from my mouth that Americanus Rex is no one to be afraid of."

Priscilla nodded solemnly.

"I doubt Dad's ever had a better student," Imogene told Ellen. "I'm very glad we met."

Ellen stood. "Ditto," she said, crumpling her paper cup in one callused hand.

"Tomorrow lunch?" Priscilla reminded her.

"We can work out the details after press thing tonight," Ellen said. "I'm sure Dr. Hume will know of a place we can go for an hour of peace tomorrow."

"Good luck with your parents," Imogene said, shaking her hand.

Ellen rolled her eyes once more, suddenly looking seventeen instead of twenty-one. "I'll need it. That'll be harder than talking to the reporters."

Imogene watched her walk off into the crowd before turning to Priscilla. "Well, we should probably head back down to—"

The rest of the sentence died on her lips as she noticed, standing in front of the *Museum Personnel Only* door at the west end of the balcony, the now familiar figure of Lord Droon. He was staring at them with a serene, almost smug, smile on his angular face.

Priscilla turned to see what had distracted her. "Is that the guy you and Ben told me about on the airplane?"

But Imogene was already three paces ahead of her, dodging museum visitors as well as she could without taking her eyes off Droon. She heard Priscilla on her heels, offering the people in Imogene's wake one polite "Excuse us" after another.

Droon did not move an inch until they broke through the edge of a line of people waiting their turn for the Tate's uppermost galleries, at which time he tipped his hat to each of them in turn.

"All right, who *are* you?" Imogene demanded as they skidded to a halt in front of him. "And how do you keep finding us?"

Instead of answering, Droon reached inside his jacket and drew out three thick envelopes, splayed in his long fingers like a Chinese paper fan. Even in her agitated state, Imogene saw that one envelope was addressed to *The Historian,* another to *The Catalyst,* and the last to *The Light of the World.*

She gasped as she read the last one, all questions of Droon's true identity momentarily gone. She reached shakily for the envelope. Here, she was sure, were the answers to every question that had vexed her since she had arrived in Accord—perhaps even since her mother had died.

Before she could touch the envelope, however, the silver wire in Droon's hatband erupted in a squeal like a throng of linked stereos playing a thrash metal album on fast-forward. Imogene clapped her hands to her ears as Droon pulled the envelope out of reach with a polite, puzzled frown.

"For her," he said, indicating Priscilla. His voice, though still oddly tinny, was clear and the formerly constant Evian bottle was nowhere to be seen.

He handed the *Light of the World* envelope to Priscilla, who accepted it wordlessly. She showed no sign of having heard the squeal.

"You are the Catalyst," Droon told Imogene as if it should have been obvious, and he handed her the corresponding envelope. Imogene noted distantly that he now seemed to be speaking with a convincing British accent. "I was rather hoping to deliver the third envelope to the Histor—"

He broke off, head cocked in a listening gesture eerily similar to the one Gary Pritchard had made at the church in Accord. After a moment he favored them with his familiar goatee-framed smile.

"Ah," he said, handing the last envelope to Priscilla with unmistakable satisfaction. "You will deliver it tonight."

Imogene was still struggling to clear her head of that horrid sound—

she had only heard it for a second or two, but during that time her head had seemed ready to splatter apart like an overripe watermelon—but she tore open the envelope Droon had given her. "Catalyst" was not a word she used in her everyday vocabulary, but she knew it meant something like the spark that ignites a bonfire. It reminded her too of what Ben had told her in Accord—that he had not seen any hints of the Men in Black or bizarre behavior from the townspeople until the day she had arrived in West Virginia.

And a very deep part of her brain resonated with Dr. Logan's question about the origin of Ben's chickenpox all those years ago: "You say Imogene brought home the infection?"

Inside the envelope she found no answers. Just two British Airways tickets for tomorrow morning, one in her name and one in Ben's, from Heathrow to Dulles…and back to Yeager International Airport in Charleston. The envelope also contained a voucher for a rental car.

She shook the tickets at Droon. "What is this?"

Droon blinked in that same polite and utterly British puzzlement. "After tonight's press conference, you will have done all you can here."

Imogene gaped at him.

"Is Gary in Paris now?" Priscilla asked, the contents of her own envelope in one hand.

Imogene saw that Priscilla had also received airline tickets, hers reserving a seat on a commuter jet between Heathrow and Charles de Gaulle airports.

"You're separating us," Imogene realized. "Why? If I've done everything I can do here, what can I possibly do in West Virginia?"

"The world is nearly ready for the Beacon," Droon said, still maddeningly pleased with himself.

Priscilla deduced his meaning first. "*My* portrait?"

Droon aimed one of his disquietingly long fingers at Imogene. "You will retrieve it."

Imogene lifted her hands and let them drop against her thighs. "You know, my brother told me that you guys like to play doomsayers, except instead of strapping the sandwich boards onto your own chests, you pass them on to people like Priscilla and Ellen and me, and you force us to do it for you."

Droon's dark eyes widened in alarm. "We force no one. Your free will is essential to our purpose."

"Did you give Gary the same choice?" Priscilla asked.

"Most definitely. In fact, the Artist has begun to surprise us."

"Which leads back to my first question," Imogene put in. "Just who are you, and who is this 'us' you're talking about? Do you call yourselves the Men in Black too, or is that just the name people like Ben have given you over the years?"

Droon considered her question for what felt like a long time. "You have heard that the wizard Merlin placed the crown on King Arthur's head?"

"Let me guess," Imogene said, unable to keep the sarcasm out of her voice. "You're going to tell me that you guys actually rule the world because you secretly select the people who take office all over the world, right? The way the Pope used to crown the Holy Roman Emperor. Or maybe you're the parent organization to the Freemasons. Just let me know when I've figured it out."

A shadow of Droon's old smile reappeared. "You misunderstand. We make a point to crown no one. Had we been in the story of Arthur and Merlin, we would have been the ones to place a wand in Merlin's hand."

"The way you put a paintbrush in Gary's hand," Priscilla said softly. Droon nodded.

"Fine, but *why?*" Imogene insisted. "I know you hope to change the outcome of the Council of Paris. You told me that much yourself on the airplane."

His goatee twitched as his smile widened. From the corner of her eye, Imogene saw Priscilla look down at her tickets again.

So the last part of your plan will happen in Paris," Imogene went on. "That makes sense for once. But with the Council of Paris only a few days away, you say you need Priscilla's portrait so badly that you're sending me back to West Virginia to get it. Why don't you just do it yourself? You seem to have plenty of resources."

Priscilla cut in almost sheepishly. "I already offered my portrait to Imogene's boss."

"Yes, I heard," Droon said. His voice sounded unperturbed enough, but he slanted his brows at Priscilla in mild reproach. To Imogene, he said, "There is more to do in Accord than simply retrieve the rock. It is as you and the Oliver Hume discussed this morning."

"How did you—"

"If you please," he interrupted, "I find it rather difficult to talk for very long, and I did not bring any water."

"We can get you some water from the restaurant," Priscilla offered.

Droon shook his head. "The paintings are only part of our job. As the Oliver Hume said, the media will decide the value and meaning of art, no matter its power or its artist's original intent." His shoulders shook suddenly with ratchety coughing. He straightened back up. "What do you think would happen right now if a sea of news reporters flooded Accord with questions about Americanus Rex?"

Imogene's mind flashed back to the zombies lining Main Street, silently waiting—perhaps hoping—for Cody Hemphill to make Gary Pritchard take his medicine for shaming their beloved Priscilla.

"Nothing good," she admitted.

"The reporters do not know of Accord today, but they will soon enough," Droon wheezed. "We cannot and should not shield Accord from the public, so we must—"

But he was interrupted again by the most violent fit of coughing Imogene had seen from him yet. The little man doubled over and hacked until Imogene smelled the strong odor of hot sulfur she had first smelled on the airplane.

Priscilla patted his back and looked up at Imogene with wide, distraught eyes. "He's burning up. We need to get him to a hospital."

Imogene reached into her pocket for her phone.

"Wait," Droon said weakly.

He straightened back up, sparing Priscilla a pained smile. He reached into his lapel pocket and pulled out an enormous pill that reminded Imogene of nothing so much as a black glossy beetle. He slid it into his mouth and swallowed with some effort. The sulfur smell dissipated instantly.

"I will be alright for a bit longer," he said. Indeed, he already sounded much better.

Priscilla continued to rub his back. "Look, I should really be the one to go back to Accord. Imogene is better at this traveling business, and I think I can make the people in town see my portrait for what it is."

Droon began shaking his head even before she finished. The wire in his hatband glinted in the bright museum lights. "You and Americanus Rex are the primary reasons for Accord's unrest. It would be dangerous for you to go back now."

"It won't be dangerous for Imogene?" Priscilla countered.

"She is the Catalyst," Droon said patiently. "You will be needed next in Paris to help the Artist. As will the Historian. You will leave tomorrow afternoon."

Despite Droon's earlier words about free will, this last statement sounded a lot like an order to Imogene. But before she could ask anything else—Imogene doubted she would ever run out of questions for this guy—he tipped his hat once more and exited through the *Museum Staff Only* door. The knob twisted easily in his grip despite the fact that he had no keycard.

9

The two women stared at the Employees Only door for several seconds before deciding to take the winding public ramps from the Tate's top level back down to the Rex exhibit. They walked most of the way in silence until Priscilla unexpectedly yanked the two envelopes Droon had given her from the back pocket of her jeans.

She smiled sheepishly at Imogene. "I suddenly thought, what if I lost the tickets? Who knows if we'll see your friend again, and he said Gary would need Ellen and me in Paris. You do think Ellen is the Historian, don't you?"

Imogene nodded. "No doubt. Although I sure wish you were coming back to Accord with Ben and me. I know Droon said it would be dangerous for you there, but it's still your home. The people know you and trust you more than they trust Ben and me."

Priscilla shook her head slowly. "I'm not sure Accord is my home anymore. At least not until the town can see and accept the part of me that's finally waking up. I can't go on letting them treat me like some kind of rare flower—you know, pretty, fragile, and useless. I treated myself that way for long enough."

The two of them slid through a knot of people jammed against the security cordon outside the Rex exhibit. Imogene flashed her museum pass at the security guard, earning several photographs from cell phones and digital cameras. She even heard her own name a few time, along with the murmured phrase "from the *Times*."

Priscilla caught her arm before she could escape into the exhibit. "Can you tell Mama I'm doing all right when you go back to Accord? I'm sure she's worried, but if I tried to call her again she would hang up before I could say two words. She's a proud woman."

"Of course."

Priscilla looked relieved. Imogene thought she was going to say something else, but she just ducked under the tent flap and disappeared into the exhibit. Imogene followed and saw immediately that Oliver's workers had been busy. Every bit of painted bathroom tile, the side and back stall walls, and even the toilet from her portrait in the Tube station had been cleaned and reconstructed on the far right corner of the platform.

Oliver and Ben sat together in the front row of seats, Ben talking and Oliver scribbling furiously in a notebook. When Ben saw her, he raised his eyebrows in a simple question that she heard as clearly as if he had asked aloud: *Everything alright?*

She nodded. *Fine.*

He nodded in return and continued whatever he had been saying to Oliver. She wondered what on earth her brother could be talking about that would demand Oliver taking notes.

"Where the hell have you been?" Teddy greeted her. He took her wrist like a kid tugging his mother to the Christmas tree. "I've been waiting all morning to show you how Oliver's crew set up your portrait."

Priscilla had located Ellen's portrait and she moved toward it immediately, drawn in as surely as ocean tides are drawn by the moon.

"Oliver's carpenters used this stuff called AboCrete to make the base," Teddy said, still clasping Imogene's wrist. "Stronger and lighter than concrete. I didn't think they'd get all those tiles in before it dried." He looked back at her with a disbelieving snort and held up his index finger. "The whole thing took them one hour."

The carpenters had also angled each of the stall walls outward slightly to make the words in Dulci's letter easier to read without changing the original basic shape of the stall. The new shape also made Imogene's portrait an even more effective focal point and left a wider field of visibility for the portrait's small details. The flex of her calves jutting from the hems of her capris, the determined cast of her eyes, her arm pointing toward the wall bearing Dulci's letter, the undeniable sense that the world would follow where she pointed.

"Oliver said you agreed to appear at the press conference tonight," Teddy said. "Answer the reporters' questions."

"If they have any."

He stared down the bridge of his nose at her for a moment. "He didn't tell you about his press conferences, did he?"

"He showed me the *Guardian* this morning and told me that some English politicians may not want a big artistic peace movement in this country during the Council of Paris. But no, he didn't give any specifics."

Teddy nodded as if he had expected as much. "I hate to be the one to tell you this, Genie, but Oliver invites his closest friends and his bitterest enemies in the media to exhibit openings. I'm sure that will be especially true for an artist as controversial as Americanus Rex. See, Oliver's got this crazy idea that if he answers reporters' most scandalous questions right away, they'll have to print his responses instead of speculating."

"Which is precisely what happened in this morning's *Guardian*," Oliver said tartly from behind them.

He and Ben had apparently finished their conversation and he was striding across the platform toward the corner with Imogene's portrait. Ben had already joined Priscilla in front of Ellen's portrait.

"It doesn't matter," Imogene said before either Teddy or Oliver could speak again. "Like I told Oliver this morning, I believe Gary's messages about women and peace are worth spreading, and I'll make any effort I can to help." She hesitated, but this was as good a time as any to share her own news. "Which is also why I'm going back to West Virginia tomorrow."

She had expected Teddy to object and she was not disappointed.

"Oh, no no no. I brought you over here to take some of the pressure from myself and Oliver for the exhibit opening, and while I could happily marry you for getting yourself painted by Americanus Rex, your portrait has also effectively doubled our workload. We still have to rewrite the official press release, redesign and redistribute publicity posters, get the photographer back in here and somehow print new postcards for the gift shop by tomorrow morning, and twenty more things I can't remember right now. This afternoon I was going to have you punch up the copy for all of the exhibit placards and get them to the printers before the press conference."

"I still can," she said. "The exhibit will be finished by the time my flight leaves."

"Oh, you already have a ticket, do you?" Teddy said, settling his hands on his hips. "I certainly hope you didn't use the business credit card for an unauthorized purchase."

"Teddy," Oliver said mildly.

"Stay out of this, Oliver. Genie's not your employee."

"Unfortunate, but true," Oliver said evenly. "I actually appreciate my best workers. And as for me staying out of this situation, I believe we burned that bridge yesterday when I arranged to have Imogene's portrait removed from the South Ealing station."

"Who paid the bill?" Teddy retorted. "And who agreed to let you show Genie's portrait in the Tate until you have to return the Dresden portrait to Germany?"

Who's going to sell my portrait the moment you get back to Los Angeles? Imogene didn't say. "I didn't use your credit card to buy my tickets."

"Then where did you get the money?" Teddy asked, turning a suspicious squint to Oliver.

Before Imogene could answer, Oliver said, "Lord Droon."

Teddy threw his hands in the air. "Who the crispy fuck is Lord Droon? One of the Tate's inbred noble benefactors?"

"A secretive Asian man who has been in consistent contact with Imogene and her brother since Americanus Rex began painting," Oliver said.

"How do you know that?" Imogene asked incredulously.

He held up the notebook he'd been scribbling in when she had entered the exhibit. "Your brother is a very interesting man. And you lead a very interesting life."

"To hell with this," Teddy said, turning to leave. "Genie, have fun in Buttcrack, Arkansas or wherever. Come back to LA as soon as you have the other portrait. I've got work to do."

"Just stop a second, please," she said, marveling at how much conflict had already arisen in the middle of what was supposed to be a peace movement. "This isn't just about the art for me. As long as so many people are paying attention to Americanus Rex, we've got an opportunity to—"

—*light a beacon of peace from the top of the world,* she almost said. But she wasn't ready to share that story with Teddy or Oliver, in large part because she had no tangible, real world concept of what that beacon of peace might look like.

Teddy wasn't listening anyway. "Okay, so once you get back to Alabama, how do you plan to get a thousand pound rock off the top of a mountain?"

"West Virginia. And, I don't know."

Teddy shook his head disgustedly as if he had expected no more. "Well, Genie, far be it from me to discourage you from a plan that could potentially fill my home with heaping sacks of money. However, you will notify me the very instant Priscilla's portrait is on its way to California. *If* you can get the rock off its mountain, of course." A pointed glance over the tops of his small square glasses broadcast his doubt in this last respect, but he said no more.

"Thank you," she said. She really couldn't have asked for easier permission from him.

"Well?" he asked, still staring over the tops of his glasses.

"Well what?" Oliver asked, but she knew.

"The copy for the placards," she said. "I'm on it."

Teddy nodded once, satisfied, and walked briskly from the tent to complete one of the other errands he'd mentioned earlier.

"As I told you before," Oliver told her, watching Teddy go. "This has been the strangest exhibit I've ever built." He faced her. "Talking of strange, your Lord Droon is unendingly interesting, but I would prefer we keep any mention of him from the exhibit placards for now."

"Of course."

"And from the press conference as well," he added, suddenly hesitant for the first time since Imogene had met him. "I must also tell you that Teddy was quite right about the conference. I hope to handle the nastiest muck the press can rake tonight myself, but I suppose they may ask you some ticklish questions as well."

"I'll be there, like I promised," she assured him. She still wasn't positive why Droon had labeled her as the Catalyst, but it didn't take a scientist to understand that a spark rarely escaped the fire it started. "I'm sorry I won't be around for the opening, though. I would've loved to see it."

Oliver made a dismissive sound through pursed lips. "Thousands of people crammed into a small space look the same no matter where you cram them."

"You should still have Ellen for the opening in the morning. Oh! And tonight. I met her today and she said she would come to the press conference too. Based on my short time with her, I think she'll be ready for those ticklish questions."

Oliver seemed unsurprised. The wide grin with which he had rewarded her this morning returned with an air of gleeful menace to it. "I'm counting on it."

10

The Tate Modern Museum shooed its final visitors out the door seven minutes after eight on Sunday night. The beige canvas tent around the Americanus Rex Exhibit fell in heavy piles on all four sides of the exhibit's second-floor platform at 8:30, after Ellen was granted a full ten minutes of solitude to view her portrait for the first time. By 8:45 a host of Tate custodians in starched gray coveralls had rolled the canvas into tight bundles to be reshelved in the museum's vast underground storage rooms.

Another team of workers, these in tasteful black attire and radio headsets, waited in the wings with silver trays of finger sandwiches, exotic cheeses, pastries, oily mounds of caviar, and champagne. Near the mouth of the platform, Imogene saw two large men carrying a table with a gleaming—and enormously heavy, from their strained expressions—espresso machine resting on the black tablecloth.

Oliver, also in a headset, stood at the head of the platform, surrounded by Teddy, Priscilla, Ellen, and the Cornells. He pulled a silver watch from the inner breast pocket of his tuxedo, clicked open its lid, and snapped it shut again with a satisfied grunt.

"Ten minutes to set up the food and drink," he calculated, "and five minutes to spare before the press arrive."

"I'm guessing less," Teddy said dryly, gesturing down to the Tate's locked front doors, through which optimistic photographers were already snapping pictures of the uncovered exhibit platform. But even with their high powered flashbulbs—Imogene wondered giddily if any of them were attached to Polaroid cameras—the inside of the Tate was too large and gloomy, and the angle of their shots too poor, for them to capture much besides the underside of the platform.

However, the gloom would not last long, Imogene knew. A third team of Tate workers, electricians this time, were currently securing long racks of stage lights to the third and fourth balconies directly above the exhibit, reminding her strongly of a Broadway production. And she supposed that actually wasn't too far from the truth. They each had their roles to play tonight, didn't they?

As if to reinforce this idea, Oliver faced the five people around him and asked, "Everyone recall your places when the press arrive?"

They all nodded, but Oliver's eyes had lost their focus, which Imogene knew meant that someone was speaking to him over the headset. He nodded once in response to a question none of them could hear, and his eyes abruptly focused again.

"Teddy, the lights on balcony four need all need new cellophane filters. They're in—"

"On it," Teddy said, already two strides closer to the *Museum Staff Only* door than when Oliver had started speaking.

"Good man," Oliver beamed, the compliment only slightly more distracted than it might have been.

He looked over Ellen and Imogene approvingly. Ellen wore a pair of white capris much like Imogene's khaki ones, except that they were made of some thin material that swished softly when she moved. She had also traded in her sleeveless top for a long sleeved baby blue lycra shirt with a white Mizuno label stitched on the left breast.

Imogene wore the same white button-down shirt she had put on this morning. "Are you sure you don't want us to look a little more formal?"

"You're perfect as you are. All of you," Oliver added with quick nods to Ellen, Priscilla, and Ben. "A few minutes of the Academy Awards or the BAFTAs on telly is enough to prove that an audience rarely pays attention to a woman's words when she's wearing an evening gown. The last thing we want is for the press to mistake you and Ellen for simple eye candy."

He ran a palm over his shining head, an oddly self-conscious gesture that Imogene guessed was a remnant of a time before he'd begun shaving his head. His final comment to the four of them, delivered casually as he left the platform to begin his own role as host, sent a shiver down Imogene's back: "We change the world in ten minutes."

As soon as he had left, Priscilla reached into the pocket of her jeans, pulled out the warped envelope Droon had given her this afternoon, and held it up to Ellen. The taller woman accepted the envelope and studied the words on it for what felt like a very long time. Finally she tore open the paper flap. Priscilla watched her, waiting for Ellen to speak before she explained what the airplane ticket meant.

Ben's arm, Imogene saw, had crept around Priscilla's waist again. He hadn't been angry this afternoon when she had told him that they were returning to Accord so soon—after his reaction to Teddy's vacation ending phone call back in Accord, she had expected a rip-roaring battle. However, he had taken every opportunity since then to be physically close to Priscilla, as if afraid he might not get the chance again.

When Imogene had asked for the third time if he was *sure* he wasn't upset about leaving London so soon, he had remarked, "Gene, I have never seen you care so much about anything. At this point you could tell me we were rowing to the North Pole in that dinghy I built with Dad in high school, and I would reach for my mittens and some superglue." The customary dryness had left his voice as he'd added, "She was my mother too."

She had hugged him hard enough to provoke a loud "Oof!" that was only part theatrics. "And you're not mad that I'm taking you away from Priscilla?" she'd whispered in his ear.

He had extracted himself from her, his expression earnest. "The way I see it, you're saving me from catching a very messy rebound. I don't have the self control to give her the alone time she needs right now."

Seeing him and Priscilla together now, though, Imogene thought the possibility of Priscilla being on the rebound from her engagement to Gary was open to debate. She certainly hadn't refused Ben's attention. And even as she explained to Ellen that they were supposedly going to Paris to help Gary with his next effort, she had sidled closer to Ben so that their hips touched.

At last Ellen tucked the envelope into her back pocket with a sense of great finality and satisfaction. "Oliver was right," she said simply.

"Does that mean you'll go?" Priscilla asked.

"You're damn straight I'll go," Ellen said. Under her mask, her cheeks rose with a smile that was somehow goofy and ruthless at the same time, the smile of a reprehensible pirate who loved her work. "When do those reporters get here anyway?"

A very short fifteen minutes later, the Tate workers had all but vanished from the platform, leaving behind gleaming platters of artful "nibbles," as Oliver had called the finger foods, and slender goblets of champagne. The remaining workers stood at attention behind the tables, all of them in the ubiquitous black uniforms.

Most of the chairs on the platform were already occupied, the reporters in them jotting preliminary notes on pads of paper or laptops while simultaneously enjoying the food and drink Oliver had provided. A jungle of cameras and electronic recording gear stood behind the two sections of chairs, leaving only enough space for people to move up and down the center aisle. Oliver was hobnobbing with his typical grace.

Imogene sat nervously in the middle of the front row of chairs. Ben and Priscilla were to her right, Ellen and Teddy to her left. Teddy was the only one who seemed unconcerned about the conference. He munched contentedly on a cracker decked with cucumber and raw tuna. Imogene ran her fingers under the circumference of her waistband, making sure her shirt was fully tucked in, then smoothed the creases in her pants as well as she could with the palms of her hands. She might have gone on doing this until the press conference started if Ben had not pinned her arms to her sides with a firm one-armed hug.

"You look great." He planted a noisy kiss on the right side of her head. "Except now your hair's messed up," he added cheerfully.

Throughout this exchange, the bank of cameras at the back of the platform flashed ceaselessly. Imogene swept a hand through her hair again, wondering if she would ever get used to people with cameras paying her so much attention and hoping she would never have to.

"Good evening," Oliver's amplified voice rolled through Tate's massive main gallery. In the last few seconds he had glided his way to the front of the platform where a team of technicians had fitted a podium with a bristling bouquet of foam topped microphones. "Thank you all for coming."

"Thanks for the invite," one of the reporters called jovially and most of his colleagues seconded him.

Imogene thought that if Oliver had truly invited his closest friends and bitterest enemies in the media tonight, the latter were the politest enemies she had ever seen. Oliver's easy smile and the champagne in his hand relieved her in any case. The atmosphere here already felt much more casual than she had expected.

"I have never prepared a more interesting or more taxing exhibit for the public, as I'm sure is evident from the fact that I took temporary possession of both paintings only yesterday."

This comment earned a flurry of clicking laptop keys and hushed whispering. The cameras flashed more rapidly as well, as if excited by Oliver's statement.

"I'm also thrilled to report that none of you need to continue inventing fictitious threats from the German Chancellor to our esteemed Prime Minister and myself regarding my acquisition of the Dresden portrait. The Chancellor has quite willingly agreed to let the Tate show the painting originally discovered in the Dresden Frauenkirche for one full month, beginning tomorrow. After this time, the painting will be returned to Germany.

"Similarly, the second Americanus Rex portrait, discovered at the South Ealing Underground Station here in London, will also remain on display at the Tate for a month, after which it will travel to the United States with its current owner and my invaluable assistant over the last three days, Teddy Roth of Roth Gallery in Los Angeles. You'll have to ask Teddy for yourselves where the portrait will be installed after that because, by his own admission, Roth Gallery is rather too small to permanently host such a well known piece."

Teddy stood and offered a brief wave to the cameras. Imogene expected a rush of shouted questions while Teddy was on his feet, but other than the echoing clicks of keyboards, the reporters held their silence.

"And I may as well finish my introductions while I'm at it," Oliver continued. "My guests and their portraits are, after all, the reasons you lot are here tonight."

Ellen grabbed Imogene's hand and squeezed so hard that Imogene had to grit her teeth against a startled shout of pain.

"Ellen Ramsey, the subject of the Dresden portrait, and Imogene Cornell, the subject of the London portrait, have most graciously agreed to appear at this event and entertain any professional and responsible questions you may have."

Imogene hardly heard anything past her own name. She stood with Ellen, almost gasping with relief when Ellen released her hand, and turned to face the reporters. Hushed chatter erupted immediately, sounding almost as horrified as it was eager. Ellen's bruises were especially dramatic under the harsh stage lights Oliver's people had erected on the third and fourth floor balconies. And even those lights suddenly seemed dim in comparison with the endless flashbulbs. Imogene also saw the small, steady red eyes of actively recording television cameras.

A sudden and impossible sense of *déjà vu* gripped her. She had never stood in front of a bank of cameras like this, but her mother had. And what the cameras had captured had defined the way people had remembered her mother for the rest of her life. Imogene waved and tried to smile, barely managing to sit back down before her knees buckled.

Ben clasped her right hand much more gently than Ellen had done and she closed her eyes, letting his emotional support flood into her through that wonderful and mysterious emotional bond they shared. Eventually her breathing returned to normal. When she opened her eyes again, she found her vision clear and bright.

She had heard nothing of what Oliver had said since he had introduced her, but his words caught her full attention now: "So I think I'll give up the floor to my guests."

11

This time it was Imogene who wanted to snag Ellen's hand, but she managed to keep both her hands calmly at her sides as they stood again and took their places beside Oliver at the podium. She focused all of her energy on not shifting her weight, stuffing her hands in her pockets, or, heaven forbid, gnawing at her fingernails. How had her mother managed to look so poised in front of a couple thousand people in a bathing suit? And at nineteen years old to boot.

"Right," Oliver began. "Our first question of the evening will come from the *Times*. Miss Hunter?"

A fifty-something woman with sweeping silver hair stood from her chair in the front row. "Miss Ramsey, did your injury occur during the painting of your portrait?"

"Just before," Ellen said. "Americanus Rex paints from photographs, as I'm sure many of you know, and the Frauenkirche's basement was quite dark, and, well, do any of you remember the end of that old Alfred Hitchcock movie *Rear Window?*"

Surprised but appreciative chuckles broke out at this. The silver haired woman from the *Times* watched Ellen for a moment, her battery powered tape recorder wavering uncertainly in her outstretched hand.

"I was flash-blinded and tripped over my own feet," Ellen clarified. "Rebroke my nose."

"Rumors have placed someone fitting your description in a Dresden hospital the same day as the portrait was discovered," the silver haired woman said. "Does that mean that your encounter with Americanus Rex forced you to seek medical attention?"

"Yes," Ellen said. "But the bones in my nose haven't been as strong since I took a volleyball spike to the face in college. That girl was huge."

Imogene had heard that line already once today, but she guessed the description was even more striking with Ellen standing at her full height, dwarfing the podium and its bristle of microphones. Several reporters laughed again, more loudly this time.

The silver haired woman was not among them. "You are saying that Americanus Rex snuck up behind you and took your picture without your permission—while you were nearly in the nude if your portrait is anything to go by—then put that image on public display, and you see nothing wrong with this?"

Ellen's valley girl persona vanished in an instant. "Look at the result." The soft tone of command in her voice turned a hundred heads toward her portrait in unison and stillness settled over the exhibit.

But Miss Hunter would not be put off. "Miss Cornell, are you so easy to forgive Americanus Rex painting your portrait unbidden, despite his sneaking into a women's lavatory to do so?"

"Like Ellen, I didn't have a choice about Americanus Rex painting me. But I do have a choice about what to do now that he has. I'm sure we've all heard the speculation that Americanus Rex is painting these portraits as a statement against the Council of Paris initiating a war with China and Russia. So if my portrait, combined with my actions here, can make a positive change for much of the world, I'll do it. To me, the fact that you're all here asking us questions only confirms that my choice is the right one."

Several hands had gone up as she spoke. "Mr. Hughes from *The Guardian* is next, I believe," Oliver said when he was sure Imogene had finished.

The reporter in question, a thin man with a hooked nose and almost as little hair as Oliver, flipped to a fresh page in his ledger and cleared his throat. "Right. Miss Cornell, before I ask my real question, I notice that the man with whom you are sharing a relieved hug on the cover of this morning's *Guardian* is present tonight, as is the young woman who was with you at the time."

She glanced at Ben and Priscilla and saw that they were holding hands. "My brother, Ben, and our friend, Priscilla Hemphill."

"Thank you," the man said, though he sounded almost disappointed with her answer. "Now you seemed quite relieved after the police arrived, as I mentioned. Why would you be so eager for rescue if Americanus Rex were as benevolent as you and Miss Ramsey have said?" He spoke with a permanent sneer that colored his pronunciation of the word "benevolent," effectively dismissing Ellen's statement as something ignorant and flimsy.

"The crowd's reaction in the subway station when I called for help was more of a threat to me than Americanus Rex's presence was. I thought they might trample me."

The man nodded mechanically, scribbling into his ledger while she spoke. "And so you believe that Americanus Rex's methods, which most trained psychologists would equate with those of a stalker, are justified by the possibility that he painted the two of you in the cause of peace."

The 'possibility,' Imogene thought, her temper flaring. "I doubt anyone could miss the powerful message of peace in both our portraits, both textually and visually."

More hands went up this time. Oliver pointed at a lanky, red haired, bearded man in the third row. "Herr Becker from *Der Spiegel*."

"It is also difficult to ignore the connection between Germany and

England to the Council of Paris, as you have already mentioned," Becker said in a crisp German accent. "Do either of you believe Americanus Rex has something specific to say about this event?"

"Very specific," Ellen said. "Americanus Rex is certainly not the first artist in popular culture to suggest that all human conflict is at some level a result of miscommunication," she said, her voice drifting through the Tate's open levels like the voice of a professor in an enormous lecture hall. "Read anything by Orson Scott Card or Timothy Zahn if you don't believe me. And while I could study my portrait for years without ever finding all of the hidden meanings, the written parts of both portraits clearly call for better communication. Therefore, it is my belief that Americanus Rex is calling for the Council of Paris to invite representatives from China and Russia to the talks."

Amid hushed muttering from most of the room, Becker jotted something down on his notepad. "The Russian and Chinese governments have refused to comment on the purpose of the Red October Sky to NATO or the UN. Would inviting them to the Council of Paris change their stance in some way?"

Ellen seemed to have an answer prepared, but Imogene spoke first. "Probably not," she said softly.

She felt Ellen's eyes fall on her, but she didn't look over. Her mind kept returning to the image of Dulci's family at supper with the two fighting boys from school and their own families; to Oliver's descriptions this morning at breakfast of people marching through the streets of European cities in support of peace; to Droon's cryptic comment the first time she'd met him: *Our greatest hope is that it has always been people like you, not governments, who instigate meaningful changes in history.*

Imogene leaned into the microphones. "Inviting China and Russia to the Council is only one part of what Americanus Rex's movement could be. I believe he is also calling upon us—Ellen and me, you journalists in attendance tonight, your readers and viewers—to take our own action. That's the only way to make any real difference. Every government on the planet must respond to the needs and actions of its people, and we need our leaders to create a peaceful solution rather than make vague threats of Armageddon."

The German man was positively scribbling now. "Surely you do not speak of revolution."

"Imagine thousands of people from all over Europe and the United States traveling to Paris between now and next Thursday, filling the streets outside Elysée Palace and the American, German, Spanish, and British Embassies."

"A war protest," Becker clarified.

Imogene's mind was racing. A comment her mother made to her father one night at dinner popped into her mind. "Protests start out angry and have way of turning violent. I'm talking about people from all over the world, not just the nations involved in the Council, gathering in good will to show the Council of Paris that we choose peace."

Several new hands shot up and Oliver once again pointed, seemingly at random. "Mr. Sommers, National Public Radio."

"The world has never existed entirely in peace," a low male voice said. "Is it not naïve to assume Americanus Rex can achieve something that no society or government in the history of our planet has achieved?"

Ellen leaned forward. "There's *already* peace between the countries involved in the Council of Paris and Russia and China. Choosing peace is no more or less complicated than choosing to go to war. I'm no artist, but even I can see that those two choices are as opposite and well defined as the contrast between light and shadow in our portraits."

Imogene addressed the man who had asked the last question. "Mr. Sommers, was it? I listen to NPR back home, and I know you guys have correspondents in both Russia and China. Get them talking to their own in-country contacts and other citizens they know. There will be room enough in Paris for them too. The alternative is to cower in fear of what might or might not happen to our own world. Americanus Rex has chosen to act, and I hope that all of us here tonight can make the same decision. We will light a beacon of peace from the top of the world!" Imogene boomed, completely lost in the moment.

Oliver stepped closer to the microphones once more. "I would once again like to thank our guests, Ellen Ramsey and Imogene Cornell."

Polite clapping pattered through the hall.

Are we done? Imogene wondered dazedly.

Oliver continued, "As per the program you all received, I would like to give everyone a chance to see the portraits up close before I take some more of your questions myself. The food tables are still fully stocked as well. When we return, our first question will come from *The Artist's Magazine*. I, for one, am anxious to explore the duality Miss Ramsey mentioned of Americanus Rex's peace message and his style of high contrast light and shadow."

Imogene blinked. She recognized the name of *The Artist's Magazine* easily enough. Not only was it one of the highest circulated art publications in the United States, but Teddy's gallery had appeared in it when he had hosted a private collection by Mexican artist Frida Kahlo.

She suddenly realized that Oliver's friends and enemies in the press weren't just from the news outlets, but from all branches of media. All of the questions so far had been related to politics, meaning that Oliver's pointing hadn't been nearly as random as it had seemed. Now he was turning the focus from the exhibit's political impact to the art itself.

He'd told her this afternoon that he would try to tackle the most difficult questions himself, but must have been referring to difficult questions related to art. All of the political questions he'd directed toward her and Ellen.

We answered them, she realized as she sat down beside her brother.

Ben reached across his seat and took her right hand again, this time to shake it rather than give comfort. "Holy hell, Gene," he breathed.

Priscilla regarded her with a species of awe that made color rise to her cheeks.

But she also realized this press conference might not be much more than a warm up for the questions she would have to answer when she and her brother flew back to Accord tomorrow. But that was just fine by her. Gary Pritchard had already lit three beacons of peace since he'd promised to do so four days ago. It was time she lit one of her own.

INTERLUDE: THE ENVOY

1

Monday, August 29, 2011

Dulci stepped out of the bookstore and back into the relentless early afternoon Spanish sunshine. She stuffed her traveler's money pouch into her backpack, where it settled between her water bottle and the book she had just bought for her father. She'd come across what seemed like several hundred editions of *Don Quijote de la Mancha* during her travels in Spain, but this one had the most interesting illustrations by far, some of which had been on posters in bookshop windows in Madrid. She suspected the modernized spelling of Quijote would annoy him (the original spelling had been "Quixote," which her father still insisted on pronouncing *Kee-show-te* as per archaic Spanish linguistic rules), but she knew he would be won over by the fact that she'd bought this edition in Alcalá de Henares, the town where the book's author, Miguel Cervantes, had supposedly been born.

Now she only had to find a gift for her brother. She wiped away the rills of sweat that had reformed in the last five minutes before sliding her sunglasses back into place through the wet hair over her ears. Even after spending her first eighteen years of life in Phoenix, she hadn't known just how brightly and with how much heat the sun could shine.

Dulci detoured around an impressive mound of dog shit baked onto the decorative grid of the sidewalk that ran along Alcalá's old Roman city wall, thinking that sidewalk poop was just about the only common denominator of Spain's wildly varied cities.

She had begun her trip in Barcelona, with its cathedrals, sprawling beaches, and science-fiction mix of gothic and ultra modern architecture. From there she had taken a train to the southern province of Andalucía, where the clipped, consonant-dropping accent had been so much heavier even than her parents' that she had barely understood a word of it. And two days ago she had traveled north once more to Madrid, a city brimming with fountains and parks alongside grand palaces and yet more cathedrals.

Her destination today, Alcalá de Henares, was not part of Madrid-proper, but still contained every reason Dulci had come to Spain: history, art, architecture, and, wrapped in all of those, culture.

"*Hola, mucha gracias,*" said a bored voice to her right as someone thrust a thin newspaper into her hands.

She had learned quickly to ignore most of the paper handouts that people on the sidewalks here frequently offered her, but she took this one and spoke her own thanks to the man who had given it to her. The newspaper, called *20 Minutos* because you could supposedly skim every article in that amount of time, was distributed for free throughout Europe everyday. During her first days in Spain, Dulci had seen *20 Minutos* offered in Spanish, French, and even Catalan, the regional language of Barcelona.

She tucked the newspaper in her backpack's elastic mesh pouch behind the paperback novel she'd finished last night in her hotel room, taking care not to bend the photograph of herself and Alexander sticking out the top of the novel. It had served as her bookmark on the trip, as well as a constant reminder that her fiancé had chosen not to join her on this trip. She had been disappointed by his decision, but she knew his parents' constant repetition of propaganda about supposed anti-American sentiments in Europe due to the Council of Paris had finally gotten to him.

"At least Spain is attending the Council," he'd said one evening while she'd been searching the internet for airline tickets. "You'll be with the good guys even if you're not in America."

Dulci had ignored the implication that anyone not in the Council must be "bad guys." She'd already shared her opinion that the Council of Paris was simply an excuse for the Department of Homeland Security to reenact, and add a few playful paragraphs to, the Patriot Act. But Alexander had never read *1984,* and she knew from experience that he didn't care to explore the implications of George Orwell's famous phrase, "War is peace."

But, Dulci reminded herself, Alexander was not the same as his parents. Proposing to her last April had been proof enough of that. His mother had threatened to disown him following their engagement announcement, sputtering that her only son would never show up to a family reunion with "little brown Mexican children."

"Well, then maybe I won't show up at my wedding with an ignorant racist mother," Alexander had retorted hotly, clasping Dulci's hand and pulling her from his parents' house.

The following week had been the worst of her life. She and Alexander had already taken five days of vacation from work with the idea of spending Holy Week, the most important holidays of the year in Dulci's family, with his parents. Instead she had drifted aimlessly around their apartment in Indianapolis, sometimes watching TV, sometimes reading a book, but always lost in her own mind. Alexander had taken over her half of the housework in addition to his own, occasionally presenting her with flowers or hot tea.

Easter Sunday his mother had finally telephoned and asked to speak to Dulci, who had sat patiently through a short, uncomfortable story about how Alexander's paternal grandfather had come from Austria and settled in northern Indiana after World War II. He too had suffered racism, Alexander's mother had said, because he couldn't speak English.

"Things eventually worked out for him, I suppose. Now Alex's grandfather is as American as they come. Hasn't spoken a word of German in thirty years," she'd said proudly. "But I'm sure you understand why I was concerned at first."

Dulci hadn't understood at all, but had said nothing in the hope that the conversation would end soon.

"And I know it's not a mother's place to tell her son who he can love," Alexander's mother had said in a wisely weary tone that had made Dulci want to scream.

Just like it's not a woman's place to choose her mother-in-law, Dulci had almost said, but had stifled the comment as vindictive and unfair.

Alexander's mother had breathed deeply into the receiver. "All of that is to say I hope that Peter and I will be welcome when you marry our son."

We all have room to grow, Dulci now reminded herself, *including me.* This trip had already proven that to her.

She followed the sidewalk through a line of trees and found herself in a sea of bright pink flowers. A large metal plaque on the side of a building read, *Plaza de Cervantes.* Up ahead, a statue of Miguel de Cervantes stood atop a tall concrete dais in the center of the square, stained a sooty gray by time and air. The statue's metallic head winked dully in the ever-present sunshine, surrounded by a sea of noisy people and noisier pigeons.

The majority of people in the silver chairs scattered throughout the square tipped back bottled Fanta or munched complimentary *tapas* from plastic baskets on their tables. One man in particular clutched a liter bottle of Evian water in each of his long-fingered hands, and Dulci could certainly understand why he would need so much water. Despite the day's temperature, the guy was wearing a two-piece black suit and a black fedora to match. And what kind of shoes did he have on? Her most hideous white nursing clogs didn't have soles as thick as his.

Dulci had enough time to feel sorry for the man, who seemed to be the only friendless person in the square besides herself, before another man brushed past her, bumping her backpack, and dropped into the chair across from him. The newcomer was just as absurdly dressed for the heat. He wore blue jeans and a long-sleeved flannel shirt below thick, tinted prescription glasses that dominated the upper half of his face. An old bulky Polaroid camera hung from a plastic strap wound under his collar like a loose tie. Both men seemed totally oblivious to their surroundings, except that the guy in the suit had the presence of mind to keep hydrated.

Okay, she thought with grim amusement, *now I'm the only one with no friends.*

But she didn't waste any time on self pity. A large hand written sign on a post at the far edge of the plaza had caught her eye: *Torrijas y Bizcochos.* Alexander would undoubtedly notice the new five pounds that had somehow gathered on her hips and thighs during this trip, but the extra miles she would have to jog once she got home were a small price to pay for real Spanish *torrijas.* She still had not found any pastries here to rival those her mother made at home, but she would continue searching in the name of science.

She still remembered the time she had mashed two hot *torrijas,* dripping with cooked sweet wine, into a manila envelope to mail to her childhood penpal, Imogene. As punishment for wasting them, her mother had forbidden her to eat from the rest of the batch, which Dulci still found unfair twenty years after the fact. Shortly after that incident, the letters from Imogene had stopped. Dulci wondered, as she did whenever she thought of her old friend, if Imogene had ever learned to speak Spanish.

"Where is this place?" she muttered to herself.

She had followed the arrow on the original sign down a much less traveled side street, where she had found another painted sign advertising the *torrijas,* this one pointing down an alley. Strange, but not unheard of. Dulci had already tracked down a group of nuns who sold baked goods from a private apartment in Madrid.

Inside the alley, the only visible door was closed, the jamb covered in dust as if it had not been opened in months.

"Probably closed," Dulci said, just to break the silence. "Taking their *siesta*."

Well, she wasn't going to spend her afternoon waiting for them to reopen. Her only decision was where she should go next. She shrugged out of her backpack and unzipped the largest pocket, where she kept all her maps. She'd picked up a very detailed one of Alcalá de Henares this morn—

Heavy shoes scraped the stones behind her. She spun around, one hand clutching the squashy shoulder strap of her backpack, the other buried inside the main pocket. The man she'd seen in Plaza de Cervantes wearing flannel and denim stood calmly at the mouth of the alley, thumbs hooked casually through his beltloops. His friend was nowhere to be seen.

Dulci instinctively grabbed the first thing she felt out of the bag and cocked it behind her ear to throw if Farmer Joe tried to get fresh. She realized with real dismay that she was holding her half empty plastic water bottle, and with that dismay came immediate shame. Had Alexander's paranoia rubbed off on her so completely that her first instinct in a surprising situation was not only self preservation, but violence?

She relaxed her throwing arm, still holding the bottle at her side. "Can I help you with something?"

The man had a pleasant, somewhat vacant face, and Dulci thought she saw a flicker of a smile play on his lips. He didn't move or speak.

Dulci tried again. "I saw you with your friend back in the plaza. I'm meeting my friends there in a few minutes too."

This was a lie, of course. She still saw no reason to start chucking the contents of her backpack at the guy, but there was also no reason he shouldn't think she might be missed, and soon.

His smile, faint to begin with, faded entirely. Now he simply looked confused, as if she weren't behaving the way he'd expected.

Good, she thought. *Surprise is the most important element of attack* and *defense.*

"You know, it's very hot today, and I couldn't help but notice that your friend wasn't sharing his water," she said, taking one step toward the alley's exit, lifting the water bottle again. "You can have some of mine if you—"

The man pulled his thumbs from his belt loops as if preparing to accept her gift, but the bottle toppled from her hand and rolled to a wobbly, sloshing stop at the scuffed toe of his work boot.

"Sorry," she said convincingly, although she had quite purposely dropped the bottle.

A refrain pounded through her head: *Pick it up, buddy. Just pick it up.* A few seconds of inattention from him and she'd be safely past him into the street, where there would be an avenue of escape if she needed one.

But the man ignored the bait. He kept his eyes on her, looking, if anything, even more confused than before.

Becoming rather desperate, she reached into her bag once more and drew out the apple she'd meant to eat as an afternoon snack. "If you're hungry too, you can have my apple. My friends will be glad to buy me someth—"

The man smiled radiantly, erasing any possibility in her mind that he might be dangerous. However, instead of reaching for the offered apple, he lifted the Polaroid to his eye and snapped a single picture. The camera spit out a broad square photograph, which the man caught between his thumb and forefinger. Then he turned on the ball of his foot and disappeared around the nearest street corner at a light jog.

2

Dulci stood where she was a moment longer before tucking the apple back into her backpack with a bemused shake of her head. She lifted the water bottle from the pavement, brushed away some street grit, and replaced it in the bag as well. She made her way back to Plaza Cervantes at a dignified stroll, trying not to speculate about the man's motivation for wanting her picture, but dwelling on it just the same.

However, all thoughts of the man temporarily vanished when she reached the plaza. Her eyes swung back and forth across the square in disbelief. The only person in sight was the grimy statue of Miguel de Cervantes. Pigeons overran every table in the square, bobbing their heads and cooing ecstatically. It looked like the hundreds of people had vacated the square and the food they'd been eating *en masse*, leaving the pigeons with a banquet.

Images of the March 11 train bombings in Madrid in 2004 flowed into her mind, embellished by her own panicked imagination. Buildings on fire, people fleeing through the streets. The rigged trains had come from Alcalá de Henares, after all. This time would it be squadrons of terrorists on hijacked airliners? Had she missed some public announcement to take shelter during her search for *torrijas?*

Stop! she commanded herself fiercely. *Do you hear sirens? Do you see smoke?* Look *with your eyes instead of running laps with them.*

Her breathing slowed, her eyes quit their dance, and she discovered that someone else remained in the square after all. She was not surprised she had overlooked him. The man was covered in pigeons from his thick-soled shoes to the peak of his felt fedora. Three birds had nestled themselves onto the hat's black brim. One pecked curiously at the tip of the silver wire sticking out of the band. The man seemed indifferent to the pigeons, though he must have known they would make a terrible mess of his black suit if he did not shoo them away.

She walked cautiously to within five feet of his table. He smiled warmly at her, his square white teeth gleaming inside the tidy triangle of his goatee. A pigeon cooed sedately on his shoulder and he stroked its head with a long, tapered finger.

"*Te estás perdiendo el espectáculo,*" he said in an odd, tinny voice. More oddly yet, his speech perfectly matched the Castilian Spanish she had heard on television in her hotel rooms.

She felt immediately racist for assuming a Chinese man couldn't speak her language properly. *You don't even know that he's Chinese,* she chastised herself.

He tipped the brim of his fedora as if she had complimented him aloud. One of the pigeons on his hat clucked in obvious irritation at the sudden jostling of its perch.

"You are missing the show," he repeated, this time in equally perfect English.

Dulci caught a distinct whiff of sulfur on his breath, as if he had swallowed a box of matches or smoked too many cigarettes. She wondered how the pigeons could tolerate the smell when it was strong enough to reach her five feet away.

"What show is that?"

He pointed a finger in the direction she had come from this morning. "Your portrait is his most daring yet, though I am sorry if he frightened you. He can be clumsy."

"My portrait?" she repeated. "You mean the picture he took? I don't think 'clumsy' covers behavior like—"

The man broke into a fit of ratchey coughing and tipped back one of the bottles of Evian into his mouth. His lips did not leave the bottle until only an inch or so of water remained in the bottom.

"Dry air," he wheezed calmly, the sulfur smell much stronger now. "Have you read today's newspaper?"

"I've got one in my bag," she said, reaching for the copy of *20 Minutos* jutting from the elastic pouch on her backpack.

But Droon was quicker. Her pulled another folded copy from his inner breast pocket and held it out to her, cover up.

She accepted the paper from him, unreality creeping over her like an ill fitting suit. A color photograph of two unusual paintings Dulci had glimpsed on the news just last night filled a quarter of the front page, but with an important difference: the women themselves stood together in the foreground, a nest of microphones jammed onto a podium in front of them.

The caption read, *Ellen Ramsey (la izquierda) e Imogene Cornell con sus retratos de Americanus Rex en el Tate Modern Museum en Londres.*

Dulci's eyes widened even as she told herself that there must be hundreds of Imogene Cornells in the world, if not thousands. Except that the Imogene Cornell in the newspaper had a beautiful tumble of dark red curly hair, just like the little girl in the wallet-sized school picture Dulci's penpal had sent with her first letter all those years ago.

Dulci's eyes flew over the article below the photograph. The two women, she read, had entertained questions for several minutes at the Tate Modern Museum last night at a press conference before the official opening of the exhibit housing their portraits. The women had theorized that Americanus Rex was calling for Chinese and Russian representatives to be invited to the Council of Paris. They based this idea on the symbolism and written messages in the two portraits.

Dulci frowned. She hadn't seen any writing on the brief news footage she'd seen. Just the painted women.

The writing in Ellen's portrait mentioned the Tower of Babel and something about a mountain, but Dulci couldn't get much more than that from the lousy Spanish translation in the newspaper. The salutation alone in Imogene's portrait, however—*Estimada amiga*—precluded the need for any translation at all.

She glanced up at the Chinese man. He nodded once, that square white smile wider than ever. Her eyes returned to the article, unable to believe that a letter she had written before her tenth birthday had become the topic of international political debate.

The British and American governments apparently felt the same way. After the press conference in London, which had taken place in the middle of the day according to US clocks, the White House Press Secretary had quickly, albeit indirectly, addressed the international attention Americanus Rex had received, claiming, "Communist states with weapons of mass destruction are just as dangerous to the United States and its allies as any terrorist organization, and have no place at an event like the Council of Paris, which was created to defend democracy and freedom."

That *didn't take long,* Dulci thought acidly. *Cry "terrorist" and let the culture of fear shepherd the American public into a bleating huddle behind the military industrial complex in the name of democracy and freedom. Forget that Russia has had a democratically elected government for over twenty years.*

The newspaper quivered in her hand like a leaf in a breeze. She had never been as angry, as *enraged,* as she was right now. As a nurse in a psychiatric hospital, she would have to be pretty lousy at her job not to see that much of her volcanic anger had been born of the anxiety she had felt back in the alley.

Not all of it, though. She also heard Alexander's voice on the day she had bought her tickets to come to Spain, her brain transforming his light tenor voice into the high, reedy *baa* of a sheep. "At least Spain is attending of the Council."

Once again she told herself she wasn't being fair. Alexander was always trying, if not always succeeding, to put the most unseemly parts of his upbringing behind him. He did want to marry her, after all.

But her imagination wouldn't listen to reason. It conjured up an image of Alexander in his pleather easy chair in front of the TV, the Press Secretary speaking his lines on Fox News while digital ticker-tape marched importantly across the bottom of the screen. Alexander turned toward her mind's eye as if looking into a camera lens. Even his pink face and third generation Austrian blonde hair, curly like his mother's, appeared sheeplike.

"You'll be with the good guys even if you're not in America!" the Alexander-sheep bawled at her.

"I'm sick of it," Dulci told the Chinese man.

He couldn't possibly have known what she was talking about, but he nodded as if he did. His long index finger made another appearance, pointing in the direction of the city wall the Romans had built two thousand years ago.

Dulci left Plaza de Cervantes at a run.

She didn't run very far before she found out he hadn't been kidding about "the show," although his Spanish description had fit even better: *el espectáculo.* This was a spectacle if she had ever seen one. Twice as many people as had been in Plaza de Cervantes were gathered before the Roman wall, and more were arriving all the time. A hushed chatter rose from the congregation, reminding Dulci of the sort of tidal white noise she'd heard yesterday in the Prado art museum in Madrid.

Whatever had caught their interest was still invisible to Dulci, hidden by the crowd. She scanned her surroundings and saw a balcony jutting off the side of a building across the street from the wall. She glanced around but no one was paying attention to her. She tightened the shoulder straps of her backpack and scrambled up the stonework onto the balcony. Just as her legs cleared the railing, she noticed two yellow-vested police officers in the street below, but they were too busy rubbernecking with everyone else to pay her any attention.

She reached up to brush off the front of her dress, but her hands fell limply to her sides when she finally saw what had drawn so many people here: two figures had been painted on the Roman wall in glittering silver.

The one on the left was a mounted cartoon knight that Dulci recognized immediately from the cover of the copy of *Don Quijote* she'd bought for her father. The new silver versions of Quijote and his horse were cast in stark light and shadow, as if standing before a powerful light source. Dulci could clearly see the jutting ribs and bulging eyes of the knight's "steed," and the knight's circular armored cap was bent and torn as though it was made of cardboard. Under the wobbly arc of armor, the knight's face looked very familiar…

A sensation like icy water splashed down her scalp and shoulders, pebbling her arms with gooseflesh. She squeezed her eyes shut. Maybe when she opened them again the horrible illusion would be gone.

Okay.

She opened her eyes to their minimum possible squint and saw, with a sick dread, that she had seen no illusion. The cardboard knight on the dying horse had Alexander's face. The curl of hair spilling over the visible part of his forehead; the close-set eyes, so deep in his face that she sometimes wondered if the bridge of his strong nose obscured his vision; the wide, knowing mouth set in a sour line like a toad's smile, as if the man who'd made this portrait had known how little Alexander liked having his picture taken.

But none of that explained how the painter had known Alexander's face to begin with.

Dulci snatched the paperback novel from her backpack's side pouch and riffled through the pages. The photograph of her and Alexander that she'd been using as a bookmark was gone. The man in flannel—almost certainly the elusive Americanus Rex, she now realized—had done more than just bump into her in the plaza.

She shoved the paperback into its pouch again, her attention once more on the painted knight who wore Alexander's face. Like the drawing of *Don Quijote,* Alexander's only pristine accessory was a long, sharp lance painted with stripes like those on a barber pole. Unlike the book cover, on which Quijote held the lance pointed skyward as if keeping it visible without actually planning to use it anytime soon, Alexander's lance pointed straight ahead toward the other figure painted on the Roman wall. This second figure held an apple toward the knight in an outstretched hand.

"She's me," Dulci whispered.

Americanus Rex had painted Dulci as she must have appeared in the alley—facing forward, but in the context of the painting, facing the knight as well—with an apple resting in her palm. The painted woman, like the knight, was thrown into dramatic light and shadow, with the apple in her hand as the apparent light source.

Dulci's painted face exuded both confidence and encouragement, as if she were telling the ridiculous knight it was okay to climb off his ragged horse and take her apple. That, even though he seemed prepared to skewer her with his lance, he had nothing to fear from her.

In contrast, the Knight wore a dangerous expression equal parts confusion and rage. Dulci recognized it well from her years at Arbor Hospital. It was the face of a paranoid schizophrenic having a very bad day.

Dulci had read *Don Quijote* enough times to recognize the portrait's literary foundation. Don Quijote, the utterly insane self proclaimed knight of Spain, travels around the country questing against progressively more ridiculous foes—famously attacking a windmill at one point, believing it to be a dragon—all for the sake of a working class girl in his village named Aldonza whom he idealizes as "Princess Dulcinea," and for whom Dulci had been named.

Except that the scene painted down on the Roman wall had not happened in the story. Quijote never introduces himself to Aldonza, and is thus able to maintain his perfect notion of her as a damsel in distress.

"What if *el Quijote* had met her, though?" Dulci recalled her father remarking in his deep smoker's voice after a nightly reading session at the dinner table. "Imagine his terrible frustration with Aldonza that she was not only oblivious to the deeds he had carried out in her name, but that she'd never needed him to begin with. Might he not turn his weapon on her in that moment for forcing him to realize his noble war was ridiculous and unnecessary?"

Dulci wanted nothing more than to study every inch of the painting up close, but she saw that the crowd below had doubled again in size since she'd climbed onto the balcony. She nearly despaired until she remembered that her father had insisted she bring his heavy Zeiss field glasses so she wouldn't miss a single saint or gargoyle carved high up into the side of a cathedral. She wrestled the field glasses from their leather case in her backpack with numb fingers and held them to her eyes.

Alexander's unhappy sneer leapt at her from under his warped helmet. She quickly swung the binoculars to the right, running her view down the striped lance aimed at the heart of the offered apple and, ultimately, her own heart.

She stopped suddenly and swung back to the left. On the three widest stripes nearest to the lance's hilt—Dulci reflected that she would have been a woefully inept student of psychology had she not recognized the lance's blatant Freudian symbolism—were three capitalized words: *WAR IS PEACE.*

She let the field glasses drop from her eyes. Americanus Rex hadn't just selected her at random. Of course he hadn't. Seeing her old letter to Imogene in the newspaper was already proof of that.

But *why?* Dulci hadn't recognized the man in the flannel shirt or the Chinese man who'd spoken to her on his friend's behalf. So how had Rex known enough about her to create such stark representations of her own internal misgivings about Alexander, her personal politics, and her father's musings on a five hundred year old book?

A good question, but one that required no answer. At least not for Dulci. The Don Quijotes of the world had quested against phantom giants and dragons in the name of supposedly helpless women for long enough. If Imogene Cornell and her tall companion in the newspaper were any indication, the Dulcineas of the world were finally questing for themselves.

And this Dulcinea, like the original, was far from helpless.

STRANGERS IN ACCORD, PART 2

1

Monday, August 29, 2011

Main Street in Accord looked just as it had the first time Imogene had seen it, except for the time of day. Faded brick façades rose on either side of the street. Sidewalks shimmered in the noonday sun, free of any speck of litter. Through the open driver's side window of her rented pickup, Imogene clearly heard the quaint creaking of the town's traffic signal on its crisscrossing wires and the soft clatter of the ancient air conditioner propped in the front window of the town diner.

"I still don't see why we couldn't have just brought the Prius," Ben groused, sinking lower in his seat.

Imogene didn't respond. Her brother had voiced this complaint several times since they had left the airport, his mood growing fouler with each repetition. But Droon's envelope had included a voucher for Enterprise Rent-A-Car, and thus far Droon hadn't seemed to do anything without a reason. So she and Ben had located the Enterprise desk after their flight, and to Ben's great dismay the only vehicle left on the lot had been a Chevrolet Silverado.

"Six-liter vee-eight," the teenager working the desk had told her reverently. "She'll haul two thousand pounds without losing more'n a second off the line. I can bolt on the hitch if you all are looking to pull a boat or camping trailer."

"Thanks, we're embarrassed enough already," Ben had said. "You sure we can't get different car?"

The kid had checked the computer after a sidelong glance that Ben bore gracelessly. "No sir. Your reservation is for a full size pickup, and the Silverado's the only one we got. I couldn't switch you to another class of vehicle either. Busy time of year with all the tourists visiting the Appalachian Trail."

Once they had climbed aboard the Silverado—a shining blue fortress of a truck with four doors and a deep cargo bed lined with hard black plastic—Imogene had reminded Ben that Priscilla's rock wouldn't fit in his Toyota, a fact which had only soured him further.

"Look on the bright side," she told him now. "People in Accord might find a new respect for you when they see you in a Chevy."

"That's what I'm afraid of," he said, his voice so grim that Imogene couldn't help laughing. He glared up at her, slouched so low in the seat that only the crown of his head would be visible from outside. "I hope you know how ridiculous you look right now," he told her. "What day is it?"

"Monday the twenty-ninth," she said. "Oliver's exhibit opened this morning. I would have liked being around for that."

"So it's the same day we left London? I'm going to fall asleep on my feet in the shower." He rubbed his eyes and sighed. "Okay, remind me what the burning bush told you again."

"If you mean Droon, he said I need to collect Priscilla's portrait from General's Peak. He acted like he already knew we were planning to send it to Los Angeles."

"Piece of cake," Ben yawned.

"And while we're at it, we need to convince the townspeople that Priscilla's portrait is both respectful and important so they don't condemn Gary as an un-American pervert when the media eventually arrive in Accord and start asking questions."

"No problem."

"Oh, and I forgot to tell you earlier that Priscilla asked if we would visit her family and tell them she's alright."

Ben's false cheer vanished and he stared out the window. "Hell," he murmured, his voice almost lost under the hum of the Chevy's tires on Main Street. "So what's our first stop?"

"You know the town better than I do, but I think we'll need somebody with influence to be on our side before we try to recruit the small army we'll need to move Priscilla's portrait."

He watched the alley leading to his apartment as Imogene drove past it. "Got anyone in mind?"

She swung the pickup into a parallel parking spot in front of Pritchard's Corner.

"Glenn Pritchard is a responsible business owner, a respected member of town, and he's Gary's dad. Good place to start?" she added self-consciously.

He looked closely at her for the first time since they had pulled onto the winding highway between Charleston and Accord. She watched him stuff away his foul temper the way he had always stuffed his toys into a clothes hamper whenever their mother had asked them to clean the room they shared.

"Yeah, it's a good place to start," he said. He even managed to stifle further comments about the Silverado as he climbed from the cab onto the sidewalk, using the side running board like a stepladder.

She met him coming around the truck's high front grill and touched his shoulder. "I know this week hasn't been what you planned."

He barked a short laugh that contained a promising dose of actual mirth. "Nobody could have planned this week. By the way, you should know that by now everyone in town will have connected the two of us with Gary Pritchard's dramatic departure from reality."

"I'm the Catalyst, remember?"

He smiled at that, though not as widely as she had hoped. He'd been uncharacteristically grave about the title Droon had written on her envelope in London.

"Yes, well," he said. "If you can do to Glenn Pritchard what you did to those reporters in the Tate, he'll be lapping his weak coffee from your cupped palms two minutes after we walk into his store."

She blushed at that. The British press had agreed with him. Before she and Ben had left London, Oliver had showered her with clippings from the morning's newspapers. Descriptions of her and Ellen's brief question-and-answer session had ranged from "formidable" to "majestic," the latter being so absurd to Imogene's thinking that she had pitched the article into Ben's lap with a derisive snort.

"That one's just getting close to the truth," he'd insisted. "You should have seen yourself up there, Gene. You and Ellen both. You just—" he'd wriggled his fingers, searching for the correct word, "—*crackled* with this energy. Like the whole room was filling up with invisible electricity."

A few writers had nonetheless pointed out that neither Ellen nor Imogene had any real authority in world politics, but even they had made note of what *The Guardian* had called the women's "lively discourse and arresting presence."

Imogene pushed these thoughts away as she entered Pritchard's Corner; she would need her full concentration and "majesty" for the task at hand. The sleigh bells hanging inside the front door jingled just as merrily as they had done the first time Imogene had entered Pritchard's Corner. Just like the town itself, the mountains of stuff neatly clogging the general store hadn't changed a whit in the last four days.

But when the saloon doors behind the main counter of Pritchard's Corner creaked open to reveal Glenn Pritchard, Imogene couldn't quite stifle a gasp. The man had aged twenty years in the last four days. The formerly broad line of his shoulders had broken, dragging the subtle stoop of his back into a full slouch. Deep vertical lines ran from the sides of his nose all the way down past the corners of his mouth.

The color of his skin gave the impression that he'd fallen into a pile of ash and not bothered to wash it off. He paled even further when he saw the identity of his customers.

"What do you want?"

Imogene had been prepared for anger, fright, or resentment from the man. She was not prepared for the husky, somehow resigned moan that came out of him now.

Then, as if remembering that he ran a business, he said, "Grill's closed today." He turned and shuffled back toward the saloon doors.

"Mr. Pritchard," she began.

He wheeled around, his eyes blazing cold fire from too deep in his face. But he wasn't looking at her. He was looking at Ben.

"You couldn't leave her alone, could you? I knew your desire for Priscilla Hemphill as well as anyone in town but I never imagined you would root through my garbage to thieve her away from Gary. Well you got her now, and my boy is gone. Take your prize and leave."

Ben took a step backward. "I was trying to help."

"We know where Gary is," Imogene said, trying to draw Glenn's attention from her brother. "He's safe. I saw him in England."

Glenn eyed her warily. "You saw him?"

She nodded. "A museum in London is showing two of his paintings right now. A lot of people believe he's doing important work."

"Gary did important work right here in this store."

Glenn turned to leave again, but Imogene stepped forward and pressed her shaking hands on the glass countertop between them. "Priscilla Hemphill is in England right now, and will soon be traveling to France because she believes Gary's actions can be made into something powerful and good. I'm asking you to do the same thing. Help us do something powerful and good right here in Accord."

Glenn half faced her with one hand resting on the top seam between the batwing doors leading into his storage room. "You all sound just like Aggie. This would've been easier if you'd stayed gone."

"No, it wouldn't have," Imogene said.

"Go talk to Aggie," Glenn said.

He pushed through the batwing doors and disappeared into the back of his store.

2

Imogene closed her eyes and took several slow breaths of the warm air outside Pritchard's Corner. She had been in the store for no more than two minutes, yet it had been enough time to chill her to the bone.

"That man thinks we ruined his life," she said quietly. She willed her hands to stop shaking.

"I completely disagree," Ben said. "He's angry. You know what Dad says about anger."

Imogene closed her eyes and sighed. "It's an honest and healthy emotion."

"And it means you're about to make a very good or very bad decision," Ben finished. "Glenn struck me as a man on the edge of a big decision and he's struggling to deal with it. He doesn't believe that tripe about his life being easier if we hadn't come back any more than we do. Now come on," he said, steering her back toward the driver's side door of the Silverado with a comforting arm around her shoulders. "Let's take his advice and pay someone else a visit."

"Agnes?"

"Couldn't hurt. And anyway, didn't she invite us over for a meal when we dropped her off that night after the hike?"

"I don't think so."

"Well, I'm sure she meant to."

Agnes lived only two blocks from Pritchard's Corner. Imogene turned right off of CR 20 and parallel parked across the street from Agnes's house. It was small, square, and solid looking, much like the woman herself. Tiny blue flowers grew in boxes fixed under the curtained windows and on either side of the narrow concrete steps leading to the door.

Ben was across the street and knocking on the front door by the time Imogene exited the pickup. She joined him in time to see the door crack open. Agnes's thick, round spectacles floated in the doorway like an owl's eyes peering from a tree trunk burrow.

Then the door was thrown wide and Agnes emerged onto the concrete stoop, squinting in the midday sun and clutching Imogene's wrist as if trying to convince herself she wasn't hallucinating.

"I saw you all on TV not three hours ago. But it said you were in England. The *painting* he made of you, dear…"

The older woman gazed at her with such unguarded wonder that Imogene felt her cheeks start to burn. "We just got into town," she said.

Agnes glanced at Ben, then at the Silverado parked at the curb. "Priscilla already gone home?"

"She decided to stay in England for now," Ben said.

Agnes grunted. "Maybe that's best." She released Imogene's wrist and hobbled back over the threshold of her front door. "Are you all hungry? I'll warn you ahead of time that I haven't entertained guests in a very long time."

Agnes's house was clean almost to the point of sterility. The three of them clustered into a short hallway that connected Agnes's kitchen and living room. In the latter, Imogene caught a glimpse of the pink afghan Agnes had worn on the two previous occasions they'd met, folded over the back of a dark wooden rocking chair that faced a fireplace. Just before Imogene turned away to follow Agnes into the kitchen, the tufted ears and large golden eyes of a cat rose above the arm of an olive green love seat to regard her with kingly interest.

The stove and refrigerator shared a similar shade of green as Agnes's (or possibly her cat's) love seat in the living room. The counter tops were white with inlaid gold star patterns. The only items in the kitchen that didn't fit the ultra clean 1970's decor were a small TV/VCR on the counter and an antique table scooted against the wall with two simple wooden chairs at its head and foot.

Agnes swept one of the table's hinged leaves up into the horizontal position and locked it. "Have a seat. You all look tired."

Ben groaned theatrically as he sat. "Guilty as charged. Fifteen hours of travel will do that to a person. Especially two times in...what?" He glanced at Imogene. "Three days?"

"Something like that."

Agnes was pulling jars from the refrigerator and setting them on the counter. "The night we met at the foot of the Peak, you told me you were interested in Priscilla's portrait because of a connection between your mother and something Gary Pritchard said, which according to town natter over the last couple days is that he would," she paused as if preparing to deliver a speech, "'light a beacon of peace from the top of the world.'"

Imogene and Ben nodded together.

"The first time I heard those words I took them for a strange figure of speech, and I would probably still take them as such except for what I heard you say on the news this morning. I don't mind telling you all I'm ready to burst with curiosity. I'd hear your part in our town's drama from the beginning, if you'd tell it."

The story came more quickly and naturally this time than it had with Teddy. Imogene began with the church service on the previous Wednesday night, breaking off to describe the 1968 Miss Washington pageant where her mother had spoken the words that had so dominated Imogene's life in the last five days. Their experiences in London came next.

Agnes stopped her partway through her description of the Tate's press conference. "Saw much of that for myself this morning," she said. "And now you all're back here for the rock."

Imogene couldn't quite suppress a guilty wince, nor could her brother. Neither had forgotten Agnes's fierce protectiveness of Priscilla's portrait the night she'd taken them up to see it.

The woman nodded as if they'd agreed aloud, her shrewd eyes calm. "When I saw you all on TV I knew the rock wouldn't stay a secret. Not that I think it should," she assured them. "Not anymore. I just couldn't believe it when I saw you on my front stoop. After the news this morning I figured you'd be on Gary Pritchard's trail in Spain. Though I suppose—"

"Spain?" Imogene interrupted. Droon himself had hinted that Gary was on his way to Paris, and Priscilla's and Ellen's airplane tickets had all but confirmed it.

"You haven't heard," Agnes said in obvious disbelief.

"Heard what?" Ben said.

"Words won't do it justice," Agnes said, lifting a small TV remote off the counter.

Agnes's cat, which Imogene now saw was the size of an adult raccoon, trotted silently into the kitchen, its bushy tail pointing straight up in the air. For such an imposing beast it mewed at Agnes in a surprisingly delicate voice.

"Not now, Simon," Agnes cooed absently. The VCR geared up into a high whine as she rewound the tape. "I record the Pet Shop show late Sunday nights to watch with Simon Monday mornings. He likes the rabbits," she explained. "Otherwise I wouldn't have had a tape ready for…here we are. You all watch while I make lunch."

Simon made no more noise, but he wove affectionate figure-eights between Agnes's legs while she chopped pickled eggs into a bowl and topped them with generous globs of mayonnaise and sweet relish. This mixture she began scooping liberally onto thick slices of homemade bread.

But Imogene hardly noticed any of this. An image of herself and Ellen on the platform in the Tate Modern had popped onto the TV screen. Now that she didn't have to worry about answering the reporters' questions, she saw for herself what the newspapers had meant. Under the harsh lights and tireless flashbulbs, she and Ellen looked like comic book superheroines, white hot and radiant with the power to move worlds.

The newscast cut to an anchor in a studio. "Only hours after the press conference in London, Americanus Rex added to his growing publicity by painting his third controversial and highly public portrait in as many days, this time near Madrid, Spain."

The image cut to a long reddish wall with what looked like thousands of people grouped before it as calmly as visitors in the Tate Modern. The camera quickly zoomed in above the people's heads to focus on the new portrait.

Imogene and Ben leaned forward together. Agnes had ceased her food preparations to watch at the screen as well.

The little TV showed a bizarre silver cartoonish knight on an equally cartoonish horse—neither was poorly drawn by any means, but aside from Gary's trademark ultra high contrast of light and shadow, the two figures were a vast change from his realistic style—aiming a long lance at a woman standing before him with one arm held out in what Imogene initially took for a defensive posture. But when the camera completed its zoom she realized that the woman's posture and expression were miles away from defense. She had large eyes full of caring and intelligence, and there was nothing tentative about the way she offered her would-be attacker a bright silver apple in her hand.

The camera swooped away well before Imogene finished her study— the painted woman seemed distantly familiar, much like Droon had seemed familiar the first time Imogene had seen him on the airplane— and resettled on the face of the cartoon knight. Rather than the simple, swooping lines of the knight's armor and horse, his face was just as realistic as that of the woman opposite him. He wore a terrible battle sneer that Imogene quickly realized was an expression closer to terror than satisfaction. His close set eyes seemed almost to shift back and forth as if he wished he could be doing anything besides jousting with the formidable woman in front of him.

Agnes set the sandwiches she'd made on the table and both of them began to eat at once. The image on TV cut back to the studio.

"The Spanish government has already granted the Reina Sofia Museum of modern art in Madrid custody of Americanus Rex's latest painting, provided that the museum will begin immediate plans to preserve and relocate the ancient Roman wall to a permanent indoor display," the anchor said.

A second anchor in the studio took over. "Of course, not all participants in the Council of Paris regard Americanus Rex's paintings so highly. This morning the Vice President spoke out against what the White House is calling 'Rex Mania.'"

The Vice President appeared on camera, looking typically well quaffed and surly. "Look, Americanus Rex might make for good television, but he doesn't have much to do with foreign policy. Name me an artist who has prevented the famine, pestilence, or death that come as natural parts of large scale war. Yet the President is in Paris to do just that right now. That kind of real world problem solving might not come in pretty silver paint, but it can help you sleep at night."

Imogene pointed at the television, outraged. "Am I the only one who just caught another apocalypse reference?"

"Famine, Pestilence, War, and Death," Agnes agreed, switching off the TV. "The Four Horsemen of the Apocalypse."

"How is *that* supposed to help people sleep at night?" Imogene demanded.

"Political balderdashery, and secondary to our business," Agnes said dismissively. She leaned back against the counter, eyes glittering behind her thick glasses. "So when do you want to get Priscilla's rock off the mountain?"

3

Ben and Imogene exchanged a glance. "That's a terrific question," Ben said slowly. "But we won't know the 'when' until we can answer the much peskier 'how.'"

Agnes waved a hand. "How we liberate the rock isn't any of your worry, as you'd know if you thought about it for any length of time."

One of Ben's eyebrows rose. "Why don't we back up a few hundred paces. You seem to know we're here for Priscilla's portrait. I can accept that. But have you also puzzled out how to carry that thing down from General's Peak?"

"All I've puzzled out, young man, is that if the rock comes off the mountain at all, it'll take more than the three of us. I just need to know when you all plan to leave town again, so I know when I have to bite the bullet and call everyone together."

"You understand that we're probably talking about selling Priscilla's portrait to the highest bidder, right?" Imogene asked. "I don't mean to be crass, but you should know the situation. You seemed pretty protective of the portrait the last time we spoke."

Agnes shifted against the counter. "At sundown on the day after you all left for London, I had my first visitor at home in almost ten years."

"Who was it?" Imogene asked.

"Calliope Garfield. Curtis's granddaddy, if that helps you."

"The one who called you to look for Curtis the night Gary painted Priscilla," Imogene clarified.

"Him, yes. After the scene that night between Gary and Cody Hemphill, word got out that Curtis had been the first to find Priscilla's rock."

"How?" Ben asked.

Agnes smiled dryly. "Word always gets out in Accord, dear. It may not reach your ears just yet, but wait until you've lived here as long as I have. I don't leave my house during the day except to the grocer once a week, and I still hear plenty of scandal whether I listen for it or not.

"At any rate," she continued, "Calliope told me Curtis cried most of the night after he saw what passed between Cody and Gary."

Imogene clicked her tongue in sympathy. "Poor kid."

Ben's jaw clenched—Imogene remembered his fury the other night when he had seen Curtis in the lineup of blank faces on Main Street—but he managed to keep silent while Anges spoke.

"Curtis kept saying he was sorry he'd found the rock and caused so much trouble, but maybe he could take other people from town up the mountain to see that it didn't make Priscilla ugly the way Cody had said."

"I'm sure that idea didn't take hold," Ben said bitterly.

"You'd be surprised," Agnes told him. "A child's despair can move people in unexpected ways. In the case of Calliope Garfield, it moved him to my doorstep. The few people in this town who still acknowledge my existence also know of my nightly excursions up the Peak, and old Cal requested that I take him along to see Priscilla's rock for himself. His eyes don't work so well in the dark anymore and he didn't fancy snapping an ankle in a sinkhole halfway up the trail."

"That's amazing," Imogene said. "That he was willing to see for himself, I mean."

"Not half as amazing as what Cal and I saw on the mountain that night," Agnes said.

"People," Ben guessed, his jaw starting to relax. "Other people in town got the same idea as Calliope Garfield and went to see for themselves, didn't they?"

Agnes smiled grimly, but with unmistakable satisfaction. "Not a one of them said boo to me or Cal, but we met fully seven other little groups either on the trail or at the summit. Looked like they'd just heard the voice of the Lord Almighty from the burning bush."

Imogene and Ben exchanged another glance.

"That doesn't make sense, though," Imogene said. "Glenn Pritchard acted like Gary had left Accord to become a bank robber or something."

"You saw Glenn today?"

"It wasn't as bad as all that, Gene," Ben said reprovingly. "Glenn was a still a little tense, that's all."

Agnes sighed. "It's not easy to go against the opinion of everyone you've ever known, even if you're siding with your son to do it. Glenn needs to make a decision."

"Ha!" Ben said triumphantly.

"He didn't seem like he was siding with Gary today," Imogene said. "Or even accepting of him. I mean, if everyone's gone up to see the portrait and thinks it's wonderful…"

"Cal and I saw at most twenty people," Agnes reminded her. "I'd say twice that many have made the trip in the days since Gary left. That leaves a couple hundred who haven't. And a couple hundred who won't buy their goods at Pritchard's Corner for fear of having to look Glenn in the eye. Small towns adore whispered scandal, but they don't do so well when it's out in the open."

Imogene set her elbows heavily on the table and rubbed her eyes. The sandwich had rejuvenated her briefly, but now a full stomach just made her want to crawl into the nearest bed.

"That won't make my job any easier," she sighed.

"Your job, dear?"

She lowered her hands to find Agnes intently watching her once more through those owlish bifocals. "I'm not just here for the rock. I'd also hoped to convince as many people as possible that Priscilla is proud of her portrait and everything else Gary is doing. Maybe get them on our side before the news cameras come to Accord."

"I can't believe the cameras aren't here *yet,*" Ben said, swallowing the last of his sandwich. "I almost expected to see a newspaper in Charleston this morning with a headline like, 'Man Threatens to Shoot Sister's Fiancé while Town Looks On.'"

Agnes grunted humorlessly. "That story will never make any newspaper."

"The whole town saw Cody try to kill Gary, including the kids," Ben growled. "They can brush off my questions about UFOs and Men in Black all they want, but they can't just tell an investigating police officer to go fly a kite. That's called obstruction of jus—"

"Police?" Agnes said loudly. "This town doesn't *have* a police force."

"Yeah, but—"

"And I promise you no one called the department in Point Pleasant. We take care of our own."

"That doesn't make any sense," Ben insisted. "There had to be some kind of report filed when Cody was checked into the hospital with gun-related injuries."

"How many young men do you think visit a doctor with powder burns or buck shot in their backsides from hunting accidents? Unless you think Cody Hemphill told the doctor the real circumstances of his injuries."

Ben had no answer to that. Imogene could see him debating whether to tell Agnes that Priscilla had also been with her brother in the ambulance, but the Priscilla Hemphill they'd known last Thursday wouldn't have told a doctor what really happened either.

"This town will ignore what it wants to ignore," Agnes said with oddly wistful finality. "I'm living proof of that."

"People here don't ignore you," Imogene objected. "Curtis Garfield talked about you breaking your leg. And Priscilla said something about you not being a demon from hell."

Ben's eyebrows knit in a pained expression. Agnes simply stared at her.

"You remember," Imogene said, her cheeks starting to burn. "In the car. That night after we hiked the mountain?"

Agnes let loose a cackle, breaking the clouds that had gathered in the kitchen. "I suppose you've got a point, dear. I'm just as guilty as the rest of them. I've ignored the rest of the town for the last ten years, nursing my self-righteous pride and waiting for an apology that will never come. I let them turn me into a ghost."

"You've called yourself that before," Imogene said. "What happened to you?"

But Agnes shook her head and began clearing the table. "I will only tell that story once today. Less, if I can help it. You all have other errands in Accord?"

"Priscilla asked us to let her family know she's alright," Imogene said.

"Now's as good a time as any," Agnes said. "We'll meet up again at the church tonight at seven. That should be time enough for me to draw a crowd."

"What are you going to do?" Ben asked.

"What any ghost does to be noticed." A mischievous gleam shone behind Agnes's bifocals. "Rattle my chains."

4

The Hemphills' ranch rested in a shallow bowl of land half a mile northeast of downtown. Yellow dust puffed around Imogene's sandals as she slid out of the pickup onto the rutted gravel lane. Up ahead, the lane emptied into a vague L shape in front of a gray two-storey house. A low wooden porch with a simple slate roof ran across the entire front of the house. Five second-floor windows, their screens caked with a layer of light brown dust, stared grimly down upon a yellowing lawn. A much newer barn painted in similar gray rose behind the house like the rump of a sleeping dragon.

"Nice place. Bit of a fixer-upper," Imogene said, just for something to say.

Ben shook his head slowly. "You should have seen the farm when I came here with my students in May. Yard was mowed, house clean. Even the dirt in the horse corral was smooth and uniform. Cody must have taken a rake and a shovel to it everyday."

She wondered where all the horses were now. This close to the house she would have expected to hear them prancing around the corral or whinnying in their stables, but except for cicadas droning in the surrounding woods, silence hung about the place like fog.

They walked passed an ancient International Harvester farm truck sitting in the front yard. Like the house, Imogene could tell someone had once taken decent care of it but now long yellow grass reached up over the running boards and rust pitted the wheel rims.

"Do you think anyone's home?" she asked in a near whisper.

She was actually grateful for the cicadas. Without them, she and Ben would be in a real-life horror movie, trapped in the seconds of dead quiet just before a monster jumped out at them.

All at once a sharp, piercing squeal erupted from somewhere behind the house. Ben and Imogene clutched each other's arms in the front yard like Hansel and Gretel before the witch's cauldron. However, the squeal dissolved into giddy laughter and two sweaty boys came tearing around the corner of the house, shushing each other dramatically as if they'd both just remembered they weren't supposed to be making noise. Imogene recognized them immediately as Curtis Garfield and Priscilla's quiet, gray eyed younger brother, Jamie.

"Masters Hemphill and Garfield, I presume," Ben said formally.

Jamie greeted them impassively. "Afternoon, Mister Cornell. Miss Cornell."

Curtis shot a nervous glance at the house, then smiled nervously at Ben and offered a quick, awkward wave to Imogene. "'Lo again, ma'am."

"Listen, Jamie," Ben said, "your sister asked us to come see your mom. Is she at home?"

"You know where Prissy's at?" Jamie asked suspiciously. He shifted his feet constantly, giving Imogene the impression that his world had gotten a lot bigger and a lot less safe in the last few days. "She said she was leavin for awhile but wouldn't tell where."

"She's fine," Ben assured him. "After what happened to your brother she thought it might be a good idea to stay out of town for a little while."

The firm line of Jamie's mouth finally quivered and he was a boy again. "You can tell me where she is," he said in a trying-to-be-brave voice that broke Imogene's heart. "Ma's still upset but I won't tell her. Prissy knows I can keep a secr—"

"*James Nehemiah Hemphill?*" a female voice bellowed from inside the house.

Curtis instantly bolted for the back yard as if a hungry mountain lion were at his heels.

"Curtis ain't here," Jamie stage whispered to Ben and Imogene once Curtis had disappeared into the trees at the edge of the property. "Wadn't *ever.*"

He raised his voice. "In the yard, Maw! We got visitors."

Moments later, one of the widest women Imogene had ever seen puffed through the front door onto the porch. A floorboard cracked like a gunshot under her weight. Ben and Imogene received a distrustful grimace, but her real attention was reserved for her youngest son.

"Emma Louise just phoned wantin Curtis. I told her he ain't been in my house since before the weekend. I weren't lyin to her, I hope."

"You told her the God's honest truth," Jamie said earnestly.

Her mouth compressed to a white scar in her hard, round face. "You finish muckin them stalls?"

"I came to greet our visitors," he said. "Can't quit bein hospitable just because—"

"Those stalls is clean by supper or you don't git none."

"Yes, ma'am." Jamie raced off in the same direction his friend had gone moments before.

Imogene shifted uneasily under Mrs. Hemphill's glare. Ben stepped cordially to the porch and held out his hand. "Afternoon, Mrs. Hemphill. Ben Cornell."

When it was obvious he wouldn't lower his hand, she slapped her own hand against her expansive apron, raising a white cloud of flour, and shook grudgingly.

"I teach at Jamie's school," Ben continued. "My room's just down the hall from Priscilla's. I'm not sure if you remember, but I came out here a few months ago to see the horses with the sixth graders?"

She eyed Imogene even more suspiciously. "I amember," she said finally. "Horses is gone, though. Glue factory up in Wheeling picked em up just this mornin. Jamie's still scrubbin the last of the gunk from the stables."

Imogene thought Ben hid his shock well. "I'm sorry to hear that... I, uh." He paused, obviously reorganizing his thoughts. "This is my sister, Imogene. It might sound strange, but Priscilla asked us to come talk to you."

As Mrs. Hemphill pondered him, time slowed to a dead stop. Scents of hot grass and dirt mingled with the sweet, welcoming odors of baking drifting from inside the house. Sunlight glinted on sharp bits of tan and black shale in the yard. Even the music of the cicadas seemed to slow. Except for Imogene's growing unease regarding the emotional stability of Mrs. Hemphill, the moment would have been idyllic.

The woman seemed to make a decision and time flowed normally again. "You all care for some pie? Come on inside."

She rotated her massive body toward the door and Imogene noticed purple stretch marks on the backs of her knees under the hem of her dress. Her skin looked taut and shiny, as if her obesity was a recent development.

"That sounds lovely," Ben said, holding the screen door open for Imogene.

They followed Mrs. Hemphill through a long dining room with a heavy table planted in the middle. Dust covered every inch of the table, the wood floor, and the simple chandelier hanging off-center over the table.

Not dust, Imogene realized, *baking flour.*

As they entered the kitchen, Imogene slipped in the flour covering the linoleum floor and would likely have cracked her tailbone if Ben hadn't caught her wrist. Mrs. Hemphill seemed not to notice. She picked up a rolling pin and set to work on one of the piles of dough on the counter. The motion obviously calmed her.

The crust beneath her rolling pin quickly became smooth and paper-thin. Three expert sweeps of the spatula separated it completely from the counter. She draped her perfect crust over a mound of what appeared to be rhubarb in a pie tin and slid the whole works into the oven behind her. Two more pies sizzled merrily inside, one of which she pulled out with a hot pad and set on a stand to cool.

"You all can take this here blackberry when you go," she said, sounding neither eager nor disappointed at the prospect of their leaving. "Glenn sells em uptown as well, bless him."

She rubbed a handful of flour up and down her rolling pin and started the process over again. Her stroke stayed steady and firm, but tears dripped from her downturned eyes. She rolled over the wet spots in the dough without pausing.

"So you all've seen my Priscilla," she continued. "Does she know I owe the hospital in Point Pleasant fifteen thousand dollars for putting my Cody back together after Gary Pritchard shot him with his own gun?"

Imogene frowned. "Gary didn't shoot anybody. It was the other way ar—"

Mrs. Hemphill's red-rimmed eyes glittered. "Cody told me what happened when he come home, so I hope you all ain't callin my boy a liar in my own house. I won't have it. Not after everything else that's happened."

"Mrs. Hemphill, we didn't come to argue or insult any member of your family," Ben said calmly. "But if you've heard enough of the truth that you're keeping Jamie away from his best friend, then you know my sister is no liar."

"How *dare* you?" Mrs. Hemphill breathed. "I invite you into my house—"

"And we appreciate it," Ben interrupted, calmer than ever. "But we also came here at the request of your daughter, as we told you. I don't quite understand it all myself, but Priscilla said that when she saw Gary's painting of her, she realized that she'd been ashamed of being a woman."

The rolling pin clattered to the counter and gouged ugly holes in Mrs. Hemphill's perfect dough. Her cheeks had gone patchy white below her eyes, which looked round and large as dinner plates.

Imogene was also staring at her brother. Priscilla had never mentioned any of this to her.

Ben seemed not to notice their reactions. "She said she tried to tell you this, but your grief over Cody's injuries were too fresh. She also said she believes you'll understand and come to terms with what she's talking about, even if it is difficult for you. She respects you a great deal, Mrs. Hemphill. After Earl passed away, I heard Priscilla say that she has never met a stronger woman than her mother."

Mrs. Hemphill studied Ben carefully for a few seconds before heaving a sigh that seemed to originate somewhere around the soles of her feet and travel all the way up her body and out her mouth.

"I reckon all three of my children is liars now." She lifted the blackberry pie from the cooling rack and handed it to Ben. "You don't want to touch the bottom of the tin just yet. Hold it here, by the lip. I appreciate you all comin out here."

5

"So that was fun," Ben said once they were back in the Silverado, driving down the dirt lane leading away from Hemphill Ranch.

"You got her attention, though," Imogene said. "Somehow I feel better about how that ended than our visit with Glenn. Where did you get that thing about Priscilla being ashamed to be a woman?"

Ben shrugged. "Priscilla started talking about it that first night in London, when you and Teddy went to the museum. She wasn't making a whole lot of sense to be honest, and like I said, I didn't understand it all." He dipped his finger into one of the decorative holes in the pie crust and tasted the filling. "Now *that's* a pie. Wow."

"At least we did what Priscilla wanted us to do."

Ben nodded, dipping his finger again. "Where to now?"

"Home," she said, running a hand through her hair. Between the hours of circulated air on the airplane, the West Virginia humidity, and the clouds of flour in Mrs. Hemphill's kitchen, it felt like steel wool. "The only thing that could keep me from a one hour bath right now is another visit from Droon, and he's back in London."

Ben leaned against the headrest and closed his eyes. "That's the most sensible thing you've said all day."

Sunlight dappled the truck's gray dashboard until Imogene pulled from the dirt lane back onto the paved road leading to town.

"What did she mean her kids were all liars?" she wondered aloud. "She obviously knew Jamie was still playing with Curtis. I suppose she was admitting that she didn't believe Gary had shot Cody after all. But what does she think Priscilla's lying about?"

"Being ashamed of being a woman?" Ben hazarded.

Imogene shook her head. "No, that definitely struck a nerve. Even if you didn't know what it meant, Priscilla's mom did."

"Maybe she thinks Priscilla is just pretending to be okay with Gary leaving her."

"Hmm," Imogene said noncommittally. "Did you ever read anything about the Men in Black seeking out people who have lived through traumatic events? How many of your contactees lost a family member or experienced some other trauma at a young age? I mean, think about the all the crap we've survived between us, Priscilla and Ellen. And Agnes, too. She broke her leg really badly when she was ten, right?"

Ben shrugged. "Every kid has some kind of traumatic experience. That's just part of being a kid. Hell, my four years of junior high were nothing but one long traumatic experience."

Imogene shook her head again. "I'm talking about a single event. For us it was when Mom died. For Ellen it was, well, she had a big one too. For Agnes it was when she broke her leg. She still climbs that mountain everyday, for heaven's sake. In one way or another, none of us have gotten over what happened when we were younger."

Ben drew a steaming blackberry from a widening hole in the pie crust and blew on it thoughtfully.

"I wonder what happened to Priscilla," Imogene said.

"You just met her mother," Ben said. "She might have a pretty healthy laundry list of traumas to choose from."

"Only one," Imogene insisted. "Something big. Remember the way she tore off her dress on her front porch the other night after church? Tell me there wasn't any emotional history behind that."

Ben said nothing.

"Don't like my theories?" she asked, trying not to sound defensive.

He shrugged again. "Psychologically, I suppose it would make sense. Maybe the Men in Black supposedly target people like us because, after the unbelievable offense of losing our mother, we're more prepared to deal with a second unbelievable scenario. My thing is, does it really matter why Droon came looking for us? Is there any answer that would make you give up being his Catalyst?"

Neither of them needed her to respond.

"It is an interesting idea, though," he allowed. "I'll need to check a few of my books back at the apartment, but you might be onto something there."

Five minutes later they trudged up the single flight of stairs to Ben's apartment, Ben wearing the backpack he'd taken to London and carrying Mrs. Hemphill's pie, Imogene with her carryall slung across her chest on its single strap. Ben dug his apartment keys out of his pocket, but when he tried to stick the key in, the door snicked open.

"That can't be good," Ben said. "Let me go in first. Take this."

Before she could object, he handed her the pie, pushed the door open the rest of the way, and strode into the apartment. She followed him immediately and almost smashed the pie against his back when he stopped dead, two steps inside.

"What the balls?" he demanded.

Imogene peeked around him and found Lord Droon sitting primly on Ben's puffy red couch with a serene smile on his face. A half empty liter bottle of Evian water sat on the coffee table. He'd even found a coaster.

"You are late," Droon said.

"How did you get in here?" Ben asked.

Droon gave him a mildly reproachful glance, as if Ben had asked how a cat is able to catch a mouse. Imogene remembered how the electronically sealed *Museum Staff Only* door had opened to his touch. But she was more interested in the questions she and Ben had just been exploring on the drive back into town. And wasn't it utterly convenient that the little man had shown up just in time to field those questions?

Or to deflect them, as he'd so deftly done in London.

But before she could ask even one of the galaxy of questions she'd been saving up, all of them fled her mind with a sudden realization.

She pointed at Droon. "Glenn Pritchard told us you were in his store to buy water everyday for a week. But you and I were on the same airplanes all day on Wednesday, and I never even saw you get off the plane in Charleston. I didn't think about it because I had a lot on my mind right then."

"You and me both," Ben murmured. "Holy *shit*."

Imogene took a deep breath. "You're a twin, aren't you?"

Droon didn't hesitate. "I am told there are—"

"—many people in the world who look like you," she finished irritably. "I want a real answer this time. Did you come to Accord with your brother?"

Droon's smile never faltered. "Yes."

"Who *are* you?" she asked, well aware that she'd asked precisely this question to the other Droon in London, and had received no real answer.

Droon seemed to like it as well. "Your brother told you days ago. I am the Smiling Man. I am a Man in Black. I am Lord Droon."

"Please just quit with the riddles!" she exploded. "In case you haven't figured it out yet, we're on your side. I believed your warnings about the Council of Paris and I've done everything you've asked me to do even though it has put people I care about in danger. Why can't you just tell me who you are, and why you're here, and why you chose me to be your Catalyst in the first place? Just tell me why *anything*."

Droon's attention was still on her brother, the triangular smile inside his goatee soft and kind. "Ask your question," he rasped.

Imogene turned to Ben in surprise. His face had gone ashy except for burning pink spots below his eyes. "Benny?"

"Why did I live?" he asked in the small voice of the boy he'd been twenty years ago. "Would Mom have lived if I'd died instead? Did you take her because of the deal I made with you?"

Imogene stared at her brother in uncomprehending shock. *She* had been the one to bring home the infection. Dr. Logan had said so. Ben and their mother had both gotten sick because of her. The idea that Ben had saved his own life by giving away Dulci's letter had seemed outlandish enough, but the idea that the same transaction had somehow killed their mother was positively moronic.

"Your mother originally caught our attention when she vowed to light a beacon of peace from the top of the world. In the seconds it took her to deliver those words, she not only meant what she said, she knew she could do it. The force of her will rebounded through the cosmos."

"You were one of the judges at Mom's pageant," Imogene said through suddenly numb lips. "You talked to her afterward and told her exactly what you just told us, didn't you?"

She expected him to grin, as he had done on previous occasions when she had correctly unlocked some part of his puzzling nature, but he simply shook his head.

"Not I. Though I understand why you might think it. A promise like your mother's cannot occur swiftly, nor without help. She never again attained such clarity of thought, though she came close when the two of you were born. We watched both of you to see if her strength would carry to another generation. It did not do so until she died."

He turned to Imogene. "Your desire to actualize your mother's dream has made you immensely persuasive, as you must know."

"I—"

"And you," he said to Ben, "could not have been drawn to Accord to tell our story without the link between your first encounter with my companion and the death of your mother."

Droon finally hefted the water bottle to his lips. The remaining half-liter of water disappeared in a few seconds. When he had finished, he addressed Imogene again. "You spoke the truth in London. We do indeed play doomsayers, although not because we like to do so. We are simply the best equipped for our roles, just as you are the best equipped for yours. You ask who I am? I communicate between people who would otherwise be silent to one another. That is my purpose and my identity."

He stood and padded toward the door on his absurdly tall and shiny shoes. "One more thing," Ben called. He didn't sound exactly like himself yet, but he at least sounded like an adult once more. Droon's eyebrows rose politely under the brim of his fedora. "What's the deal with the Evian?"

Droon regarded him evenly. "Sulfide reactors require a great deal of cooling, as I think you well know."

He tipped his hat and latched the door behind him.

6

Ben watched the door for several seconds after Droon left, as if waiting for the little man to return. When Droon stayed gone, he shrugged his backpack onto the floor and collapsed into his desk chair.

"What is a sulfide reactor?" Imogene asked.

Ben smiled wanly. "Another fairytale. Like a sharktopus or cold fusion."

"I don't get it."

"My Men in Black book isn't the first one I've written. It's just the first one I got serious about."

"You never told me that."

He waved her comment away irritably. "In college I started this crappy sci-fi novel about a robot built by invisible aliens who lived on earth with us. The only way they could communicate with human beings is through this robot they built and sent to our dimension with the help of a sulfide reactor."

"So what is that? Like some kind of nuclear pow—"

"It's *nothing*," he interrupted, an almost desperate edge to his voice. "I made it up. And when the book's main character learns the robot's true identity, the robot tells him, 'Sulfide reactors require a great deal of cooling.' Droon was just proving one more time that he's been watching us for a long time. Not that he needed to."

"Did your robot drink Evian water all the time?"

His lip twitched. "No, I had him taking these big shiny capsules filled with liquid nitrogen whenever he started to overheat."

Imogene said nothing. She remembered well enough that Droon had taken a large pill to stop his coughing in the Tate, and Priscilla telling her, *He's burning up.* If she had believed telling her brother these things would cheer him up—what aspiring science fiction writer wouldn't be proud that the real life Men in Black seemed to be borrowing his ideas?—she would have done so in an instant, but he seemed beyond cheering up right now. He was staring down between his knees at a spot on the floor. She wondered how hard it had been for him to ask Droon about their mother's death. How much energy he had wasted over the last twenty years keeping his guilt hidden from her.

She laid her own bag next to his and sat cross legged on the hard floor in front of him. "He's right, Benny. Mom's death had nothing to do with you."

He took a shaky breath. "The logical part of my brain has been telling me that for twenty years. But the part of me that *feels*…Gene, I didn't even stop having the dream until high school."

She didn't need him to say which dream he meant, because she had suffered the same dream herself for years after their mother had died. In this dream, their mother hadn't died at all—hadn't even been sick, in fact—and her *death* had been the dream. In that dream, her mother had squeezed her and smiled at her with such unbounded love that Imogene had finally been convinced she would get to keep on having a mother until she had kids of her own and beyond. The worst part was that Imogene had always emerged from the dream with breath stealing relief, only to have her breath stolen again moments later when she woke completely to reality.

"It was in high school," Ben continued, "that I read that Smiling Man article I told you about."

She nodded.

"Suddenly Mom's death was like a mystery to be solved. I thought maybe if I found the Smiling Man again, I could finally ask him the question I've been asking myself for the last twenty years."

"Why did you live?" Imogene whispered.

"Why did I live?" he agreed.

She was trying to come up with some comforting words to tell her brother when her cell phone erupted into its grating electronic rendition of "It's Raining Men." Ben was on his feet before he realized the sound had come from her carryall.

"It's Teddy," she apologized. "I'll call him back later."

Ben rubbed the back of his head, a ghost of a smile on his lips. "Don't worry about it. I think I'll have a shower as long as I'm up."

She clicked the answer button on her phone before "It's Raining Men" got to its second electronic *Hallelujah!*

"Genie?" Teddy yelled over roaring crowd noise in the background. "You make it back to Mississippi alright?"

"West Virginia," she corrected automatically. "We got here this morning. Where are you?"

"We're just closing down for the day. There hasn't been a quiet moment in the exhibit since we opened this morning. I assume you heard about the new portrait in Spain?"

"I saw a quick shot of it on the news."

"Did you also see there was a march today in Madrid to protest the Spanish government's involvement in the Council of Paris?"

"Really?"

"Just like you suggested at the conference," Teddy said proudly. "To be fair, Oliver says people in Spain take to the streets if they get the wrong soup order at a restaurant, but the point is that public perception of Americanus Rex has changed. They're already calling the portrait in Spain 'The Redemption of Eve.'"

"All that happened today? Over here they're talking still about the Council of Paris in terms of the end of the world."

"Nothing but sour grapes," Teddy grumbled. "Yesterday Americanus Rex was a controversial artist at best and a pervert at worst. Today he's a revolutionary for peace. And he owes no small thanks to you."

"Me? What do you mean?"

"Oh come on," Teddy laughed. "The British media are calling you and Ellen the Rexie Chicks. Cute, huh? Good thing you haven't put out a CD or people in Texas would be chucking it into bonfires."

"The Rexie Chicks," Imogene repeated.

"Today I've gotten calls from HBO, Hallmark, and Lifetime, all wanting to buy the film rights to your story," Teddy went on. "You're a celebrity, Genie. Whatever we make off your portrait in LA is going to look like peanuts compared to the royalty checks you could be pulling after this is all over."

"What did you tell them?"

"That they'll need to talk to you, of course. I can sell your portrait out of my gallery, but you're the only one who can sign away your own story. Anyway, I didn't give them your number for now. I figured you had your hands full with the rock."

She didn't miss the implied question in his statement. "Well, I talked to a few people already. I hope to have a more formal plan by tonight."

Actually she hoped that *Agnes* would have a plan by tonight, but she saw no reason to make such a distinction to Teddy.

"Swell. Buzz me when you figure it all out. Be careful, okay?"

This was such an un-Teddy-like comment that Imogene thought she'd misheard him. "Careful?"

He seemed to hesitate on the other end of the line. The roar of the Tate's visitors abruptly dropped to a whisper as if Teddy had just closed himself into a separate room.

"I also heard from Amanda today," he said. Amanda was the secretary at Teddy's gallery and took all of his business calls when he was out of LA. "She's gotten a few anonymous threatening calls that if the gallery shows your portrait or anything else by Americanus Rex, they'll bombard us with Molotov Cocktails and other clever stuff like that. Rednecks and NRA nutjobs, I'm sure, but if they're rallying in LA they can't be far away from you in the Carolinas."

"West Virginia. Thanks for the heads up, but I'll be fine," she told him, trying not to think about Cody Hemphill.

"Okay, gotta run, babe. Call me when you can."

7

Imogene followed Ben up the steps to the high wooden doors of the First Pentecostal Church of Accord at 7:04. Only fifteen minutes earlier, she had woken up on her brother's puffy red couch, her feet on the floor and her head kinked painfully against the armrest, the position in which she'd keeled over after her conversation with Teddy. Sleep had come over her so suddenly that her telephone had still been clutched in her hand when Ben had shaken her awake. She'd had just enough time to rinse off in the shower, shove half a turkey sandwich down her gullet, and tame her hair into a pony tail before Agnes's meeting at the church.

"I still can't believe I fell asleep," she told him for at least the third time since they'd left his apartment.

"I'm jealous," he said, holding the heavy door open for her. "I feel like I could sleep for a week."

The first thing Imogene noticed when she stepped inside the sanctuary was the oppressive silence. Last Wednesday night the congregants had sat quietly for the service, but had still generated the typical sounds Imogene remembered from her own church growing up: stifled coughing, swishing fabric and creaking wood as people shifted their weight in the pews, the rhythmic whisper of people fanning themselves with the service program. Tonight the sanctuary was emptier than it had been last Wednesday—the fifty or so attendees barely filled a quarter of the pews—but even so small a group still should have made some noise.

These people aren't reporters, she reminded herself. And if any of them put up a fight they way the reporters had, she knew, they would be that much tougher to convince because they would actually believe what they were saying rather than trying to startle Imogene into blubbering out a newsworthy quote.

"I suppose that's everyone," Agnes announced abruptly as Imogene and Ben entered, rising from her place in the front pew.

The pews finally creaked as several heads turned toward the Cornells. Imogene saw at least as many women in attendance as men, ranging in age from twenty to seventy. Agnes was standing to the right side of the pulpit. Her bifocals shone as she swept the people with her gaze. Amazingly, she seemed about to cry. Imogene thought it must be a trick of the light until Agnes spoke again and her voice cracked with obvious emotion.

"I don't know if you all are here because you've seen what Gary Pritchard done on the Peak, or as a favor to Glenn there. Shoot, maybe you're just plain curious to see what could rouse old Aggie Mills out of her den after ten years."

Imogene shot her brother a startled look and mouthed, *Glenn Pritchard is here?* Except for Cody Hemphill, Glenn was the last person she would have expected to attend a meeting like this. Ben pointed discreetly between several heads and, sure enough, Imogene saw Glenn's broad shoulders and cropped silver hair above the front pew.

"Whatever the reason," Agnes continued, "you all have my thanks. I admit that I expected less of this town, and I ask you to forgive me for it."

She paused to swipe a gnarled finger under her glasses. When she lowered her hand, her familiar grim determination had returned.

"How many of you saw Ben Cornell's sister on television this morning? The lovely redhead beside Ben there."

Heads turned toward Imogene and Ben again. A few pairs of eyes lingered and narrowed, and suddenly Imogene wondered if she should have taken Teddy's warning to be careful more seriously. But soon enough everyone's attention returned to Agnes and nearly every hand in the sanctuary went up.

Agnes nodded. "Good. Now if you think what Miss Cornell said on television was ugly or cowardly or un-American, go on and excuse yourselves now. The rest of us will leave you to your opinion if you leave us to ours."

Pews creaked again as people shifted uncomfortably, but no one got up.

"Anyone missed the connection that the artist calling himself Americanus Rex is our own Gary Pritchard?"

Imogene saw Glenn Pritchard shift in his seat, but still no one made a sound.

Agnes sniffed purposefully. "In that case, I'll cut to the heart of the thing. The Cornells, Glenn Pritchard, and I are planning to carry the boulder with Priscilla Hemphill's face down off yonder mountaintop and introduce it to the world."

Agnes's knuckles went white on top of her cane. "And we would like your help."

A tall man Imogene recognized as Pastor Wallop from last Wednesday's service stood slowly from the second pew on the left side of the sanctuary. His pale face looked all the more pale under his gleaming sweep of black hair.

"Introduce it to the world," he repeated, his voice quaking with outrage. "For God's sake, *why?*"

Agnes swiveled on her cane to regard him. "Ephraim, I'm glad you felt called to join us tonight, but—"

"You of all people, after what you nearly put their family through ten years ago…" Wallop interrupted. Harsh bolts of color on the sides of his neck rose with his voice.

A few rows ahead of Imogene and Ben, an older man in starched overalls stirred. Imogene recognized him as the man who had been sitting with Curtis Garfield and Jamie Hemphill during last Wednesday's service—Curtis's grandfather, Calliope, if Imogene remembered correctly.

"Ephraim," Calliope said, his voice so gravelly that the pastor's name sounded like a particularly messy throat clearing.

Wallop took no heed. "Did you believe I would allow you to use my pulpit against the Hemphills just because Earl is four months buried?" He raked the congregation with his dark eyes, apparently unable even in his righteous ire to keep from sermonizing. "With poor Cody disfigured by accident, and lovely Priscilla disgraced by a fiancé run mad—"

Glenn Pritchard rose from the front pew and faced Wallop. "Fiancé run mad," he repeated in a dangerously quiet voice.

Ben leaned over to whisper in Imogene's ear. "Remember how Aggie said Glenn needed to make a decision? I think he just made it."

Before Wallop could respond, Calliope Garfield rocked backward in his pew and used the resulting forward momentum to propel himself into a standing position. "No one is misusing your pulpit tonight, Ephraim. If anything, our sister Agnes is trying to clean up a few names that we've all helped lately to soil."

Wallop's eyes bugged at the older man. "Calliope, that rock is the sin of lust incarnate. I cannot understand why you would want young Curtis to suffer more shame for discovering it than he already has."

"So you would try to heap shame on Curtis Garfield as well as my Gary," Glenn said, still quiet, but calmer now. He might have been commenting on a mild shift in the weather.

Wallop smiled sardonically. "Let me tell you about shame. When I began my ministry here, Agnes was the church secretary and the only woman who worked in the building." He paused meaningfully. "Until

Priscilla Hemphill turned seventeen and became our song leader. Agnes and I always maintained a professional relationship, but I suppose that it was only natural for her to be jealous when we brought Priscilla into the church."

The congregation's hushed attention to this narrative made Agnes's interruption all the harsher. "I was there, Ephraim."

"What?" Wallop said, all traces of soothe and smooth gone.

"The night you told seventeen-year-old Priscilla that her canary voice and sunny presence had brought more than one lost sheep back to the flock, but that some of the men in the church had confessed to impure thoughts about her and maybe it was time she started wearing more modest dresses at the pulpit."

"That was a private conversation," Wallop gasped. "You had no right to—"

"But that was just the beginning. Your admonition moved Priscilla to tell you her daddy had touched her, and you said—I'll never forget it, no matter how much I want to—'Sometimes men have trouble controlling themselves around a beautiful woman like the one you've become, even their daddies. Take care in the display of your body at home as well as in church, lest you encourage this kind of behavior.'"

Agnes gazed at Wallop over the heads of fifty people more hushed than the space between lightning and thunder.

"My mistake, Ephraim, was that I tried to save you from *your* mistake. You were new to the church and new to the town. I called for Priscilla to be removed from the church so that she could at least be out from under the greedy stares of the men in this congregation every Sunday and Wednesday. But in return, you requested my removal to the deacons because I 'spit and hissed at you like a she-demon from hell,' if I recall your phraseology correctly."

Wallop clutched mutely at the pew in front of him, his expression blank and distant.

Agnes returned her focus to the congregation. "My next mistake was leaving the church without telling anyone what I had heard. I thought that if Wallop wouldn't deal with Earl Hemphill, then Priscilla at least deserved the right to find her own solution in peace. I have continued to make that mistake everyday since."

Agnes's story made Imogene feel like she'd fallen into a vat of live cockroaches. She herself had suggested to Ben that whatever trauma Priscilla had suffered to attract Droon's notice must have been a single event, much like the death of their mother. However, she knew from discussions with her father that sexual abuse among acquaintances often lasted years, and the same was doubly true with family members.

"No more," Agnes said severely. "If Priscilla ever lost the strength and confidence inside her, she's rediscovered them in the days since Gary painted her, by God. Priscilla's as much a part of the Americanus Rex movement as Imogene Cornell or even Gary Pritchard himself. And we have the unique chance to help a daughter and son of Accord change the world for the better.

"So." She squared her shoulders and assumed her full, if unspectacular, height. "How are we going to do this thing?"

8

Imogene had seen the people of Accord ignore some outlandish events during her brief tenure here, but when they decided *not* to ignore something, they wasted no time on the decision. The echo of Agnes's question had barely died in the sanctuary's dark rafters when a middle aged man with thick forearms stood from the pew behind the immobile Pastor Wallop.

"I seen the rock last night. Nora and me did."

Wallop, who had finally sat down again, glanced at him blearily.

"Can't weigh more'n half a ton," the man went on. "What if we tip it over and slide it down like a log jamb? I got enough old lumber in my shed to shore up a simple path to stop it rolling side to side."

"Trail's longer than you think just by walking it, Herb," Glenn said. "It would take an awful lot of two-by-eights to fence a log slide from top to bottom. And a lot of time. But it's not a bad idea. We'll keep it in mind."

Herb nodded and sat back down.

"We could use some of Herb's lumber to rig up a travois," suggested a young woman five rows back from the front. "Wouldn't take more than five or six of us on a strong rope to anchor it from behind. Another two or three up front to steer."

Glenn nodded approvingly. "I've got three-thousand pound climbing rope at the store we could use. Same stuff you and Stuart bought last year to rappel in the Poconos, Emma Louise," he added to the woman who had spoken. "Remember though that the trail dips up and down and even breaks at a few points. I hate to think of all us old goats in here trying to lift a thousand pound sled out of a mountain crack."

A few dry chuckles greeted this.

Calliope Garfield spoke next. "What are your appliance carts rated at, Glenn?"

Glenn considered. "The big upright is tested for twelve hundred pounds. Probably weighs sixty by itself, though."

"Then how about we put ten men on your climbing rope behind it, just to be safe," Calliope said decisively. "Then we could steer around any tricky spots."

"Don't worry yourselves about the trail," Agnes spoke up, still beside the pulpit. She fixed Calliope with a hard stare. "You think Curtis would help me navigate the best route? My eyes aren't what they once were."

Calliope harrumphed an affirmative. "So long's his mama don't mind."

"She doesn't," Emma Louise said, smiling at Calliope. The smile turned shy but did not fade completely when she saw Ben.

Glenn nodded once more, a quick, satisfied gesture. "We'll need everyone here who's able to help. Even with ten men," he looked meaningfully at Agnes, "and women on the rope at a time, we'll have to switch often to avoid fatigue. Make sure you all wear your heaviest shoes and leather work gloves if you have them. Canvas gloves will suffice if you don't."

Agnes shifted her gaze to take in the whole crowd. "It's eight o'clock now," she said. "Is it too late to start tonight?"

"Give us thirty minutes," said Emma Louise. "Curtis and I will see you all at the trailhead."

Amid quiet murmurs of excitement, the people stood and filed out of the church just as they had done last Wednesday. Except this time, to Imogene's relief, determination had replaced the vacant sheep's stares they had worn that night.

Two minutes later, only four people remained in the sanctuary of First Pentecostal Church of Accord: Agnes, Ben, Imogene, and Pastor Wallop.

"I'm sorry Ephraim," Agnes said. She opened her mouth to say more, but closed it again.

Wallop stood and walked slowly down the center aisle through the heavy wooden doors without so much as a glance at Agnes or the Cornells.

Agnes heaved a sigh. "I never meant to break him. Not ten years ago, and not tonight. But fear can make a good man do ugly things."

Imogene doubted she would ever have the grace to call Wallop a good man after the story Agnes had told tonight.

"I wish Priscilla could have seen what you did for her tonight, Ag," Ben said. "I never thought my life would be so full of powerful women."

Agnes smiled faintly. "Not too intimidating, are we?"

"Of course not. I'm just tired of being on the sidelines. Come on, Gene," he said, standing. "Let's go see if we can dig up some work gloves."

The digital clock in the Silverado's dashboard read 7:58 when Imogene pulled slowly into the gravel turnout and shut off the engine. Ben whistled softly. The fifty people from church had brought friends, with latecomers still trickling into the clearing behind their pickup.

"A lot of these people are more than twice our age," Imogene said wonderingly.

Ben nodded. "There's no such thing as retirement in Accord. Most of these people will keep working until they're either dead or too infirm to leave their beds."

The trail would be well illuminated, Imogene saw. Most of the people carried heavy flashlights, and several of the older men, she noted with amusement and surprising affection, wore what looked like mining helmets with powerful spotlights above their plastic brims. Light and shadow flitted through the spruce trees surrounding the clearing like a festival of glimmering pixies.

Agnes stood gravely at the trailhead in her pink afghan. To her right, Glenn Pritchard was holding a sturdy orange appliance dolly with what looked like rubber tank treads on its back. To her left, a very excited Curtis Garfield was practically dancing on his tiptoes. At first Imogene thought he was simply trying to pick out familiar faces in the crowd, but suddenly he shouted, "*Jamie!*"

The chatter in the clearing, hushed to begin with, died as Priscilla's slim little brother found himself the focal point of a hundred flashlight beams. He raised a forearm over his eyes, his step faltering.

Curtis ran forward. "All right! How'd you sneak past your mama?" he wanted to know, obviously impressed.

Agnes's stern voice carried easily through the quiet clearing. "James, we are all glad you were moved to join our efforts tonight, but your first responsibility is to obey your mother. I'm sure one of these kind people will take you back—"

"Mama said I could come," Jamie interrupted, and Imogene recognized very well the look of proud defiance in his gray eyes. "She and Cody…they argued."

Curtis grabbed his friend's arm. "Well come on. We're climbing the Peak to get your sister's picture."

"I know," Jamie said in the slightly annoyed tone only twelve year old children can pull off. "Mama's been talking about it since we started getting the calls this afternoon." Now at the trailhead with Agnes and Glenn, he turned and addressed the crowd in a surprisingly clear voice. "She's glad you all are trying to do something nice for Priscilla, even if Cody ain't so glad."

"Thank you, James," Agnes said warmly. "With your mother's blessing, we welcome you. Perhaps you would help Curtis and me lead everyone up the trail?"

Jamie nodded, smiling for the first time. He and Curtis began whispering excitedly. The rest of the crowd followed suit as Agnes thumped her way over to Imogene and Ben.

"I'm not sure what you all said to Meredith Hemphill, but I'm starting to believe you're a mobile version of the Damascus Road."

Glenn Pritchard came up behind Agnes, and announced briskly, "I think it's time we get started. Ben, would you and your sister mind helping me with the dolly? We'll come up last, then. Wouldn't want anyone behind us if we lose the dolly to gravity."

They followed Glenn back to the appliance dolly perched at the trailhead. Lengths of black climbing rope were secured at several points below the dolly's handgrips. Glenn had knotted several loops into the longest piece of rope, but he ignored these for now. He directed Ben and Imogene to grab the two shortest loops.

"These short ones will be our steering wheel on the way down as well," he informed them. He started to turn away, but abruptly faced Imogene. "I also need to apologize for my behavior earlier today."

"Don't worry about it," she said.

He squinted at her. "I've earned this humility, young lady, and I'll see it through if you don't mind. I won't pretend to understand what Gary is doing with all this, but I also won't pretend you have done anything besides help my boy. If you see him before I do…" He snorted into a handkerchief, which he folded awkwardly before stuffing it back in his pocket. "I'm proud of what he's doing."

Imogene considered hugging him, but stayed herself. Glenn Pritchard didn't seem like a man used to hugs from strange women.

"I'll tell him."

Without another word, he took for himself a third loop of black rope, this one attached to the longest bit of rope fastened to the central crossbar at the top of the dolly.

"If you or Ben lose your grip I want you to make a big fuss about it so I know to let go myself."

"No problem," Ben said. "Gene's great at making fusses, aren't you Gene?"

Glenn's eyes crinkled again, this time with a smile. "That she is."

"Single file!" Agnes bawled to the crowd, which quieted quickly. "Anyone without a light should walk with someone who does. The dolly's coming up last, so there's no need for the rest of us to hurry. It's possible to misstep even if you stick to the trail, and it's no fun when you do." She twirled her cane meaningfully in the air. "Believe me."

9

The trip to the summit of General's Peak seemed less tiring than it had a few days ago, despite the added burden of Glenn's appliance dolly. Perhaps it was the excited chatter rising from the people of Accord like the first birdsong of spring; perhaps it was the realization that she and Ben, admittedly with help, had in a single day drummed up the support they needed from the people of Accord.

Near the top of the trail—around the time she, Glenn, and Ben were navigating the dolly through the little stand of spruce trees to the right of the famous stone gap in the trail—the crowd's soft chatter died. The process began immediately behind Agnes and the boys and washed down the line of hikers like a cold front sweeping over a winding river.

"What's the matter?" Ben asked.

Glenn didn't even raise his head. "They've spotted it. Mind your wheel," he added when Ben, craning his neck to look ahead, thumped his side of the dolly against a tree.

Another minute brought the three of them to the same spot in the trail where the rock finally peeked above the artificial horizon of the summit like a cool white sunrise. Through the row of Spruce trees lining this final stretch of the trail, Imogene could see the people gathering before Priscilla's portrait in the helpless wonder.

And as the crowd parted to allow the dolly's passage, Imogene found herself just as unprepared for the portrait's simple perfection. Now that she knew Priscilla better, the likeness was even more striking. The hard determination in her eyes, the subtle jut of her chin under rosebud lips. This was Priscilla at her best and most commanding. Priscilla gearing up to move a mountain.

And yet, as overwhelming as the portrait was, Imogene realized it was still only a shade of the real woman. The floating head of Oz the Great and Terrible may have captivated Dorothy and her friends, but Oz the *man* had been the one to take Dorothy back home. Unlike the real Priscilla, this portrait would not be able to cope with a reneging fiancé or adapt to a new culture any more than Oz's smoke and mirrors could have transported Dorothy back to Kansas.

"I think I know why Priscilla didn't mind giving her portrait to Teddy," she told Ben.

He nodded slowly. "She knows she doesn't need it. She's not the only one."

"I know." Imogene eased her side of the dolly into a standing position as Glenn and her brother did the same. "Okay, Glenn. What's your plan?"

"One! Two! *Three!*" Glenn hollered, and two young men who at one time had likely played important roles on their high school football teams strained against the top half of the boulder's flat painted face. Four men opposite them, including Ben and the thick armed man named Herb, supported the rock as it tilted backward. Once they had raised the rock's base a few inches, Glenn slid the steel lip of the appliance dolly underneath it. The hundred fifty or so people in attendance applauded, whistled, and catcalled.

Imogene and Emma Louise Garfield ran thick canvas straps attached to one side of the dolly around the circumference of the boulder and cinched them down in long steel hoops on the other side.

"I can see the *Accord Tribune's* headline now," Emma Louise told Imogene, grinning. "'Town Plays Tug-of-War against Gravity.'"

"I never heard the title of Accord's newspaper," Imogene said. "Who writes for it?"

"I do," Emma Louise said, giving her strap a final tug. "So where's this thing going?"

"Los Angeles. I work for an art gallery that will make sure Priscilla's portrait gets a lot of attention. You know, when we get back down to ground level you should take a picture for your front page. Has the Associated Press ever bought a picture from your newspaper?"

"They sure haven't," Emma Louise said, her eyes glittering. "But I reckon it's time they did."

Glenn paced a full circle around the rock and dolly before addressing the group once more. "And you all thought this would be tough."

Laughter and a fresh smattering of applause greeted this.

"The good news is that this here rock doesn't weigh any thousand pounds. We probably could manage her with six people at a time since a burden becomes exponentially lighter with each person lifting, but she still ain't a feather. Besides the steering loops, I've tied ten more into the rope as handholds just to be safe. They're big enough to fit your hands inside, but you should still be able to let go easily enough if the dolly gets away from your group."

He grew more serious. "It's important, what we're doing tonight, but let's not forget that it's unorthodox and potentially dangerous. Don't take any chances."

When he had received a satisfactory amount of nods and spoken affirmatives, he set the two former football stars on the steering loops and handpicked ten others of similar size from the waiting crowd.

"You ten hold your positions on the rope, and I'd like another two directly supporting each side of the dolly until we get to the trail,"

Glenn instructed. "The hardest part of this might well be wheeling across the flat ground up here since gravity will be on our side later on, so the rest of you I didn't pick shouldn't feel left out. We'll switch out every five minutes to avoid fatigue, so with less than fifteen groups of ten, plus two for steering, you all will get your chance. Okay, boys, remember to let your legs bear the weight."

The men crowded around the dolly grunted and puffed as they staggered over to the edge of the summit where the trail began, though Imogene guessed most of their straining stemmed from the awkward positions in which they walked rather than the actual weight. The ten strong-arms Glenn had assigned to the rope shuffled behind, clutching the limp rope, shrugging their shoulders, and taking deep breaths in anticipation of the nearing slope.

"If anyone loses your footing, call out so the rest can let go!" Glenn reminded them through gritted teeth. "We're heading downhill... now!"

A hundred fifty people held their breath as the dolly's rubber wheels rolled slowly onto the trail. The long rope straightened, became taut. The ten men dug in their heels, grimaces tightening all of their faces. They seemed to be waiting for the weight to become unbearable.

After a moment, a burly teenager Glenn had placed near the front of the rope said, "This is it?" He actually sounded disappointed.

The waiting crowd broke into hoots of relieved laughter.

"Toldja it weren't no thousand pounds!" Glenn hollered gleefully. "She'll weigh plenty after your five minutes are up, though. Remember to walk slow and keep your footing. Those of you not on the rope, it'll be your job to illuminate as much of the path as possible."

"Genius," Ben said into Imogene's ear.

"What do you mean?" she asked, mirroring his quiet tone.

"Do you really think this is the best or even the simplest way to get the rock down to ground level? I'm sure it's safe enough, or Glenn wouldn't have allowed it, but twelve people at a time on a daisy chain?"

"He's giving them ownership," Imogene realized. "*All* of them. It wasn't enough that they agreed to help in the church, they had to plan and do all this together."

"For a bunch of reasons," Ben agreed. "Here we go."

Agnes, Curtis, and Jamie were taking their positions at the front of the group, but well clear of any possible path the dolly could take if the carriers lost control. The first five minutes of the hike saw them past the wide gap near the top of the trail. Rather than vaulting across on her cane as she had done before, Agnes cut left through the opening in the trees. She and the boys held branches out of the way while the train of carriers passed.

"We've got a stretch of shallow grade ahead," Agnes announced over her shoulder to Glenn on the other side of the gap. "Want to switch out your hauling crew?"

Glenn nodded and wiped his forehead with the back of one gloved hand. "Ten new people on the rope!" he called. "Trade positions one at a time, from back to front!"

Within two minutes the dolly was inching its way down the trail again. And so it progressed for the next hour. No group stayed on the rope for more than seven minutes even though nearly everyone commented on how easy their shift had been. Only Glenn Pritchard maintained his position on the first central loop all the way down the mountain. No one complained or even commented on this fact. Imogene supposed that in a town as deeply family oriented as Accord was, everyone respected Glenn's desire and right to lead his son's artwork out of the wilderness, as it were.

Imogene and Ben took their turns in the final group, making sure all of the longtime townspeople had their chance first. Like everyone else, she was immediately surprised at how little the dolly seemed to weigh. But as Glenn had warned, after her five minutes she felt a new tightness in her thighs and the small of her back. These were only minor discomforts, however. She avoided real injury—the most immediate danger being loose stones on the trail—thanks to over a hundred dedicated flashlights constantly playing over her feet and the trail.

"*Terra firma!*" Agnes crowed ahead.

Imogene glanced up to see twenty flashlight beams swing into the clearing to reflect brightly off the waxed sides of her rented Silverado. Another glint of silver on the periphery of the clearing caught her attention as well. She squinted in an effort to make out exactly what had made the flash—it had looked like the bumper of a second vehicle, but she and Ben had been the only ones to drive—and in that moment a large, flat stone slid under her heel. She sat down hard on the stony trail, yanking the rope from the hands of the people directly behind and ahead of her.

Five feet of rope, suddenly free of any resistance, snapped hard enough to wrench two more loops free. The others anchoring and steering the dolly either saw Imogene go down or felt the sudden surge in weight and, as Glenn had instructed, released their grips and called out that they were doing so. The dolly, trailing twenty feet of black rope behind it, skidded noisily down the rest of the trail and came to a rest in a cloud of white gravel dust at the feet of Cody Hemphill.

10

Flashlights swung up to illuminate Cody's face. Imogene remembered too well the gout of smoke and flame that had enveloped Cody's head when his gun had backfired, but she could not have imagined the black and red volcanic tundra his face would become only a few days later. Thickets of charred hair stood out from his scalp. Around his eyes were circular patches of bright red, taut and shining like the surfaces of overfilled balloons.

As more people trained their flashlights on the newcomer, Imogene's shock subsided into uneasy pity. Cody's two friends—Wash and JT if she remembered correctly—stood slightly behind and to either side of him, as if waiting to catch him should he topple over. Indeed he seemed ready to do just that. His blistered head swayed and his boots crunched lightly on the gravel with his constant unbalanced shifting.

"Cody, dear, what happened to you?" Agnes breathed.

"I been shit on," Cody said matter-of-factly, squinting into the barrage of flashlights. His voice sounded parched and cracked, as if he'd inhaled as much of the smoke and flame as had burned him so badly. "But as long as I'm alive, one person in this town will have the courage to stand against Pilate's horde."

"'Pilate's horde?'" Agnes repeated. Suddenly she thumped across the gravel until she was in front of Cody, Priscilla's prone portrait creating a low fence between them. "And where *is* the Ephraim the Good Shepherd? If he's so courageous, why did he drag you off your sickbed instead of confronting the 'horde' himself?"

Cody smiled. "Aggie Mills. Wallop said you'd slunk out of hibernation like an old grizzly to spread lies about my daddy rapin Prissy. You shoulda stayed in your den, she-bear. You look like blue hell."

In the deeply contrasted light and dark from the flashlights, the tendons stood out on Agnes's hands like a row of pencils as she gripped her cane.

"Cody, I did your family disservice a long time ago and I extend my apology to you, along with an invitation to help us help your sister. She's a strong girl and it's time we give her the resp—"

"*Don't!*" Cody screamed, his head swaying more than ever with the effort. "Don't you talk about my Prissy like you know her."

"Look around you, Cody," Glenn said, stepping to Agnes's side. "Look at the people who turned out to help your sister."

Cody swayed a moment longer before turning to the taller of his friends. "JT, get my drill."

JT obliged immediately, albeit with a few nervous glances at Cody's back. In this he was not alone. Cody's other friend Wash had remained mostly unnoticed by the roving flashlights, but his eyes danced down to Cody's lower back every few seconds as well.

Another gun? Imogene wondered.

"Here, Cody." JT shoved an enormous antique hand operated drill into Cody's hand and stepped away so swiftly that Cody almost dropped it. He staggered a few feet to his left before he recovered.

"Dumb shit," he wheezed.

The red mess covering his head seemed to have gone blotchier in the harsh lighting. When he recovered his balance, he set himself in front of the fallen rock and dolly once more, the heavy drill clutched in both hands.

"For heaven's sake, child, what are you doing?" Agnes nearly pleaded.

If Cody heard the sympathy in her voice, he chose to ignore it. He fell to his knees in front of the rock and set the drill's heavy bit against it.

An uneasy murmur rolled through the crowd, but no one moved. Imogene took a quick step toward him, but Ben laid a restraining hand on her forearm. She realized almost at once what everyone else had already known: whatever reason Cody had to drill a hole in the rock, he no longer had the strength to back it up. The ancient drill bit skittered across the surface of the rock, leaving barely a scratch.

"Help me, you peckerholes," he gasped to his friends.

Neither moved. Like the rest of the silent crowd, they seemed too stunned by what they were seeing to move an inch.

"That's enough, son," Glenn said gently, reaching down for the drill, which Cody yanked out of reach and flung to the gravel. "Wash and JT here will take you back home now, won't you, boys?"

Wash nodded slowly, but JT's eyes never strayed from Cody's back.

Cody climbed to his feet again, grabbing JT's shirt for balance with one hand. The other hand went behind his back.

"Look out, Glenn!" someone shouted, and the semicircle of people closed around Cody and the rock. Imogene and Ben surged forward on the inner edge of the human tide.

If Cody had been carrying a gun, he would likely have gotten off a few shots before being disarmed, but everyone froze when they saw what he pulled from his belt. Imogene had never actually seen a stick of dynamite, but the thin cylinder in Cody's hand looked close enough to its cartoon counterpart in old Bugs Bunny cartoons, right down to the long fuse curling from one end like a possum's tail, that she had no trouble identifying it.

"Everyone move away right now!" Ben commanded in what Imogene thought of as his teacher voice. "Cody, put that down slowly."

Still clutching a handful of JT's shirt, Cody grinned. "You'd like that, wouldn't you Cornell? If I blow up this here smut you won't be able to set it up by your bed and jerk off to it every night. I ain't forgot what you said about my Prissy the other night, just like I ain't forgot that she left town the next morning. So I think I'll just drill my blasting hole and vaporize this here rock from the inside out."

"Listen to me," Ben said in the same tone. "I don't know where you found that thing, but it's old enough to be sweating nitroglycerin. Those little crystals on the side there? Simple pressure, or even the oils in your skin, could act as a catalyst for an explosive reaction. If that happens, you won't get away with a few burns this time. None of us will."

Imogene stepped past her brother. She had no doubt he was right about the dynamite, but detailing the extreme danger of the situation for everyone to hear would only put more power in Cody's court, and Cody had already achieved too much power through violence and fear in the last few days.

"Jamie said you and your mom argued earlier," she said. "Did she tell you not to destroy this rock?"

Cody eyed her disinterestedly. "Ain't no reason for a pretty lady like you to get uglied up by standin too close to this rock when she goes up in smoke."

Imogene took another step. "Priscilla told us that seeing this rock made her stop being ashamed of who she is. Do you think she'd want you to destroy something so important to her?"

She sensed Ben behind her, ready to yank her backward if Cody made any sudden moves, but she didn't think that would be necessary. Cody glanced at the crowd of people, five deep on every side of him, and licked his cracked lips, giving the impression of a swimmer who has realized just how far away from shore the tide has carried him.

He pointedly raised the dynamite higher again, making sure everyone around him could see it. "You ain't doin this to my sister. None of you are. Maybe I can't get rid of the rock with you all around, but I can make damn sure none of you take it with you either."

"No, you can't," Imogene said matter-of-factly.

Cody's eyes widened in obvious outrage, but now she saw even more of the doubt she had glimpsed a moment ago. She was almost there.

"Cody, all these people are here to help Priscilla stop a war that could kill millions of people from ever starting. Let's say you set off that dynamite in your hand and kill ten people, including you and me. All you've done is make sure that everyone else here believes even more strongly in getting this rock to the public so that more people in the world will listen to your sister talk about peace."

"*I will stop this!*" Cody raged.

"A madman only has as much power as people give him." Imogene straightened up, hoping to convey more confidence than she felt. "We'll give you none."

Cody stared at her as if she were an apparition. The Boogeyman, or perhaps the Easter Bunny.

Over Cody's shoulder, Imogene saw a hulking teenage kid—he was mostly in shadow, but she thought he was the one who had been disappointed that the rock wasn't any heavier—take a menacing step toward Cody. The kid's hands were flexing like the jaws of hungry piranha.

"*Stop!*" Imogene roared.

Cody was so startled that he almost dropped the dynamite. It slipped from his grip and he just barely caught it by its long, curling fuse. He wrapped a sweating hand around the stick again, the unburned skin on his face and neck ashen.

"Nobody here is going to *touch* Cody Hemphill," Imogene said fiercely. "Don't you understand why we're doing this?"

The hand holding the stick of dynamite fell slowly back to Cody's side. He wore a new smirk that Imogene didn't care for in the least.

"I reckon I'm not the only, ah, 'madman' here after all."

"Anger is an honest and healthy emotion," Imogene said automatically. "And it usually means you're about to make a very good or very bad choice."

Cody's smirk widened. "That's real cute. I'll let you know which one you made soon enough."

He tossed the stick of dynamite to Ben, who, despite his surprise, caught it deftly in one hand.

"Come on, boys," Cody called, as if his friends were right beside him instead of cowering halfway between him and the pickup at the mouth of the clearing. "The mob has spoken, and baby gets her bottle for tonight."

Agnes was the first to find her voice after Cody's taillights vanished around the corner that led to the Hemphills' ranch. "Well," she said, "I think we all know what we're about now. Let's finish what we came to do."

INTERLUDE: FRANÇAIS THE EASY WAY

1

Tuesday, August 30, 2011

Imogene drove the winding hour of road between Accord and Charleston while Ben rode shotgun in amiable, if exhausted, silence. They stopped at the first motel they found, and Ben went inside to rent a room for the night while Imogene stayed in the truck and phoned Teddy. He whooped into her ear when she told him the rock was in their possession.

"Where is it now?" he demanded.

"In the back of the truck, lashed to an appliance dolly. I can see it in my rearview mirror."

"Don't tell me you're leaving it there all night?" Teddy spluttered. "What if someone tries to steal it?"

She tried not to sigh. "No one around here knows that we have it or that it even exists. And if anyone *did* know, how would they go about stealing a six foot rock that weighs almost half a ton?"

But Teddy wasn't satisfied until she explained that the townspeople had covered Priscilla's portrait with heavy canvas tarps, transforming it from an impossibly lovely glowing rock into a rather uninteresting lump that might have been a pile of old shovels, a farming implement, or a mound of fertilizer.

She didn't mention the trouble with Priscilla's brother, but she wasn't terribly worried about any more trouble from Cody tonight. There was only one road between Accord and Charleston and several people, including Glenn Pritchard, had vowed that Cody and his friends would not leave town before morning.

"We'll find a trucking company in Charleston to ship the rock first thing in the morning," she promised, stifling a yawn with the back of her free hand. "I'll insure it for, what, five hundred thousand?"

"Two million," Teddy corrected at once. "Or however much they'll let you do. The hype around these portraits has grown so much in the last twelve hours that any one of them might go for twice that amount next week."

"Two million, then," she said. "After that, Ben and I are leaving for Paris, like we talked about."

Teddy made a disgruntled *harrumph* into her ear, but any irritation he might have had was more habit than genuine emotion. "Go back to California as soon as you're done. We've got a sale to promote in LA— *two* now," he amended, the joviality creeping back into his voice.

Ben opened the truck door and climbed back into the passenger seat. He jingled a key hanging from a large plastic diamond with a number on it. "Room's on the north side," he whispered.

Imogene nodded. "Okay, Teddy, I'm going to bed. Have a good night."

"It's almost morning over here, babe," he said. "Sleep well. You deserve it."

She located the room with Ben's help and backed the truck into a parking space directly in front of their window. She checked over Priscilla's portrait one last time before following Ben into the room.

The canvas lump in the pickup's bed looked unremarkable indeed, bathed as it was in harsh yellow light from a McDonald's sign across from the hotel.

Ben was brushing his teeth when she entered the room. Imogene doubted she had the energy to do even that much. She managed to undress before collapsing into bed, but just barely. She was asleep seconds after her head hit the lumpy pillow.

She woke shortly after dawn, the sliver of sky visible through the hotel curtains a deep, pleasant shade of orange. Ben was already sitting up, shirtless and tousled, scratching notes onto a yellow legal pad with one of the complimentary motel pens that had been on the nightstand the night before. He grinned when he saw that she was awake.

"Morning. I've figured out a title for my Men in Black book." He held up his hands as if showcasing a film marquee. "*We Come in Peace.*"

She fell back onto her pillow and stretched her arms and legs luxuriantly, wriggling her fingers and toes. "You're incredible."

"I've got to do something to keep up with my sister."

She sat up again and attempted to wrestle her hair back into a rubber band. "I'm not sure you noticed, but I was the only one who lost my footing carrying the rock last night. And Aggie and Glenn were the ones who called the troops into action, not me."

Ben threw his pen disgustedly onto the bedspread. "You know, at first I thought you were just being modest about all this, but I'm starting to wonder if you're really just a moron."

"What?"

"Come on, Gene. Cody Hemphill showed up to play ball last night, and you sent him home in the first inning. Warm up the bus, son, the visiting team is pitching a shutout. Plus you stopped Jeremy Biggs—that big linebacker kid from the high school—from pounding Cody into the ground, all without even a hint of physical force. Do you understand what that meant to the people who were there? That you risked your life to create the type of peaceful resolution they heard you talking about on TV?"

"None of them mentioned the news. Except for Glenn and Aggie, no one said a word to me."

"That's because they're in awe of you."

"It's a little too early in the morning for flattery, Benny."

"Think about it—besides you being on TV like a celebrity, you also impressed them last night, and people in Accord aren't used to being impressed by strangers."

Imogene stared down at the lumps of her knees rising below the bedspread, unsure of what to say.

"I'm not saying these things to make you uncomfortable, I just don't want you to be embarrassed when you read all the great stuff I write about you in my book."

"You're putting *me* in your book?"

"Gene, please. You're the heroine." He turned away abruptly, his cheeks reddening. "Unless you'd rather have the Hallmark Channel or whoever tell your story like Teddy suggested. In fact, that would make sense in a lot of ways. I didn't mean to—"

"Benny. I wouldn't dream of letting anyone else tell this story."

He nodded, still not looking at her. He slid his legs off the bed and walked to the window in his boxer shorts. Imogene had the strangest idea that he was trying not to cry.

But when he spoke again his voice was even. "Priscilla's portrait is still there. The tarps are still tied the way we left…Oh hell, you'd better see this."

She padded across the room and peered over his shoulder. A familiar brown pickup was parked fifty yards away in the McDonald's parking lot, three heads inside silhouetted against a backdrop of early morning light.

"So much for there only being one route out of Accord," Ben said grimly. "Okay, let's do a quick run-through of our plan, such as it is. First order of business, we hit the Yellow Pages for a trucking company to ship the rock to Los Angeles."

"Where Teddy's people will build a display for it to be auctioned off, thereby filling Teddy's house with sacks of money, as he put it," Imogene finished.

"Classy as always," Ben said. "So after we get the rock sent, you and I hop on an airplane to Paris, where we will…" He twirled his hand helplessly in the air. "I guess that's the part where things get a little fuzzy for me."

"Back in London, Droon basically told Priscilla and me that Gary would be doing something big in Paris."

"Which you then delivered as genuine prophecy at Oliver's press conference."

An unpleasant thrill shot through her stomach. "Right. So all we have to do is reconnect with Priscilla and Ellen in Paris, figure out together where Gary is most likely to light his beacon of peace, and then gather the thousands of people I invited to Paris into a peace rally to stop World War Three."

"But before any of that can happen, we still have to avoid whatever petty revenge Cody and his pocket Einsteins out there have cooked up," Ben added, rubbing his upper lip in his old thinking gesture. "I can be ready to leave in ten minutes, how about you?"

"I need to shower, so…" She grinned. "Five."

They found a trucking company about ten miles from the airport that agreed to Imogene's packing and shipping specifications for the rock, as well as the two million dollars of insurance that Teddy had demanded. Imogene guessed that Roth Gallery had just dished out enough money to pay the truck driver a year's salary, but she knew Teddy wouldn't mind. He was a firm believer in the you-have-to-spend-money-to-make-money school of business.

Cody's pickup had followed Imogene and Ben to the trucking company, but Cody and his buddies seemed content to continue watching them from afar, this time parking patiently across the street at a branch of the Charleston BMV. The only excitement came when Cody's pickup roared out of the BMV's parking lot, coming within in inches of sideswiping a sleek black Cadillac that was turning into the trucking company's parking lot as Imogene and Ben were leaving it. Cody followed them all the way to the airport.

"It's just an intimidation tactic," Ben said, glaring into the passenger side mirror. "And not a very good one. Cody wants to show you and his buddies that he's not afraid of you, but deep down he *is* afraid of you, which only makes him angrier. What a dick."

Imogene wasn't particularly frightened of Cody but neither was she convinced, as Ben seemed to be, that he would be content simply to escort her to the airport and then go home. His terrible sneer from the night before kept rising in her mind, the vow to inform her whether her anger had led to a good or bad decision.

But by the time she and Ben returned the Silverado to the rental depot at the airport, the brown pickup had disappeared somewhere in Charleston's morning rush hour. And like most things out of sight, Cody left Imogene's mind as well. At the counter in the airport, she paid for two one way tickets from Yeager to Charles de Gaulle in Paris. Imogene balked when she saw they would have three hours to kill at Dulles International outside Washington, DC, but Ben pointed out that they would still arrive in Paris by the next morning.

"I'm sure that whatever replaced the Concorde could probably get us there by two a.m. or so," he told her, "but it's not like Ellen and Priscilla will be wandering around the city that late. I'd rather sleep on an airplane than try to find a motel in Paris in the middle of the night."

After a moment's tortured consideration, she acquiesced.

"We'll grab a bite in Dulles," Ben went on. "Make a date of it. Maybe we'll even find you a little book in the airport bookstore to help you bone up on your French from high school. It'll kill time for you, and who knows, it might even come in handy while we're roaming around Paris."

2

Fifteen hours later—forty minutes' flight time outside Charles de Gaulle International Airport—Imogene closed the little language book Ben had found in a bookstore during their layover at Dulles. The book's last pages contained no concluding remarks from the author or biographical information, and the back cover was empty gloss white. The front cover showed only the title printed in plain purple letters: *Français the Easy Way.* And if you could be hoodwinked into believing that learning any language could be easy, the book's subtitle made an even more ridiculous claim.

"*A no nonsense guide to speaking conversational French in 10 hours of study,*" Imogene read now, her voice barely audible over the the 777's massive jet engine droning outside her window like the world's largest beehive.

On the same shelf as this book, Ben had shown her other equally ridiculous language study guides, the worst offender guaranteeing tourists functional French after a single 75 minute audio program. Despite *Français the Easy Way* boasting a completely nondescript cover in a sea of brightly colored books and CDs vying for attention—she and Ben had both glanced over it several times before it had caught his eye—a tiny logo centered at the bottom of the front cover had instantly convinced Imogene that this book might deliver what it promised.

She now ran her fingertip across the logo, a simply drawn hand that was holding a torch. Below this she saw the words *Beacon Press*. And in case Imogene had needed any other hint that the book had been meant for her, the title page offered the following information about the publisher:

Beacon Press
A Division of DroonCorp
Picking up the pieces of the fallen Tower of Babel since 2011

Ben was leaning forward over his knees with his face buried in the little rectangular pillow the flight attendants had passed out as they boarded. It was the only position in which Imogene had ever seen her brother sleep on an airplane. She patted his shoulder. He sat up and groaned.

"Is it time for the next movie to start?"

She held up the book. "I finished it."

His drowsiness evaporated. "And? Did anything come back to your from high school French?"

"A little bit each chapter," she said cautiously.

Un peu chaque chapitre, her mind automatically translated.

"Well, hey, that's something. Even if you've got some key phrases back, that'll help us get around the city more easily."

"No, you don't understand," she said.

Vous no comprenez pas, her mind helpfully supplied.

"Any unit we covered in high school could fit in a chapter introduction in this book. You know how Dad sometimes talks about the language center in the brain that works like crazy for the first few years of life and then either disappears or slows way down?"

Ben nodded.

"It's like Droon or his people figured out how to turn it back on. The first few pages instruct you in creating the sounds you'll use to emulate the accent, then every following chapter makes you use vocabulary and grammar from the previous one in a new colloquial way while introducing *more* vocabulary and grammar."

"I guessed it was something like that," Ben said, stretching his arms as well as he could without bumping the ceiling or other passengers. "You've been whispering to yourself since you opened the book at our gate in Dulles."

"The last chapter contains a reading from *Notre Dame de Paris* by Victor Hugo, and I understood *every word*, Benny."

He smiled tiredly. "So the next time I buy a build-it-yourself computer desk, you can use the French instructions to put it together. It'll probably be easier than the English ones."

She shook her head and pointed to the cover. "It says *conversational* French and that's exactly what it means. I think I could walk up to anyone on the street in Paris and ask directions, or talk about the weather or my job. I could translate exactly what I'm saying to you right now in French if I wanted to." Her brain was, in fact, doing just that as she spoke. "But I don't have any specialty vocabulary. Unless there's a Volume Two. Man, I can't wait to show this thing to Dad."

"I'll be honest, Gene, I doubt this book will be the most exciting news you have for him when he gets back from the Boundary Waters." Ben slid the book from her grasp and studied it with enormous satisfaction. "However, it is proof that Gary isn't the only contactee in this mess."

"Why?"

"Did you ever see that movie *Phenomenon,* with John Travolta?"

"I don't think so."

"Well, at the end of it, John Travolta's character learns Portuguese in like twenty minutes, which is another case of art mimicking reality. Twenty minutes is a little extreme, but you certainly aren't the first contactee to pick up a second language more quickly than normal. And to my way of thinking, relearning French from a book is a lot less strange than Gary learning to paint basically overnight."

Stated so simply, Imogene had no argument this time. She was a contactee. She arrived at this admission with a startling level of contentment.

*If the shoe fits...*she thought.

Then: *Qui se sent morveux, qu'il se mouche.*

Not a direct translation, but she already understood that the best ones never were. She leaned back and tried to sleep away the last half hour of the flight.

REUNION IN PARIS

1

Clearing customs at Charles de Gaulle was more of an open air affair than the cramped hallways at Heathrow had been, with high ceilings and windows surrounding a long bank of bulletproof glass booths that reminded Imogene of the lottery stands she'd seen dotting the sidewalks in London. Although the lines were all full, Imogene and Ben neared their respective checkpoints quickly. They had decided that they should go through on their own so that Imogene could try out her French on a native speaker without any other audience.

"Duration of stay?" the French customs official asked boredly.

It was a more complicated question than the officer knew. Imogene had only bought one way tickets to Paris even though the Council of Paris was supposed to end tomorrow. That meant Gary would almost certainly have to do whatever he planned to do today or tomorrow.

She leaned toward the circular patch of mesh in the bulletproof glass between her and the customs official. "*Je reste pendant peut-être deux jours.*"

His eyebrows went up. He looked her up and down, obviously studying her clothing, hairstyle, and any other clue he could find to determine her culture of origin. "*Etes-vous américaine, no?*"

Imogene suppressed an idiotic grin. "*Oui.*"

"Your accent is very good, *mademoiselle*," he said, returning to English. "Please enjoy your two days in Paris."

"*Merci.*" He nodded smartly, stamped her passport, and waved her through.

"How'd it go?" Ben asked on the other side of the checkpoint.

"*Magnifique,*" she said happily. They piled onto an escalator leading down to the airport's exit with the other travelers. "The guy could hardly believe I was from…" she trailed off.

"What's the matter?" Ben asked, seeing her expression.

He followed her line of sight across the crowded terminal. The woman who had caught Imogene's attention looked close to Imogene's age and was very short with a handsomely tanned complexion. She had thick black hair piled in a loose bun supported with two decorative hair sticks in the shape of an X. She smiled at Imogene and Ben, wearing an expression of timid, almost disbelieving recognition. Imogene might have taken her as simply another fan—a cell phone raised to take a picture would have sealed the deal—except for the white rectangle of poster board in the woman's hands with Imogene's name printed on it.

"Holy crap, that's the lady from the Spain portrait," Ben said. "How in the boiling lake of hell did she know we were coming here?"

Imogene had only seen the Spain portrait for a few seconds on the news, but that had been enough for her to see now that Gary's rendition had been as accurate as ever. The large eyes, the full lips, the sharp nose—the woman's whole appearance was instantly recognizable and somehow familiar.

The woman met Ben and Imogene at the foot of the elevator, smiling nervously. She shook hands with both of them. "Imogene? Hi.

And you must be Ben. I'd always hoped I would meet you someday, but I never dreamed I'd have to wait twenty years."

Imogene's mouth made the connection before her mind did. "Dulci? How in the world?"

Dulci didn't answer and Imogene didn't bother asking again. She simply stepped forward and hugged her old friend for the first time.

"You were the fourth portrait," Imogene said, pulling away from Dulci. "Of course you were."

"How did you know we were coming to Paris?" Ben asked.

"Your friend Oliver called Ellen and told her. He knew your flight number and everything."

"I'm sure Teddy told Oliver the very instant he hung up with me," Imogene said, but then her brain caught up with what Dulci had just said. "Wait, you know Ellen?"

"She and Priscilla and I have been staying together at this ritzy hotel in central Paris since we all got here. They were going to come with me to the airport, but I wanted to meet you for the first time by myself. I know it's selfish," she added meekly.

"It's wonderful," Imogene said. "Where are they now?"

Dulci smiled. "Back at the hotel. We've been watching the news and reading newspapers in any language we can understand for a sign of Gary. Until today, pretty much all we've heard is political bickering. Did you hear the Vice President make that reference to the Horsemen of the Apocalypse?"

Imogene nodded impatiently. "What do you mean 'until today'? What happened today?"

"Ellen called me about a half hour ago while I was on my way here. I guess she and Priscilla saw some footage of Gary on TV, but they sounded pretty confused about what they saw. Apparently Gary was dumping paint on a sidewalk somewhere, and the police showed up."

"Police?" Imogene asked, pulse quickening. If Gary had been arrested—

"Hey guys," Ben broke in, pointing at one of the large flat-screen televisions hanging all along the length of the airport terminal. "I think we're about to see for ourselves."

The television showed a small man in jeans and a faded flannel shirt, hunched over as if sick to his stomach and running backwards down a wide patch of sidewalk. In his hands was a five gallon bucket of what looked like DayGlo yellow paint, which he was spilling in a splattery line down the middle of the sidewalk. Tourists and other walkers around the man gave him a wide berth, as if worried he might chuck the rest of his bucket of paint at them.

As Dulci had mentioned, three police officers stepped into the picture, and Gary Pritchard's pale, heavily stubbled bespectacled face finally rose into focus just before one of the officers covered the camera's lens with his palm.

"Hey!" Imogene called, raising her arm and taking a single panicky step forward.

Several passersby glanced at her and kept on moving. Two college age girls, amid much pointing and whispering, lifted identical pink cell phones and snapped her picture.

"So what do we do now?" Dulci asked, the same edge of panic in her own voice.

Imogene forced herself to calm down. "Look, the ticker at the bottom of the TV screen up there says that this footage was shot over an hour ago."

"You know French?" Dulci said.

"A little," Imogene said dismissively. Now wasn't the time for that conversation. "It says Gary was someplace called Parc du Champ de Mars."

"That's the park around the Eiffel Tower," Dulci said.

Up on the screen, the newscast had returned to the studio. A sleek female anchor with her hair tied back in a gleaming ponytail and bright pink lips spoke sternly into the camera, but no sound came from the TV, and Imogene's new understanding of the French language didn't seem to extend to lip reading.

"We've got to get there now," she said.

Dulci nodded. "Do you have any more luggage?" The Cornells

shook their heads. "Okay, there's a car outside."

She started off at once with Imogene and Ben on her heels. Outside, Imogene started scanning the line of yellow and white taxis spanning the long canyon of highway that ran through the center of the airport's six terminals. Most drivers leaned against the passenger doors of their cars, smoking nonchalantly as they waited for fares.

Imogene was raising her hand to hail the nearest driver when Dulci called, "Hey, Steve!"

The man who waved back to her stood before a gleaming black Mercedes limousine. He wore a black suit ill tailored to both his limited height and snowman-like girth. Under his chauffer's cap, his eyes crinkled to the point where they disappeared altogether when he saw Imogene.

"Miss Cornell? You are even lovelier in person than on the television. And who is your friend?"

"This is my brother Ben," Imogene said, utterly taken aback.

The driver stepped forward smartly—the peak of his hat came dangerously close to whacking Imogene's forehead as he nodded to her and Ben in turn—simultaneously shaking her hand and relieving her of her carryall.

"My name is Étienne, but it will be easier for you to call me Steve like your friends, yes?" He sounded nearly giddy at the prospect of being called Steve. "The journey to the Plaza Athénée will last perhaps one hour. You and your friends may take whatever you wish from the mini bar. Monsieur Roth has covered all fees including the gratuity."

"Teddy sprung for a limo, huh?" Ben said, impressed.

"Thank you," Imogene told the driver. She rarely heard Teddy called by his surname, and the driver's thick accent made it sound almost like *Goth*.

"We're not going back to the hotel, Steve," Dulci said, swinging open the rear door. "How close can you get us to the Eiffel Tower? I know that the afternoon rush hour will be starting soon."

Steve's button nose rose haughtily. "Traffic is of no importance, Mademoiselle. If not for the law forbidding automobiles to drive on the sidewalk, I could deposit you on Eiffel's steel toes. Although that journey will last a bit longer than the other. Now, if you will enter the limousine, *s'il vous plait.*"

"Thanks, Steve-O," Ben said gamely, crawling through the door Dulci had opened.

Once Imogene and Dulci had followed suit, belting themselves into tan leather seats so soft they almost felt like suede, Steve clapped the door shut behind them and marched to his own door. He immediately eased the long limousine into the continuous stream of taxis and other travelers heading back toward the city.

Imogene turned to Dulci. "We should call Ellen and Priscilla to let them know where we're going."

"On it," Dulci said, pulling a cell phone from her pocket and started tapping buttons.

She pressed the call button and held the phone to her ear. Someone on the other end picked up right away. "Hey…yeah, they got here on time. We're already on our way to—" She broke off and listened for several seconds. "Okay, we'll meet you there."

Dulci closed the phone with a satisfied snap and turned back to the Cornells. "The Eiffel Tower is within walking distance of the hotel, so they'll probably beat us there."

Imogene finally sat back against the plush leather seat and took a deep breath. "Over an hour, huh? I suppose that will give you time to tell us how you got painted and met up with Ellen and Priscilla."

Dulci smiled apologetically. "I'm not sure this ride will be long enough for those stories, especially since they'll probably just raise more questions for you."

"I wouldn't worry about that," Ben said dryly. "Our lives are ruled by questions."

2

With late afternoon Paris rush hour traffic coalescing around them—and Steve the limo driver navigating it with the ruthless grace of a dolphin zooming through a school of tuna—Dulci began her story.

"Well, you know that Americanus Rex—Gary," she amended, "painted me in Spain. And that's also where I met the Chinese guy. Priscilla says you call him something like 'Drool,' but she couldn't remember any better than that."

Ben grinned. "We don't know his real name. Gene and I just started calling him Lord Droon after a character in this old book."

"Droon!" Dulci laughed. "That's perfect. From *The King's Stilts*, right? Dr. Seuss? Hey, don't look so surprised. I come from a family of readers. My mother used to read me and my brother that book all the time. Freaky."

She shook her head in amusement. "Anyway, your Lord Droon pointed me toward my portrait, which I finally saw by climbing up the side of a building onto a balcony. I don't know how long I spent staring at my portrait. I just…" she shrugged.

"You couldn't quit looking," Imogene supplied.

"I did eventually," Dulci said. "Droon had also given me a newspaper with a picture of you and Ellen onstage at the museum in London, but I hadn't read the whole article yet. And when I opened it back up, an envelope fell out."

"Containing one airplane ticket to Paris," Imogene guessed. "The rest of us got envelopes too. Did Droon give you a nickname too?"

"*The Envoy*," Dulci enunciated. "It means like an ambassador or diplomat. I honestly didn't pay much attention right then because, according to the ticket, I had less than two hours to get to the Madrid airport for my flight. That was Monday."

"The same day the Americanus Rex exhibit opened at the Tate," Imogene calculated. "That seems like forever ago."

"And the same day Ellen and Priscilla flew to Paris themselves," Ben added. "Let me guess: you guys all just happened to meet up at the airport."

Dulci nodded. "Our flights got in at almost the same time, and by some miscommunication in the airport, our bags wound up at the same carousel. I recognized Ellen right away from her picture in the newspaper. How could you not?"

"How could you not?" Imogene agreed helplessly.

"So Ellen rented us a suite at the hotel I told you about, the Plaza Athénée. Her parents are footing the bill."

"And since Monday, you guys have been keeping an eye on all the news media for signs of Gary," Imogene finished for her.

"We've also visited some likely hotspots in the city."

"Hotspots?" Ben asked.

"The Louvre was our first stop," Dulci said. "We thought, what better place for a modern master of art than the most famous art museum in the world?"

The high wail of a police siren rose outside the limo. All three of them peered out the tinted windows as Steve rapidly crossed three lanes of traffic onto the highway's shoulder. Moments later two motorcycles bearing the green stripes of the Paris Prefecture of Police zoomed past, tailed by an armored bank truck.

"This is the world!" Steve bawled at the windshield. "Thousands of living, breathing passengers must make way so that satchels of money will not arrive late to their destination!"

Imogene bit her lower lip to keep from laughing, and saw Ben and Dulci exercising similar restraint as Steve slid the limo back onto the highway.

Ben cleared his throat. "So you started looking for Gary at the Louvre. No dice, I take it?"

"No dice," Dulci confirmed. "Next Ellen suggested Notre Dame since she'd been painted in the best known cathedral in Dresden. The crowds there were even worse than in the Louvre," Dulci reported darkly. "Ellen doesn't mind crowds, and you guys probably don't either, but when you're as short as I am…"

Her glare was so ill tempered that Imogene couldn't help laughing.

"We stuck our heads into a few other churches as well, but none of them made as much sense to us as Notre Dame had. I mean, Gary has mostly worked near busy places. Tourist traps. Your portrait was in a heavily traveled station, even if most tourists don't go to London to see—where was it?"

"South Ealing," Imogene said.

"Next we took the cue from my portrait," Dulci went on. "Gary painted me on an old Roman city wall in Alcalá de Henares, so we visited all the Roman ruins we could get to in an afternoon, popping our heads into any churches en route. We've seen more of this city than I would have thought possible in two days."

"I guess so," Imogene said, shaking her head in admiration.

"This morning, before we heard you were on your way, we were pretty much grasping at straws. We were going to leaf through the English, Spanish, and German newspapers on sale at the kiosk outside the hotel. None of us speak French, unfortunately, or we would've read those too."

"Gene's got you covered there," Ben said, hands laced comfortably behind his head. "Meaning that now our little group has some proficiency in all the languages spoken by the countries currently involved in the Council of Paris. That's handy, isn't it?"

"That's not going to help us if Gary's been thrown in jail or something," Imogene said, trying not to sound as frustrated as she felt. "We're meeting Ellen and Priscilla at the Eiffel Tower?"

Before Dulci could answer, they heard the electronic chitter of a cell phone up in the limo's cockpit. Steve immediately began speaking softly into a headset fastened to his ample cheek.

"*Oui. Je comprends, oui. Merci. Au revois.*" He tilted his head back through the driver's partition without taking his eyes from the road. "My friends, I am afraid the Prefecture of Police have closed all roads around the *Tour Eiffel.* I can leave you at Avenue Silvestre de Sacy. That is the boundary of Parc du Champ de Mars. You will have perhaps a two blocks walk to the tower," he finished, disgust evident in his voice.

"Why have the police closed the roads?" Imogene asked, although she already had a decent idea.

"My friend did not explain to me," Steve said, his shoulders slumping noticeably with this latest failure. "However, I will guess it is related to the *Conseil de Paris,* which I am sure you know ends tomorrow. I know that airplanes and helicopters have been limited in their ability to fly over Paris during the *Conseil.*" He waved a meaty hand in a surprisingly prissy gesture of irritation. "*Perhaps they will close all of the damned roads tonight!*"

Imogene smiled. "*You are doing a fine job,*" she assured him.

Dulci and Ben turned to stare at her—even Steve finally took his small, but sharp eyes from the road to watch her in the rear view mirror.

"What's the matter?" she asked.

A funny little smile played at Ben's lips. "You didn't even realize, did you? You were speaking in French just now."

Dulci's expression had taken on a new appraising quality. "I'd better reevaluate my own bias. Frankly, when you said you spoke a little French I thought you meant it the way most Americans do when they say they can speak a second language. Like, they can say hello, good-bye, please pass the cheese. Things like that. But you sound like a native speaker. Or you did right then anyway."

"This is the truth," Steve agreed decisively from the front seat.

Imogene blushed. "Thank you."

"Ben was right. How handy is that?" Dulci said. "If we see the police at the road block, you can ask them where they took Gary."

"Handy," Imogene said.

3

Streetlights had begun to dot on throughout the city by the time Steve maneuvered the limousine from the crawling A1 highway onto smaller, equally well traveled city streets leading ever deeper into the heart of Paris. When Steve crossed the eight lane Avenue des Champs-Elysées—"The most beautiful and famous avenue in all of Europe!" he boasted through the partition—Imogene and Ben pressed their faces to the limousine's windows like astonished children.

Dulci pointed out the Seine River curling off to the southwest. "The Eiffel Tower and Parc du Champ de Mars are right off the river, a few miles south of here."

Sure enough, a few minutes later, traveling west along the southern edge of the river, a low patch in the cityscape finally revealed an uninterrupted view of the Eiffel Tower. Against the hazy purple-orange of dusk, the tower looked like the dirty brown skeleton of some ancient, terrifying amusement park attraction.

The illusion abruptly evaporated as twenty thousand lights along the tower's entire height exploded to life, bathing it from top to bottom in brilliant yellow light. Only the tower's highest point, a round complexity of steel that looked like a puffy hat, or perhaps a pincushion, remained dark.

"Does it always do that?" Imogene wanted to know.

"At dusk," Dulci confirmed.

Ben whistled through his teeth. "I'd hate to pay their electric bill. It's nice, though, isn't it?"

Dulci leaned over so she could see better. "I wonder why they haven't turned on the Beacon yet."

Imogene grabbed Dulci's forearm, her cheeks and scalp suddenly tingling. Out of the corner of her eye she saw Ben's head snap around. "What did you just say?"

Dulci grinned. "Priscilla had that same look on her face this morning at breakfast when she was reading about the Eiffel Tower in a travel book. There are four extremely powerful spotlights at the top of the tower that rotate like the lenses in a lighthouse. Their rotation is controlled by a computer so that instead of seeing four individual lights, you only ever see two shining in opposite directions. It's a really neat effect."

"And they're called the Beacon?" Ben asked. He had the same expression on his face as when Droon had mentioned sulfide reactors.

Dulci nodded. "Priscilla and Ellen told me all about the thing with your mom. The Beacon of Peace," she clarified. "I didn't know she'd died. I'm sorry."

"Thanks," Imogene mumbled.

Her mind was racing. The Beacon. Another fabulous coincidence in a long trail of them, leading her ever onward like Hansel and Gretel's breadcrumbs. Except that the breadcrumbs in this case had been leading her *away* from anything as safe and familiar as a home.

"How soon will we be there?" she called through the partition.

Steve uttered a series of guttural sounding words that had not appeared in *Français the Easy Way* as he braked hard to avoid rear-ending a little Citroën hatchback that had just cut into the lane ahead of him.

"Forgive me, Madamoiselle, but the traffic is far worse than normal due to the closed roads. It may be faster for you to disembark and make the rest of your journey by foot," he finished in a tone of voice a doctor might use to prescribe an amputation.

"We know you're doing your best," Dulci soothed.

Steve didn't respond, but he relaxed minutely and looked slightly less like a bear driving a car.

"I should probably call Teddy anyway," Imogene said. "I'm sure he'll want to know that Gary really is in Paris. I don't think he much liked the idea of me coming here."

"Yeah, it's not like you've done anything for *him* lately," Ben muttered.

She found Teddy's number and dialed. Teddy picked up on the first ring.

"Genie. So I guess you're in Paris." He sounded tense.

"Yeah, we made it just fine. Thank you for the limo. The driver is excellent."

Silence on the other end. "Amanda called a few hours ago for me to approve a hefty charge from a trucking company in West Virginia."

"Good. Priscilla's portrait will come right to the gallery sometime next week in a discreetly marked semi and crate. I can't wait for you to see it, Teddy."

"Oh, I can see it just fine right now. Big as life on every channel of British television with that little weirdo you call Lord Droon. I don't think *discreet* is the word for it."

Imogene swallowed. The cell phone suddenly felt slippery in her sweating grip. "I'm sorry, I don't think I'm following you."

Teddy barked a laugh. "I'm sorry too. You were a hell of a good assistant until you started flaking out in London. But even then I thought you had more integrity than this. The armored truck was a nice touch. Am I going to get a bill for that too?"

"What truck? Teddy, what are you—"

But even before she could finish the sentence, her mind made the connection to the armored bank truck and motorcycle police escort that had sped past the limousine shortly after they'd left the airport. On the heels of this, two previously unrelated memories fell into place as well: the black Cadillac that had pulled into the parking lot of the trucking company in Charleston as she and Ben had been leaving and Glenn Pritchard telling her and Ben how Droon's "sort" had driven black Cadillacs around Accord and asked funny questions back in 1967.

"Oh no," she breathed.

"Oh yes!" Teddy hissed triumphantly, believing that he had just heard some type of confession.

"Teddy," Imogene said sternly. "I don't know what you saw on television, but I haven't stolen anything. You know I'm smarter than that."

"Please," Teddy snorted. "I've been in LA long enough to know that even the best relationships can go sour over this much money. I've at least got the insurance on Priscilla's portrait, though I don't know how you can sleep knowing the trucking company ponied up for your theft."

"Teddy, listen—"

"I'll have Amanda box up your shit and mail it to your dad's place in Seattle. Enjoy the rest of your limo ride."

"Wait!"

But Teddy was gone. The words *Call Ended* flashed on her phone's LCD screen.

"What was that all about?" Ben asked. He and Dulci were watching her with identical wide eyed expressions. "What got stolen?"

"I just got fired," Imogene said, trying to decide whether she was more shocked or furious.

"Wait, Teddy fired *you?*"

"Who's Teddy again?" Dulci asked.

"He's Gene's boss and an arrogant, ungrateful assbag," Ben explained before turning back to Imogene. "But even he knows he can't tie his shoes without you to show him how. What happened?"

Imogene relayed Teddy's half of the conversation, finishing with his comments about the armored truck and Droon's apparent cameo.

"Armored truck?" Dulci repeated, recognition filling her dark eyes.

"Yeah." Imogene rotated in her seat and called to Steve through the partition. "Was that truck with the police escort coming from the airport?"

"Most likely," Steve answered at once. "Many valuable things travel through Charles de Gaulle. I would not be surprised if the Prefecture of Police keeps such trucks at the airport at all times."

"I wish I'd asked Ellen and Priscilla to stick around the hotel and watch the news a little longer," Dulci said. "I'm sure they're already at the park."

"Got a TV anywhere in this thing, Steve-O?" Ben called.

"I am sorry, Monsieur," Steve reported, sounding sorry indeed, as if the absence of a television were yet another personal failure in a string of them this evening.

"We don't need a TV," Imogene said loudly enough for Steve to hear.

Teddy would certainly cancel her phone service, but that might not go through for a few hours yet if she was lucky. She scrolled through her list of phone numbers, selected Oliver's, and hit the *Call* button.

Oliver's phone rang twice. "Hume."

"Oliver, it's Imogene. Have you talked to Teddy today?" she asked without preamble.

A brief pause gave her all the answer she needed.

"Did he tell you he thinks I stole Priscilla's portrait for myself?"

"Yes. The footage appeared on the news only minutes ago, and I must admit that the evidence against you is quite damning. I take it Teddy terminated your employment."

"That's about the size of it," Imogene agreed. "What did this 'footage' show?"

"It's all terribly mysterious to me," Oliver admitted. "Essentially, an armored lorry was escorted through the police barrier, after which it backed up to the base of the Eiffel Tower, where several men relieved it of what appeared to be a large shipping crate. The television cameras were behind the police barrier, but they managed to sustain a reasonable view."

"What about the shipping crate?" Imogene redirected.

"That was puzzling," Oliver said slowly. "The men who unloaded the crate seemed to place it purposefully in plain sight, where the television cameras would be able to see it. Then another man fitting your brother's description of Lord Droon removed the front panel of the crate with a crowbar, and gave the cameras a moment to zoom in. I quite easily recognized the image of Miss Hemphill inside," he finished. "Masterfully done, as usual."

"No wonder Teddy jumped to the wrong conclusion," Imogene said fitfully. "Was there anything else?"

"Your Lord Droon and his companions carried the stone onto one of the lifts in the Eiffel Tower's legs, and that's the last anyone saw of it. The reporters are making all sorts of mad speculations, naturally." He paused. "I don't suppose you *can* offer any insight about how Miss Hemphill's portrait wound up in Paris?"

"I have my guesses," Imogene admitted, "but they're just that: guesses. I hope to have actual answers in the next couple hours."

"Indeed," Oliver said. "And when you find your answers, they will be worth far more to me than the ten thousand Pounds I already owe you."

"Ten thousand?"

"Surely you haven't forgotten about your reward for, ah, discovering a new Americanus Rex portrait."

She *had* forgotten. It seemed like very long ago indeed that she, Ben, and Priscilla had read about the reward in the *Times*.

"You don't need to give me any money," she said.

"In that case, consider the ten thousand as a signing bonus for the new position I've just created for you at the Tate," Oliver said cheerfully. "I've had a hard go creating a close partnership between the Tate Modern and the Louvre since I began as curator. A full time liaison between London and Paris would go a long way toward building that bridge."

"You're offering me a job?" she asked incredulously. Ben's head snapped up.

"I'm offering one *possibility* for a job," Oliver corrected. "I won't lie and say it will be easy. You would have to learn some French, though I doubt that would be a problem for someone as resourceful as yourself. Still, if you don't like this job I'll invent another."

"*Je parle français,*" she said numbly. "I speak French, I mean."

"*Sousestimation!*" Steve bellowed from the driver's seat. Even in her current state, the internal translation arrived instantly: *understatement.*

"Brilliant!" Oliver said at the same time. "I'm not surprised, actually. That only illustrates my point that you're too valuable for me to let you get away the way Teddy did. I've seen how big things happen around you. *Because* of you. Anyone who wouldn't want someone like that in his employ is either a coward or an absolute twat. Possibly both."

"I don't know what to say."

"Say you'll think about it," he supplied. "Although if you would prefer never to work for a man again I would understand. We can be a right dodgy lot."

"I'll think about it," she promised.

"For as long as you need," Oliver said, not bothering to mask the satisfaction in his voice. "Americanus Rex is the main dish on your plate at the moment, as he should be."

"Thank you for everything," Imogene said.

"No, love, thank *you.* I'll see you on television shortly then, will I?"

"It's a date."

4

Ben watched her power down the cell phone and stuff it back into her carryall. "So Oliver wants you to work for him now?" he prompted when she said nothing. "Every hour I spend with you makes my book grow another chapter."

"What did he say about Priscilla's portrait?" Dulci asked. "Was it really in that armored truck that passed us back on the highway?"

"Yes," Imogene said. "Hey Steve, how far are we from the Eiffel Tower on foot?"

"Ten minutes, maximum," he said. He glared out the windshield at the acres of stopped, honking traffic and added, "Walking will be faster than driving, I am sorry to say."

He aimed one short, thick finger through the windshield at the mouth of a narrow street leading into a tunnel of leafy trees lit from underneath by quaintly glowing streetlamps. Bright orange sawhorses adorned with flashing lights blocked the street from automotive traffic, but the uniformed men behind them made no move to stop the scores of pedestrians milling past.

"Avenue Silvestre de Sacy," Steve announced, "presently becomes Avenue Gustave Eiffel. Regardless, this close to the *Tour Eiffel* you may simply look to the sky and you cannot become lost."

"Thank you," Dulci said, clicking open the door handle.

Imogene slid toward the door as well. "Can you park somewhere nearby and wait for us? It might be a few hours," she warned.

Steve nodded severely. "I wait with the bells on."

Stepping out of the car, Imogene immediately saw that Steve had been dead right about them not getting lost. Even without the steady, enthusiastic trickle of foot traffic following signs to Parc du Champ, the brightly lit Eiffel Tower seemed to dominate fully half visible sky.

Five minutes into their walk down the narrow street, Imogene, Ben, and Dulci came upon an even narrower crossroad. A meandering, two foot wide line of luminous yellow paint ran down the center of this new street, vanishing around gentle curves a block or so away in either direction. It was a toss-up whether the streetlamps or the yellow streak of paint provided more ambient light. People all around had stopped to take photographs.

"I guess the policemen we saw on TV let Gary finish what he was doing after all," Ben said. "Criminy, how many gallons of paint must this have taken?"

"Do you think this line goes all the way around the tower?" Dulci asked.

"We'll find out in a little bit," Imogene said.

But soon their progress toward the tower was impeded by a vast sea of curious onlookers. Police officers in full riot gear guarded the inner edges of the crowd, creating a barricade that prematurely dead-ended Avenue Gustave Eiffel and separating the growing knot of spectators from the square at the base of the tower.

"This crowd has got to be twenty people deep," Ben said, squinting first to the right, then to the left. "And it looks like that might be true all the way around the tower. Lovely night for the pickpockets, I imagine."

Dulci stood on tiptoe, which only brought her eye level to Imogene's chin. "You think Ellen and Priscilla are in there somewhere?"

Before Imogene could answer, the people closest to the sawhorses began to ripple outward until a wide section of crowd had parted like the Red Sea before Moses. Except in this case, the role of Moses had gone to Lord Droon. He glided forward, a full head shorter than most of the people watching him pass. Added to his trademark tailored black wardrobe was a silver badge hanging from his breast pocket. Imogene read the words *Préfecture de Police de Paris* in gleaming silver as he stepped before her.

"*Nous vous avions attendu, Mademoiselle Cornell,*" he said cheerfully.

"I've been waiting to see you too," Imogene said. "Did you really hijack Priscilla's portrait somehow and bring it to Paris?"

Droon only smiled. "*Vous comprenez?* I am pleased that Droon-Corp's first venture in publishing was a success," he said in English, turning politely to Ben and Dulci. "We have also been waiting for your friends, naturally."

Imogene was confounded to hear that his English was now tinged with a distinct French accent. "You're the other brother?" she asked. "The one Priscilla and I met in London."

Droon dipped his head once, a gesture full of impatience. "*S'il vous plaît,*" he said, moving aside and indicating with a sweep of his arm that they should follow him.

Without waiting to see if they would obey or not, he began walking toward the base of the Eiffel Tower. Ben and Dulci looked to Imogene, who set off at once.

Before she caught up to him, however, Imogene was startled by a woman's joyous shout from somewhere in the crowd: "We came to Paris! Just like you asked!"

Localized rushes of applause and similar shouts greeted this announcement. Imogene waved awkwardly in the direction of the first voice as she trotted past. The now familiar cameras and cell phones clicked and flashed. At the edges of the crowd, field reporters speaking in at least three different languages recited into their cameras the names and descriptions of Imogene and her companions.

"Americanus Rex has been working for much of the day," Droon informed them briskly. He spread his short arms in a grand gesture that encompassed the Eiffel Tower and its surrounding real estate. "*Roue de Guerre!*"

"The Wheel of War," Imogene translated automatically for the others. She turned back to Droon. "Can you tell us what happened to Priscilla's portrait after we left West Virginia?"

"We paid all monetary fees due for the transgression," Droon said. "We typically do not steal what is not ours, but the Wheel of War could not be completed without your friend's portrait."

He pulled a folded piece of paper from his lapel pocket and handed it to Imogene. Ben and Dulci crowded at her shoulders as she unfolded it. The thousands of lights glaring from the Eiffel Tower's steel skeleton provided ample light to study the picture scrawled on the paper:

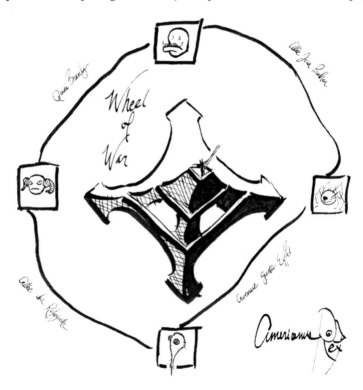

The cartoony, high contrast sketch of the Eiffel Tower was far cruder than Gary's typical style, but Imogene still didn't need the signature at the bottom to understand that he'd drawn the picture himself.

"Do the tower's legs really point north, south, east, and west like this?" Ben asked, looking up and frowning as he tried to get his bearings.

Droon stopped walking and pointed a long finger to the curve running between the tower's eastern and southern feet. "We are now here, west of Avenue Gustav Eiffel."

"So Gary's a cartographer now too?" Ben said, shaking his head. "What are these four frowny face things at the end of each leg of the tower?"

"They will be clearly visible from the tower's higher levels," Droon said.

"Hang on," Dulci said. "Are you saying this is like a blueprint or sketch of Gary's lifesize painting? I mean, that yellow line on the street that we saw walking in—did Gary actually paint a gigantic circle around the Eiffel Tower?"

"As I said, he has been busy most of the day," Droon said.

Imogene frowned. "Gary hasn't done first drafts before, has he?"

Droon's dark eyes bored into hers. "Wheel of War is not like his other work."

After a moment he set off again. Ben caught up to him easily this time. "So you're really a French cop? I have to admit, I never saw that coming. Most of the literature says the Men in Black are Air Force, CIA, or maybe NSA. But then again, you guys operate all over the world, don't you? How is it that a single organization most people don't even believe exists can infiltrate high levels of governments all over the world?"

"We are what we must be," Droon replied. He coughed once, grimaced, and took a brief pull on the small glass Evian bottle hidden in his coat before adding to Ben, "Though you are correct that our role here is less subtle than on previous occasions."

Ben laughed and clapped Droon on the shoulder. "I hate to break it to you, pal, but you guys are about as subtle as a Godzilla movie."

"Strange, then, that you say no one believes we exist."

Ben was spared from coming up with a retort when Droon banked right and led them under the massive archway spanning between the Eiffel Tower's eastern and southern legs—the spot he had shown them on Gary's drawing. Directly beneath the main rise of the tower, all four legs met in a dark square vortex two hundred fifty feet above the ground.

Head tilted back, mouth open, Imogene thought the tower's complicated steel innards looked like nothing so much as an upside down whirlpool.

"Reminds me of a vaulted ceiling in a church," Dulci murmured.

At the same time Ben said, "Biggest damn spider web I've ever seen."

A high voice suddenly echoed through the open air cavern under the Eiffel Tower. "*Imogene!*"

Imogene pulled her gaze down from the steel warren and saw Ellen loping toward her across the concrete like a gazelle, with Priscilla and the other Droon trailing behind at a jog. Imogene had time to register the way the tower's yellow lights slid rapidly across the slick surface of Ellen's mask and to see that the swelling in her face seemed to have gone down a little. Then Ellen yanked her off her feet in an enthusiastic and ridiculously painful bear hug that slammed the side of her head against a hard slab of shoulder muscle.

"Can you believe we're all here?" Ellen roared in her ear. "Feels like weeks since we saw you last."

The two Droons, together for the first time since Imogene had met them, nodded politely in greeting to one another as the rest of the group exchanged various giddy salutations.

When Priscilla had extricated herself from Ben, she turned the bright gray lamps of her eyes to Imogene. "They were unloading my portrait from a truck when Ellen and I got here. I thought you were sending it to Los Angeles."

"So did I."

Priscilla nodded as if she understood. "Were there any problems at home? Cody?" she added almost reluctantly.

"Your mom's managing," Ben answered. "Cody was less than thrilled when we moved your portrait, but a hundred fifty people in town took up our cause once they found out that we had your blessing. Agnes and Glenn had a lot to do with it too."

Priscilla opened her mouth to ask something else, but was interrupted by a loud mechanical squeal that drifted down between the tower's legs from somewhere far above.

"What the hell was that?" Ellen demanded, looking wildly up into the tower's steel guts.

"We must go quickly," said the Droon with the badge. "Even we cannot ensure your privacy in this place indefinitely."

He led them beneath the tower's center spire to a tourist hub of sorts, where signs posted in five languages directed visitors to various ticket booths, gift shops, staircases, and elevators. The elevator toward which Droon led them was housed in the western leg.

Priscilla glanced upward again when a second squeal echoed down from the tower's upper levels. "It sounds like a table saw."

"Your guide," Droon said pleasantly as the elevator doors opened.

Dulci looked inside and emitted a complicated little chirp.

Unfazed, Ben muttered, "I should have known."

The elevator's interior was lit with harsh white light and lined with rectangular windows. Standing beside the control box, one hand wrapped protectively around a water bottle, a third Droon tipped his hat in greeting. "Going up?"

5

Ellen's head swung back and forth between the three Droons, reflected light rippling across her mask. "There's *three* of you?"

The new Droon's smile widened. "I am told there are many people in the world who look like me."

For the first time since Imogene had met her, Priscilla seemed to be losing patience. "Will you take us to see Gary now?"

Droon stepped forward, clasped her small hand in his long, delicate fingers, and ushered her inside the elevator, where she leaned calmly against one of the wooden handrails running along the walls.

Imogene followed them without another word. Shortly each of them had taken places inside the elevator car, much to the Droons' collective delight. Only the newest Droon remained in the car with Imogene and the others. He opened the elevator's simple control box, which contained four large buttons. When he pressed the green one, the doors slid closed and the car jerked upward into a relatively smooth diagonal ascent through the tower's leg. Steel beams flashed past the windows. Soft thumps and clanks echoed from above as the thick cable supporting the lift ran along its system of spinning pulleys.

"Would you look at that," Ellen breathed.

The enormous yellow circle painted on the streets around the tower was becoming more visible as they ascended. It gave Imogene the impression that a bicycle-riding giant with wet paint on his tires had raced all the way around Parc du Champ de Mars leaving a luminescent trail behind him.

"I see you guys have the police keeping Quai Banley empty as well," Ellen said to Droon, pointing at an empty six-lane boulevard tracing the bank of the Seine River.

Actually it was not quite empty, Imogene saw. Straight west, a team of men was unrolling a two hundred foot square of heavy canvas like an immense area rug. They worked quickly, and when they were finished the canvas covered a patch of land where the boulevard butted up against green parkland. The giant canvas had been painted too, but Imogene had no success detecting a pattern; the steel beams flashing past the window created a dizzying strobe effect.

"What is that thing?" Priscilla asked.

"I don't know, but there's another one," Dulci said, pointing. "Straight south. It looks like they're rolling it open across the top of a grove of trees in front of those apartment buildings."

The elevator abruptly shuddered. The cityscape vanished and a dimly lit pavilion came into view in the tower's interior before falling away a few seconds later.

"First level," Droon announced, proper as any department store elevator operator. "The horsemen will be more visible from the second level, if you wish to study them."

"Horsemen?" Ellen asked.

Ben turned to Droon. "You're referring to whatever is painted on those big canvas squares, right? I'm no expert in art composition, but given that we can see one horseman to the west and one to the south, I assume there are two more. And with a name like 'Wheel of War'..."

"The Four Horsemen of the Apocalypse," said Dulci authoritatively. "Is this a jab at what the Vice President said the other day, or are you and your buddies just suckers for literary symbolism?"

"None of this is our design," Droon croaked.

Ellen looked away from the window. "If you can't make out any of Gary's painting from the ground, why aren't there twenty news helicopters circling us right now, spamming Wheel of War live on every network?"

"The Council of Paris doesn't end until tomorrow," Droon reminded her smugly. "With so many high profile dignitaries in Paris, most of the city is restricted airspace for all besides French defense forces. And, of course," his goatee twitched, "our own aircraft."

Ben raised his own eyebrows. "What, did you guys empty the flying saucer Park-N-Ride at Area 51?"

Another goatee twitch. "Police helicopters."

"Whose pilots and crews will undoubtedly take pictures and videos that you'll leak to the press as you see fit?" Ben supplied.

Ellen shook her head in open wonder. "You guys must be the most organized group on the planet."

Droon didn't argue. His mouth was occupied with chugging the rest of his water bottle, that same earnest expression in his dark eyes. For the first time since they had boarded the elevator, Imogene caught the smell of sulfur in the enclosed space.

"Are you going to be okay?" she asked.

Droon waved her off and slid the empty bottle into his hip pocket. Another impenetrable web of steel fell across the windows and blocked out their view of the city. Droon pushed a button and the elevator eased to a stop, swinging slowly forward, then back. Imogene heard another of those soft clanks and the doors rolled silently open.

"Level Two," Droon said pleasantly.

6

The elevator dumped them into a darkened ultramodern restaurant called *Le Jules Verne,* according to a handsome placard mounted on the wall. The four women and Ben followed Droon's winding course across soft carpet, past empty tables and ergonomic rolling chairs that Imogene was sure would be packed with wealthy diners on a normal evening. Just glimpsing the various balcony exits, she reckoned the view alone would probably be enough to merit a hundred bucks a plate.

"You said we could get a better look at your horsemen from up here, right?" Ben asked Droon, indicating the nearest balcony. "Do we have time for a quick peek?"

Droon tilted his head in the now familiar listening gesture before answering. "Certainly."

The restaurant's glass outer door slid peaceably open under Droon's touch. A stiff summer breeze swept into the restaurant, ruffling tablecloths and raising gooseflesh on Imogene's bare arms.

They exited single file onto the corner where this level's western and southern balconies met. A manmade pond, perfectly black but for the glimmering reflection of the tower, spread across the ground to the south. Strings of streetlamps cut hazy orange trails throughout Parc du Champ de Mars.

It only took Imogene a few seconds to pick out the wide path around the tower that glowed a brighter yellow than the rest, marking the outer arc of the Wheel of War. Like the drawing Droon had given them, the actual "wheel" wasn't terribly round, due perhaps to Gary's exhaustion, which had been plainly evident in the few seconds of news footage they'd seen at the airport, or the simple fact that there was no perfect circle of roads circumscribing the Eiffel Tower.

But Imogene's real attention was divided between the creatures— the horsemen—Gary had painted on the two visible squares of canvas, now fully unrolled, at ground level to the south and west.

"Weirdsville," Ellen said, rubbing her forearm with her hand. "Am I the only one getting a creepy vibe right now?"

"No," Dulci said. "Those things aren't like Gary's sketches on the map at all. Those were almost cute."

"Did Gary do all of this by himself?" Priscilla asked.

"The man is intense," Droon answered.

"Droon, old boy," Ben interjected. "I know you called the things painted on those canvas squares the horsemen, but I'm struggling to pick out either horse or man. Care to explain? You can start with the wicked witch of the west."

He pointed down at the square of canvas that had been unrolled half in the street and half in the park.

"Americanus Rex has not told us his intentions for the horsemen," Droon husked. "He requested the materials and began painting immediately after his arrival in Paris. Only today did he instruct us to place them equidistantly from the Eiffel tower at the four points of the compass, as you can see in the drawing we gave you."

"But what *is* that thing?" Dulci asked, wrinkling her nose at the painting Ben had called the wicked witch of the west. "Is it supposed to be some kind of animal?"

Imogene's brain rebelled at the sight of it, but she forced the image into the context of a horseman and was able to discern some kind of creature with crooked, muscular legs and a heavy horned head lowered against a great burden. An armored rider sat astride its humped back, seeming to grow out of the creature's body like a human shaped tumor. This rider carried a long staff bearing many banners that seemed to flap in the night's cool breeze. But the ultimate unreality, the nail in the coffin of rationality, was that one of the banners on the rider's staff very clearly bore a Coca-Cola logo.

"Gary didn't take any Polaroids of that thing," Ellen said, sounding almost sick to her stomach.

Droon harrumphed into his delicate fist, expelling a heavy odor of sulfur into the breeze. "Even we could not have predicted that he would begin to paint his dreams."

Priscilla turned her attention to the other visible patch of canvas spread across the treetops to the south. "Gary's had dreams about these things?" She sounded horrified.

The southern canvas contained a soft, shiny creature whose body was segmented into leaking rolls of fat. On its back was a crouched man shape with an equally bloated belly and a mosquito-like facial proboscis sunken deep into the neck of its mount.

"We must leave here now," Droon wheezed.

Imogene turned gratefully away from the horsemen, not terribly eager to see their northern and eastern fellows, and followed Droon back inside the restaurant. He led them to a new elevator located behind a partition of diamond-shaped windows. When he pressed the button, the sleek outer door rolled open to reveal a much smaller lift.

Dulci was first in line to enter, but she hesitated at the threshold, watching Droon anxiously. Imogene looked too. Despite the restaurant's almost nonexistent lighting, she thought she could see thin curls of vapor drifting up from the corners of Droon's mouth.

"Are you sure you're alright?" Dulci finally asked.

Ben strode over to an upright cooler much like the one in Pritchard's Corner, opened a bottle of Perrier from the top shelf, and brought it back to Droon. "No Evian in there. Sorry."

Droon blinked in plain surprise, but accepted the green bottle in his long fingers and took a brief swig. "Your ride to the top will be brief," he said, sounding a little better.

Before they could ask anything else he turned and marched back the way they'd come.

"Hey, see you later," Ben called.

Droon's head snapped around and he studied Ben with wide eyes. "Perhaps," he finally said, and he disappeared around the restaurant's partition.

"Huh," Ben said. "That's not the answer I was expecting."

"Have you expected anything that's come out of that guy's mouth?" Ellen muttered disinterestedly.

Without waiting for an answer, she ducked into the new elevator. Ben gestured for the other three women to go on ahead before boarding himself.

"Do you guys see a button or someth—" he began, but as soon as he'd cleared the doorway, the lift closed itself and leapt upward, traveling at least twice as fast as the previous elevator had done.

Dulci giggled nervously. "Going up, I guess?"

This lift ran through the tower's central spire and therefore offered its occupants a 360 degree view of the surrounding landscape. Imogene immediately noted that the northern and eastern horsemen were in place, and a few seconds of study granted more detail than she needed.

The northern "horse" seemed to be composed of rotten, festering cuts of meat, its rider's face a pile of slippery organs with shallow indentions for eyes, and an unbearable drooping mouth. The creature to the east resembled a horribly mutated buffalo with a filthy, shaggy coat and a jutting fan of spiked bones rising from its back. Its rider's many-jointed arms and legs were embedded deep in its fleshy sides with hands and feet like curling fishhooks.

"I bet you that's the kind of crap HP Lovecraft saw whenever he closed his eyes," Ben said.

Dulci cleared her throat. "At Arbor Hospital, where I work, there's a little boy with chronic insomnia who draws stuff like that whenever someone gives him a crayon. He gets two ground up Indiplon in his applesauce at night so he can sleep for more than ten minutes without waking up screaming."

"Cheery," Ellen said. "Not to change the subject, but have you guys noticed the flags those things are all carrying?"

"Like the one that said Coca-Cola?" Ben said. "Yeah, I'm still trying to figure them out."

"I think each horseman has a different theme," Ellen said slowly. "It looks like the eastern one has the American flag and Britain's Union Jack. Its other flags are harder to identify because they're all painted in yellow, but from the contrast and position of the stripes on the next one down, I'd say it's Germany."

"The one below that is Spain's," Dulci said authoritatively. "France, Iraq…"

"Why would Gary give that horseman a flag with the Christian cross on it?" Priscilla asked, pointing at the northern figure.

"Same reason he gave it the Star of David and the crescent moon of Islam?" Ellen suggested.

"The fat, slimy guy seems to be the businessman of the group," Ben observed from the southern window. "Exxon Mobile, Microsoft, Gap, World Bank. I can keep reading if anyone still hasn't gotten the point."

Dulci had made her way to the western window. "How's this for a bowl of alphabet soup: CIA, GRU, SOA, SS, ETA, NRA, PLF, AQIM…"

Ellen was frowning. "I can't say I'd put all those in the same category, but it's certainly not hard to see where he's going with all this."

"The Four Horsemen of the Apocolypse carrying banners of church, state, corporation, and other political organizations," Dulci said, tallying the bullets one by one on her fingers, "all with histories of creating or endorsing violence or inequality, and all connected by a giant misshapen circle?"

"'Wheel of War,'" Ben finished for her. "Truth in advertising strikes again."

The elevator was beginning to slow. The tremendous vista afforded by the elevator's windows darkened a final time in a thick web of steel.

And here we come, Imogene thought, *to the top of the world, to light a beacon of peace.*

She suddenly couldn't bear anymore waiting. She stepped in front of the door, and when it rolled open at the top level of the Eiffel Tower, she was the first outside.

7

The highest level of the tower was open to the air, but wrapped in a ten foot high cocoon of wire mesh that curved inward at the top, presumably to keep overambitious (or possibly drunk) tourists from climbing the railing and toppling to their deaths. Despite its obvious safety advantages, the widely spaced mesh did nothing to obstruct the staggering view of the city. Buildings and moving cars below seemed impossibly small and far away. The brightly lit Arc de Triomphe, the monolithic archway through which a French pilot famously flew his fighter to celebrate the end of World War I, looked no larger than a Lego block. Its powerful ghost lighting, in concert with the other seemingly endless light sources throughout the city, cast a permanent orange twilight into the Parisian sky.

But all of this was mere window dressing. Compared to the ambient light of the city, Gary's glowing yellow Wheel of War down on the ground seemed corrupt and cancerous, the color of radioactive pus.

Over half the wheel, including three of the four horsemen, was visible from Imogene's spot at the railing. A pair of binoculars would have given her a fantastic detailed study of the northern horseman in particular, and pure artistic interest made her consider popping a Euro coin into one of the heavy telescopic viewing stations scattered around the platform. However, upon further consideration, the regular human part of her wasn't sure she really *wanted* a closer view of any of the horsemen.

"Do you like it?" a high male voice asked behind her. "It's not quite done."

Imogene spun around to discover Gary Pritchard standing no more than ten feet away. Starlight sparkled in the enormous lenses of his Coke-bottle glasses. The round face behind them was unlined and impassive.

"*Baby,*" Priscilla gasped.

Ellen and Dulci only stared at the man for whom they had ceaselessly searched for most of the past week. Even Ben seemed struck dumb by his sudden presence.

"I've seen you before," Gary told Imogene, oblivious to the shock his appearance had caused. "I'm Gary."

"I know," Imogene said, a sense of unreality creeping over her like the shadow of a storm cloud. "We've never really been introduced. My name is Imogene Cornell."

He cocked his head to one side the same way a gecko might scrutinize a cricket. "I painted you," he said suddenly, as if arriving at a great epiphany.

"Yes, in London."

"Gary?"

He turned casually to face Priscilla. "I've seen you too!" he cried, adding, "All of you!"

Priscilla seemed taken aback, but she persisted. "I understand now why you left me, and I think we're both better people because of it. But I also wanted to say I...I'll take mostly good memories from our time together."

A troubled fissure ran upward from between Gary's eyebrows to the center of his forehead. He looked like a man fighting either to retrieve or block a particularly potent memory.

Dulci took a step away from the railing, her dark eyes fixed on Gary's face. "I postponed my wedding, maybe forever." After revealing this tidbit she seemed to become self-conscious. "I thought you should know."

Gary's forehead smoothed and he beamed at her. He spun around on the toe of his work boot and beckoned. "I want to show you all something."

"Hang on," Imogene said.

Gary twisted around to face her, eyebrows raised impatiently.

"You said you would light a beacon of peace from the top of the world. Where did you hear that? How have you been able to do all this? I mean, how did you make the connection between my family and Ellen and Dulci? How did you *find* us?"

Gary looked troubled again. His eyes flitted across her face, then to his surroundings, as if he had just woken up in a strange place.

"You don't know, do you?" Ben said, coming around from behind Imogene. "The Droons just poleaxed you with a ten trillion watt lamp, then handed you a Polaroid and a paintbrush. They told you to get to work and, boom, you got to work."

When it was clear Gary wouldn't entertain their questions, Imogene prompted, "You were going to show us something?"

Gary nodded pleasantly and started off again, clearly meaning for them to follow. "As I was saying, Wheel of War isn't finished yet. I've done everything I can do by myself. Now I need your help."

They followed him in a haphazard line like ducklings behind their mother. Deep in thought, Imogene walked behind Ellen, eyes on the scuffed and pitted concrete ground. Without warning, Ben grabbed her arm and steered her to the right just in time to prevent her from blundering into a thick metal counterweight hanging off the back of an industrial spotlight.

"Thanks."

"I barely saw it myself," Ben said. "That's a terrible place for a big piece of equipment like that. It's a lawsuit waiting to happen."

But judging from the fresh scrapes in the concrete, Imogene thought someone had recently scooted the spotlight into the corner where the northeastern and southeastern handrails met. Four feet in diameter, the spotlight reminded her of a newer variant on the powerful spots that swung long light trails across the sky over Mann's Chinese Theater on big premiere nights, except this light had an extra rectangular steel frame extending from its face.

Imogene was about to ask Dulci if this was one of the Beacons she had mentioned in the limo, but Gary stopped abruptly in front of a door to a women's restroom. A crude paper sign had been taped to the door, declaring in five languages that the toilets were *Out of Order*.

"I've been living here for days now!" Gary said happily.

"Where else?" Ben said wryly, just loud enough for Imogene to hear. "Bruce Wayne has the Bat Cave and Gary Pritchard has a women's bathroom."

Priscilla was the first inside, but she stopped so suddenly that Ellen bumped into her.

"Hey, what's the hold up?" Dulci asked from behind them. She whacked Ellen on the rump. "Get a move on, Tiny Tim. The rest of want to see too."

Priscilla and Ellen hurried forward, allowing the others to follow them inside a surprisingly spacious restroom. Propped along the wall of an open area just inside the door were three milky stone rectangles, two feet wide, six inches thick, and of slightly varying heights. The rectangles' tall faces were polished, but blank. A green flannel sleeping bag lay before them on the tile floor.

As they fully entered the restroom, a fourth and final rectangle became visible, standing against the wall to behind the open door. This one contained Priscilla's original portrait from General's Peak, glossy, perfect, and unmarked.

Ellen whistled softly. "This thing makes Pleiades look like a Power Puff Girl."

"Gary, how did you cut the rock like this?" Ben asked. "You divided the original stone we took off General's Peak into these four rectangular segments, right?

"*I* didn't cut anything," Gary corrected primly. "The Droons used a special saw and took four vertical cuts from the stone as easily as if I'd asked them to slice up a loaf of bread the long way instead of normal. They're quite clever with machines, you know."

"So they hauled an industrial stone saw to the top of the Eiffel Tower to make your cuts?" Ben asked. "Why didn't they just do it on the ground?"

Gary seemed to be losing interest in the conversation. "Too much trouble."

"That makes sense," Ben said brightly, rolling his eyes.

"The 'Droons'?" Imogene whispered to Ben.

He gave his head a little shake, and she understood. Asking Gary where he'd heard the name Droon almost certainly wouldn't result in a sensible answer. Gary seemed to have little interest in the whys or what-might've-beens of his situation.

Priscilla had moved in front of her portrait as she'd done on General's Peak, spine straight as a yardstick, shoulders squared. Gary kicked aside the green sleeping bag and took his place beside her. For a moment they looked like the wedding couple they would have been, standing before the altar.

They made a lovely image, but after just a few seconds Gary left her again and disappeared inside one of the toilet stalls.

Dulci walked over to one of the blank stones and ran her thumb down one smooth edge. "I thought so. That's no regular stone. Alexander, my old fiancé, has a few chunks of this stuff at home. His company has spent the last several years laying fiber optic cable under the city for internet and cable lines." She rapped the hard surface with her knuckles. "Or in this case, fiber optic crystal. It's a special kind of ultra pure glass that transmits light the way a pipe transmits water, except at the speed of light and with zero resistance. Look, you can see individual flecks of dirt in the tile grout through six inches of this stuff. It's lighter than it looks too. They use it to make those fake Christmas trees with glowing needles."

"That's quite a sales pitch," Ellen said, smirking. "I'm thinking of buying a big hunk of it myself."

"Har har," Dulci said. "I've heard Alexander's spiel enough times that I could give it to a customer myself. I wonder where Gary or Droon—the Droons, I mean," she corrected herself, "found such a big piece of it. It's not like this stuff happens in nature. You can't mine for it or anything."

Ellen turned toward the stall into which Gary had vanished. "Hey, what are you going to do with the other three stones? The blank ones?"

"I said I wasn't finished, didn't I?" Gary's voice drifted from inside the stall. "I've been practicing for this. Come look."

They clustered around the entrance to the stall. If the green sleeping bag on the hard tile floor had been acting as Gary's bedroom, this stall must have been his workshop. Drawn on the high inner partitions and back wall were perhaps fifty vague circles similar to the sketch Droon had given them earlier. The drawings ranged from six inches to two feet wide, glowing silver in the bathroom's low light and adorned with countless appalling variations of the four horsemen.

"I started having bad dreams before the Droons came to me. Ugly, confusing things," Gary said pensively. "They've been giving me places to paint my nightmares. At first I didn't like it, but the first time I saw this tower, I understood how to make the ugly things go away. I understood how to light my beacon of peace."

He sidled a little farther into the stall to showcase a small, simple drawing Imogene hadn't noticed before:

The Beacon

"That wasn't all," he said, stepping back in front of the drawing. "I realized I was painting from my imagination." His eyes shone behind his Coke-bottle glasses. "*I don't need the camera anymore. Watch.*"

He leaned down and selected a calligrapher's paintbrush and one of the white tubes of paint that were scattered around the floor of the stall like a messy child's toys before leading them all back to one of the slabs of fiber optic crystal. Imogene watched, fascinated, as he squeezed a glob of paint like liquid mercury onto every surface of the brush, looking for all the world like a little kid squirting too much toothpaste onto his toothbrush.

"You first," he said to Dulci, positioning himself with his back to the shortest of the blank slabs. "All of your faces have changed since the first time I painted you. Except you," he added offhandedly to Priscilla. "Your face told me you had already made a decision, so the original still works as the final portrait."

Gary giggled as if this idea were quite funny. Priscilla simply accepted it in stoic silence.

"The rest of you needed a little more prodding, but you're ready now," Gary declared, and began an intense study of Dulci's face.

Dulci reddened, but bore his laser-fine scrutiny for a full twenty seconds before speaking. "Can I ask you something?"

"Please," Gary said, though he still seemed far more interested in every detail of her face than in any question she might ask.

"How did you know so much about me? I mean, the *Don Quixote* painting, the doubts I've had about Alexander. For that matter, how did you know where to find me in Alcalá? How did—" She sighed. "I'm not asking the right questions. I think I just want to know why you picked *me*."

"She already asked me that," Gary said, pointing offhandedly at Imogene with the wooden handle of his brush. "All of you have always wanted to act on your deepest beliefs but have never known how, and so the cosmos conspired to help you figure it out. You offered me an apple. What more reason did I need to choose you?"

"But that answer could apply to any of us," Dulci argued. "Or anyone at all, for that matter."

"Then you understand...*finally*," Gary muttered, plenty loud for all of them to hear. He pivoted toward his unusual canvas, brush raised.

Deep down, Imogene had never fully believed Curtis Garfield's story about how Gary had painted Priscilla's portrait using side-to-side robotic arm movements like the cartridge of a dot-matrix printer. That Gary's painting method would turn out to be unorthodox she'd had no doubt, but she was more than astonished to find that Curtis's impression had been spot on. Gary held his arm straight out in front of his body and swung it back and forth, varying only the pressure he applied to the stone's smooth surface to create heavy or light marks, lifting the brush entirely to leave blank spots. Every so often he reloaded the calligraphy brush with a new glob of paint.

In this way a new life size, two dimensional Dulci emerged inch by inch under his brush. This new Dulci held out a shining apple in the same pose as her portrait in Spain, but was garbed in Dulci's current wardrobe, right down to the decorative tooling on the twin sticks holding her hair in place and the simple hank of leather tied around her left ankle. Her facial expression looked as it had when she had introduced herself to Imogene earlier today: plainly hopeful, but with an undercurrent of fierce determination that turned her natural beauty into something both otherworldly and fearsome.

Two more passes of Gary's brush completed Dulci's toes and the front lip of her sandals, not fifty seconds after he had begun.

He straightened up. "Who's next?"

8

Ellen came next. Imogene wondered if Gary would include Ellen's mask and fading bruises or paint her face as it had been when he'd initially seen her, but she didn't have to wonder for very long. Ten seconds after the initial brush stroke, Ellen's head and neck had materialized on the flat surface of the stone, plastic facemask and all. Yet something was different about it. With only a few quick highlights, Gary had transformed the mask from a functional hunk of plastic to a reflective second skin like some kind of celestial armor.

Although Ellen was a good six inches taller than her designated slab of stone, Gary managed to scale her down so that her portrait spanned her whole body from the crown of her head to the worn soles of her Mizuno volleyball shoes. And where the pose of her original portrait had spread its arms wide in a protective gesture, this time around Gary had to lower her arms several degrees to accommodate the narrower painting surface. If anything, this new compact pose made the painted

Ellen seem like an even more effective guardian.

Gary stood once more and dusted his hands. "Last one." He shifted his disconcerting visual analysis to Imogene without any other preamble, but immediately the deep, troubled vertical line reformed between his eyebrows, cutting higher into his forehead with every passing second.

Imogene stuffed her hands self consciously into her pockets. "Is something the matter?"

Gary's frown broke and he made a long, pleased sound: "*Ahhh.*"

"What?"

He squeezed another long silver bead of paint onto his brush and set to work on the final stone rectangle. Her first clue that Gary planned to alter her portrait more than he had done with the other two was her hair. On the airplane she had tied it back in a ponytail just to keep it somewhat tidy for travel. Gary's dot matrix movements unbound the ponytail to spill a mass of curly hair down to her painted shoulders, which, Imogene was surprised to see, were bare save for single straps of fabric that eventually led down to a conservatively cut v-neck. The cut, however, was the only thing conservative about her portrait's clothing.

"How are you doing this?" Ben asked huskily.

Imogene turned to him, frowning. "Doing what?"

"*Look,* Gene."

She looked. But she only became more confused as the portrait grew downward. The painted shoulders, for example, were narrower than hers and led to thicker, somehow more youthful upper arms. The highly defined bust swelled more fully than hers under the skintight top. Not until Gary passed below the line of her hips did she understand, and then her eyes leapt back up to the painted face to make sure it was indeed hers.

And it was…mostly. She suddenly seemed to lose control of her eyes; they flitted up and down the portrait, drinking in the hybrid Imogene whose legs Gary was now finishing. They were as long as her own legs, but with an added fullness Imogene now remembered from her mother's Miss Washington videotape. Gary had somehow mixed the two of them, Imogene and her mother, into a single image on the stone.

Gary stood a final time, pressed his hands to the small of his back, and grimaced, seemingly unaware of the miracle he had just performed.

"The paint will be dry enough for you to move these slabs in a few seconds. They look pretty heavy, but the five of you working together won't have any—"

His voice cut off as Imogene seized wads of his shirt in her sweating hands. "Why did you do this?"

"Yeah," Ellen agreed. "That hardly looks like Imogene."

Gary batted Imogene's hands away distastefully. "*You're* the one who brought her along with you," he told Imogene tartly, as if she should have known this already.

"Brought who?" Ellen asked.

"Our mom," Ben answered, sounding much more under control. "Somehow he combined Gene and Mom into one portrait."

"Now," Gary said, leaning over and stuffing his brush and paint carelessly into the mouth of the sleeping bag, "as I was saying, you should all be able to move these where they need to go if you help each other. Droon lifted one by himself, but…" He twirled his hand at them as if to say, *You know how* that *goes.*

"We, uh…" Imogene blinked hard and tried to clear her mind for the task at hand. "A group of around ten carried the original stone off a mountain, and that was with a heavy dolly attached."

"And it was still in one piece, right?" Priscilla said.

"I think you have seen the spotlights outside," Gary interrupted. "We passed by one of them on the way here. Each one of them has an added steel frame on the front, designed to hold one of the portraits." He pointed to Priscilla's, resting nearest to the door. "We'll take this one first since it goes the farthest, to the spotlight at the western corner."

He gazed expectantly at Ellen, who offered him a firm, business-like nod. "Priscilla's first, huh? Okay, I'll take the end that's on the floor now. Dulci, you take the upper end." The corner of her mouth twitched. "If you can reach it."

"Laugh all you want," Dulci said, slipping herself between the stone and the wall. "I bet I can squat more weight than you can, string bean."

Priscilla took her place on one long side of her portrait, and Imogene and Ben took the other.

"Backs straight, lift with your legs," Ellen ordered. "I'll get it off the ground on my own if I can, but you guys keep your hands on it in case it starts to slip. Watch your toes, and if it starts to fall, get the hell out of the way," she admonished in an unwitting imitation of Glenn Pritchard's speech to the people of Accord when they had moved Priscilla's portrait for the first time.

Ellen hunkered at the painted Priscilla's stone feet, laid her strong fingers on the stone slab's underside, breathed once—in through her nose and out her mouth—and tensed her legs. Deep, alarming ropes of muscle contracted beneath the skin of her thighs and calves.

The stone rose off the floor more easily than any of them had expected. Its top edge did indeed slip against the smooth tile wall, and Priscilla and Ben slid their hands a foot upward to compensate. Dulci made a deft movement of her own that took advantage of the stone's downward momentum, but also slowed it to the point that she could keep her grip when the top edge had fallen to her waist level.

She grinned a little wildly. "This is nothing compared to managing someone having a grand mal seizure."

"Or my first roommate's eight-foot couch," Ellen agreed. "You weren't kidding about this stuff being lighter than it looks, Dulci."

"Follow me!" Gary cried in a jubilant voice. He left the room at a quick waddle.

They carried Priscilla's portrait face-up between them like a legless table. Ellen led the group easily enough despite having to walk backwards. Imogene and Ben had to tilt their side upward to create the necessary clearance to fit through the doorway, but otherwise carrying the portrait was a piece of cake.

Now that they were outside again, the milky stone glowed like a crystal ball in a movie. The image of Priscilla, facing the sky as the four women carried her, gleamed with cool, silver light.

"How is it glowing?" Dulci asked, staring downward at the portrait. "The yellow paint down on the ground was doing the same thing."

"I've been thinking about that," Ben said. "Biologists and chemists have been working to duplicate the bioluminescent reaction that happens in fireflies and several kinds of deep sea fish. They can make a single bacterium light up like Times Square in a dark petri dish. Maybe the Droons figured out how to make a stable and prolonged bioluminescent reaction. Now, how they made their glowing paint 'nonremovable' is a true mystery."

"Priscilla said you teach middle school biology?" Ellen asked doubtfully.

"I also keep an ear open to the speculative sciences," he said, but he was watching Priscilla, and Imogene could tell he was pleased that she'd mentioned him to her friends.

Priscilla's cheeks flushed in the light radiating upward from her portrait. "Ben's one of our best teachers."

"Here we are," Gary announced, directing them with a maître d's flourish to a large modified spotlight shoved into the western corner of the walkway.

"Are these spotlights part of the Beacon you mentioned, Dulci?" Imogene finally asked.

"I don't think so," Priscilla answered. "Those are supposed to be mounted a ways above us on the top spire and controlled by computers, but this one has big handholds on the back."

"The other ones we passed did too," Dulci said.

"Just slide it into the frame here," Gary directed. He grabbed the handholds Priscilla had pointed out and swiveled the front of the spotlight toward them. "You can fasten it down with the extra braces there on the ground."

"Set it down a second, guys," Ellen suggested. "Let's get a look at this thing."

The spotlight had a concave face that was four feet across and glossy enough to reflect a clear, upside down image of the six of them. The frame Gary had mentioned consisted of four reinforced steel arms extending outward from four points on the light's circumference. These four arms were connected to each other by four more crossbars—two long vertical ones on the sides and two shorter horizontal ones at the top and bottom. Extra crossbars of identical size lay at Gary's feet, along with a large socket wrench and a set of bolts as thick as Imogene's thumb. Imogene had no doubt this new added framework would perfectly accommodate Priscilla's portrait.

Small lumps of solder on all the joints of the added framework and handholds betrayed the work of a skilled welder. They looked fresh.

"Gary, did you take apart the Eiffel Tower Beacon to get these lights?" Priscilla asked gently. "Is that why it never turned on tonight?"

"*I* didn't take anything apart," Gary said, but he spoke with a guilty child's impish grin.

Ben was rubbing his upper lip. "I'll be honest, Gary. I'm a little confused about our next step here.

Gary sighed theatrically before digging in his pocket and bringing out a crumpled sheet of paper. "Okay, I've got one more drawing to show you. It's not as good as the other ones, but I was in a hurry."

He smoothed the page against his chest and held it out while the others gathered around it in a semicircle.

"Got it," Ben said at once. "We set the portraits in those frames, turn on the spotlights, and we've got instant Bat Signals. Except instead of the Batman logo in the sky over Gotham City, you get four handsome women floating above Paris like a team of twenty-first century angels."

Priscilla turned to the others, an excited fire flickering behind her eyes. "I read that each of these spotlights can penetrate over fifty miles through the air."

Imogene looked up doubtfully at the sky. There were a few wispy clouds overhead, but nothing that would really show the type of projection Ben was talking about. For some reason her mind returned to the bizarre dream sketches Gary had shown them inside the bathroom stall.

Ellen settled her hands against the sides of Priscilla's portrait. "Makes sense to me. Up again on three."

The five of them set themselves in place and lifted the portrait into the brackets. It slid into place with pleasing tightness.

"Wonderful!" Gary cried.

"You guys hold it there and I'll fix the crossbars," Ellen said.

"Let me do that," Ben said, hefting the big socket wrench. "You really don't need a fifth person to carry the portraits, and it will only take one of us to put the rest of this contraption together."

"Are you sure?" Priscilla asked.

"Course," Ben said easily. "I don't mean to brag, but I used to assemble furniture for the IKEA in Seattle."

Priscilla touched his arm. "Thank you."

His nonchalance faded, his eyes fixed on hers. "You're welcome."

Gary clapped once, briskly, breaking the tractor beam holding Ben's and Priscilla's attention on each other. Priscilla glanced guiltily at Gary, but he seemed deeply uninterested in the soulful look his former fiancé had just shared with another man.

"Three more portraits, people," he barked.

Priscilla fell into step at Imogene's side as they walked back to Gary's headquarters. "In your brother's kitchen, when you were telling me about how you thought Gary's beacon of peace was connected to your mama, did you imagine any of this?"

"You mean painted sidewalks and lug nuts and spotlights?" Imogene said wanly. Priscilla only watched her. "No, I never could have imagined anything like this."

Ahead of them, Dulci mused, "What do you guys think it will look like when we switch on those spotlights with our portraits in front of them? Fifty miles…"

Ellen glanced up at the mostly clear sky again. "Three more trips to the can and we'll find out."

9

They moved Imogene's portrait last because it had to travel the shortest distance from the bathroom to the eastern spotlight. As they were fitting the stone into its steel frame Ben strolled up to them with the socket wrench slung over his shoulder.

"Dulci's portrait is all set up," he said. "Guess that leaves this one."

Ellen began threading the bolts into their respective crossbars and Ben secured them with the wrench. Gary capered around them on his tiptoes, seemingly unable to contain his excitement this close to completing his vision.

"Aren't you finished?" he squeaked at Ben's elbow after a few moments.

"Nervous little guy, aren't you?" Ben said, his voice changing to a growl with the effort of tightening a bolt into the frame.

"He never was," Priscilla said softly at Imogene's left shoulder. "Our wedding was supposed to be today, did you know that?"

"I'm sorry," Imogene said. "Do you think..."

Do you think you'll try to start over? had been her original question, but she realized it would be impolite for her to ask such a thing, and not just because Ben was standing a few paces away.

"That's not my Gary," Priscilla said, as if Imogene had asked anyway. "I knew it the moment he walked into church the other Wednesday. And to be honest, I'm not his Priscilla either. Not anymore."

Out of the corner of her eye, Imogene saw Ben pause in his work and tilt his head in their direction before turning back to the last bolt.

Gary heaved an impatient sigh as Ben stood and laid the big wrench over his shoulder again. "Finally. Each of you needs to go back to your own portrait. Do you need help finding them again?" he added pointedly when they didn't all leap into action.

"We're going, baby," Priscilla soothed, though her use of the word *baby* sounded like nothing more than an endearment for a child. "But why don't you tell us what we're supposed to do before we go."

"Yes, of course," Gary said.

He seized the black handled lever on the side of Imogene's spotlight and yanked it upward. Imogene's knees nearly buckled against an assault of pure white light. Webs of spidery red veins pulsed in her eyelids, which suddenly seemed no thicker than tissue paper.

Ellen cried out as if Gary had slapped her bruised face. "Aim that thing somewhere else!"

Gary didn't answer, but the unbearable light dimmed. It took Imogene a few moments of utterly dazzled blinking to realize that Gary had simply shut off the light.

Ellen had actually gone to her hands and knees. "That's the third time I've gone flash blind in the last week. Hell," she added thickly.

"You teach her that kind of language, Pritchard?" said a voice from behind the darkened spotlight.

Imogene's pupils still hadn't regained their full nighttime dilation, but she could see a blurry figure towering over Gary, who had backed up against the railing, his hand still resting on the spotlight's power lever.

"Cody?" Priscilla said uncertainly.

"Prissy," he grunted, shuffling forward.

As Imogene's eyes readjusted, she could see knotted burn scars like continents across his face and scalp. The reddish skin around his eyes seemed especially tight and swollen, perhaps because his uneven beard softened the lower half of his face. His eyes sparkled deep within their sockets like tiny diamonds.

"Aw, Prissy, thank God I found you. I was so worried that—"

His frame shuddered with a fit of sharp, dry coughing. When he settled down again, a high whistling sound accompanied his every intake of breath. Imogene wondered how his condition could have worsened so dramatically in the hours since he had accosted the group at the base of General's Peak.

"Just get on that elevator back there and don't give me any lip," he wheezed. "I have something to take care of."

Gary dug in the back pocket of his jeans and pulled out a warped Polaroid photograph. "I *knew* you'd forget," he said, holding the photograph out to Cody. "You should probably see this before you do it again."

"Don't you touch me," Cody said, shying back from the photo in Gary's outstretched hand.

Priscilla reached a shaking hand toward her brother. "Oh, Cody, what have you done to yourself?"

His head snapped up. "What've *I* done? I'll tell you what I done. I emptied the cash safe at the garage and followed Cornell and his slut sister to Charleston so that I could sit on an airplane puking my guts out in a steel vacuum toilet for God knows how many hours in the hope of rescuing you."

He straightened to his full height and aimed a condemning finger at Gary, who had apparently bored of Cody Hemphill's accusations. He was avidly watching something down on the ground, the fingers of both hands hooked through the wire mesh at either side of his head. The photo he'd offered to Cody skittered across the concrete in the wind and came to rest against the foot of Imogene's spotlight.

"Whereas *that* sorry sack of shit," Cody continued, still pointing, "brought ruination on our family and you followed him here like a puppy don't know who its master is. He showed you naked, Prissy. If that ain't bad enough, Glenn and Aggie Mills got the town pissing on Daddy's grave about some lie that Daddy raped you. So I sure hope you asked Pritchard what *he* done when you caught up with him."

Priscilla took another step toward her brother, steadier this time. "Look around, Cody. Thousands of people down on the ground have come to see what Gary painted today, and if I'm right about these big spotlights, we're about to make angels appear in the sky. *Look.*"

Though her voice was as gentle as ever, her tone was so commanding that Cody's head creaked, as if against its own will, toward the images on the ground beyond the railing.

Imogene took advantage of his hesitation and grabbed the handholds on her spotlight, swinging its new painted face outward and upward. At the top of its swing, she pulled up on the lever Gary had used. She could not have hoped for a more dramatic result. The shocking hybrid that Gary had created of her and her mother sprang to hazy life on the lower surface of a patch of thin, high clouds. Imogene couldn't be sure, but she thought she heard a rush of crowd noise from the ground, just barely audible over the constant wind.

"What did I tell you?" Ben said in hushed awe. "Americanus Rex presents the Bat Signal."

Cody watched the delicate figure swim across the sky, mouth hanging open in helpless fascination.

Priscilla took her cue perfectly. "See what I'm part of now? This is bigger than our family."

"Yes," Gary agreed loudly, finally moving away from the railing. "The Four Horsemen below are quaking in their boots, powerless against even the single angel keeping watch above them."

Dulci joined in next, moving closer to Cody. "Let's get you back indoors. Maybe we can find you some food in the restaurant down on the second level, settle your stomach. When we've finished here, we can all eat together and talk this all out. How's that sound?" Her voice contained a measured, almost clinical ratio of respect and empathy.

She thinks he's crazy, Imogene thought.

Which of course he was. Still, Imogene considered this new bewildered crazy to be better than the murderous crazy she'd seen from him previously.

Cody's eyes regained their focus and settled on Dulci. "I'm going to eat a steak dinner every night for a month when I get back home, but I ain't doing it in any pussy bullfrog restaurant."

He turned back to Priscilla and pointed at the elevator. "Now you get in that elevator and you wait for me."

"Wait just a minute," Ellen said heatedly.

"I am still the head of this family," Cody went on, raising his voice over hers, "and you all—"

"The head of this family?" Priscilla demanded. "You mean the way Daddy was the head of the family, right? You mean you're going to work yourself to death so the rest of us have money for food and clothes, while Mama and I stay home and keep your house? Jamie will also be expected to find work when he starts high school, and when he turns eighteen, he'll go fight and die in this war we're trying to stop. Because that's what men *do,* right?"

Cody blinked in surprise, but backed down not an inch. "Prissy, there is a decent and proper order to a family, which you should know plenty about after all the time you've spent at church."

"What order is that? Daddy's version of order meant Mama couldn't open a bakery in town for extra money, but when we needed the new barn, he paid for it with the money they'd put away for our educations. Yours and mine and Jamie's. All because he couldn't bear the shame of a wife working outside the home."

"A man has the responsibility to do what's right by his family. You went to college on Daddy's dime in the end anyway. And what happened then? Instead of being grateful, you got your teaching job and moved out of the only home you'd ever had."

Priscilla's whole body went still except for her chest, which rose and fell with increasing rapidity. Her eyes had widened to the point where

Imogene could see stark white all the way around the pale gray irises. Cody took a step back from her. They all did.

"You wanna know why Daddy paid for my college? After Mama bought me my first training bra, Daddy came to me in the barn while I was laying fresh hay in the stalls. Lifted up my shirt because he said he wanted to see what kind of a woman his baby girl was becoming."

"Don't you say that," Cody said, but his voice was little more than a whisper.

"He touched my breasts for the first time that day, and over and over for four years. One night when I was seventeen I found him waiting in my room when I got out of the shower. It was the only time he touched me while I was fully unclothed."

"Daddy *never* raped you," Cody snarled.

"He didn't have to," Priscilla said. "You can't know what it does to a girl's mind when her father whispers sweet words into her ear and explores her body with a lover's hands."

Gusts of cool breeze, seemingly in perfect time with Priscilla's own deep breathing, whistled through the tower's zigzagging girders and rattled the protective wire mesh against the handrail. The dual image of Imogene and her mother flashed onto another passing cloud, all but forgotten in the shadow of Priscilla's terrible, stark vitality.

"I went to Wallop after that, thinking the church would help me. And maybe it did. Wallop acted like he wouldn't say anything, but he must have because Daddy came to me in the barn again. This time he had a riding crop in his hands."

"Prissy, don't," Cody moaned.

"My breasts were black with bruises for a month. It was the only place he hit me," Priscilla said. "Mama wrapped my chest in gauze every morning because that was the only way I could even walk without crying. She threatened to leave him after that, but he asked her what if he talked to Glenn Pritchard about setting up a rack in the store for her to sell pies. He promised to put me through college. Anything to keep her from leaving. Anything to avoid the shame of a publicly broken family."

A fat tear broke over Cody's eyelid. It ran crookedly down his scarred cheek and disappeared into his beard.

"No one—not Mama, not even the man I promised to marry—has seen my chest uncovered since then," Priscilla said. "The night Gary left me for good, the night I knelt in the grass and begged him not to leave, I disrobed in full view of God and the whole world for the first time in my life. I bared my body because I decided it was mine again. Not my fiancé's, not my Daddy's, but mine. No grass stains on my knees, no shame or regret that I possessed a woman's full figure."

She took one last deep breath and let it out again. "That's the moment Gary showed to people. Showed to *me*. The wildest, most profound moment in my whole life. I had a choice whether or not to make something right out of what Gary did, just like these three wonderful women who have become my best friends."

She pointed to the vision of Imogene shimmering over the Paris skyline. "If Gary wants to use these moments as symbols for the strength and beauty of a world in peace, then I choose to help him do it. I choose to fly my face and my woman's body in the sky with Imogene's and Ellen's and Dulci's."

Cody's chin dropped to his chest. His hands hung limply at his sides, and his shoulders shook with silent, uncontrolled sobs. Without raising his head, he loosed a terrible wail, the sound of a man being buried alive in the falling rubble at the end of the world.

At last Priscilla closed the gap between them, laid her hand on the back of his neck, and drew his forehead gently to her shoulder. Cody sagged against her. All the strength seemed to have left him. He seemed incapable even of raising his arms to return his sister's embrace.

A scrape of shoes on concrete tore Imogene's attention from the Hemphills. Despite the drama of the last few minutes, Gary had maintained his watch through the mesh, and now he had apparently found what he'd been looking for. Without a word to any of them, he took off running. In a moment he'd disappeared around the corner to the north.

"Now where's he going?" Ellen asked in a voice that was still thick, but for a different reason now.

Gary's voice floated to them from around the corner, almost lost in the soft, steady roar of wind. "*They're here!*"

Something in that cry set Imogene's teeth on edge. He didn't sound scared or desperate. He sounded happy, deliriously so.

Dulci confirmed her fear with a simple, "Uh oh."

Even Cody raised his head shakily in the direction of Gary's voice. "Stay here for a minute," Priscilla told him.

The rest of them trotted around the corner, Imogene and Priscilla in the lead, to find Gary balanced on top of the handrail, his fingertips and chin pulled awkwardly above the curved upper boundary of the protective wire mesh like a little boy peering over the kitchen counter to watch his mother make his birthday cake. One of his bootlaces had come untied and flapped wildly against the cuff of his jeans in the strengthening wind.

He faced them, lines of moisture glittering on his smooth cheeks. "You can finish it on your own now," he told them. "There's not much left to do, and it's all pretty obvious. I'll get you started."

He swung his foot downward and hooked the toe of his boot under the lever that switched on Ellen's spotlight. Cold white light shot straight up into the sky. There were no clouds directly overhead, so it was impossible to make out the shape of Ellen's portrait against the clean backdrop of stars and blackness.

Gary didn't even look up. He had focused his gaze once more on the ground. Imogene looked down too, and saw that the Droons' blockade had failed. Thousands—*tens* of thousands—of people crowded in a wide circle directly under and around the tower. Cameras flashed relentlessly. Lining Avenue Gustave Eiffel were perhaps twenty tiny news vans swinging generator powered spotlights— compared to the Beacon spotlights, these seemed about as powerful as the dying flashlight Ben kept in his kitchen—across the crowds and up at the tower.

Far in the distance, Imogene heard one of the helicopters Droon had mentioned earlier.

"A second ago you said somebody was here," she called up to Gary.

"*Who's* here? Did you mean the press? Did you call the press?"

Gary ignored her. He muscled his body over the top edge of the wire mesh with startling speed and agility. He might have been a small man, but like Priscilla and Cody, a lifetime of hard work had given him tremendous natural strength.

Priscilla and Imogene, who were still closest to him, lunged forward together to pull him back down. Gary's foot, however, was still caught under the spotlight lever, and when he yanked it upward the whole spotlight rotated down and to the right. Imogene just managed to shift her momentum in time to avoid what would have been a nasty uppercut from the steel encased corner of Ellen's portrait. After that, everything was lost in irresistible, torrential light.

10

Someone was shaking her shoulder. She must've hit the ground harder than she'd thought; all of the muscles in the left side of her body were tingling as if they'd fallen asleep. She blinked several times before she could make her eyes focus on anything that made sense. The first thing she saw was Priscilla's pale, round face.

"Gary's gone."

Imogene struggled to a sitting position. The top of the wire mesh above the spotlight was buckled and bent where Gary had pulled himself up. A few feet away, Ellen was also sitting on the ground in a daze. Ben and Dulci were standing together at the railing.

"No screams," Dulci observed. "No one down there saw him fall."

"You sure?" Ben asked. "It'd be pretty hard to tell from up here. Maybe he didn't..." He swallowed hard. "Maybe he didn't make it all the way to the ground. The tower flares outward as it goes down. Maybe he landed on one of the lower levels. Oh man."

"No," Dulci said with great certainty. "There would be panic down there. We'd see little pockets of turmoil in the crowd like whirlpools. Surges in one direction or the other. And you'd better believe that at least one of those news lights would have picked him up. It would've taken no more than a second or two for the rest to follow."

"Then where'd he go?" Ellen asked. She had made it to her feet, but she clung to the hand rail as if afraid she might topple over herself.

Dulci turned around. "Did any of you see him fall? Or even jump? I didn't."

Imogene spun around and faced the elevator, suddenly positive that Droon would be inside, grinning serenely in his black suit, his slender hand on the controls. But the elevator door was closed.

"I know someone we can ask," Ben said, as if reading Imogene's mind.

"Droon?" Dulci asked. "He didn't seem all that helpful before."

"It's a place to start," Priscilla said. "Let me get Cody and we'll all go back down."

As if on cue Cody shuffled around the corner, his face even redder and puffier than before. The bent photograph Gary had offered him earlier was clutched in one fist. He winced at the unbearably bright reflection shining up from the ground a few feet in front of him. "Where's Pritchard?"

"We don't know," Priscilla said. "We're going down to find out."

"Hang on, if we go down to the ground with that crowd, we'll never make it back up here by ourselves," Imogene said. "I don't want to sound heartless, but we have a job to do before we leave. Even Gary said it was up to us to finish before he...Am I being a jerk?"

"No," Priscilla said.

Ellen and Dulci were shaking their heads in agreement, but neither of them moved. They were all looking to Imogene.

To their Catalyst, she thought, and realized that she didn't just accept this truth, she welcomed it.

"Gary said finishing the Wheel of War would be obvious. All that's obvious to me is that there are four of us, four beacons, and four of those disgusting things on the ground. The horsemen. There's no doubt that Gary meant for this painting to be as densely symbolic as his other ones, and the most obvious symbolism is for us to cover up the horsemen with our beacons. Pointing the beacons into the sky never sat well with me, and I've just figured out why. Gary's own drawing that he labeled The Beacon back in the bathroom showed the light rays pointing down, not up. Remember?"

Dulci was nodding. "They can't be more than a couple thousand feet away, and we already know the beacons reach fifty miles. They should easily outshine the yellow paint he used for the horsemen."

"So we cover them up," Ellen agreed. "Then what?"

Imogene hesitated. "That's less obvious, at least to me. Maybe we should fix the spotlights on the horsemen until sunrise?" she guessed. "There's good symbolism there, if maybe a little clichéd. But maybe Wheel of War was only ever supposed to be a one night deal. I can't imagine how anyone would preserve everything Gary set up here and on the ground with thousands of tourists crawling all over it day after day."

"We won't know until we try," Dulci announced, heading off in the direction of her portrait. "I'm on the southern corner."

Imogene and Priscilla followed suit. Ellen took up the steering handles on her spotlight with a quick warning to Ben and Cody to look somewhere else while she spun it outward again. Imogene had just reached her own beacon when Ellen started shouting.

"That guy had one messed up concept of the term obvious! No, don't come back here, go to your own," Ellen said when she saw Dulci heading back in her direction. "You'll see for yourself."

Imogene seized the handles on her spotlight and dipped it down over a patch of the diseased yellow thread that made up the Wheel of War. She didn't shout as Ellen had done, but Ben, who was standing just behind her, did.

"Pritchard, you sly dog!" he whooped.

Where her light struck the distorted circle of the Wheel, new glowing patterns emerged in cool, soothing blue so light that it was almost white. These new patterns twisted like ivy around the single yellow line of the Wheel of War, dimming it, choking it the way healthy grass will grow over an abandoned and rusted railroad track.

Imogene didn't waste time staring. She eased her beacon across the wheel's curve toward the perverse eastern horseman. She could almost hear its terrified, spidery cry as her light spilled over the edge of its canvas. And then her face (her mother's face) was sliding over the horseman's terrible face, blotting it out almost completely.

More of those strange organic shapes appeared on the canvas now as well, coaxed out of the heavy material by Imogene's light. The new shapes looked like a cross between crawling plants and licking flames. After only a few seconds of playing her spotlight across the painted canvas square below, the horseman was effectively imprisoned in clean blue-white flora. Its ghastly eyes were obscured by two flamboyant flowers of the sort that hula dancers wore behind their ears. Tiny, delicate blooms like upside down bells lined the reins running from the horseman's hands to the bit in his mount's tortured mouth. It was as if rider and beast had died mid-gallop and life itself had begun to defile their corpses by making beautiful things grow from them.

"Make sure you get the whole wheel, not just the horsemen!" Imogene called first to Dulci, then to Ellen.

Ellen shouted an affirmative before passing the message on to Priscilla.

Dulci didn't answer at all. She was shrieking with uncontrollable laughter. Ben immediately left Imogene's side to see for himself what had set her off. He returned moments later with his own case of the giggles.

"Remember how Dulci's horseman was that horrible gross fat thing?"

"Okay…" Imogene didn't see what was so funny about that, but his laughter had begun to infect her as it always did.

"Well, now there's a big springy bouquet of daisies growing out of its belly button," he relayed, wiping his eyes. "It's the happiest, most ridiculous thing I've ever seen."

Imogene didn't have to ask what he meant. She had just discovered Gary's now famous Americanus Rex signature at the bottom corner of her horseman's canvas sheet. The bouncing cartoon breasts still rounded out the upper half of the *R* in *Rex,* but this time Gary had slipped a drawing of a rose jauntily into the cleavage between them.

She pointed the rose out to Ben, who fell into fresh tumbles of laughter at the sight of it.

"It's more whimsical than funny," she chided, and she came off sounding so absurdly prissy that soon they were both rubbing their streaming eyes like drowsy children.

"That Gary sure knew how to make an exit," Ben remarked hoarsely.

His comment sobered them a little, but Imogene also thought Gary wouldn't have minded their joy in his final painting. On the contrary, she believed he'd meant this last stage of Wheel of War to be epic and grave, but also happy, funny, and even a touch preposterous. It was his last painting's startling salvation.

"Okay," she said as sternly as she could manage. "I've got to finish my part of this."

Ben hiccupped once and crossed his forearms on the handrail. "Knock yourself out."

She swept the light away from the horseman. Without the beam directly on him, he was still very much visible, but the new white-blue glowing vines and flowers winding around, across, and through him had completely robbed his fundamental menace and horror.

"Alright, science guy," she said to Ben. "How did Gary pull this off? Making the flowery lines invisible until our lights touched them."

"Oh, that's much easier to explain than the original glowing yellow paint. The Droons just made a liquid compound of the same chemicals that go into any glow-in-the-dark toy. Remember my little toy dinosaur I used to hold up to a light bulb and then shut myself inside the closet and pretend it was a *radioactive* dinosaur."

He spread his arms wide toward the ground. "*Voila!* The glow-in-the-dark stuff Gary used is definitely more powerful than what a toy company could put in a toy dinosaur, but that shouldn't surprise any of us. The spotlights you guys are shooting down there are also a hell of a lot stronger than a sixty watt light bulb."

"Your dinosaur faded out after a few minutes," Imogene reminded him. "Do you think we'll have to stay up here all night with the spotlights?"

Ben shook his head. "Look at the first glowing spot you activated. It's not a whit dimmer now than in the moment it started to glow. I think if you get all of the invisible stuff glowing with that light of yours, it'll keep glowing as bright or brighter than the yellow wheel and horsemen until morning. After that, I'd guess a whole day of sunshine tomorrow will fuel it enough to keep it lit tomorrow night, and so on. It could very well go on forever. Or at least until the Parisians get tired of having four giant canvas squares draped over their city. No matter what, you guys were the ones who lit it for the first time."

He took one step forward and unexpectedly pulled her in one of his breath stealing bear hugs. "You did it, Gene."

11

Ben made rounds to the other three women while Imogene double checked that she had illuminated everything Gary had left behind to illuminate. To her surprise, there was no extra glow-in-the-dark scrolling around the numerous banners the horsemen carried. She was still mulling this over when Ben reappeared beside her. Dulci, Ellen, Priscilla, and Cody were with him.

"We left our spotlights on," Ellen said. "I aimed mine at a clearing down the park so the whole portrait is visible from the sky. For the cameras," she added, extending her index finger at the sky. The helicopter Imogene had heard earlier had arrived and been joined by a second one. The two of them circled far above, hovering and flashing as if in counterpoint the constant flashing of lights and cameras down on the ground.

Imogene aimed her spotlight down at the nearest patch of grass that the expanding throng of humanity below still hadn't reached, perhaps half a mile to the east, before releasing the spotlight's handholds.

"So what do we do now?" Ellen asked. "I mean, holy cow, we don't even know if Gary is still alive. The whole damn planet is waiting down there for him. I thought tonight he might finally get his audience."

Imogene shook her head slowly. She'd been thinking about this. "The public was never meant to see him."

The three women and Ben raised their eyebrows in unison. Cody only stared at his feet.

"Priscilla said it herself. That wasn't her Gary up here. Imagine what would happen if you stuck that guy in front of a TV camera. It'd be like tossing a duckling into a den of feral cats."

"Is that why…" Priscilla began. She clenched her jaw, but after a very brief internal battle her chin firmed and rose like a queen's. "Did Gary jump so that he wouldn't have to talk to the news people?"

"No," Dulci said firmly. "Whatever happened to him at the end there, suicide was the furthest thing from his mind. It was almost like…" She stopped, obviously unsure how to finish that sentence.

"Like he thought he was going somewhere," Ben supplied. "That's what he looked like to me anyway. Most contactees carry a firm belief that their alien friends will be back to collect them after they've completed their task, whatever that might be."

Imogene hadn't discussed much of Ben's and her metaphysical musings with the others, but she also thought it was rather late in the game to pussyfoot around any topic related to Gary, even one so strange as alien contact.

"Right after he ran away from us, he said, 'They're here,'" Imogene recalled. "Did you guys hear him?"

All of them nodded, even Cody.

"I'm not quite as convinced as Ben that Gary was taking orders from aliens," she continued, "but it doesn't matter much what I think if Gary thought aliens were talking to him. Hopefully we can ask Droon what happened to Gary once we get down to the ground level. Or, if he actually did jump, I think we'll know pretty quickly from the questions we get asked."

"He didn't jump," Dulci said stubbornly. "I don't care if my only other option for his disappearance is that he was picked up by a UFO."

"Is that what we're going to tell everyone when they start asking where Americanus Rex went?" Ellen demanded incredulously. "That his pals from outer space gave him a lift to Alpha Centauri?"

"You guys are missing the point," Ben said. "Gene's right, those people down there didn't come to Paris to see Americanus Rex in person at long last. They came to Paris because in London Imogene and Ellen asked them to, and because they want to see the Council of Paris end without a new war, just like we do. I mean, there's got to be twenty thousand people down there."

"Not to mention the ones watching this on TV," Dulci added, nodding. "Those news vans wouldn't be here if they thought no one would tune in."

"So what do we do?" Ellen asked. "A little bit ago we made some guesses about the symbolism Gary may have intended with all this, but we don't know anything concrete. Let alone how Wheel of War will actually affect the Council of Paris."

None of them spoke for a few moments. In the silence, faint snatches of music and cheering drifted up from below. Imogene looked down through the mesh and saw that the crowd had noticeably grown in size even since she had last looked. In addition to the news vans and run of the mill rubberneckers clogging the square, many people were also carrying signs.

"We need to get down there," she decided. "Let's head back to the elevator. We can talk about all this on the way down."

Cody and Priscilla led the others back to the elevator, and all six of them piled in. Cody yanked open one of the sliding windows near the top of the car. "I ain't showered in awhile," he muttered, possibly in apology.

Priscilla slid a comforting hand along his upper arm, but this gesture was only reflex. Her staring gray eyes mirrored the shell shocked silence echoing through the elevator. No one seemed to know what to say. Each of them stood before one of the windows, marveling at the crowd that had now spilled over the boundaries of Parc du Champ de Mars into the streets around the Eiffel Tower.

At the restaurant on the second level, the six of them exited quickly and made their way to the first elevator that had brought them up from the ground. This time Imogene had no expectation to find Droon waiting for them, and he wasn't. Ellen operated the elevator's simple controls.

Once they were rolling Imogene spoke up. "I've got an idea. Remember Oliver's whole first strike policy on dealing with the press? The gist of it was to let the media ask tough questions as soon as something happens so they don't have a chance to speculate. Luckily for us, we don't have a choice about that since the Council of Paris is supposed to end tomorrow."

"I've got my doubts about that," Dulci said. "My guess is that the people behind the Council were hoping so many heads of state in one place could force either Russia's or China's hand. Since that hasn't happened, I'm guessing the Council will be extended for at least another week."

Ellen snorted. "Or else they'll make a rash decision just so they can prove they accomplished something. The lack of information from the Council only makes me more nervous."

"Which means," Imogene broke in, "that we'll have to get our messages right the first time."

Cody surprised them all with a coughing fit that threatened to buckle his knees, hands clenched in a shaking knot in front of his mouth.

"First thing, we have to get Cody to a doctor," Priscilla said.

His face turned upward, a pale pink mess framed in straw-colored hair. "I don't need any doctor."

Priscilla hushed him with a gentle hand on his back. "Do you all think an ambulance will be able to get through the crowds?"

"The city police are still down there," Dulci said, pointing out the window. "I'm sure they'll be able to get some kind of medical help for us."

Priscilla eyed white and green police cars doubtfully.

"And if they don't understand English," Dulci went on, "Imogene can talk to them."

And with that single statement, the final piece of the puzzle fell into place in Imogene's mind with an almost audible click. She saw Droon's smiling face as he led them toward the tower, heard his rasping voice as he complimented her French: "I am pleased that DroonCorp's first venture in publishing was a success."

I can talk to them, came the thought, delirious in its clarity. *I speak French. I can talk to them.*

"Guys, this is even bigger than we thought," she heard Ellen say. "Check out that van down there with the blue lettering on the side."

"What's D-W-T-V?" Dulci asked, squinting.

"*Deutsche Welle,*" Ellen explained excitedly. "It's Germany's international television company, kind of like the BBC in England. Those aren't just the pissant local channels down there."

Dulci craned her neck. "You're not kidding. *Cuatro* and *Univisión* are both here too. That takes care of the biggest networks in Spain and most of Central America."

Imogene recognized three French network logos on news vans— they had appeared in one of the popular culture lessons in *Français the Easy Way*—as well as vans representing CNN and the BBC. A few moments later, after they had dipped below the tower's first level of girders and concrete, Imogene could make out several reporters elbowing their way toward the base of the leg where the elevator would end up. Camera operators and technicians trailed behind them with heavy rigs on their shoulders and powerful lights on metal tripods.

Ellen's eyes were wide and startled behind her mask. "This is going to be a free for all as soon as the elevator opens. We'll be lucky not to be smashed to a fine paste."

Imogene hardly heard her. The sight of the reporters and their cameras, the thousands of people all watching them, had transported her once again. Not to a time or place but to a television image. It filled her mind like an endless, two dimensional square universe: her mother, nineteen years old, in a light blue bathing suit; a long microphone topped with a round hunk of foam like a snowman's head; an eternally grinning man in a dark suit holding the fat snowman's head at her mother's mouth; the unforgettable bounce of her red curls as she tossed her head in preparation to deliver the sentence that would reverberate in ever widening circles for the next thirty years until it became true halfway around the world.

"*I will light a beacon of peace from the top of the world,*" Imogene heard her mother declare across all that time and space.

The others turned toward her as if she had spoken the words herself. Maybe she had. It didn't matter. She was the Catalyst.

The elevator was perhaps a hundred feet off the ground now. Certainly no more than a minute until the doors slid open to let in a sea of tourists, sign wavers, and reporters like some inside out Pandora's Box.

"Listen carefully. Whatever they ask first, tell them we need an ambulance for Cody. When they ask who he is, tell them he's Priscilla's brother. If they don't recognize her from her portrait tonight, they'll certainly remember she was in London with us. Ben too."

They all nodded.

"Come to think of it, a doctor don't sound too bad," Cody said weakly, punctuating his statement with a spate of dry coughing.

"We'll find one together," Ben told him. "Can't be that tough, right?"

Cody eyed him for a moment, as if trying to detect a joke or mockery in Ben's voice, but apparently he decided Ben was serious and answered with a single nod.

They had maybe forty-five seconds now.

Imogene resumed, "When we're convinced Cody and Ben are headed in the right direction, we'll answer the rest of the reporters' questions. When they ask what happened to Gary, we'll tell them we don't know. Because we don't."

They all nodded.

"Wheel of War was never about the painting, maybe not even for

Gary. It's stunning and symbolic and wonderful, but the real purpose was to focus the attention of an enormous amount of people on Paris on the Council's last night. We'll use the cameras the same way we did at the press conference in London: to call everyone listening into action. One of the first things Droon ever told me was that people like us, and like everyone waiting out there, are the ones who shape history. We'll ask everyone out there not just to rally, which they're already doing, but to write letters to their leaders and ask their friends and relatives to do the same thing."

Ellen said, "Teachers and university professors could collect creative and nonviolent responses to the Red October Sky from their students, and hold national contests for the best ideas."

"Beautiful," Imogene said. "Even if the Council does end tomorrow with a military option in place, it'll take a while to get going, and during that time we can encourage the people to continue working for an alternative."

"Okay. Who do we talk to first?" Dulci asked. "You know everybody's going to make a big deal about who gets the first interview."

Imogene's heart pounded with undiluted exhilaration. "All of them."

The press conference, the impassioned speech to the gathered population of Accord, the little French book the Droons had planted in the airport—all of those things had only been preparation for this moment.

If I ever see any of the Droons again I'll buy them enough Evian water to fill an Olympic swimming pool, Imogene vowed madly.

Aloud she said, "I'll take the French reporters."

A wide, wonderful smile appeared under the bottom curve of Ellen's mask. "I guess I've got the Germans."

Dulci actually laughed. "Bring em on! *Antenna Tres, Telemundo,* whoever. *No tengo miedo.*"

"Priscilla, that leaves you with the American and British crews. Is that alright?"

Priscilla shrugged. "I've made more difficult speeches."

No one contradicted her.

The elevator eased into its cradle inside the base of the Eiffel Tower's western leg. Hundreds of cameras created a lightning storm inside the elevator. Bodies banged against the outside of the car. Reporters bellowed questions and mashed their microphones against the elevator's windows as the car finally settled to the ground with a series of brief shudders.

Ellen glanced down at Dulci. "You need a box or something to stand on so they can see you?"

"Try not to whack your head on the door frame on the way out," Dulci replied, reaching up to give Ellen's wrist a companionable, if anxious, squeeze.

Priscilla had also taken one of Ben's hands in hers and was wringing the heck out of it with a small, white knuckled fist. Her face, in contrast, was a study in composure.

Without letting go of Priscilla, Ben leaned forward and pressed his mouth close to Imogene's ear to be heard over the frenzy outside. "I don't know how you do it, Queen Gene, but you make everyone around you better. When I grow up I want to be just like you."

Before she could respond, the elevator doors slid open and the noise level inside the car instantly increased tenfold. The people, rather than rushing inside as Ellen had worried they might do, formed a small arc outside the car so the six of them had room to exit. Imogene took this as a good sign. Knowing the others would follow, she led the way out.

LIFE AFTER REX

From the Epilogue of *We Come in Peace*

By H. Benjamin Cornell

I've heard the same arguments you've heard about my sister and her friends, the same tasteless lesbian jokes. I've heard the four women and their hard work casually dismissed by people who label them as "hot." And then there's my favorite, the acidic accusation that, despite the dramatic shifts in international policy following the unveiling of Wheel of War, world peace is just as much a fairy tale now as it was when the first beauty pageant contestant wished for it on live television. The implication in each of these cases is that the Americanus Rex movement accomplished nothing.

Fine. In fact, here, let me make your arguments for you: bullies still pound the smallest kids they can find in school hallways and playgrounds; Israelis and Palestinians still kill each other over rights to the Holy Land; suicide bombers still target schools and police stations in Iraq, Afghanistan, and many other troubled countries; multinational companies continue to enslave whole populations of undeveloped nations to make expensive sneakers and designer clothing; so called "small scale" genocide continues in Africa, South America, Eastern Europe, the Middle East, and, yes, the United States, though the latter involves the attempted suppression and destruction of immigrant cultures rather than of people's lives.

Such arguments permanently exist for those who persist in negativity. What strikes me about the case of Americanus Rex is how much of the world has chosen to focus on the *good*. Ironically, this trend began with a public call to negative thinking on September 1, the day after Gary Pritchard created his Wheel of War on and around the Eiffel Tower.

In a televised press conference from the White House, the Vice President of the United States declared that the heads of state in the Council of Paris wouldn't be swayed by what he described as "harshly anti-American graffiti." The White House had already been, in his words, "endlessly patient with the international attention to one man's public perversion. Americanus Rex has nothing to do with protecting the American or European people from nuclear war, and it's time we rein ourselves back in to reality."

It was the first instance since the crash of the Red October Sky that any politician had uttered the phrase "nuclear war," and the public response was immediate and dramatic. Thousands of protestors—one of whom created a stir of his own when he handcuffed himself to the working gears of one of the four elevators at the base of the Eiffel Tower and lost an arm before he could be sawed free—flocked to the tower in another impromptu rally. Several prominent European and American conflict resolution specialists who were already in Paris appeared throughout the day to educate the protestors about the ways governments throughout history have used fear mongering and propaganda to create popular support for military campaigns.

The Parisian riot police maintained their positions around the tower—the squads from the night before had never left entirely even though they'd changed shifts a few times—but to their credit, and to the credit of the protestors, the event remained peaceful.

As Imogene and Ellen had predicted during the press conference at the Tate Modern, the masses did indeed garner the attention of the Council of Paris. In particular, the French President's dismissal of the Vice President's talk of nuclear war turned out to be even more jovial than an infamous appearance he had made at a G8 Summit while obviously drunk.

"Even if France could ignore the world's cries for peace," he joked with his trademark impish smile, "why would we ignore a new claim to fame for the world's most famous landmark, the *Tour Eiffel?* Furthermore, the four American women featured in the Americanus Rex portraits have rightfully earned new respect for Americans in a Europe which in the last decade has lost sight of Americans as anything but loud, pushy tourists."

Later, in a compliment whose gravity you might have to be French to appreciate, the nationally beloved singer/supermodel/First Lady of France added, "I have never heard an American speak better French than Mademoiselle Cornell in her interviews beneath the Eiffel Tower."

And Imogene certainly wasn't the only one who received such praise. September 1, the streets of Spanish speaking cities from Madrid to Mexico City filled with jubilant citizens cheering for the revamped Council of Paris and carrying posters of Dulci, the American who had rallied for peace in their native language.

The Germans don't share the Spanish custom of marching in the streets, but the scads of political television chat shows that run daily in Germany heaped terse praise on Ellen and the others for their shrewd method of dealing with the European media.

Priscilla, on the other hand, began the night as the least known of the four. She performed her interviews under one of the many streetlamps dotting the square around the Eiffel Tower, so that the contrast between darkness around her and light directly above created the impression that she—unlike the other three, who stood in heaving, noisy pockets of humanity with microphones thrust under their noses—appeared to be utterly alone. Priscilla freely admits that she looked the least comfortable in front of the cameras, but the *London Times* described her as "all the more enrapturing for her quiet intensity."

America-side, in the most visual culture on the planet, Priscilla in her stark shaft of light surrounded by darkness struck tones of American individuality and perseverance that rang from the Bible Belt to Long

Island. I've even seen Priscilla's portrait screen-printed onto a black t-shirt, above the words *Regina Americana,* which I can only guess is a Latin derived female version of Americanus Rex.

At about ten o'clock (Greenwich Mean Time) on the evening of the second Eiffel Tower rally, the BBC broke the story that the Chinese President had arrived at the Chinese Embassy in Paris, answering a joint invitation from the British Prime Minister and German Chancellor. Not only that, he'd brought along Russia's highest ranking Air Force officer. Together they revealed that the Red October Sky was indeed an experimental aircraft, it just hadn't been designed to attack anyone. Their countries had collectively spent over a trillion dollars on the prototype of a landing and exploratory craft for humanity's first manned mission to Mars. Their governments had remained tight lipped about the project, even under threat of violence from the West, because the materials and processes used to construct the Red October Sky's fission reactor violated a distressing number of international laws and treaties. Unfortunately for the insatiable news media, any other details about these violations or the Red October Sky itself were too highly classified to repeat outside the Council's meeting chambers.

The Council of Paris closed its last session on September 11, 2011. Our President, who weeks earlier had introduced the Council from the White House, closed the Council with a speech to a packed room of reporters at a press conference in the American Embassy in Paris. I'm sure it was no coincidence that his tie perfectly mirrored the blue of the United Nations flags hanging behind him.

"We have arrived at a point in human evolution where we have the ability and obligation to quit responding to international problems by simply putting up our dukes. We are more enlightened about our planet and our psychology than anytime in history, and it's becoming clear that Americanus Rex, along with the staggering amount of people who stepped up to support the message of his artwork, is asking the governments of the world to act our age."

If his opening remarks sounded too good to be true, the rest of his speech only got better.

"I've said a lot about globalization in the last couple weeks, and I won't quit anytime soon. The Council of Paris is just a stepping stone to new patterns of behavior and cooperation between governments all over the world. I'm not talking about just the rich and powerful nations creating some new world order for our exclusive benefit, either. If we're to establish a true global community, the wealthiest and most powerful nations in the world must also welcome input and participation from developing nations. In a world as small as ours is becoming, what affects one of us affects us all."

In the days following this speech, the President further surprised everyone by putting his money where his mouth was, at last pledging full American support for the 2002 Monterey Conference, in which the 22 wealthiest countries in the world agreed to donate at least 0.7% of their national income to the world's poorest countries each year. The number rose to 24 countries at the end of the Council when China and Russia threw in their lots as well.

But by far the most radical result of the Council was a detailed proposal of the International Violence Tax. And because I firmly believe the President's speech on this subject can't ever be repeated enough times to do it justice, I've recorded what I consider to be the most poignant passages below.

"There has been too much violence throughout history for the Council's goal to be the immediate cease of all large scale conflict in the world. Recommendations from the foremost specialists in mediation and conflict resolution led us to create a preventative resolution that places a heavy taxation on any nation that initiates conflict with or retaliates against another nation for any reason. A separate tax would be applied to a nation which produces weaponry for itself or for sale to foreign militaries or militias.

"In the spirit of growing a broader global community, however, we understood that the Council of Paris was too limited a forum to create such a fundamental change for the entire planet. For that reason, the violence tax will be a main point of discussion at the next full meeting of the United Nations, where it will ultimately face a vote.

"Some of you may worry that these actions will result in a weaker America. It's an accusation I've heard many times in the few years I've been President. So let me lay your fears to rest. The United States military has been the best trained, best equipped fighting force on the planet since the founding of our nation. Our first President, George Washington, was so impressed by his own military that he recommended dismantling it, lest it become too powerful. President Eisenhower, a highly decorated general himself, expressed similar views when he left office.

"Unlike those great men, I'm not suggesting we dissolve the military that has helped to shape America into what it is today. Instead we will train our bravest men and women first and foremost to be peacekeepers and peace builders. We will reshape military philosophy so that no fellow human being can ever be considered a true enemy, deserving only of death at our hands. No more black and white lines will be drawn between good guys and bad guys. I don't promise that other soldiers will view us in the same way, but we will conduct ourselves with honor befitting our nation's fortune and the responsibility that goes along with it."

The President's closing lines below led as many newscasters and television viewers to tears as his Presidential acceptance speech three years previous.

"The era of the rifle and bayonet has ended. The new breed of soldier will carry brick and mortar, seed and spade, and an extra ration of food for whomever needs it. Today, on the ten year anniversary of the heinous attacks of September 11, 2001, I can think of no greater honor for us to bestow on the memory of those who died in New York, Washington, and Pennsylvania than the adjournment of the most dramatic international peace conference in human history."

While much of NATO and the UN applauded the President's sentiments, the backlash from political conservatives and military organizations on this side of the Atlantic was immediate and wrathful. More than one conservative pundit latched onto the fact that the President wore flag pins representing each of the countries involved in the

Council, unhesitatingly questioning his patriotism and dedication to the United States.

None of this negative publicity prevented the Violence Tax proposal from sweeping through the UN and passing into international law with an overwhelming 83% approval. In typical bureaucratic fashion, even the initial policies of the Violence Tax will not take effect until 2016, but progress is progress.

These are all things you know unless you lived in a cave for the last quarter of 2011 with your eyes squeezed shut and your fingers in your ears. You've all seen, for example, the photographs of our President sitting between the Chinese and Russian Presidents at a green table adorned with a bank of black and gold pens, one for each of the representatives present. And now, less than a year later, you'd be hard pressed to find a citizen in any country with functioning news media who has never heard of the New Paris Peace Accords, as the Council of Paris came to be called.

But enough of that. If you've made it this far in my book, chances are you're waiting to hear what happened to the main players in the weeklong saga of Americanus Rex. I'll start with the stories of Ellen Ramsey, Dulcinea Montero de Frutas, Priscilla Hemphill, and Imogene Cornell, all of which are delightfully easy to explain.

At the time of this writing, Dulci is in her first semester of doctoral study in psychiatric medicine at the IU School of Medicine. As far as I know, she and her former fiancé are still on speaking terms, but she has no plans to get married to him or anyone else in the near future.

Ellen is working as my dad's research assistant at the University of Washington (Go Huskies!). Dad—who scarcely ate, slept, or bathed for a full week after he got home from his kayaking trip, lest he miss a single second of coverage about his daughter and former student and the Council of Paris—wrote a successful grant proposal for a new book about women's roles in both art and peacemaking in the last century, and how those roles have affected, or been affected by, the women's liberation movement. Both Ellen and the UW Public Relations Department were pleased as punch when Dad invited her to assist him with the book.

Next fall Priscilla will begin a Masters of Divinity program at Eastern Mennonite Seminary across the Virginia border in Harrisonburg. There were options nearer to home, but upon learning of the Mennonites' focus on peacemaking and justice, and their openness toward female clergy, she was completely sold. She'll come home for the major holidays, during which we'll be planning our wedding.

Because of her new job, I actually haven't seen my sister since I hugged her goodbye at Aéropuerto Charles de Gaulle early last September, though she did take several days in late September to fly back to Seattle to see Dad. During the last week of the Council of Paris—before anyone began calling it the New Paris Peace Accords—France's First Lady invited Imogene to the palace at Versailles for an intimate lunch. ("Intimate" in this case meant that only one reporter from every national French news outlet was invited.) Imogene understood the lunch to be the publicity stunt that was, but she did *not* expect the French Ambassador to the United States to attend as well. Nor did she expect him to award her with honorary knighthood in the *Légion d'Honneur* "for initiating unprecedented progress in international peacemaking." Whenever I speak to her on the telephone now, I cannot help addressing her as *Chevaliére,* the French female equivalent of the British "Sir" title, and she cannot help pretending to be annoyed.

Following the relentlessly televised event at Versailles, Oliver Hume had no trouble convincing the Louvre to install Imogene as Liaison to the Tate Modern and Head of English Speaking Public Relations. Imogene was never one to believe the lie that a woman needs a man to be complete, but she has admitted that she and Oliver are spending considerably more time together than would be necessary to maintain a professional relationship. I would agree, since they take turns riding the Chunnel between Paris and London to meet every weekend.

Now, with regard to Gary Pritchard and the enigmatic Lords Droon, I'm afraid you'll find little satisfaction in the information I can give you. No one ever did find Gary Pritchard's body, although that isn't terribly surprising since the Paris authorities conducted no search for him. Based on the conspicuous lack of questions we received about a man who may or may not have thrown himself off the Eiffel Tower, we all eventually deduced, as Dulci had from the start, that no one below had seen Gary fall or hit the ground. The reporters did, however, ask what that bright flash had been about ten minutes before we reached ground level.

And in that flash lies the first of my unsatisfying answers. In theory, the light could have come from Ellen's beacon, which Gary accidentally kicked our direction during his jungle gym scramble up the wire barrier, or from one of the helicopters circling over us. However, it is tremendously unlikely that either of these could have blinded all of us so completely at precisely the same moment as Gary vanished.

Any UFO nut could tell you without looking up from his Dungeons & Dragons manual that a bright flash is one of the unfailing commonalities in abduction tales. The implication is clear: a flying saucer swooped down from space, snatched Gary out of midair, and swooped right back into space, leaving behind only the telltale bright aerial lights. And Priscilla and Imogene both woke the next morning with puffy eyes—conjunctivitis being one of the symptoms that researchers use to tell whether a "close encounter" could be legitimate or just another prank—but that could easily have been a result of exhaustion, especially since the rest of us suffered no eye problems at all.

Having gone on record with even crazier ideas in this book, I do believe Gary has entered the mystifying annals of human abductees. Every era and civilization in human history describes inhuman, yet clearly sentient beings who appear on our world with us. They've always been a fretful lot, warning us in Biblical times against incurring the wrath of God or of the hazards of an afterlife in hell. As technology has advanced, so have the warnings. In the decades after Truman signed the document to vaporize Hiroshima and Nagasaki, these same beings ceaselessly warned humanity that the end of the world was imminent unless we gave up nuclear weapons research. The motivation for their concern seems to be that if we blow up our world, we blow up theirs too.

It's very handy for these entities that regular old people, like Imogene and her friends, are always the ones to instigate change. The Men in Black never have to step out from behind the curtain to take credit for their goals reaching fruition. I would love to point this out to Droon himself, but in classic Men in Black form, I haven't so much as glimpsed Droon since we parted company with him in the Jules Verne restaurant, nor have any of the others who knew him. This mental merry-go-round is yet another common thread running through all genuine modern studies of unexplained phenomena. So let me assure you that I'm just as frustrated by my lack of concrete answers as you might be reading this.

Still, every time I get too upset by what I don't know, I remember how much Imogene, Priscilla, Ellen, and Dulci accomplished while operating on a most reckless and wonderful combination of intuition and faith. And in the spirit of positive thinking, I will be forever grateful that I got to take part in their story.

Ben Cornell
Accord, West Virginia
June 19, 2012

ACKNOWLEDGMENTS

Publishing a book is not the job of any single person, and *Americanus Rex* simply would not exist without the patience and hard work of several people. The most patient by far is my wife, Kate, who should be nominated for sainthood in the world's major religions for her years of unfailing support as I wrote and rewrote this book until I was happy with it. Which leads nicely to the next most patient person, my editor, Alan Rinzler. Alan wasn't content simply to improve my book, but sternly forced me into becoming a better writer and storyteller. I've never met anyone with a lower tolerance for bullshit.

I must also thank Charlene Potterbaum, who shared my belief that "coincidence" is a fool's word, and who stepped out of her comfort zone to publish my first book, *The Island of Misfit Toys*. Still with me from that time is graphic designer Alison King, to whom I continue to owe my thanks for her work on this book.

Lastly, I have employed probably a score of test readers over the last few years (and drafts) of *Americanus Rex*, and I to extend my thanks to all of them. Whether I received pages of careful notes, a few quick words, or prolonged dead silence, each one of them taught me something about my book.

Naturally, all of you reading this now are a different sort of test reader, and I am humbled that each of you has picked up this book and seen it through to the end. I thank you as well, and I hope we meet again across the pages of my future projects.

ABOUT THE AUTHOR

André Swartley lives in Ohio with his wife and two cats. His first book, *The Island of Misfit Toys*, was a finalist for the 2005 Indiana Book Award and was nominated to the Elliot Rosewater Booklist. When he is not writing, André teaches English as a Second Language.

Breinigsville, PA USA
29 September 2009
224891BV00004B/3/P